Deemed 'the father of the sc:
Austin Freeman had a long a.
a writer of detective fiction. He was born in Lᴏɴᴅ.
tailor who went on to train as a pharmacist. After graduating as a
surgeon at the Middlesex Hospital Medical College, Freeman
taught for a while and joined the colonial service, offering his skills
as an assistant surgeon along the Gold Coast of Africa. He became
embroiled in a diplomatic mission when a British expeditionary
party was sent to investigate the activities of the French. Through
his tact and formidable intelligence, a massacre was narrowly
avoided. His future was assured in the colonial service. However,
after becoming ill with black-water fever, Freeman was sent back
to England to recover and, finding his finances precarious,
embarked on a career as acting physician in Holloway Prison. In
desperation, he turned to writing and went on to dominate the
world of British detective fiction, taking pride in testing different
criminal techniques. So keen were his powers as a writer that part
of one of his best novels was written in a bomb shelter.

BY THE SAME AUTHOR
ALL PUBLISHED BY HOUSE OF STRATUS

A Certain Dr Thorndyke

The D'Arblay Mystery

Dr Thorndyke Intervenes

Dr Thorndyke's Casebook

The Eye of Osiris

Felo De Se

Flighty Phyllis

The Golden Pool: A Story of a Forgotten Mine

The Great Portrait Mystery

Helen Vardon's Confession

John Thorndyke's Cases

Mr Polton Explains

Mr Pottermack's Oversight

The Mystery of 31 New Inn

The Mystery of Angelina Frood

The Penrose Mystery

The Puzzle Lock

The Red Thumb Mark

The Shadow of the Wolf

The Singing Bone

A Silent Witness

THE UNWILLING ADVENTURER

R Austin Freeman

HOUSE OF
STRATUS

This edition published in 2001 by House of Stratus, an imprint of Stratus Holdings plc, 24c Old Burlington Street, London, W1X 1RL, UK.

www.houseofstratus.com

Typeset, printed and bound by House of Stratus.

A catalogue record for this book is available from the British Library.

ISBN 0-7551-0381-5

To My Sons
John and Lawrence

CONTENTS

Chapter 1	In which the Reader makes a Genteel Acquaintance	1
Chapter 2	In which I become involved in a Tragedy	14
Chapter 3	In which I am Cast Away	26
Chapter 4	In which I meet Friends both New and Old	38
Chapter 5	In which I enter the Abode of Godliness	49
Chapter 6	In which I meet a Wolf in Sheep's Clothing	63
Chapter 7	In which I experience changes of Fortune	76
Chapter 8	In which I am Presented to my Cousin Percival	90
Chapter 9	In which I discover a New Enemy	104
Chapter 10	In which I have a Narrow Escape	117
Chapter 11	In which we approach a Strange Island	133
Chapter 12	In which the Pirate shows his Wit and his Heels	147
Chapter 13	In which I am Marooned	161
Chapter 14	In which I explore my New Territory	176
Chapter 15	In which I find a Key to unlock my Prison	192
Chapter 16	In which I play the Eavesdropper	207
Chapter 17	In which I encounter a most Genteel Rascal	225
Chapter 18	In which the Schooner is brought to her Berth	243
Chapter 19	In which Captain Parradine calls Checkmate	259
Chapter 20	In which I show much Valour and little discretion	278
Chapter 21	In which Mr Murking pilots the *Charity* to her last Berth	295
Chapter 22	In which I return to an Old Haunt	311
Chapter 23	In which I come to an Anchor at the Bell Inn	330
Chapter 24	In which my Cousin Percival makes a Discovery	348
Chapter 25	In which the Bells are rung in Shorne Steeple	365

CHAPTER ONE

In which the reader makes
a Genteel Acquaintance

The wayfarer on life's highway who has reached that stage of this earthly pilgrimage which is graciously miscalled middle age – a period when the full-blooded green of summer begins to show certain sere and yellow adumbrations of approaching autumn; when the silvery frost of age has begun to gather on the temples and Time has written, in many a lined inscription, the epitaph of passions dead and gone, of sorrows buried and forgotten; if he should pause to look back and retrace in memory the stages of his journey, will surely let his eye roam fondly over the fairer scenes – the shady dells, the flower sprinkled meadows, the quiet streams by which he has rested in joy and peace – rather than the dismal wilderness through which he has struggled, despairing and dismayed.

And so, if he should take up the pen, to set down for the eye of others, those things that have befallen him by the way, it is needful that he should hold with a firm hand the reins of memory, lest, like a mere gossip, he should but talk for his own pleasure and so weary the reader. For, left to his own inclinations he will tend to let his thoughts turn back to the springtime of his life, when this old and outworn world was a thing newly discovered, its simplest and commonest pleasures as yet unstaled by custom, and its illusions unspoiled by disappointment; when the future loomed far ahead with the uncertain beauty of a mirage, and no weary journeys lay behind. For even when the wheels of life begin to run stiffly through the wear and rust of age, when pleasures have become dull and the future is but an empty coffer wide agape, still memory can raise the ghosts of dead-and-gone delights until they seem to live again and the world is once more young.

But I should seem a dull historian if I should fill these pages with an account of my childhood or even of my youth; which, to speak the truth, were as little eventful as those of other country-bred lads, so I shall pass over these early days and come to that period when my misfortunes and adventures began.

Yet it is necessary for me shortly to inform the reader as to my condition, that I may not come before him as a complete stranger; for otherwise would much of that which follows be barely intelligible.

My father, then, was a Kentish yeoman, or gentleman farmer as they say nowadays, of a good family though of slender means, and a very agreeable and cultivated man, as I have been told. But I have no clear recollection of him, for he died before I was yet five years old, and was followed a few months later by my mother; when, as my high relations would have none of me, I came to live with a kinsman of my mother, Mr Roger Leigh of Shorne, in Kent. And at Shorne I remained up to the time at which this history opens, finding in Mr Leigh and his wife the kindest and most indulgent of parents, and in their daughter Prudence, a loyal and affectionate sister.

At the time of the opening of this history I was just twenty years of age; indeed this chronicle commences with the day following my twentieth birthday, on which day it had been arranged that I should make a journey to London, partly as a sort of birthday treat and partly to transact some business for my uncle – as I called Mr Leigh – with the hop-merchants of Southwark. It was no uncommon thing for me to spend a day or so in London, for the town was but little more than twenty miles distant, and what with the stage-wagons and coaches from Rochester and the tilt-boats at Gravesend, there was no difficulty in making the journey; and my own custom was to walk up to town, and return by water, either in a tilt-boat or on some hoy or other craft with whose master I was friendly. Yet, accustomed as I was to these journeys, and often as they had occurred, the incidents of this day are impressed on my memory with the most singular vividness; and the very aspect of the house, as I came down from my chamber in the grey dawn, rises before me now clear in every detail, although, God knows, I little suspected then that I was bidding a long farewell to the familiar scene.

I can see the old kitchen, wide and low-ceiled, and crossed by age-blackened beams, as it was revealed when I threw back the shutters and let in the wan morning light: the clean brick floor, the yawning fireplace with the great hook swinging above it, the polished pewter ware and blue china platters ranged above the dresser; the copper warming-pan glistening on the wall beside the painted bellows. With especial distinctness do I recall the old black-faced clock that hung in its sheltered corner solemnly counting out the seconds, while the little wooden smith on top of it hammered away with noiseless stroke at the red shoe on his anvil: and I remember finding something whimsically solemn in the thought that all through the dead hours of the night, when the silent house was wrapped in darkness and its inmates in slumber, the little tireless figure was thus pursuing his labours, unseen by mortal eye.

When I had breakfasted heartily and drunk a cup of ale, I thrust into my pocket the parcel of provisions that my aunt – as I called Mrs Leigh – had set ready for me, and let myself out, closing the door silently behind me. The sun was already up when I came out into the lane, and the world was waking to the beauty of a perfect summer's day. A lark was carolling aloft in the blue sky, the voices of countless birds resounded from the shady woods on the hill and an unseen crow-boy was springing his rattle far away among the corn.

Along the footpath, between walls of fast-ripening wheat, all sprinkled with drowsy poppies and blue-eyed speedwell, I strode with a gay heart, singing aloud as I went, until I crossed the stile into the Dover road.

Early as it was, I was not the only person afoot. Near to the manor house of Parrock I overtook old Tom Staples with a cartload of grain that he was taking to the Gravesend mill, and when I passed the Prince of Orange Tavern the shutters were already open, and there was the landlord himself taking his morning draught at the open door. By the time I reached Northfleet the business of the day was in full swing; a couple of wagons stood outside the Leather Bottel and from the shipyard under the cliff came the din of beaten trunnles and the ring of the caulkers' mallets.

I halted for a few minutes to gaze upon the ever new spectacle of the busy river. The tide was beginning to flow, and already the anchorage was studded with the white sails of vessels bound for London, while a pair of large line-of-battleships went sidling up Northfleet Hope, backing and filling their great topsails as they drove to and fro across the river.

When I had watched the two warships turn round into Fiddler's Reach I resumed my journey, stepping out very briskly, for the morning was still cool and fresh; but although I loitered nowhere, the clock of St George's Church was striking ten when I turned out of the Dover road into High Street, Southwark.

At first I was disposed to go and dispatch my business out of hand, that I might have the day free before me; but reflecting that the coaches and wagons would be presently arriving, I hastened to the George Inn by London Bridge to bespeak a bed, and to wash and brush off the white dust of the chalky Kentish road. When I had finished my ablutions I stepped out on to the gallery, and, leaning my elbows on the wooden parapet, fell to watching the scene of bustle and business in the inn-yard below, where the Guildford coach was preparing to start.

For some minutes I remained absorbed in idle contemplation of the departing travellers, when I was startled by feeling my hat twitched from my head, and, springing round, mighty fierce, as may be supposed, was not a little amazed to find the gallery empty and my hat lying on the floor. But as I gazed around in search of the cause of this phenomenon, my eye caught a loop of thin cord rapidly ascending in front of the gallery, and, on leaning out over the balustrade and looking up, I was confronted by a pair of grinning faces thrust over the rail of the gallery above, each as round, as red and as shining as a copper warming-pan. Almost instantly, however, the grin on one of them faded into an apologetic smirk and its owner hailed me in a voice like the below of a shorthorn bull.

"Save us Master Hawke, but who'd a thought to see you here in the old George! I ask your pardon, sir, for the liberty, but d' ye see this here shipmate of mine, which is an unmannerly son of a gun, to go a skylarking with the quality – "

"What!" roars the other, "me a-skylarking! Fine talk this, shipmate, when you done it yourself. Look at him, master, with the spunyarn in his fist at this very moment, and trying to cast the blame on to a innocent man."

The two faces suddenly vanished, and, immediately after, a pair of uncommonly massive legs appeared dangling over the balustrade, and the astonished people in the inn-yard were regaled with the sight of a square-built, pursy little man coming hand over hand with monkey-like agility down the pillar that supported the upper gallery. As he stepped lightly down from the rail of the balustrade he held out a square, tar-stained hand.

"And what might you be doing up in London, Master Robert?" he asked, as I grasped his great, rough paw. "I thought you were down among the cornfields and hop-gardens at Shorne."

"So I was this morning," I replied; and I then told him what had brought me to town.

"As to me, Master Robert," said my friend, "perhaps you mightn't think I'd come up to pay my respects to the Comptroller of Customs."

"No, indeed," I replied, with a laugh; for Toby Rooke was master of the cutter *Tally Ho*, the most bare-faced smuggler on the south coast.

At this moment Toby's companion made his appearance, having condescended to walk down the stairs like an ordinary mortal, and stood a few paces away, grinning shyly and staring into his hat which he held in his hands, the very picture of embarrassment.

Toby proceeded to do the honours of introduction.

"This here swab what you sees before you," said he, "is Bill Muffin. Billy, come and show yourself."

Thereupon Bill Muffin advanced, hunched up his back, and gave a tug at his forelock, as though he were pulling a bell-rope.

"It's all on account of Bill, here, that I came up to London," said Toby. "You see, I heard that a Guineaman was fitting out in the Pool and that her master was on the look-out for a mate; and as Bill thought he would like to have a change from our trade and try his luck in deep water, I sent word to the captain that I knew the very man to suit him, so he sends me word back asking me as a favour to meet him here today at eight bells, and bring my mate with me; and here I am and here's Bill."

"The captain is mighty careful to take so much trouble in choosing a mate," I remarked.

"So I was thinking myself," replied Toby; "but it's a queer trade, d'ye see, sir, is the Guinea trade. Gold dust and ivory are costly stuffs, and you want to know the men as is a-going to handle 'em."

Here our conversation was interrupted, for a stranger appeared at the head of the stairs and advanced along the gallery towards us, attracting our attention immediately by the oddity of his appearance. He was a somewhat tall man and immensely fat, not alone in his paunch – which was like a terrestrial globe – but in his face and limbs; yet notwithstanding his great size, he walked with a light, springy step, and as silently as a cat.

His aspect impressed me disagreeably at once, I could hardly say why, except that he was excessively uncomely. His large, puffy face was of a tallowy paleness with a long mouth stretched across it, of which the lips were so rolled in that it seemed but a great wrinkle under his nose. He had, moreover, what sailors call a swivel eye, so that one could not tell at what he was looking, and his grey wig fitted so ill that it listed over to one side exposing a tuft of red hair above his ear.

We drew up against the balustrade to let him pass, but when he came opposite to us he halted and bent his gaze upon Toby, or Bill Muffin, or both of them at once – for it was impossible to be certain upon the matter.

"I take you to be a mariner, friend," said he.

"Right, master," said Toby; "that is if you mean me," he added hastily.

"I do," replied the fat man sourly, "or I should not have addressed you."

"No offence I hope, master, but I wasn't certain, d'ye see," said Toby.

"I came here," pursued the stranger, ignoring the apology, "to seek one, Tobias Rooke."

"Then you've made your port at the first cast," said Toby, "for that's my name; and I'll make bold to say that I am talking to master Enoch Murking."

"You are," replied the stranger, "and I suppose one of these friends of yours is the mate you sent me word of."

Here he fixed a cold grey eye upon me, and I lifted my hat and bowed; but as he paid no regard to my salutation, I concluded that the other eye was the one in use at the moment, and that it was directed at Bill Muffin, for that bold mariner had become suddenly covered with embarrassment and hung his head until his well-greased queue stuck out behind like a pump handle.

I thought this a good opportunity to make my escape, so I excused myself, observing that I must go to settle my business and leave them to theirs; but Toby would not be satisfied until I had promised to return anon and take a bite with him. Accordingly, when I had finished with the hop-merchants, I came back to the 'George,' and, having inquired of the drawer for Mr Rooke, was directed to the coffee-room, where I found Toby and the other two seated at a table awaiting my arrival. They had kept back the meal for me but they were not without refreshment, for a jug of pop-in — a liquor compounded of a quart of strong ale and a quartern of brandy — stood on the table three parts empty; and I could perceive by the complexions of my friends and the sprightliness of their talk that it had not been consumed in vain.

Under the influence of an excellent dinner and a further supply of liquor, even the austere Captain Murking relaxed somewhat and related many strange things concerning the countries that he had visited. For it seemed he commanded the ship *Charity* in which he had for many years traded to the Guinea Coast; a land that, he assured us, by no means merited its evil reputation; and he rounded up his encomiums upon this ill-omened coast by asking me, rather suddenly, if I should not like to see its wonders and beauties for myself.

"If it were only the matter of my own inclinations," I replied, "I should be disposed to say yes; but as I have both means and occupation at home I have no excuse for roving."

"Wisely spoken and like a godly youth," said Captain Murking, smiling greasily and filling his glass afresh; "The call of duty is louder than that of pleasure to the righteous man. Still 'tis a pleasant life in Guinea, where the summer never wanes, and where flowers bloom and fruit ripens all the year round. 'Tis a profitable life too," he added thoughtfully; "for nowhere in the world may a man grow rich so quickly as there, where the very dust of the earth and ooze of the river sparkles with the good red gold."

The picture thus drawn by this strange unsailorlike shipmaster of the far-away African coasts, impressed me, I am free to confess, not a little; for I was but a mere country lad, and my imagination had already been set a-roving by the white sailed Argosies that stole into the river on every tide. Yet I could not but reflect that Captain Murking had, on his own showing, spent many years on the Guinea Coast, whence it should follow that he was either very rich or very unfortunate; and I was on the point of saying somewhat to that effect when the captain rose – the meal being now finished and all the liquor drunk – and hoisting a great globular copper watch out of his fob, declared that he must get on board his ship.

"Is Bill a-coming with you, master?" asked Toby.

"William Muffin had better come on board now," replied Murking, "that I may show him his berth and give him directions about the cargo. And I trust," he added, "That I shall find him, as you say, a careful seaman, and a God-fearing man who will set a profitable example to the crew."

"You will find Bill Muffin as good a seaman as ever stepped a plank," said Toby a little sulkily; "but as to t'other matter, why d'ye see we h'ant no call for it in our trade."

"No," assented Murking, "'tis a godless traffic as you say. Howsoever, I wish you a good day Master Rooke, with many thanks for your good offices. And you also, young sir, I wish you God speed; and should you desire a sight of my craft before she sails, I am always to be heard of at the 'Ship Aground' in Redriff."

I thanked him for his courtesy and accompanied him out into the yard, where Toby and I stood watching him as he took his way through the arch, followed by the reluctant Bill Muffin, the latter winking and grimacing at us over his shoulder as he went.

"There's a hypocritical, psalm-singing old slush pot for you," exclaimed Toby, as the two men turned into the High Street. "God-fearing, forsooth! Show me a pious shipmaster and I'll show you a damned rascal."

I laughed at Toby's prejudice (though, to be sure, I was little prepossessed by the captain's piety myself), and proposed that, now we were rid of Bill and the captain, we should cross the bridge and take a look at the town, as I was desirous of buying one or two little presents for Prudence and my aunt and uncle.

Accordingly we took our way towards the city across the bridge, stopping to lean over the parapet for a while and watch the watermen from the Pool shooting the rapids through the narrow arches, on the flood tide.

When I had made my purchases, we sauntered away westward, gazing about us with infinite relish at the novelties around, and mightily diverted by all the life and bustle of the town; and then, when we had gazed our fill at the crowded streets, the fine ladies and modishly dressed dandies, we must needs go to the play, where we were nearly stifled by the heat; and so at last back to our inn as tired and happy as a pair of children.

"How do you travel home tomorrow, Master Robert? asked Toby, as we turned into the inn-yard. "Is it shank's mare or the Rochester coach or the tilt boat?"

"I told my cousin that I should come down on board the Margate hoy," I replied. "'Tis more pleasant to sit on the hoy's deck than to huddle amongst the straw in a tilt-boat, and I know the master of the *Susan Solly*, the hoy that sails tomorrow – a genial, honest man who will gladly give you a passage down, I have no doubt."

"Then," said Toby, "We may lie late tomorrow, for 'twill not be high water until half-past ten. But we must not be too sluggardly, neither, since the hoy will haul out on the top of the tide, for certain. So pleasant dreams to you, Master Robert, and a fair wind home."

With this he turned into the staircase (for he lay in a room on the upper gallery), and I betook myself to my chamber.

On the following morning, when we had breakfasted and paid the reckoning, we made our way over the bridge to the Wool Quay, near to the Custom House, where the *Susan Solly* was lying; and we were none too soon, for we had hardly stepped on to the deck when the bell at Billingsgate began to ring and we saw the tilt-boat push out from the quay, while the master of our own vessel began to cast off his shore ropes and get the square sail hoisted.

As the tilt-boat pulled past – for they had not yet hoisted the sail – I noticed Toby casting a very searching glance at her passengers, who were all in sight, the tilt being rolled up on the bails because of the heat; and on my asking him what he was regarding so earnestly, he pointed out three rather ill-looking fellows in the stern.

"I am wondering what has been a-doing at Gravesend," said he; "for if those three rascals are not Bow Street runners, may I never land another keg."

"They may not be going to Gravesend at all," I said, looking at the men with a new interest nevertheless; "perhaps they are going to meet the Rochester tide-coach. There are plenty of doubtful characters about there and Chatham."

"That's true," replied Toby, and as the tilt-boat vanished among the shipping in the Pool and the hoy moved out into the stream, the matter dropped.

The breeze blew light but steady from the west, to the great satisfaction of the captain; for these hoys are none of the speediest of craft, and a breeze setting fair over the taffrail suits them better than any other. With her big square sail set, and a three-cornered topsail above it, her main sheet trailing in a bight over the side, and her head sails blowing out like Cherubim's cheeks, the *Susan Solly* shoved her way through the slack water in such style that she had fetched Limehouse Hole before the ebb began to overtake her.

Once clear of the crowded Pool, the company began to settle themselves for the voyage; and soon from the crowded deck arose a very babel of noise, as jests and laughter mingled with the crying of infants, the squeaking of a fiddle, the shouts of the sailors, and the drawing of corks. The *Susan* was a large hoy – near upon a hundred tons burthen – but the fifty or sixty passengers on her deck left mighty little room for walking about, and I was glad to find a seat upon an upturned barrel near the stern, where I could sit and listen to the sea gossip of Toby and the captain, or watch the seamen trimming the sails as the course was changed, and the white-capped, white-aproned cook bustling to and fro, now busy with preparations for dinner, and now stopping to coil down a rope or take a pull at a jib-sheet.

Most of the passengers were Londoners, and many of them had evidently never been afloat before, as appeared from the many odd and diverting questions they put to the sailors. They were all simple citizens – for the people of fashion travel down by the coach – and were full of high spirits and good humour, so that to watch them and listen to their talk was as good as being at a play; and I was so well entertained by them and by looking at the ships of all nations in the river and the moving panorama on the banks, that when we came to the end of Long Reach, and the Swanscombe marshes appeared just ahead, the familiar sights impressed me with surprise at the manner in which the time had slipped by.

We had just passed the village of Grays Thurrock and were heading down Northfleet Hope, when, from my perch in the stern, I observed a waterman's towing-hook rise above the bulwark and lay hold of the lanyards of the main shrouds. Immediately afterwards the weather-beaten visage of old Simeon Speed, one of the Gravesend watermen, appeared above the rail and began peering amongst the passengers as though looking for someone. I hailed him by name, and as soon as he saw me he beckoned.

"Why Simeon," said I, as I stepped across to the side, "what brings you aboard of the Margate hoy?

The old man leaned inboard and said in a low voice.

"Miss Leigh, sir, is alongside, and she bid me ask you to please step into the boat with her; she has some matters of importance to tell you about."

I looked over the side and saw my cousin Prudence sitting in the boat with her hood drawn nearly over her face; so with a few hurried words of explanation, I bid adieu to the captain and Toby Rooke, and, climbing over the high bulwark, let myself down into the boat.

"Well, Cousin Prue," said I, sitting down by her side, while Simeon unhitched his hook, "what wonderful piece of news is this that would not keep till I reached home?"

"A piece of news, Robert," she answered gravely, "more wonderful than pleasant. But I shall not tell it you now. I want you to land at the jetty here, and do exactly as I bid you. I shall go on shore at Grays and call at one or two shops; then I shall take the way to Chadwell, and I wish you to meet me on the road near to Grays; but if you see anyone coming along the road keep out of sight if you can."

"This is all very mysterious," said I, with a strong feeling of uneasiness.

"It will all be made clear when you meet me," she replied; "and now go ashore and do as I have said."

Simeon had brought the boat up alongside a little wooden stage, and he now steadied her with his hook as I mounted the slippery steps. Prudence waved her hand as the boat pushed off, and I turned away across the Chadwell marshes, disturbed no less by my cousin's pale and anxious face than by the strange directions she had given me.

I strolled off at an easy pace across the marshes, for I knew that the boat would take some time pulling up to Grays against the strong tide that sets into the bight at the top of Northfleet Hope; indeed I could see her creeping slowly upstream, and could contrast her sluggish movement with the swift progress of the hoy, the bellying sails of

which I could perceive over the low land, slipping down Gravesend
Reach, borne forward by wind and tide. Presently I struck a small
cart-road that crossed the marshes to the west of the hamlet of Little
Thurrock, and proceeding along this, at length came out into the high
road from Grays to Chadwell St Mary, within a couple of hundred
yards of the former. In accordance with my cousin's directions, I had
kept a bright look-out, but had not encountered a single person upon
the marshes. Here, however, on the high road, there were several foot
passengers in sight, as well as a wagon; so in order to keep out of sight
and yet maintain a watch for my cousin's approach, I took my station
behind a thin part of the hedge, at a bend in the road, where I could
command, through the branches, a view right into the village, and sat
down to wait.

CHAPTER TWO

In which I become involved in a Tragedy

I remained sitting in my ambush on the bank under the hedge for near upon half an hour; and never in my life have I known time to pass with such wearisome slowness. For, as I sat, alternately peering down the road and round the fields, my mind seethed with a hundred wild and disturbing conjectures.

The few mysterious words that my cousin had uttered were, indeed, enough to fill me with uneasiness, and even alarm, and I continued to cudgel my brains for a clue to their meaning until I was nearly beside myself with impatience and bewilderment; but beyond the too-obvious fact that some serious mischance had befallen, I could conceive no explanation.

At length, as I was peering out for the fiftieth time, through the opening in the hedge, I saw Prudence coming quickly along the road with a little basket upon her arm; and, as there happened to be no other person approaching, I emerged from my hiding place and set out to meet her. She came up to me near to the cart-road by which I had come, and down this we turned and walked towards the marshes.

"I fear I have kept you waiting a long time," she said, as I took her basket and drew her arm through mine, "though I made the best speed I could, knowing that you would be impatient to hear my news."

"Truly, cousin," I replied, "I am on tenter-hooks and pray you to end my suspense as quickly as you can."

"Well, then," said Prudence, "to begin with, I must tell you that a very dreadful thing has happened. Young Will Colville was found yesterday morning shot through the heart."

"Good God!" I exclaimed, "This is terrible news indeed. Is it known who fired the shot?"

"I was going to tell you," replied Prudence. "He was found lying among the corn beside the path that leads down to the stile by the Dover road. He was shot through the heart, as I said, and he had been shot from behind, for the ball had entered his back below the shoulder. A little way off the men who found him picked up a pistol – a small pistol with a silver lion's head on the butt."

"A lion's head!" I exclaimed, starting. "Why, that is like the pistol I had from my Uncle James!"

My cousin laid both her hands on my arm.

"Robert," says she, "it was your pistol; your name was on the plate."

At this my heart seemed to stand still, and I halted, staring at her, speechless with horror. Then the full significance of her statement burst upon me, and I took her roughly by the arm.

"Prudence!" I exclaimed, "you think I murdered young Colville!"

"That I do not," she replied, "or I should surely not be here. But I fear I am the only living soul who does not hold you to be guilty."

"Do my uncle and aunt, then, think me a murderer?"

"Consider a moment before you blame them," said Prudence, gently. "Here is a man who was not only your sworn enemy, but whom, no longer since than last week, you threatened, before several witnesses, to shoot. Now he is found, within an hour of your leaving the house, lying dead on the path you were known to have taken, shot with your own pistol. What marvel is it if folk name you as his murderer?"

"You put the case with most damnable clearness, cousin," said I, gloomily, "and it only puzzles me to promises to set sail at once, if Toby will agree – which no doubt he will – and get off on the ebb tide. And now is because I know you as none of these others do. Because we have played together as little children, have rambled together hand in hand in the country as boy and girl, nesting in the woods or nutting in the lanes. Because as we have grown older, I have learned to look to you for a brother's love, to find in you my faithful champion, always brave and chivalrous and true. And that is how I know that when Will Colville was shot in the back with your pistol, it was not your finger that drew the trigger."

I was deeply affected by my cousin's words, to which I could make no reply but to doff my hat and raise her hand to my lips. Her confidence in me was indeed quite unreasonable. But when the world of a sudden turns its back upon a man, and he feels himself the victim of false appearances, the unreasoning faith that springs up in a woman's heart may seem more precious than the wisdom of judges or philosophers.

"I suppose," said I, "the hue and cry is out by now?"

"Faith but it is, and your cousin shouting the loudest of all!"

"My cousin!" I exclaimed.

"Yes; I forgot to tell you, having such a budget of ill news, that a couple of hours after you left, your cousin Percival came to our house. I do not know what business had brought him to Shorne, but he had already heard of the murder, and was ready enough to believe it was your handiwork."

"Yes, the blackguard," I assented bitterly; "he always hated me. You see I stand between him and his miserable chance of becoming Sir Percival – which he would never be in any case. So he raised the hue and cry, did he?"

"That he did," replied Prudence, flushing with anger at the recollection; "and what is more, he sent off a horseman to London for the Bow Street runners. No doubt they are at Gravesend by this time."

"They are," said I, "for I saw them start in the tilt-boat; and scurvy-looking knaves they are. Is there a warrant out, think you?"

"I know there is," answered Prudence. "Old Colville is the justice of the district, and he issued a warrant out of hand directly he heard of the disaster."

"Then," I said, "I may take it that the instant I make my appearance on the other side of the water I shall be haled before the old man, and clapped into the cage at Gravesend."

"You would be," corrected Prudence, "if you were such a madman as to show yourself."

"Show myself!" I exclaimed. "And what else could I do? You do not suppose that I, an innocent man, am going to skulk and hide myself as though I were indeed the murderer."

"I suppose you are going to act like a man of some sense," answered Prudence severely.

"And should I not do so by coming forward and boldly proclaiming my innocence?" I demanded.

"What folly you are talking!" exclaimed Prudence. "You know quite well that Mr Colville will send you for trial to Maidstone, where the assizes commence next week, and what chance would you have before a jury of strangers, think you, when even your dearest friends are convinced of your guilt? You would proclaim your innocence, you say, but what proof would you offer? What defence would you make?"

I had to admit that I had nothing but my bare statement to offer. "Still," I said, "if the worst happens, I can at least meet my death like a gentleman, and leave posterity to do me justice."

"And that you cannot," replied Prudence, "for 'tis a most ungentlemanly thing to be turned off from the gallows by the common hangman in company with a parcel of sheep-stealers and pickpockets; and as to posterity, it would do you the honour of setting you a-dangling from a gibbet by the Dover road."

"But you would not have me run off at the first scent of danger?" I protested, a good deal shaken, nevertheless, by my cousin's blunt statement of the case, of which I could not but recognise the truth. "You would not have me play the coward, Prue?"

"Fiddle-dee!" exclaimed Prudence impatiently. "A live dog, my dear cousin, is better than a dead lion, and either is better than an ass. You say you are an innocent man, which I have never doubted, then have no fear but the truth will come out if you but give it time; and meanwhile do you get away to some place of safety. I promise you no stone shall be left unturned, no effort spared to clear you during your absence, and I have little doubt but you will soon be able to return with your honour re-established. But meanwhile, as I say, you must look to your safety."

I was mightily astonished to hear my cousin talk in this strain, for she was ordinarily the meekest and quietest of maids, and had been my humble follower and disciple from the time when we were children together; though always a sober-minded sensible girl. But her judgement and self possession in these critical circumstances filled me with admiration and made me a little ashamed of my own rashness.

"I will do whatever you bid me," I said humbly.

"Then listen to me," she replied, "for I have arranged everything. As soon as I heard of the trouble, and knew what it meant to you, I rode over to Cliffe Creek, where I learnt privately the *Tally Ho* was lying. Unfortunately, Toby Rooke was away at London – "

"I know. He came down with me on the hoy," said I.

"If I had only known!" she exclaimed in a tone of vexation. "However, I saw Long Jack, who is now the mate, and made no bones of telling him the whole story, seeing that it is the talk of the countryside."

"And what said my friend Jack?"

"He said a good deal that I need not repeat," replied Prudence, smiling at the recollection of Long Jack's discourse, "but the substance of it is this:

"It will be high water in the creek at a quarter-past ten o'clock tonight, when it is proposed to warp the vessel out into the river. It was Toby's intention to anchor for the night and sail at daybreak, but Jack promises to set sail at once, if Toby will agree – which no doubt he will – and get off on the ebb-tide. And now as to picking you up. Jack promises that as soon as it is dusk he will put off in a boat, row down the Hope and pull back along the Essex shore to the little jetty at East Tilbury. As soon as the boat is made fast he will fall to whistling 'Why should we quarrel for riches?' so that you may know the boat is his. Then he will row you across and put you on board the *Tally Ho*, and may God speed you and carry you safely to St Malo."

"Prue," said I, after a pause, in which I meditated with renewed astonishment on the marvellous readiness and coolness with which my pretty cousin had dealt with this alarming crisis, "Prue, you are a wonder. You have forgotten nothing."

"Nothing," she answered with a smile; "not even your dinner. Look!"

She lifted the lid of her basket, which I was still carrying, revealing a solid-looking pie and a flagon of ale; at the sight whereof I suddenly became conscious of the fact that I had eaten nothing since my breakfast. So without more ado we sat down under a thorn bush at the side of a ditch and fell to upon the victuals, and being both prodigiously sharp-set, we ate for some time without speaking.

All this time I was as one in a dream, so suddenly had the blow fallen upon me in the midst of my careless gaiety. And though all my life was changed in a moment, everything seemed unaltered. Here I sat amidst the well-known scenes with my home almost in sight – for the blue shape of Shorne hill rose, distinctly visible, even to the mill on its crown, out of the level lands across the river. There was the old house by the side of the lane, there my little room in the end gable, with the clematis growing in at the window; there was my bed made ready for my home-coming, with my rod and gun on the wall above, my very clothes waiting for me to put them on. All the homely surroundings of my life were unchanged and near at hand, and yet they would know me no more. This very night would see me an outcast wanderer, borne on the dark sea towards an unknown shore.

And with the old life that was thus slipping from my grasp, went all whom I loved and all from whom I could bespeak love. All my friends and gay companions, the kind foster-parents who had dealt with me so tenderly from my early childhood, and, above all – far above all – Prudence herself. Even in the hurry and agitation of the moment, I dimly realised that this was the loss that really touched me. From my older kinsfolk I could, perhaps, part with the lightness of youth; and doubtless in new surroundings, new friends might easily replace the old ones. But Prudence held a place apart, which none other could fill; and, as I stole a glance at my companion and noted how trim and dainty she looked, as I reflected upon her resolute courage, her resourcefulness and her unswerving loyalty, I thought there was surely no one in the world like her. Yet who could say when, if ever, I should look upon her again?

It seemed that while I was meditating in this gloomy fashion, my cousin had been following out a somewhat similar train of thought, for, as she shook from her lap the crumbs of her frugal meal, she turned to me with a face that was very serious and wistful.

"How long, I wonder," said she, "will it be before we take another meal together?"

"Long enough, I fear," was my rather despondent reply. "But who can tell?" I added more cheerfully; "the mystery may be cleared up tomorrow, for the murderer is probably not far off."

"He is most likely in the village," said Prudence; "Colville had a good many enemies, and this thing does not look like the work of a casual stranger. By the way, can you account for the murderer having gained possession of your pistol?"

"I think I can," I replied. "Last Saturday I went, as you know, to Rochester, and as it was raining when I started I put on my surtout. Knowing that I should be returning late by way of Gad's Hill, I dropped the little pistol into the outside pocket. The evening, you may remember, was quite fine and very warm, so on my way back at night, I carried the surtout on my arm.

"As I turned out of the Dover road to come up the hill, I felt a sharp stone in my shoe and sat down on the grass by the roadside to shake it out, throwing my surtout down by my side; and when I had shaken out the stone I rose, and, catching the coat by the skirt, flung it over my arm. The pistol must have slipped out on to the grass as I picked up the coat, for when I sought it in the pocket next morning it was not there. I went at once to the place where I supposed I had lost it, but it was nowhere to be seen; and I have no doubt that some rascal had already picked it up."

"And you never mentioned your loss to anyone I suppose?" asked Prudence.

"No," I replied. "The thing was but a toy, although I was sorry enough to lose it; but it was gone, and there was an end of the matter."

My cousin was silent for a space; then she suddenly rose to her feet, casting upon me a look of deep concern.

"Robert," said she, "I fear it is time for me to go back, loath as I am to leave you. Old Simeon is waiting for me at his sister's house and he will be growing impatient. Besides, you have to make your way to East Tilbury before dusk."

I rose, and, catching up the empty basket, drew her arm through mine; and we set out to retrace our steps, slowly and reluctantly towards the road. But creep as we would, the short distance was covered all too quickly, and we found ourselves at the spot where the cart-track joined the high road.

Here Prudence halted, and, having peered cautiously up and down the road, which was now deserted, laid her hands on my shoulders.

"You must leave me now, dear," she said, "and hasten to keep your tryst. May God go with you and make you brave and patient as you need be in this dreadful trouble."

"Prue," I replied, "you have held my life in your hands today; and I should be a dull scholar indeed if I had learned no lesson of courage and patience from you, or of love and faithfulness either. Though, God knows 'tis hard enough to sneak away like a thief, and harder still to say goodbye to my little cousin."

"'Tis hard for us both," said she, "who have never parted since we were children; and what the house will be without you I dare not think. But it cannot be for long, for the truth will surely make itself manifest. Let us trust that it shall be as the Scripture says; 'He that goeth forth and weepeth shall doubtless come again with rejoicing.'"

The sound of a horse's hoofs upon the road now warned us to bring our interview to a close.

Setting down the basket, I took her hands in mine and kissed her; and so we stood for some seconds with hearts too full for speech. Suddenly she disengaged herself, and, catching up the basket without a word, hurried away down the road.

I watched her, from the shelter of the hedge, until the horseman had overtaken and passed her, when she turned and waved her hand. And I still watched as she grew small in the distance till the turn of the road into the village hid her from my sight. Then I emerged from my cover, and taking once more to the cart-track, strode off across the marshes.

It was by this time getting pretty late in the afternoon, and there lay before me a good five miles of very rough ground before I should reach the landing-stage below East Tilbury. It would not do for the boat to arrive before me, for the sailors might conclude that I did not intend to keep the appointment, and return without me; so I set forward at a brisk pace, and, finding that the cart-track seemed to lead towards the hamlet of Little Thurrock, I turned off from it across the meadows.

There were very few people in this part of the country, and often, as I walked along the top of the high banks that bordered the ditches, and surveyed the vast expanse of level land, there was not a soul in sight. Whenever a figure became visible in the distance I changed my course, if necessary, to avoid coming nearer than about a quarter of a mile, and so I accomplished my journey without being seen by anyone except at such a distance that recognition would be impossible.

As I come out upon the flats below East Tilbury I observed a boat approaching the landing-stage, which the rising tide had only just reached. In no little anxiety lest I should miss my rescuers after all, I set off at a run, but I presently perceived that this could not be the *Tally Ho*'s boat, for not only was it much too early for the appointment – being scarcely half-past seven by my watch – but the boat was too large, rowing four oars, and having the appearance of a ship's quarter-boat.

I now began to be assailed by fears of another kind. What if news of my escape from the hoy had reached Gravesend and this should turn out to be a boat from a government vessel sent to intercept me?

Some fifty yards from the jetty a clump of small thorn trees grew beside a ditch, forming the only cover in the whole dead level of the marsh. These trees I carefully kept between myself and the boat, and, by hurrying forward, I contrived to gain their shelter before the craft had reached the jetty. Of the latter I was then able to get a good view by peering between the branches, and as the boat came alongside and the man in the bow made fast the painter to an iron ring, I saw at once that my fears were groundless. The man in the stern was clearly no king's officer, and the seamen were unmistakably merchant sailors.

Nevertheless, the presence of this boat might prove a source of danger to me, for the *Tally Ho*'s people would hardly risk taking me off while these strangers were about, and what their business was or how long they were likely to stay, I could not guess. They would hardly be taking in stores from the village, with the town of Gravesend close aboard.

The mystery of their presence, however, was shortly resolved by the appearance of a cart, which came jolting down the rough track that led to the jetty; for when it drew up, the driver jumped down and began to hand out a number of wicker-covered demijohns, which I surmised were full of the famous Tilbury water. Doubtless the boat belonged to some passenger ship, bound for the Indies.

I watched the stowing of the demijohns in the boat with the keenest interest, and as the last one was lowered into the bows, I breathed a sigh of relief. But, to my deep mortification, the sailors, instead of putting off, sauntered away in a body towards the village, leaving the carter in charge of the boat.

My anxiety was now redoubled, for it was already past eight o'clock and the sailors had set off with an exasperatingly leisurely air.

Crouching in my hiding-place, I groaned and swore with impatience, peeping out continually through the branches in a vain search for the jolly-boat of the *Tally Ho*, and casting many a malevolent glance at the unconscious carter. At length, after a full half-hour had passed (although it seemed to me like several hours) the sailors reappeared in high spirits, but more slothful than ever; the carter mounted to his seat and drove off, the mariners, slowly and with much talk and merriment, took their places in the boat, and at last I had the satisfaction of seeing them cast off and pull away towards Gravesend.

They had scarcely rounded Coalhouse Point, when I observed, in the now gathering dusk, a small boat pulled by two men, creeping up the Hope, close in to the Essex shore. It was the only boat in sight (for the one that had just put off had by this time vanished behind the land) and I had no doubt that it was Toby's boat, although I thought it wise still to keep out of sight. The men were paddling easily, but the boat, borne on the strong flood tide, came on at a good pace and was soon alongside the jetty, when one of the occupants, having secured the painter, stepped up on the stage and looked about on all sides. The figure of the man seemed familiar to me, but the light was now too feeble for recognition at that distance, and I determined to wait for the signal.

The seaman, having looked up the track and across the marshes in every direction, began to pace the jetty with an air of impatience. When he reached the end he sang out to his comrade in the boat. I could not hear what he said nor could I catch the reply, but immediately afterwards he stepped briskly to the foot of the jetty, and taking from his pocket what appeared to be a small flageolet, began to play, very skilfully and melodiously, the air of "Why should we quarrel for riches?"

On this I came forth from my ambush, and, running up to the jetty, found the minstrel to be, as I had thought, my old friend Long Jack.

"Well to be sure!" exclaimed he, in great astonishment at my sudden appearance, "ye've not been long a larnin' your noo trade, Master Robert."

"And what might that be, Jack?" I inquired.

"Why, a-makin' yerself scarce," he answered. "I'd a' swore there warn't a soul within half a mile, and here you comes, a-poppin' up out o' nowheres like one of these here Jack-in-the-boxes!"

The man in the boat appeared highly diverted by these observations. "He's a pretty fellow, master, is Long Jack," he chuckled, "to send on a job like this. Why, darned if he didn't forget all about piping the chanty till I reminded him."

I was glad that Jack had not come alone, and said so; and with that I jumped down into the boat and took my place in the stern, shipping the rudder while Jack cast off the rope.

There being a light breeze blowing from the south, we stepped the mast and hoisted a sail, with the aid of which, by steering diagonally across the tide, we were carried pretty rapidly towards the Kentish side of the river.

In spite of having to dodge one or two vessels which were beating up the tide, I managed to hit off the entrance to Cliffe Creek pretty exactly, and, it being now about an hour before high tide, there was a good depth of water over the bar at its mouth. So we lowered the mast and sail and pulled into the creek, and in a few minutes came in sight of the *Tally Ho* lying alongside the quay.

CHAPTER THREE

In which I am Cast Away

As we drew near the cutter, I noticed signs of considerable bustle and activity on board, and presently observed the head of Toby craning over the bulwark.

"Oh! you are there, then, master Robert," said he. "Thank God for that; I was fearing they might have missed you."

He gave me a hand up the side, and, as I stepped on deck, said in a low voice: "This here's a sad business for you, Master Robert; damned sad; and no one more sorry about it than Toby Rooke. Little we thought when we see them there rascals in the tilt-boat this morning, what their errand was."

"No," said I gloomily. "This morning I was a gentleman, a man of reputation. What am I now?"

"I hopes you're a gentleman still," replied Toby, with a grin; "and as to reputation, you've enough and to spare with two Bow Street runners attending on you and half the town criers in the country a-talking about you. But there," he added, seeing that I received his jest somewhat dryly, "we has our ups and we has our downs. I've been in the jug twice myself and stand to be grabbed again any day. But it all comes right in the end. Have ye got the sails loosed, Tom?"

"Aye," answered Tom, the acting mate during Long Jack's absence, "they're all ready for a-h'istin'."

"Then," said Toby, "you'd better cast off the shore ropes and carry a line out ahead. It's time we began to move out into the river."

Two of the men stepped on to the quay and unhitched the shore ropes from their posts; and while this was being done, the end of a long, thin warp was made fast to the bitts and the rest made up into a large coil which two of the seamen carried ashore and paid out, as they walked along the bank.

They had hardly gone a dozen yards from the cutter when Toby suddenly held up his hand.

"Listen!" said he. "What's that?"

I turned my head and listened. For a few moments I could make out nothing beyond the bleating of the sheep out on the marshes; then there came down the wind, faintly but distinctly, the sound of galloping horses.

"Come back!" roared Toby. "Bring that line aboard again. There's no time to warp out; we must sail out and risk it. Now lads, stand by to hoist."

The crew, well trained to rapid manoeuvres, took their places at the mainsail halyards immediately and began to hoist with a will, while the two men, having thrown the warp on board, proceeded to run up the foresail and jib.

The shore ropes were already cast off, so Toby, to prevent the vessel from blowing over to the lee shore of the creek before her sails were set, now flung the bight of a rope over a post and belayed the ends to two cleats; and he stood with one end ready to cast off, gazing into the darkness over the stern and listening with one hand hollowed behind his ear. It will be readily believed that I took my place on the throat halyards and hauled with the best of them; and by slow – incredibly slow – degrees, with many a complaining creak of block or parrel or mast hoop, the great sail began to creep aloft. From my position I could see Toby standing motionless and alert, with the rope in his hand, and I listened intently for the sound of the approaching horsemen amidst the noises of the gear.

The mainsail was about two-thirds hoisted when the men paused for a moment to take breath; and in the silence, the clatter of hoofs on rough ground could be heard with ominous distinctness.

"Heave away, for God's sake!" shouted Toby; and, as he spoke, I saw him cast off one end of the rope and haul it on board by the other.

The vessel was now free, but the light breeze, largely intercepted by the buildings beside the wharf, had so little effect on the partly hoisted sail that for some time she did not appear to move; but as the canvas rose higher and caught more of the wind, the cutter began to creep, inch by inch, away from the quay.

At last the mainsail was fully hoisted; and even as the men were belaying the peak halyards, the loud clatter of hoofs and scattering of gravel and stones changed to a thunderous stamping as the horses rushed out on to the planking of the quay.

"Down below!" exclaimed Toby; and pushing me towards the companion hatch, he ran forward to the bows, leaving Long Jack at the tiller.

I dropped hastily down the ladder but kept my head above the deck so that I could see and hear although concealed by the hood of the hatch; and I had but barely hidden myself, when four horsemen appeared at the edge of the quay standing black and gigantic against the dim sky. They looked as though they could have stepped on board, for the cutter had even now drawn away barely a dozen feet from the quay, and I shrank further down the hatchway for fear I should be seen.

"Tobias Rooke!" one of the horsemen called out in a loud authoritative voice, "I call upon you in the King's name to bring your vessel to the quay."

"What for?" inquired Toby, gruffly.

"You have on board one Robert Hawke, who is charged with murder, and for whose arrest we hold a warrant," replied the other.

"You're mistook, master," said Toby. "There ain't no such person aboard this craft."

"I command you to come to the quay, that my officers may search your vessel," exclaimed the horseman, sternly.

"And supposing I refuse?" suggested Toby.

"You do so at your peril," replied the other. "My name is Colville, one of His Majesty's justices of the peace, and I command you to bring your vessel to the quay that I may have the warrant executed. You know what is the penalty for assisting a murderer to escape."

"No, I don't," said Toby; "and I tell you we haven't got no murderers on board. We're in ballast, we are."

During this colloquy the cutter had been drawing slowly ahead, and she at length emerged from the shelter of the buildings, when her sails filled and she began to move more rapidly.

"Are you going to bring up?" shouted Mr Colville.

"No, I ain't," replied Toby. "Luff her up a bit, Jack. Steady. Look out for the bend. Now! Up hellum and round she goes, Steady!"

The horsemen trotted along the bank abreast of the cutter, and Mr Colville once more raised his voice.

"If you don't bring up instantly, I shall fire into you."

At this the crew, with one accord, flopped down under cover of the bulwarks, while Long Jack, falling flat on the deck, stuck his long legs up in the air and held on to the tiller with his heels.

The few seconds' silence that followed was suddenly broken by the explosion of a blunderbuss accompanied by a shower of slugs and buckshot, which rattled about the deck like a shovelful of gravel.

A chorus of groans and smothered laughter from the crew followed the discharge; and Toby, who had taken shelter behind the mast, called out:

"Look out, Jack! Starboard a little – steady – she'll be out in a jiffy,"

"You infernal smuggling villain!" roared Mr Colville, "I'll lay you by the heels yet. You shall pay dearly for this."

"Aye, aye, sir," replied Toby. "Now, Jack, bear away, we're outside at last. Ease that boom over as she jibs."

On hearing that we were out of the creek the men rose to their feet, and I ventured to creep up on to the deck and look round. We were fairly out in the river, and, as I looked back at the creek, I could see the group of horsemen standing by a beacon at the entrance; and even as I looked, they turned and galloped away.

"They're off somewhere in a devil of a hurry," remarked Toby, who had been watching them also. "I wonder what their game is."

"It can't matter much to us," said I.

"Oh, can't it?" answered Toby. "That's where you mistake, my friend. We're not out of the wood yet by a long way. The tide will be running up for another half hour and there's hardly enough wind to carry us over it. No, I'll feel safe when I see the Calais cliffs, and not much before."

He walked away to give some orders to the seamen, leaving me, as may be imagined, not a little cast down. I hoped, indeed, that he was taking a needlessly gloomy view of our condition, but this much I could see for myself: that now we had our head pointed down, against the tide, we were hardly moving forward at all, as I could judge by watching an anchored vessel close by.

"Come, this won't do," exclaimed Toby. "We might as well have the anchor down for all the way we're making. Get the squares'l set and the tops'l over it." He took the tiller from Long Jack, who went forward to carry out his order, and very soon the great square-sail was bellying out in the breeze, and a three-cornered top-sail set from the yard to the topmast head. Under this spread of canvas, the cutter began to move perceptibly forward, although her pace was still uncommonly sedate.

When we were about half-way down the Hope and pretty close in to the Kentish shore, I observed a small vessel at anchor right ahead, and a large ship that was drifting up, backing and filling, left us so little room that we were obliged to pass within a few yards of the anchored craft. As we came near to the little vessel, Toby suddenly began to swear in the most alarming manner, and as I perceived a man on the stranger's deck holding a lantern I retreated precipitately to the companion hatch.

"Fine night, Toby," sang out a brassy penetrating voice. "You seem to be in a bit of a hurry."

"I got my living to earn," replied Toby, gruffly; "I ain't a king's officer."

"True, true!" exclaimed the other. "Art is long, life is short, hey Toby?" He have a loud cackling laugh and then added: "When shall we see you again, my hearty?"

"Next time," answered Toby sulkily.

"I knew it!" exclaimed the officer – as I judged him to be – with another cackle; "we'll see you on the homeward trip then,"

"You'll know me when you do see me," growled Toby.

"Oh, yes, I shall know you. I never forget my friends."

The voice and the bleating laugh that accompanied it, grew thin in the increasing distance, and I came up on to the deck again.

"There's an accursed piece of luck for you," exclaimed Toby, as I appeared. "That's the *Cormorant*, revenue cutter, and that old jackdaw that you heard is her commander, Lieutenant Gimlet, the worst of the whole preventive gang."

"Well," said I, soothingly, "he knows you have nothing contraband on board now."

"That's all very well," replied Toby, "but you see, there's our friend Colville and his crew. The cutter's at her regular moorings, and if Mr Colville knows she's there, he may be hailing her from the shore at any moment. You saw the way they galloped off."

"But could the cutter overtake us?" I asked, in considerable alarm.

"Depends on what start we got," was the reply. "She's bigger than the Tally Ho and carries more canvas. If she starts in our wake within the next hour we shall have all our work to get away."

"But surely," said I, "they would not be able to find us in the dark?"

"'Taint' such a particular dark night," replied Toby, "and we shall be in narrow waters until we're past the Nore. But let us hope old Colville don't know she's at her moorings."

This hope I did most earnestly entertain, but still Toby's suggestion was a highly uncomfortable one. However, there was one comfort; the ebb-tide was now setting in and we could soon see by the way in which we swept past vessels at anchor, that the *Tally Ho* was mending her pace considerably. As we turned into the sea reach the square-sail was lowered – for the wind was now brought full on our beam – and a large gaff-topsail hoisted; and with this, and the main sheet well in, the cutter was in her best sailing trim.

We sailed on for a couple of hours without any incident, for the wind remained steady, and the night, although moonless, was clear and light enough to enable us to avoid the numerous vessels which lay at anchor near the fairway. During this time Toby had kept a very bright look-out, not only ahead, but also astern, peering frequently into the darkness or probing its depths with a big wooden-barrelled night-glass. But nothing had overtaken us or hove into sight astern, and now, with the steady breeze and the swift tide, we were drawing near to the Nore – indeed the glimmer of the lantern on the new light-vessel was already visible at no great distance.

"As soon as we are past the Nore," said Toby, who knew the ins and outs of the estuary better than any pilot, "I shall turn north-east across the Warp, run past the Ooze Sand, through the Knob Channel, round the Shingles and out through the Bullock Channel. No one will ever look for the *Tally Ho* out there."

"Isn't that your usual course?" I inquired, for these names were all Dutch to me.

"Lord bless you, no!" he answered. "We mostly crosses the Kentish flats and hugs the shore till we're round the foreland. This other's a deep-sea channel what the big ships use."

"I'm sorry to put you about so much, Toby," I said, "and most grateful to you for taking so much trouble on my account."

"'Tain't nothing, sir, 'tain't nothing," he answered quickly. "We're used to dodging about. Now this here new floating light what you sees ahead" – he pointed to the light-ship, the big lantern of which threw a red glare across the water – "she'll be wonderful useful to mariners."

He was proceeding to enlarge on the advantages of this invention, when, glancing astern, he stopped suddenly, peered intently into the darkness and then ran to the companion hatch for the night-glass.

He stood for fully half a minute with the telescope pointed directly astern – in which direction I could now perceive a small faint smudge of darkness; then, taking the tiller from Long Jack, he silently handed him the glass.

"Well?" he asked as Jack, at length, lowered the instrument.

"Looks like her," said the latter, as he passed the telescope to me, and resumed his place at the tiller.

I pointed the glass at the dim, dark spot, which was immediately resolved into a fore and aft rigged vessel – apparently a cutter – dead end on in our wake.

"We'll soon see what she is," said Toby. "Get the squares'l and tops'l hoisted my lads and you, Jack bear away four points."

He ran to slack off the main sheet as the helm was put up, and, as the cutter fell off on to her new course, he picked up the night-glass and fell to observing narrowly the vessel astern of us; and, before the square-sail was fairly set, he broke into a torrent of curses, and held the telescope out to me.

I pointed it at the shadowy object, and, as I caught the magnified image, my heart sank. The vessel – which I could now see was a cutter – had fallen off on to a course nearly parallel with ours, but slightly closing in, and already she had set a large square-sail with a high square top-sail over it.

"The game's up, Master Robert," said Toby, gloomily. "We'll be cage-birds, will you and me, afore another couple of hours is gone."

I was filled with consternation. To tell the truth, I had, up to now, given very little thought to the risk to which I was exposing Toby; and now it was too late.

"You have no doubt, I suppose?" I asked feebly.

"Not a morsel," was the reply. "We knows the *Cormorant* as well as they knows us – and that's saying something."

I pondered awhile in the deepest dejection.

"How far are we from land?" I asked suddenly.

"Good five mile from either shore," he replied.

"Five miles," I repeated. "I wonder if I could swim it. I am a good swimmer."

"No, you couldn't," replied Toby decidedly. "The tide'll be running down for full four hours yet and you'd be carried right out to sea and drownded."

"Well," said I, "have you a spare spar or anything that I could keep afloat with?"

"Don't you think of it, Master Robert," urged Toby. "It 'ud be just throwing your life away."

"As to that," I said, "you know what is likely to happen if I am taken."

"Why yes," he replied; "if you puts it that way, p'raps you're right. Might as well be drownded as turned off the cart. And after all you may get picked up by some outward-bound craft."

"Quite so," said I. "And if I am to go overboard I had better go before our friends get near enough to see me."

"And that's true, too," he agreed. "Well now let me think."

He considered for a moment and then darted down below, returning almost immediately with two small tubs and a couple of fathoms of thin rope. The tubs were of the kind used by smugglers on horseback to attach to the saddle; being miniature casks, holding, perhaps, half a gallon, and each fitted with lashings of cord and a becket or loop to sling it by.

"Here's the very thing," said Toby, as he passed the rope through the beckets and knotted the ends together. "These two empty tubs would have to go overboard in any case, if we are going to be overhauled, and they'll keep you afloat, and a dozen more like you if necessary. All you've got to do is to keep hold of the beckets, or you can lash yourself to the tubs with the rope, if you like. I shall keep on the same course for a mile or two so as to lead the *Cormorant* well away from the place where you'll be drifting about; and I hopes you may have the luck to be picked up at daybreak by something bound foreign."

He took up the glass and once more inspected the revenue cutter.

"She's keeping on much the same course as us," said he. "I shall run on through the Knob and round the Shingles, and that will take her right out of your neighbourhood, for I reckon she won't pick us up until we're into the Bullock Channel."

I thanked him once more for all he had done for me, and, picking up the tubs which he had laid on the deck, shook him heartily by the hand. I then bade farewell to Long Jack and the seamen, who were gathered in the waist to see me launched, and catching one of the weather shrouds with my free hand climbed on to the bulwark and stepped down on to the channel.

Now that the moment had come I felt mighty nervous about making the plunge, and glanced down apprehensively at the dark water as it slopped against the vessel's side. But it had to be done, so, while the hoarse voices wishing me good luck still sounded in my ears, I let go and jumped clear of the vessel.

I dropped into the water with a sounding splash and soused over head and ears; but instinctively drawing the tubs to my breast, I soon bobbed up, with my mouth full of sea-water and snorting like a grampus.

The *Tally Ho* loomed above me, shadowy and vast, and as I shook the water out of my ears, I heard her people singing out a rough but hearty farewell.

I kept my head low in the water as the cutter slipped past me, that I might not be visible to watchers on the pursuing vessel, and so I remained for several minutes, with the water washing into my ears and round my chin; by which time I considered that I must be well out of the area of observation and proceeded to make some arrangements for greater comfort.

The rope connecting the tubs was, as I have mentioned, about two fathoms, or twelve feet long, and being passed through the beckets and the ends knotted together, the tubs were joined by a double rope six feet long. This left them too far apart, as I had to hold on the beckets and the rope gave no support; so, without letting go the tubs, I managed to unfasten Toby's knot, and, passing the ends of the rope once more through the beckets, I again knotted them together. The tubs were now joined by a fourfold rope about three feet long, and, by separating the four parts of the rope, I was able to make a kind of cat's cradle in which I could sit quite comfortably with my head and shoulders out of water, and the tubs clasped on either side of my breast.

The wind being light and from the south, there was very little sea, and, although I bobbed up and down rather like an empty bottle, my head kept quite dry. Nor did it, at first, seem particularly cold, for the water was tepid with the heat of the sun through the long summer day, and had the immersion been merely temporary it would not have been unpleasant.

The *Tally Ho* soon disappeared, for, owing to my low position, my field of view was circumscribed by the summit of the nearest wave, and behind this horizon the dark shape of the cutter sank rapidly until it vanished.

Then I was alone – alone with the black unresting waters and the few stars that twinkled out through rifts in the cloudy sky; and very soon the loneliness of that vast, unseen expanse began to weigh upon my spirits and chill my heart, as the tepid water was beginning to chill my body. My situation was certainly not one to beget cheerful meditation. I was drifting, I knew, on the ebb-tide, out into the great estuary where, even by daylight, I should be but a speck on the wide surface; a thing for inquisitive seabirds to wheel round and scream over but not to attract the notice of a mariner unless thrown by chance right against his vessel. What, I speculated, was to be the end of this adventure, and how soon would that end come? And even as I meditated, I seemed to see a little group of people on a sandy shore at low tide, gathered round some object cast up by the fretting surf.

And then my thoughts turned to Prudence and I recalled with renewed wonder her bravery, her resource, her self-possession and her loyalty to her old playmate. She would be thinking of me as snugly berthed on the *Tally Ho*, speeding over the sea to exile and safety; or perhaps she had already heard of my escape and the pursuit, and was waiting in fear and trembling for the news of my arrest. Then I fell to cursing the coward who had thus treacherously cast upon me the burden of his vengeance; and so my mind flitted from one matter to another as my mood changed, now plunging me in bitter grief, now filling me with anger and thirst for revenge, and yet again leaving me with anger and thirst for revenge, and yet again leaving me in black despair and utter despondency. And so the time passed on, interminably as it seemed, and still the darkness hung over the sea with never a hint of dawn, and still I drifted on, with chattering teeth and limbs that ached with the cold, sick with bodily suffering and despair of heart.

On a sudden I became aware of a sound breaking through the dreadful silence of the sea, and so clear and distinct was it that I marvelled I had not noticed it before. It was most evidently the murmur of waves breaking upon a beach; and yet, as I listened, the thing seemed to me impossible; for was I not out in the midst of the estuary miles away from any land?

Yet the sound could not be mistaken, and indeed it seemed to come from no great distance; for even while I was pondering upon the strangeness of it I began to distinguish the breaking of separate waves. Full of wonder and reviving hope, I craned up to see if I could make out any sign of foam through the darkness; and, at times, when I rose on the summit of one of the little waves that ruffled the quiet sea, I thought I could distinguish a faint glimmer of whiteness ahead.

A sudden impatience of my position took possession of me and an eagerness to be once more on solid earth. With the intention of striking out for the shore, I turned over on the supporting ropes; but, as I extended myself to my full length, my feet struck on a sandy bottom and I stood up with the water barely reaching to my armpits.

Numbed as I was with the cold, I walked forward stiffly and with difficulty, grasping my trusty floats in my hand. Now that my eyes were somewhat higher above the water, I could plainly make out the glimmer of the surf, although at some distance; and in fact, the shore shelved so gradually, that I had walked more than a quarter of a mile before I felt the little breakers dashing against my legs; and even then I seemed to be a long distance from the beach. But I plodded on, with the tubs now dangling from my hand, and at last stepped out of the surf on to a low shore of smooth, level sand.

I stood at the margin of the surf looking into the darkness on all sides, but everywhere the flat beach faded away into the gloom. Reflecting, however, that if I walked away from the sea I must needs come to the land, I set off at as brisk a pace as my stiffened limbs would permit of, in that direction.

CHAPTER FOUR

In which I meet Friends both New and Old

I walked on for some minutes over the smooth sand, looking forward very earnestly for some signs of human habitations or even of solid earth, but still nothing but sand was visible. Presently, however, I observed a number of dark, upright objects, which I took to be the piles of some decayed landing-place and I hailed them with relief as indications that I was near high-water mark.

The largest of these objects lay right in my path, and I was just passing it, within a few paces, when I was considerably startled by observing a woman standing close up against it; and I was at once astonished and disturbed by her unusually great stature, and a strange, fixed stare with she seemed to be regarding me.

So startled was I that I stood, for some moments stock still, without speaking, until, of a sudden, the explanation of this strange appearance flashed upon me. These posts were, of course, the timbers of some old wreck, and this large one her stem-post with the figure-head still attached and held upright by the buried keel. That this was the case, closer inspection made clear; and, having examined the great wooden figure, all draped with seaweed, and encrusted with barnacles, I resumed my walk, smiling with grim amusement at the start it had given me.

And yet it was not a pleasant encounter, for there was, in the aspect of this bare skeleton of the old ship, something very sad and solemn, very full of the suggestion of disaster and death; and as I plodded on through the darkness, my thoughts continually reverted to this pathetic memorial of a forgotten ocean tragedy.

Presently, as I walked on, I found the sand becoming more moist, and deeply ribbed by the waves, with little pools of water in the furrows, which made me suspect that I was taking the wrong direction; so, as a faint amethyst glow in the eastern sky heralded the approach of dawn, I returned to the drier sand and sat down to wait for daybreak.

The fatigues and excitements of the long day that had passed had left me, as may be supposed, very weary and exhausted; indeed, so utterly worn out was I that I had hardly sat down on the hard sand when I began to doze.

I must have fallen sound asleep, for I was presently awakened with a start by falling over; and when I opened my eyes it was broad daylight. A thin gauzy haze hung over the sea, concealing the horizon, where sky and water melted together into one unbroken expanse of pale primrose yellow.

I stood up, yawning and stretching my stiffened limbs, and looked round anxiously for the land. And that one glance sufficed to reveal the dreadful truth to me; for, in every direction, the smooth sand shelved away to the sea, and not a vestige of land was in sight. This, which I stood upon, was no beach, but one of those sandbanks that lurk beneath the surface far out at sea, ready to engulf the unwary mariner, and at low tide take on a mocking semblance of solid earth.

When I realised my situation, which I did, as I have said, at a single glance, I began eagerly to search the sea, so far as it was visible, for ships; for I reflected that I should be very conspicuous, even from a distance, on the level sandbank, and that no mariner would be so inhuman as to pass by and leave me to my fate.

At present there was but a single vessel in sight – a small craft about a mile distant, apparently at anchor with all sail set, for the morning was dead calm and the sea like a mirror. As I observed the little vessel my hopes rose, since when the tide turned and she got under way, she would probably pass quite near to the sandbank, and I could hardly fail to be seen, or even heard, if I shouted. But when I looked at her more closely I began to have strange misgivings. I could see that she had but one mast, and that she carried a large square-sail with a high square top-sail over it, and I began to be uncomfortably reminded of the vision I had seen through Toby's telescope. She lay, it is true, but a shadowy shape of pale grey against the yellow eastern sky; but the more I looked at her, the more I became convinced that it was indeed the *Cormorant* returning, no doubt, from her fruitless chase.

As I reached this conviction, it dawned upon me that my position was one of great peril; for my conspicuousness, upon which I had congratulated myself, was a source of imminent danger. As soon as the haze cleared, I should certainly be seen – if I had not been observed already – and escape from this island there was none. I gazed helplessly around and my eye was immediately caught by the wreck, the black timbers of which stood out against the pinkish-yellow surface of the sand with startling distinctness, showing me at once the need and the means of concealment. Picking up the tubs, I ran across the sand as fast as my weariness would let me, until I reached the wreck, the large timbers of which I saw would easily conceal me if I were not already discovered. I examined, with some curiosity, the figurehead that had so startled me in the darkness, and felt little surprised at the effect it had produced; for, as it stood, owing to the falling in of the bows, nearly upright, with its feet on the level of the sand, it had even by daylight a singularly lifelike appearance. The figure was larger than life and very finely wrought, but its beauty was sadly faded; a thin veil of sea grass gave a ghastly pallor to the face, and the painting and gilding of the dress was almost hidden by bunches of brown seaweed and clusters of barnacles.

After gazing for some moments at the great, staring figure, I sat down on the sand beside the stem timber, and, leaning my back against it, almost immediately fell asleep. I must have remained asleep in this easy and restful position for some considerable time, for I was at length aroused by a feeling of cold, and when I opened my eyes I perceived that the sand where I was sitting was already covered with water to a depth of two or three inches, and I could see the tide creeping with that swift but stealthy movement that one may mark when the sea is calm, over the flat surface of the bank. I was about to rise to my feet when I caught, very distinctly, the sound of voices; and when I peeped with the utmost caution round the timber, there was the vessel I had seen – now unmistakably the revenue cutter – drifting past on the young flood within a quarter of a mile of the sand. The morning was still calm and the cutter's sails, which hung down from the spars straight and motionless, were reflected in the smooth water as in a mirror, while the voices of the men on board came through the still air with startling distinctness.

I drew back and shifted my position as the vessel slowly moved by, keeping behind the timber, for it was quite likely that someone on board might point a telescope at the wreck. As I looked back at the sandbank, I was astonished at the rapidity with which the tide had covered it. Where, but a short while since, the level sands had stretched away for near upon a mile, there was now but a little round patch that dwindled even as I watched it until at last it vanished; and then the sea, save for the timbers of the wreck, was an unbroken expanse as far as the eye could see, in every direction.

I peered round the timber at the cutter – standing now up to my knees in water – watching her with great anxiety, for she moved but slowly and was still quite near; presently the timbers of the wreck would be submerged and then I, floating on the calm sea, should be visible for miles. At this moment, however, I noticed a darkening of the surface to the southward indicating an approaching breeze, and this gradually spread northward until the water around me began to be stirred by little ripples, and I saw the cutter's sails fill. The breeze was but a light one, but I hailed it with profound relief; for not only did the *Cormorant* now begin to draw pretty rapidly away from my neighbourhood, but I saw that on the ripple-broken surface I should be much less conspicuous.

As the water rose, I arranged my floats as on the previous night, but as I floated, still held on to the timber with my legs, craning round from time to time to catch a glimpse of the fast-diminishing cutter. It was while I was making one of these observations that I felt my knee slip from the timber, and before I could recover my hold, I had turned round and drifted clear. For a moment or two I remained stationary, caught in an eddy of the tide, and then began to move slowly away; and as I looked back at the dwindling wreck, I could see the pallid green face of the figure-head staring at the rising waters and looking like some sickly mermaiden.

The cutter soon ceased to give me any uneasiness, for she continued to draw ahead rapidly, and at length disappeared into the haze; but before she vanished I would almost have taken the chances of capture, so wretched and despairing was my condition. Faint from lack of food, tortured with thirst, and utterly spent with fatigue, I seemed farther from relief or rescue than ever. I was not, it is true, in unfrequented waters, and as time went on I saw several ships sail by; but none of them came within a couple of miles of me, and as, one by one, they rose above my low horizon, drew abreast of me and then vanished ahead, I began to give up all hope of being seen until the tide turned and carried me right out to sea.

I cannot tell how long I drifted about, for I had no measure of time; but it seemed a very eternity of misery. The hot sun beat down upon my uncovered head and its reflection from the ripples dazzled my eyes, while the cold water chilled me to the very marrow of my bones.

After a time I fell into a state of semi-consciousness – something between dozing and swooning – from which I was once aroused by a party of sea-gulls circling round my head and screaming in my face; but, at length, I must have lapsed into complete insensibility, for I have no recollection of how I got out of the water.

When I returned to consciousness it appeared to be night, and as I opened my eyes I beheld a stout, elderly woman in a white cap sitting at a small table knitting, by the light of a candle. I was still drowsy and dull, so that I blinked at this apparition with incurious and un-speculative eyes; but as soon as she perceived that I was awake, she rose and hurried out of the room – apparently through a hole in the floor. Through this same aperture she presently returned, rising like some beneficent demon from the under-world, and bearing a large bowl from which steam arose and a wooden spoon projected. She set the bowl down upon a stool by the bed or pallet upon which I lay, and putting her arm round my neck, hoisted me into a sitting posture and held me thus while, with the other hand grasping the wooden spoon, she began to shovel the contents of the bowl into my mouth. All this time not a word was spoken on either side. As to me, if I would have spoken I had no opportunity, for I must needs bolt the food as fast as I could to avoid being choked; while she, regardless of my splutterings, shovelled away doggedly as though she were filling a sack.

At length the bowl, which had contained some kind of porridge fortified with Hollands, was scraped clean, and I was allowed to sink back on to my pillow; but before I had time to thank my benefactress, she had whipped up the bowl and spoon, and retiring to a corner of the room, vanished in the same mysterious way through the floor.

Immediately after this I must have fallen into a deep sleep, since, when I again awoke, it was broad daylight and the sun was shining into the room through a small, low window. The long rest and the food had so refreshed me that I now felt quite restored and very curious to know where I was. That the apartment in which I lay, was the cabin of some vessel I judged by the fact that the bed I occupied was like a ship's bunk, and that the flower-pots on the deep sills of the tiny, lace-curtained windows were secured by lashings; but the little interior was as exquisitely clean and dainty as a lady's chamber, in which it differed remarkably from any ship's cabin that I had ever seen.

As there was no one present to satisfy my curiosity, I drew myself up on to my knees, bringing my face to a level with the window that was above the bed, and, using great care not to disarrange the plants as I drew back the curtain, I looked out; and never in my life have I received a greater or more disagreeable surprise; for the very first object that my eye fell upon was the steeple of Limehouse Church.

I was yet gazing with the deepest consternation at this building when my attention was attracted by a vessel that lay close alongside. Only her bows were visible through the window, for she was not twenty yards away; but they were quite distinctive, being very bluff and bearing a high bowsprit, fully rigged in the fashion of twenty years before. Under the bowsprit was what sailors call a family-head, that is, a group of figures, and it was this group that had attracted my notice. It represented a buxom female with a very full bust, administering nourishment in maternal fashion to two nude children whole figures certainly did abundant credit to their diet. The whole group rested upon a base, on the front of which was written in large gold letters: CHARITY.

This, then, would seem to be the vessel commanded by the gross and corpulent Captain Murking, who might indeed have been the parent of the two children in the group; and if any confirmation of the ship's identity were needed, it was supplied by a figure that appeared on the forecastle as I gazed; which figure was that of none other than my friend Bill Muffin.

My observations were here interrupted by someone entering the cabin, and, turning my head, I beheld my benefactress of the previous night, a motherly-looking woman of about fifty with a round, rosy face, surmounted by a snow-white cap, and little pale blue eyes that twinkled with good humour.

As I was fully dressed, but for my coat and shoes, I leaped from the bunk and made her a profound obeisance.

"Permit me, madam," said I, "to offer my humble and heartfelt thanks for your charity, but for which I should, doubtless, by this time, be floating out to sea a lifeless corpse."

The matron smiled very pleasantly and nodded her head several times, but evidently did not understand what I had said, and after murmuring some words in a language which was no more intelligible to me than mine was to her, she went to the door and called out loudly "Johann!"

In answer to her summons a man – apparently her husband – appeared and accompanied her back into the cabin; and a fine portly, jolly-looking fellow he was, with a round smiling face and the most enormous pair of breeches that I have ever seen. As soon as saw me he advanced and slapped me playfully on the shoulder, addressing some evidently jocose remarks to me in what I took to be Dutch; and then he fell to laughing with such infinite good nature and high spirits that I could not forbear to laugh also.

Laughter, however, is but an indifferent medium of conversation, and I ventured to revert to my native speech.

"Your good lady," said I, "does not appear to speak English."

"Yaw, yaw," he replied, "Ich speak not English." He laughed again heartily, as though he found something very droll in the circumstance; and certainly the situation began to be somewhat absurd.

Communication being evidently impossible, as soon as I had donned my coat and shoes, we all drifted out on to the deck, when I perceived the vessel to be, as I had suspected, a Dutch schuyt with a deck-house on the poop. She was moored near to the Redriff shore not far below the Cherry Gardens, and the *Charity*, as I have said, lay only a few yards farther out in the stream.

As we came out on to the deck, I observed that Bill Muffin was still on the *Charity*'s forecastle so I hailed him by name.

"Hallo!" he sang out, failing to recognise me at first.

"Can you send a boat across?" I asked. "I want to come on board of you."

He stared hard at me for a moment, and then suddenly remembering me, he ran off aft and shortly appeared round the *Charity*'s bows sculling a heavy boat.

"Well, well," exclaimed Bill, as he stepped on board and politely doffed his hat to the lady, "and who'd a-thought of seeing of you aboard of a Dutch galli-ot? You ain't a-going to sea in her I hopes."

"Why no," I replied. "The fact is, these good people picked me up at sea, half drowned, and brought me to life again, and I don't know enough Dutch to thank them."

"Then talk to 'em in your own lingo," said Bill. "Folk what can make out that darned gibberish ought to be able to understand plain English."

Here the lady addressed a few words in Dutch to Bill, who pulled his forelock respectfully but turned to me with the air of an injured man.

"Now what's the good of a-jabbering stuff like that there to a Christian?" said he. "Why can't they talk sense?"

The jolly skipper, seeing how matters stood, now interposed with a deep chuckle, and seizing Bill and me by the arms, dragged us into the cabin, where, producing from a locker a great squat bottle and four glasses, he proceeded to fill the latter with aromatic-smelling Schnapps.

"Now I calls this here business," observed Bill, as he wiped his mouth with the back of his hand and beamed on the glasses. "Any man can understand a dram of good liquor, whereas palaverin' in heathen tongues is sheer folly."

The skipper handed the glasses round, and we all raised them and clinked.

"Hoch!" exclaimed the skipper, and he tipped his liquor expertly down his throat.

"Hoke it is master," responded Bill, "and the same to you, madam, and many of 'em," and he set down his empty glass with a wistful glance at the big bottle.

My own attempt to dispose of the liquor was not so successful, for it ended in copious tears and a violent fit of coughing; which so delighted my hosts that we all sallied forth from the cabin in high good humour.

As we came out on to the deck, I drew the skipper aside and rather shyly produced my purse; but in response to his indignant gestures I hastily put it away again and murmured an apology, while I felt my face grow very red. He was not offended, however, for when we came to the gangway he shook me very heartily by the hand as I wished him farewell, while the warm-hearted dame bestowed upon me a sounding kiss; whereat a waterman's apprentice, who was passing in a skiff, smacked his lips loudly and grinned, to my utter confusion and Bill Muffin's undissembled joy.

As we pulled away from the Schuyt – on whole quarter I could now read the appropriate name *Vriendschap* – I observed that Bill Muffin was eyeing me somewhat strangely; and, concluding that he had heard something of my affairs, I opened the matter at once and gave him a full account of all that had happened since I last saw him; to all of which he listened with profound attention, paddling the boat a little way down stream that I might finish before we came on board.

"'Tis a bad look-out for you, Mr Hawke," said he, when I had concluded, "and a pity the Dutchman weren't homeward bound. I heerd two Gravesend watermen a-talkin' about the job yesterday morning in the 'Old Margate' in Redriff, and they was a-saying as the hue and cry was out and all the town a-talkin' of the murder."

"So I had supposed," said I.

"Well now," he asked, "What might you be a-going to do, sir?"

"I propose to ask Captain Murking for a place of some kind on his ship," I replied.

Bill stopped rowing and stared at me with his mouth open.

"You're a-going to sail pretty close to the wind, aren't you?" he said at length.

"Why," I answered, "I don't suppose Captain Murking has heard of the murder, and if he has it's no affair of his. Besides which he doesn't know who I am."

"Didn't Toby tell him your name?" asked Bill.

"No," I replied, "for I remember that when he bid me farewell he called me 'Mr Robert,' so I propose to call myself Roberts – James Roberts."

"Well, you knows your own business best," Bill rejoined dubiously. "We sails out this day week, and when once our moorings is let go, you'll be safe. But for God's sake keep an eye on Mr Murking, which is a swivel-eyed old porpus and as sly as the devil."

I promised to use the greatest caution in my dealings with the captain, and then asked if he was then on board.

"Why no, he aren't," replied Bill. "He's at home this morning, so if you're bent on a-seein' of him, I'll put you ashore at the King's Stairs."

I said that I was still of the same mind, so Bill put the boat's head towards the stairs, which were nearly opposite the ship's berth.

"The old fox lives in Paradise Street," said Bill. "You goes straight from the stairs and turns sharp to your left and walks on till you comes to a ship-chandler's shop. The house is two doors farther on; green door with a brass knocker made like a lion's head holding a grommet in his mouth."

I thanked Bill for these explicit directions, and as he brought the boat alongside, I stepped on to the causeway and ascended the stairs. On the top of these I turned to look back. Bill was still holding on to the causeway and watching me, and as I looked past him I could see my two friends on the *Vriendschap* also looking my way; so taking out my handkerchief I waved them a last farewell, and turned up the passage at the head of the stairs.

CHAPTER FIVE

In which I enter the Abode of Godliness

As soon as I came out of the passage into the street, it became impressed upon me, by the uncommon attention with which passers-by regarded me, that I must cut a very unusual figure. Which, indeed, was manifest enough when it is considered that not only were my disordered clothes all stained with sea-water and sparkling with salt, but the little cloth cap, which the genial Dutchman had given me that I might not depart bareheaded, was uncouth in fashion and quite out of character with the rest of my apparel.

As I reflected upon this fact, I began to waver in my resolution of calling upon Mr Murking, for I could not but perceive that my condition was one to awaken suspicion, even if none previously existed; indeed I cannot now tell why I was so set upon reviving this acquaintance, excepting that the ship was on the point of sailing, and that no other means of escape presented itself. Still, as I have said, I began to be doubtful of the wisdom of my errand, so that when I, at length, reached the ship-chandler's shop, I halted to look in the window whilst I was making up my mind.

I had stood for some time gazing absently at a fine brass-hooded binnacle that was exhibited in the window, when a gruff voice hailed me, and I perceived a stout, red-faced man in a glazed hat standing in the doorway.

"Hillo, brother!" says he, "why, what's amiss? You look as salt as if you'd just come out of the harness cask."

"I've been overboard," I replied.

"Darned if I didn't think so," he rejoined, chuckling. "How did you come to do that, mate?"

"I'll tell you all about it next time we meet," said I. "I must get a shift of clothes now."

"Ah," said he, "you do want a bit of a swab down. Which way are you bound?"

"Two doors off," I replied. "Mr Murking's."

"What! old Charity?" he exclaimed, laughing. "I'd like to see you, mate, when you get a suit of his on."

I could not forbear laughing at the absurd picture thus presented, although I wished my new acquaintance at the bottom of the sea, for as he now sauntered by my side, I had no choice but to go boldly up to the door and knock.

As I lifted the brass grommet, or ring, of the knocker, I became aware of a pair of eyes looking over the blind of a bay window above; and as one of the eyes was fixed upon me, while the other apparently regarded the grinning seaman who was watching, I concluded that they belonged to Mr Murking.

I had just reached this conclusion when the door opened and a fierce-looking elderly woman confronted me with a wrathful stare.

"Well!" said she.

"Is Mr Murking within?" I inquired, nervously.

"And what affair is that of yours?" she demanded.

"I have called at his invitation and on business," I replied, somewhat nettled by her manner.

"Business!" exclaimed she, with a sniff; "more likely you are come to rob the house. But I'll tell him," and she slammed the door in my face.

Presently she returned, and, flinging the door wide open, said, "Come in and wipe your feet."

I obeyed her command, and she then ascended the stairs, directing me to follow and keep my hands off the banister-rails.

"Here he is," said she, opening a door and pushing me into a room; and having thus introduced me, she retired and shut the door; and, in the silence that ensued, I could hear the sound of her breathing through the keyhole.

Mr Murking was seated at a table on which were spread a number of papers. As I entered, he leaned back in his chair and regarded me with a look of inquiry, which in a few seconds changed to one of recognition, and he rose from his seat with his hand extended.

"Of course, of course!" he exclaimed. "For a moment I failed to recollect you – I see so many faces."

I took his proffered hand, and was foolishly wondering how many faces he could see at once, when he continued:

"Yes, I knew I had met you Mr – Mr – "

"Roberts," said I. "James Roberts."

"To be sure, Mr Roberts, I remember the name very well now; and so you have come to see me after all?"

"Yes," I answered. "And what is more, I have come to ask for employment on your ship."

"So!" said he. "But that is business, which we can talk over anon. For the present, I have not yet broken my fast, so I shall beg you to share my homely and frugal meal."

I assented cheerfully to this proposal, being by now as hungry as a hunter, so Mr Murking, having gathered up his papers and put them away in a cupboard, opened the door and put his head over the banister.

"Rebecca!" he called out, "I am ready for breakfast now."

"Is he gone then?" the woman bawled up the stairs.

"No; he is remaining to breakfast," replied Murking.

"What?" shouted the woman.

"I say," repeated Mr Murking severely, "that the young gentleman will take breakfast with me."

"But there ain't enough for two," roared Rebecca. "You know there ain't."

Mr Murking closed the door, and I heard him softly descending the stairs. Presently he silently re-entered the room and I noticed that his lips were rolled in to such an extent that his nose appeared to rest on his chin, which gave him a very singular and disagreeable appearance. He was shortly followed by Rebecca, who bore a large wooden tray which she set on the floor while she proceeded to lay the table, taking no notice either of me or Murking, but preserving a countenance as fixed and rigid as that of some acid-tempered sphinx.

When the meal was at length ready, and Rebecca had stalked out of the room and banged the door after her, Mr Murking drew two chairs to the table and we took our seats.

There were two dishes on the table, each concealed by a brass cover, and I must confess to some anxiety as to their contents, after Rebecca's warning, until my host raised one of the covers, when I was quite reassured by the appearance of a most substantial roll-shaped pudding.

As he raised the cover, Mr Murking leaned over the pudding and sniffed; then he rolled in his lips and murmured "Ha!" in a tone of deep satisfaction and attacked it with a large knife; when, to my astonishment and dismay, there oozed out on to the dish a quantity of liquid fat. Having laid on a plate an oily slab, embedded in which I detected several pieces of excessively fat bacon, my host raised his hand, and, turning up his eyes so that they regarded opposite corners of the ceiling, invoked the blessing of Heaven on our repast; praying that "this sustenance might be even as the manna in the wilderness," in which sentiment I sincerely acquiesced, and only wished that the prayer had been uttered somewhat earlier.

Sharp-set as I was, I could make no headway with the pudding, and was fain to sit and watch Mr Murking demolish it; which he did with horrible gusto, his chin shining with grease and his eyes half-closed in gluttonous ecstasy.

All my hopes were now centred in the second dish – for I was still ravenous; but when, at last, my host raised the cover, lo! It was filled with slices of black pudding, swimming in fat. So I had, after all, to make my meal mostly of bread, with a good draught of small beer.

When I had finished and Mr Murking had wiped up with a soft crust the last drop of fat from the dish, my host pushed back his chair and drew a deep breath.

"You seem to have but a poor appetite, Mr Roberts," said he.

I assured him that I had made an excellent meal, and he then rose, and, taking a boatswain's pipe from a hook by the fireplace, put his head out of the door and blew a shrill blast. In answer to this summons Mrs Rebecca presently appeared and began to clear the table, preserving the same glowering, immovable countenance as before.

"When we have talked over our little business," said Mr Murking, "I shall have to leave you for a little, but later I may ask you to accompany me on one or two visits that I have to make."

I thanked him for his consideration and begged that I might not be allowed to occasion him any inconvenience; and then we relapsed into silence until his handmaid had left the room, when he drew his chair opposite to mine and opened the subject of my application to him.

"I understood you to say, Mr Roberts," said he, "that you wished to be employed on my vessel?"

"That is so," I replied.

"I will not ask you," he continued, "how it comes that you have so suddenly changed your views. At my age, one has learned to mind one's own concerns, and this is none of mine. I hinted that I might find an office for you on my ship if you wished to make a voyage, and I still believe that you might be useful to me."

Here he paused and turned his head as though listening intently for some sound; then, to my amazement, he began to rise slowly from his chair, as though lifted by invisible clockwork, until he stood erect, when he stole on tip-toe across the room, as silently as a cat. As he approached the door, his arm extended in the same slow, noiseless manner until his hand was within an inch of the latch when he suddenly grasped the knob and flung the door wide open.

Apparently there was nobody outside, for he closed the door and returned to his chair, looking rather foolish.

"Walls," he remarked, "are said to have ears, and if that is so, I take it that they are in the form of keyholes. However, to return to our affairs, have you any acquaintance with seafaring matters?"

"None," I replied.

"Have you any knowledge of the keeping of accounts?" he inquired.

"I have helped my uncle to keep his farm accounts," I answered, "but of other kinds of bookkeeping I am but indifferently informed."

"I dare say," said he, "that, with a little help, you could learn to keep such books and accounts as I use. But we shall have to talk of this later, I think, for" – here he pulled out his watch – "yes, it is time for me to go, and I strive always to be punctual."

He rose, and, opening the cupboard in which he had stowed his papers, took out his hat. As he was moving towards the door he stopped and turned to me.

"By the way," he said, "you have brought no baggage or outfit with you, I suppose?"

"I have brought nothing," I replied.

"And you came by water, I observe," he continued, with a fat, cynical smile, "and look none the better for the journey."

"I should certainly be the better for a change of clothing," I admitted.

"Yes," said he. "But we can talk of that anon; and now adieu! Should you find the time hang heavy whilst I am away, there are some excellent godly books upon the shelf, which will make the time pass both pleasantly and with profit."

With this he departed, and from the bay window I saw him go down the street with a light, active step that was singularly incongruous with his great bulk.

I was still watching his receding figure when I heard the door open, and, turning round, saw Mistress Rebecca standing with her hands under her apron, regarding me with an expression of great disfavour.

"What's your name, young man?" she asked abruptly.

"James Roberts," I replied.

"Oh! James Roberts, hey!" she repeated. "Hum! And where do you come from, Master Roberts?"

I was disposed strongly to resent the woman's inquisitiveness, but, not wishing to make an enemy, I replied civilly:

"From Rochester."

"Ah," said she, "Rochester; that's in Kent. I know. You ain't a seaman, are you?"

"No," I answered, "but I shall be soon. I am going to sea in Mr Murking's ship."

"Oh, are you," she rejoined; then, after a pause she asked:

"Why don't you wash yourself?"

I ventured to point out that the room did not offer any facilities for ablution beyond an ink-pot on the mantel-shelf; whereupon she turned and walked out of the room, beckoning to me to follow.

She preceded me up two pairs of stairs, and opening a door, ushered me into a small but very neat and clean bedchamber.

"There," said she, "you have water and soap and towels and brushes. Wash yourself and brush your clothes and shoes and make yourself look less like poor Jack o' the causeway."

She stalked out of the room and slammed the door, leaving me to my work of purification, which I commenced at once with enthusiasm. When I had thoroughly cleansed my own person, I examined my clothing, which was certainly disreputable to the last degree, being so stained, and dusted with salt and creased by being slept in, that the whole suit might have come from Rag Fair. However, when I had well beaten and brushed the garments and finally rubbed them with a wet towel, their appearance was marvellously improved.

These labours occupied me a considerable time and I had barely completed them when there came a soft knock at the door, and on my opening it and peeping out I beheld Mr Murking holding in his hand a small parcel.

"I am glad to see you repairing the effects of your journey," said he, "and I have brought you something that will further improve your condition; for I bethought me that your shirt was soiled by the water past wearing, and so I have brought you a new one of fine cambric."

I was filled with delight and gratitude, for my shirt had resisted all my efforts to better its condition, and thanked my host most profusely for his kindness, at which, to tell the truth, I was not a little astonished.

"Pray do not speak of such a trifle," he protested, placing the parcel in my hands, "'tis no matter for thanks. But I will ask of you a favour, and that is to put on the clean linen without delay, as I have to go forth again, and would be glad of your company."

I lost no time in obeying his instructions, being glad enough to exchange the soiled garment, stiff with salt and gritty with sand, for the fine new cambric; and in a few minutes I came down the stairs to the living-room, where Mr Murking was waiting for me.

"We must get you a hat," said he, as I took up the uncouth Dutch cap, "and then you will be clothed well enough, at least to start on a voyage."

This fatherly solicitude on Mr Murking's part was a matter upon which I reflected with renewed surprise as I walked at his side through the narrow streets of Redriff. I had certainly not credited him, at our first meeting, with a specially benevolent disposition, and I now began to wonder if I had misjudged him, and allowed my mind to be set against him by the uncomeliness of his person. The readiness too with which he had taken me as a guest into his house seemed unaccountable (for I had expected to be sent to live on the ship), as did the consideration with which he treated me, a mere youth and a stranger coming to him to ask employment as a raw apprentice. My education apparently made me of some use to him, but clerks were not so scarce that he need set any great store excepting on the supposition that he was a much better-natured man than I had taken him for.

When I had got myself a new hat at a shop near the Dockhead, and put the absurd cap in my pocket, I felt that my appearance was somewhat restored, and stepped out with more confidence, for I was now only shabby, which was not a rare condition in this part of London.

We had walked a short distance down Tooley Street when Mr Murking drew his watch out of his fob and looked at it.

"Why, bless me!" he exclaimed, "my watch has stopped; I must have forgot to wind it. Can you give me the time?"

"That I cannot," I replied, "for my watch, too, has stopped."

"Ah! to be sure," said he, "doubtless the water got into it. But I think there is not enough time to walk round by London Bridge to Tower Hill, whither I am bound, so we will ferry across the river."

We turned down a side street and walked on until we came to some stairs near the end of Shad Thames, where Mr Murking hailed a waterman who was paddling by in his wherry. As we sat down in the boat, my host drew out his watch, and having taken it from its case examined it critically.

"Why," he exclaimed, "it has started again, and I see it was wound, for the chain is on the fusee. 'Tis strange what tricks a watch will play upon one. By the way, let us see what is amiss with yours."

"Doubtless the sea water has got into it, as you say," I replied, unwilling to show the watch because of the crest and motto engraved on the back of it.

"I can tell you if it is so," said he, "for I am used to the care of chronometers."

He held out his hand for the watch, and as I had no pretext for refusing, I drew it reluctantly from my fob and handed it to him, face uppermost.

"A fine timepiece this, Mr Roberts," said he, "and prettily engraved," he added as he turned it over and examined the back, "though 'tis an odd custom to mark one's belongings with the picture of an eagle or a phoenix instead of writing one's name in plain letters."

I thought that it was well for me, in the present instance, that my name had been indicated by signs rather than letters, and was congratulating myself that the engraver's hawk had passed with my host for an eagle or a phoenix when a sudden thought flashed into my mind and over whelmed me with dismay; for I now remembered, for the first time, that the shirt that I had so cheerfully cast off and left folded on the bed, bore, embroidered in red silk as plainly as letters could be made, the incriminating inscription R. Hawke.

I say that I was overwhelmed with dismay; but more than this, for a sudden flood of suspicion surged over me when I recollected how Mr Murking had hurried me from the house the instant I had made the change. I looked at him as he sat with his great flabby face bent over the timepiece that he held in his hand, and seeming by reason of his squint, to watch me furtively out of the corner of his eye, and all my dislike of him and disgust at his hideousness revived.

"I see no rust in the works," said he, closing the watch and handing it back to me, "but I notice that it has not run down, although I cannot start it, so the water must have got into the movement."

He then proceeded to advise me about having it cleaned, and went on to discourse at some length on watches and chronometers in general, but my consternation was so great that I could pay but little attention; indeed I think that he must have noticed my confusion, for he presently fell silent, though I caught him once or twice eyeing me very shrewdly.

We landed at some stairs near the Tower and made our way to a house in a small street off Great Tower Hill where Mr Murking took me with him into the office of the merchant with whom he had business, bidding me sit in a corner of the room until he had finished. From thence he carried me to a tavern in Eastcheap where we dined in a chamber alone, although there was an ordinary kept at the house, and after resting awhile, we set out for Redriff by way of London Bridge.

All this time I was in a whirl of confusion, and so preoccupied by my thoughts that I found it difficult to carry on a connected conversation. One moment I felt convinced that Murking had deliberately tricked me, and that he, at least, suspected my identity; the next I scouted as absurd the idea that he should be acquainted with the doings in an obscure Kentish village, or, even if he had heard of the murder, that he should connect me – a stranger – with the affair.

On one point, however, my mind was made up. I would, at all hazards, regain possession of the incriminating garment immediately on my arrival at the house, and I would take uncommon care that my host should have no chance of examining it. I was still revolving in my mind the various ways in which I might carry out this resolution, when we turned into Paradise Street not far from Mr Murking's house. We had just come abreast of the ship-chandler's shop when my host suddenly halted and looked in at the door.

"Pray step in here with me, Mr Roberts," said he; "I have ordered some fittings for my ship and they should be ready by now."

As we entered the ship, a small, grimy old man who was weighing a coil of rope in a corner on an immense pair of scales, came forward and saluted my companion.

"Ah! Master Murking, sir," says he, "you've come about that there joolery of yourn, I suppose?" Here he grinned and winked at me.

"I have," replied Murking drily. "Is it ready?"

"The bilboes and the bracelets was finished this morning," answered the old man, "and the screws and gags ought to be done. Step through, sir, and you can see them."

He opened a door at the back of the shop and beckoning to us to follow, preceded us down a passage that led into a large shed which appeared to be occupied by a ship-smith, for I perceived two forges – one of unusual size – three anvils and a variety of tongs, sledge-hammers and other smith's ironmongery, from a mighty anchor that lay by itself in a corner, to small fittings such as sister-hooks, staysail-hanks or cranse irons.

As we entered, a man who was working at a bench looked round, and I noticed that he was working a screw tap into some implement that was held in a vice.

"Here you are, Thomas," said our guide, "here's Mr Murking hisself come to fetch his pretty little trinkets."

"I'm a-finishing the last of 'em now," replied the smith, gruffly, "and I can't work no faster"; and with this he applied a drop of oil to the tap with his finger, and fell to turning the level.

"How long will you be finishing it?" asked Murking.

"About a quarter of an hour," replied the smith.

"Then," said Murking, "in that case I will come in again, as I have to make a call that I had forgotten, close by. But if they should be finished before I return, you may give the screws and gags to this young gentleman. The bilboes and handcuffs you had better send on board. And," he added, turning to me, "you need not wait for me, but take them to my house. I may be detained longer than I expect."

He then departed, leaving me in some little anxiety as to whether I should be able to get home before him.

As soon as he was gone, the old man fetched a piece of sacking which he laid on the floor and placed on it a number of well-oiled iron implements, the like of which I had never seen.

"What are these things?" I asked, picking up one of them.

"I'll show you," answered the old man; and taking the implement from my hand, he held it towards me.

"You see them two holes?" he asked, pointing to two round apertures, each an inch in diameter; "well, just put your thumbs in them."

I did as he directed and he then turned a winged screw, when I immediately felt my thumbs tightly gripped. He looked at me with a sly smile and gave the screw another turn, by which my thumbs were squeezed so horribly that I shouted to him to release me. When he had unscrewed the hideous instrument, he picked up another, shaped like a very massive pair of compasses, with a screw at the joint, and asked if I would like to try it; but I assured him that a verbal description would satisfy me. He then explained that this was a screw gag, and was used for forcibly opening the jaws; which was done by introducing the points between the teeth, and separating them by turning the screw.

"But what, in the name of God, can Mr Murking want with these dreadful things?" I asked in horrified amazement.

"Why, he's in the Guinea trade, ain't he?" was the answer. "All the Guinea traders carries screws and gags and bilboes and bracelets too. Come and see 'em."

He carried me to another shed where he showed me two great heaps, one of leg-fetters and the other of handcuffs or manacles.

"These are the things to keep a ship's crew in order," said he.

"But," I objected, "there are two or three hundred fetters here, and the crew numbers not more than thirty."

"Ah! you have me there, master," he replied with a grin and a wink, but he vouched no further explanation; and as the thumb-screws and gags were now ready, he wrapped them up in the sacking and gave them to me.

I made the best of my way home with my burden, anxiously wondering whether Mr Murking had preceded me. But my speculations were soon put an end to when I knocked at the door, for it was opened by my host himself.

Instantly my suspicions returned in full force, and so angry was I at the trick I deemed he had played me, that I pushed by without a word, and, striding up the stairs, flung the bundle down on the living-room floor.

However, he took no notice of my surly manner, but proceeded to explain at great length the reasons for carrying the diabolical instruments that I had seen, pointing out the turbulent and bloodthirsty character of the common seamen who sail to the Guinea Coasts, and, in conclusion, thanking Heaven most piously that he had never had occasion to use such barbarous means to preserve discipline.

I listened with scant patience to this discourse, which I knew to be a parcel of hypocritical lies, and took the first chance of retiring to the bedroom which had been allotted to me. As I entered the room the first object my eyes lighted on was the fatal shirt, lying neatly folded, on a chest; and I could see at a glance that it had been washed and roughly dried, for it was perfectly clean and white.

I took up the garment and shook it out, turning it over mechanically to look at the marking.

To my amazement the name was not there.

Hardly able to believe the evidence of my eyesight, I turned the garment about and examined every part of it, but no vestige of a mark could I find. For a moment I thought that some other shirt must have been substituted for it, but on more closely scrutinising it I could see that it was really my own.

Then I supposed that it must have been left unmarked, although this seemed most unlikely, seeing that Prudence – that paragon of housewives – had always overlooked my linen, as well as that of my uncle and aunt.

At length, on carefully examining the yoke, behind the neck, where the marking was usually put, I detected a number of minute holes in the linen with here and there a tiny pink stain; and then the mystery was solved.

The silken marking had been carefully and neatly picked out!

I say the mystery was solved, but its solution only left the matter more mysterious. For who could have done this? And with what object?

Of one thing I felt pretty confident. The mark had not been picked out by Mr Murking; for even if he had come direct from the smith's, there would not have been time. And reaching this conclusion with no little relief, I folded up the shirt and took my way down the stairs.

Half-way down I met Mistress Rebecca and took the opportunity to thank her very civilly for having provided me with a change of linen; whereupon she grunted and gruffly expressed the hope that she might never again have to wash such a filthy rag; which, she assured me, "might have been worn for a month by a Wapping mud-lark."

My confidence being somewhat restored, I suppose I was more placable in my manner to Mr Murking, for he was certainly extremely friendly and confidential with me, giving me many particulars (mostly untrue I am sure) of his life on the Guinea Coast, and finally reading aloud several Chapters from the book of Exodus with appropriate commentaries.

We supped early (on corned pork and chitterlings) and after more pious reading and protracted prayers, separated for the night.

CHAPTER SIX

In which I meet a Wolf in Sheep's Clothing

I was somewhat late on the following morning, having, as I suppose, not entirely recovered from my late fatigues, and when I came down into the living-room, Rebecca was already laying the table for breakfast.

"Good morrow, Mr Roberts," said Murking as I entered the room; "you are late this morning, and I am early, for I have a full day before me."

As he said this I noticed that Rebecca bestowed on him a glance of the most intense malignancy and then glanced quickly at me as she left the room.

"I trust I have not inconvenienced you by playing the sluggard," said I.

"By no means," he replied, "for you see that breakfast is even now scarcely ready. But since you are well rested, you will doubtless be the more spry, and I have much occupation for you today."

There was now wafted into the room a most savoury odour, and Rebecca entered with the tray on which were the two brass dish-covers. But despite the appeal to my nostrils, I viewed the covers with deep foreboding, sorrowful experience leading me to suspect them of concealing some new culinary horror. Great, therefore, was my relief when Mr Murking lifted them and disclosed a pile of goodly gammon rashers and another of grilled kidneys.

After the customary prayer that "this nourishment might be consecrated with thankfulness to the support of our sinful and unworthy bodies," we fell to, and each strove to out-do the other in pious devotion to this work of consecration.

"You have quite a fine twist this morning, Mr Roberts," observed my host as he mopped up the bacon fat with a cube of bread. "'Tis wonderful how the appetite awakes when the body is rested and the mind tranquil."

He drained a large beaker of ale, and, rising from the table glanced at the chronometer on the mantelshelf and compared it with his watch.

"Dear, dear," said he, "how the time speeds when one is pleasantly employed. 'Tis near eight o'clock. I must run away immediately, but first I will give you your instructions. Today I shall be working on the ship, for we have but a few more days in which to finish our preparations for the voyage. I shall carry you with me that you may begin to learn your duties, but, as I have to do some business before I go on board, I shall ask you to take the parcel that you brought yesterday from the smith's and await me at the 'Ship Aground,' a tavern on the Strand hard by the Cherry Gardens. You may expect me at the tavern at about half-past eight, so you need not start for a quarter of an hour or more, for it is but five minutes walk from this house."

He drew his hat from the cupboard, and, having dusted it with his handkerchief and relocked the cupboard, took his departure.

He had hardly left the house before Rebecca appeared, and began briskly to remove the debris of our meal. I bid her "good morning" as she entered (at which I thought she looked at me very oddly), and asked if I might help her to carry the things downstairs.

"Why," she replied, "'tis no more than a great hulking fellow like you should do, to stir your lazy bones now that you have filled your belly; so you may carry this tray to the kitchen, and, if you drop anything, God help you."

I picked up the tray and bore it off to the kitchen, whither Rebecca followed with the remaining articles.

"Now," said she, suddenly squaring at me with her arms akimbo, "what are you going to do?"

"I am going to the 'Ship Aground' to await Mr Murking who is to meet me there."

"Don't go," said she.

"Why should I not go?" I inquired.

"I say, don't go!" she answered angrily. "Am I to stand here a-bandying words with a great, hulking, overfed loblolly-boy? I say don't go!"

"But I agreed to go," I objected, greatly puzzled and not a little disturbed by her manner.

"Listen to me," she exclaimed. "I am now going out a-marketing and I shall lock the front door and take the key. If you want to leave the house, you must climb over the wall at the bottom of the garden and drop down into the lane at the back."

"But," I protested, "I – "

"Listen and don't chatter," said she, shaking her fist at me. "You see that blue jar at the end of the shelf. In it is a key. That key will open the cupboard in the room upstairs. If you take it out of the jar, put it back. And I say again, don't go to the 'Ship Aground.' "

With this she caught up a grey shawl that lay on a chair, took down a great key from a hook on the wall, and stalked out of the kitchen; and a moment later the front door slammed, and I heard the key grate in the lock.

I stood in the kitchen in utter bewilderment and filled with an uneasy sense of impending danger. If I were going to the tavern, it was time for me to start; yet how could I go in the face of Rebecca's emphatic if enigmatical warning. I looked at the blue jar, but all the instincts of a gentleman cried out against the baseness of breaking into a stranger's secret receptacle with a false key.

And yet, if Murking should be plotting to betray me! Surely I should be justified in consulting my safety. Again the woman's dark hints recurred to me and my fears and suspicions grew, until at last they overcame my scruples and I boldly thrust my hand into the jar, and, drawing out the key, bounded up the stairs.

I had the cupboard open in a twinkling, but, when my eye fell upon the sextant cases, the rolled charts, log-books and other harmless properties of a shipmaster, I was so ashamed that I was on the point of shutting the door. A pile of letters lay on the single shelf and beside them a large folded paper. With the former I had not the hardihood to meddle, but the large sheet I partly unfolded; when I saw that it contained printed matter, for at the bottom, which was all I could see, I read "God save the King."

This being, then, evidently no private document, I ventured to open it out and examine it; but before I had fairly glanced through it, my hands were shaking and my heart throbbing with fear and anger, so that I must needs lay it on the table to read it.

It ran, as far as I can remember, somewhat thus:

"TWO HUNDRED GUINEAS REWARD

"WHEREAS on the 21st day of July in this present year of Our Lord, 1791, William Colville of Shorne in the Country of Kent, Gentleman, was foully and treacherously murdered and WHEREAS suspicion hath fallen upon ROBERT HAWKE of Shorne aforesaid for whose arrest a warrant hath been issued

"NOW BE IT KNOWN UNTO ALL MEN by these presents that I, the undersigned, John Colville of Shorne aforesaid Justice of the Peace, do hereby undertake to pay the sum of Two Hundred Guineas to any person who shall give such information as shall lead to the apprehension of the said Robert Hawke.

"Given under my hand this 21st day of July in the year of our Lord 1791.

"John Colville, J.P."
"SHORNE, KENT.

"The following is the description of the above mentioned Robert Hawke. He is twenty years of age, stoutly built, about five feet ten inches in height, hath a brown complexion, chestnut hair and grey eyes. On the right cheek he beareth a small scar. When last seen he wore a blue coat with gilt basket buttons, a laced waistcoat of yellow silk, white kerseymere breeches and white stockings. He is known to carry a gold watch on the back whereof is engraved a hawk with spread wings, and his linen is marked R. Hawke in red silk thread.

"GOD SAVE THE KING"

When I had read through this precious document I folded it and replaced it in the cupboard, locking the latter and taking out the key. So overcome was I with the horror of my position that I was as one in a dream, and stood with the key in my hand and fury and hatred in my heart, meditating upon the malice of my cousin Percival (who had evidently supplied the description), and the incredible treachery and villainy of Murking.

I was aroused by a soft knock at the street door.

With a new-born wariness, I stepped to the bay window and, drawing the muslin half-blind a fraction of an inch aside, peeped out through the chink.

The person who had knocked, had squeezed himself so flat against the door that he was entirely invisible excepting the toes of his shoes and the peak of his hat; but a dozen paces down the street I could see two ill-looking fellows making believe to study the ship-chandler's window, but very evidently watching our street door. Moreover I noticed that one or two men on the opposite side of the street, had stopped to look, and that heads were beginning to appear at the windows of the houses that faced ours.

While I was peering out, the man at the door turned to ply the knocker, which he did this time more sharply; and I now saw that he carried a formidable bludgeon. At the same time the two other men approached the house and I observed that they were similarly provided.

I waited to see no more, but, snatching up my hat, ran lightly down the stairs. As I passed through the kitchen I paused to drop the key into the blue jar; and as I did so, I heard the men trying, apparently with their united weights, to force the street door.

I ran out into the garden and took my way down a narrow path that led round a well and between beds filled with flowers. The loftiness of the walls somewhat dismayed me, for they were near upon nine feet high and the carefully trained fruit trees that covered them, seemed to afford but an insecure foothold. Moreover, the garden seemed to slope down towards the end so that the wall there would be the highest. But here, Fortune – or someone else – favoured me, for when I had pushed my way between two great clumps of hollyhocks, I found a light ladder placed against the end wall and reaching nearly to the top. Quickly ascending this I looked over into a narrow lane that ran between two high blank walls. Not a soul was in sight at present, so, sitting astride on the wall, I hoisted up the ladder and lowered it on the other side. Then I descended into the lane, and, laying the ladder on the ground beside the wall, walked away swiftly.

Presently the lane turned sharply to the left and a short distance further on opened into Rotherhithe Street. Judging that my pursuers had come from the west, I turned towards the east and walked on as rapidly as I could without attracting attention. But I had no idea whither I was flying, the neighbourhood being quite strange to me; and, indeed, such was the black despair in which I was now plunged, and so aimless and hopeless did my flight appear, that I was half disposed to give myself up and take the chances of my trial.

I had just passed St Mary's Church (which I knew by having seen it from the river) when I observed a man come out from the door of a tavern and cross the road. He bore in one hand a bundle enclosed in a coloured handkerchief and in the other a large stone jar, and by his dress and rolling gait appeared to be a sailor. But more than this I noticed, for the fellow's figure seemed familiar to me, so that, when he set down the jar on the ground whilst he counted some money in his hand, and turned his face towards me, I was not surprised, though greatly rejoiced, to recognise my friend, Bill Muffin.

He observed me at the same moment and immediately dropped his bundle and staggered back several paces with a droll pretence of being overcome with amazement. Then he proceeded to execute a few steps of the hornpipe while he whistled an accompaniment, and so came dancing towards me with his arms akimbo and his thick shoes making a most infernal clatter on the road.

This performance, which brought laughing spectators to every shop door, did not suit me at all, for he was like to bring the whole neighbourhood about us; so I eyed him somewhat severely and bade him behave with more decorum in a public place.

But Bill was in great spirits this morning – I mean no play upon the word, although, to speak the truth, I think he had refreshed somewhat too freely – and rather boisterous withal; so when I held out my hand, he grasped it and would have had me join in his absurd antics; whereupon, being quite out of patience with his ill-timed foolery, I caught up his bundle and jar, and, without more ado, set off up the street as hard as I could go, leaving him to follow as he pleased. But I gained little by this manoeuvre, for, although he certainly did follow, yet I gathered from the sound of his whistling and the laughter and cheers of the spectators, that his progress was neither dignified nor decorous; so, as it seemed that by carrying his burdens I but left him free to play the fool, I set them down and walked on.

This seemed to have the desired effect, for the whistling ceased and he presently overtook me, quite calm and sober.

"I asks your pardon, Master Roberts," says he, "for a-bein' gay and free as you might say, but d'ye see, I'm on a holiday jaunt, I am."

"There's no need to go up the street like a dancing bear, if you are on a holiday jaunt," I replied.

"No, there ain't," he agreed; "but it was the surprise wot done it; the surprise at seeing you – and the joy – and the joy."

He made as if he would set down his burden again, but I dragged him forward, suspecting his intention.

"But how comes you here, shipmate?" he asked. "Why ain't you aboard the ship along of old Bare-bones?"

I looked at him doubtfully, wondering whether it was safe to speak of my affairs to him.

"Look ye, Bill," said I, "I've something to tell you; but first I want to know, are you drunk or are you sober?"

"Why, d'ye see," he answered, in no wise offended at the question, "as to that, it's a matter of a quartern o' Jamaica rum and a small drop of Hollands; and if you think that a man of my position could get drunk on a quartern o' rum and a dram of Hollands, you're doing me a great injustice."

"I crave your pardon, Bill," said I, "but you must confess that you are a trifle flighty in your manner this morning, and the matter of which I have to speak is no light one."

I then gave him an account of Murking's treachery and my escape from the tipstaves, to which he listened with deep interest, and many exclamations of anger and disgust.

"Well I'm darned!" he ejaculated, as I finished my narrative, "to think of him a-sittin' there like some great, bloated spider and a-spinning of his web round you, as might be some poor devil of an unsuspecting fly – but there! It ain't no more than wot I'd have expected, and I did warn you to keep your weather eye a-liftin', now didn't I?"

"You did," I answered; "and I was half disposed not to go to him after what you said. But, of course, if I had known about this reward being offered, and so great a sum too, I should never have trusted myself near him."

"I deserve to be kicked for a damned fool not to have told you," said Bill, penitently, "but I thought you knowed about it."

"You knew of the reward then?" I asked.

"Why, to be sure, I did," he replied, "when the bills was stuck up in all the taverns in Redriff, and elsewhere too for all I knows."

"And you never thought of making yourself a rich man, Bill?" said I, not a little affected to think of the unselfishness of this simple, careless seaman.

"What do you mean?" he demanded rather huffily. "D'ye suppose I'm the sort o' swab as would soil his fingers with blood-money, and that the price of a comrade's life?"

"No, no," I replied. "I only mean that you've been a better friend to me and a truer comrade than I knew of."

"Avast talkin' foolishness, mate," said he, gruffly, "and tell us where you're bound for now?"

"God knows," I replied, "for I don't. Whither are *you* bound, Bill?"

"Me?" said he. "Why I'm a-going for to drop down with the tide to Gravesend."

"Gravesend!" I exclaimed.

"Gravesend it is," he replied, "and this here's my port of departure," he added, as we drew up by the entrance to Hanover Stairs.

"The fact is," he continued, with an embarrassed air, and blushing to the colour of a pickled cabbage, "I'm a-going down for to see a friend – sort of farewell visit, d'ye see – and I was just a-thinking that you'd best step aboard and I could put you ashore somewheres down the river; you'll do well to give Redriff a wide berth, for these here tipstaves may be on your heels this very moment."

"You're right, Bill," said I, considerably disturbed at his suggestion, "I'll come on board with you gladly if you'll have me."

"I've got a passenger," said he, as we walked down the alley that led to the stairs, "but he ain't no account. He's as deaf as a post."

"You seem to have chosen a lively companion for a holiday jaunt," said I smiling.

"Well, d'ye see, he's her brother; that's how it is," explained Bill, grinning and blushing in great confusion; "but here we are and here he is."

A large wherry was drawn up close to the stairs – for the tide was more than half-way up – and I perceived a smallish, round-faced young man in a waterman's dress, sitting in the stern. He rose when he saw us, and, taking the bundle and jar from Bill's hands, set them down in the bows; then, when we had stepped into the boat, he unhitched the painter from the ring and pushed off.

"This here's a friend of mine wot's a-coming part of the way with us," shouted Bill indicating me with his thumb; whereupon the waterman smiled and nodded, being too much occupied in getting the boat into the river, for more formal salutations.

As the tide was still running up strongly we were compelled to hug the shore – which I would rather have avoided; but although Bill and the waterman (who was named Jacob Thorpe) each took an oar while I steered, yet, owing to the tide and the number of lighters, barges, hoys and other small craft amongst which we had to pick our way, it

71

was near upon half an hour before we were well round Cuckold's Point.

The river being more free of shipping now that we were clear of the Pool, Bill and his friend cast in their oars and stepped the mast, on which they hoisted a large lug-sail.

As soon as the oars were stowed and the sail set, my two companions came aft and took their seats, Thorpe holding the sheet and steering whilst Bill took his ease and beguiled the time with conversation. I found Thorpe an excessively embarrassing companion, for he was very deaf but yet would join in our talk; and as he never heard what was said to him but guessed at its purport and always guessed wrong, we were continually at cross purposes. As to Bill, he was full of good humour and gaiety, so much so, indeed, that I was compelled to restrain him; for he would hail every boat that we passed with some quip or jest, so that I feared he would make us more remarkable than would be safe for me.

About noon, by which time we had managed, by keeping close in shore, to get as far as Bugsby's Reach, he fetched the bundle and the jar from the bows and unfastened the former; which proved to contain a supply of boiled beef and ship's bread and a leathern drinking-cup. The jar was next broached and I was rejoiced to find that the liquor was nothing more potent than strong ale; with which, and the beef and bread, we contrived to make an excellent meal.

As Bill was replenishing the cup for the fifth time, he said to me, in a low voice: "Have you made up your mind as to where you're going ashore?"

Now the fact is I had been considering this question ever since we started; and the more I thought upon it, and the more I looked at the familiar, homely river, with its burden of ships that seemed to greet me as old friends; the more did I become affected with a terrible home-sickness and a yearning to be near the places and the people that I loved. In the instant that Bill had pronounced the word "Gravesend," there had sprung up before me the picture of the old home and its inmates that were so dear, and especially the image of that sweet maid who, alone, had seen into my heart and knew it to be free from guilt. And so it fell out that my wishes begot the thought that actuated my reply.

"I have made up my mind, Bill," I answered. "I shall go ashore with you at Gravesend."

"At Gravesend!" exclaimed Bill, letting the ale trickle on to the boat's floor in the extremity of his amazement. "Are you mad?"

"Steady there!" bawled Jacob. "You're a-running all the ale into the bilge; are we a-going to lap it up like cats?"

"All's right, mate," said Bill, handing him the brimming cup to stop his mouth, and turning to me with a look of dismay.

"Has this here trouble turned your brain, Mr Roberts?" he asked.

"By no means," I answered. "If you come to think over the matter, you will see that Gravesend is as safe as anywhere, for 'tis the last place in which anyone would look to find me. Moreover, I know very few people there, and as the town is always full of strangers, I am likely to be little remarked."

"But why go there when there are other places where you are quite unknown?" he urged. "You don't mean to stay there, do you?"

"Certainly not," I replied. "My idea is this: there will be several outward-bound packets waiting there tonight ready to get under way on the ebb-tide. I can remain hid in the town until nightfall and then go aboard one of them and so be clear away by daybreak."

"That's true," Bill agreed doubtfully. "But it do seem a terrible venturesome thing to do."

"Then there is another matter," said I. My cousin, Miss Leigh, will have heard that I was not on board the *Tally Ho* and when she meets Toby and hears that I went overboard, she will think I was drowned. Now if I go to Gravesend I can send her a note by hand so that she will know that I am safe."

"There ain't no need of that," replied Bill, "for she's bound to hear about this job at Redriff. Besides, I could send her a message myself. Howsoever, you must steer your own craft and whatever tack you chooses to sail on, why, Bill Muffin'll stand by to lend a hand."

I pressed his great brown paw and told him how grateful I was to find in him so true and faithful a friend.

"'Tain't nothing, mate, as one man wouldn't do for another, without he was a darned swab," said he. "But now as to a-stowing you away in the town. I'm a-lying tonight at the 'Mermaid' in West Street, which you'll easily reckernise by a graven image of a young woman with a fish's tail, wot's set up on the front of the house. My friend wot I'm a-going to see, she lives there she do. That's why I'm a-going there. Now wot I says is this here. When we comes to the stairs, you and me nips ashore without speaking to no one, and makes for the 'Mermaid.' Then I takes you up to my chamber, which is No. 18 at the top of the house, and there you lies snug. Then I goes and finds out if there's any packet in the anchorage bound for France or Spain or any foreign port not too far away. If I find a craft that will do, I shall go off and take a passage for you, and then, as soon as it is dark, Jacob and me will put you aboard. How will that do?"

I said it would do admirably and thanked him again, from my heart, for his staunch friendship. I then asked him where he should land.

"The 'Pope's Head' stairs, I expect," said he, "but I'll ask Jacob." He put both hands to his mouth and roared out, as though hailing a ship:

"It's the 'Pope's Head' stairs, aren't it, Jacob? Hey? The 'Pope's Head' stairs?"

Jacob turned on us a bland and benevolent smile.

"I should say," said he, "as it was near upon three quarters of a hour."

"Are we going to the 'Pope's Head' stairs?" bellowed Bill, with a purple face and distended veins.

"I know," said Jacob, grinning. "I could see it directly you come into the alley."

Bill groaned. "It's no go," said he. "But we shall see when we get there."

About this time the ebb set in, and I could soon see, by the way in which the banks slipped by, that we were travelling at a good pace. One by one, the familiar landmarks came in sight and were passed; Erith, Purfleet with its solitary wooded hill, the pretty village of Greenhithe, Grays Thurrock at the bottom of St Clement's Reach, and then we turned round Broadness into Northfleet Hope. A whole lifetime of misery seemed to have elapsed since I last looked across the level expanse of Chadwell and Tilbury marshes, and yet it was but five days ago that I landed, all unsuspecting of the calamity that had befallen me, at the little jetty of which we were now drawing abreast. As I gazed at the low shore, the events of these miserable days came crowding before me like some hideous dream, until I was suddenly aroused from my reverie by the voice of Bill Muffin.

"If I was you, I'd let down the flaps of your hat. Folk do, very often, when they travel on the water, if the sun's hot."

I at once saw the wisdom of his suggestion and acted on it, lowering the brim of my hat until it partially hid my face.

As we turned swiftly round Tilbury Ness and swept along in the fairway by the north shore, Bill began to look anxiously towards Gravesend.

"Ain't it time to cross, Jacob?" he asked, as the town rose on our bow; but, Jacob, according to his custom, made some quite irrelevant reply and sailed straight on until we had covered more than half the distance from Northfleet, when he put the boat's head across the stream. The river was now pretty full of shipping, sailing or drifting down on the tide, and among the numerous vessels Jacob threaded his way with skill born of long practice.

At length we ran clear of the craft in the fairway and headed inshore with the town right ahead.

"Why darn me if he ain't a-making for the Town Quay!" exclaimed Bill. "This won't never do," and he proceeded to roar out remonstrances to the bland and smiling Jacob. But before that worthy could be made to understand Bill's objections and demands, the boat was alongside the stairs, with Jacob's hook firmly grasping a post of the handrail.

"There's nothing for it now but to jump ashore," exclaimed Bill, "and quicker the better."

He jumped out on to the stone step and I instantly followed; and, without a word of explanation to Jacob, we pushed our way through a group of watermen and ran up the stairs.

CHAPTER SEVEN

In which I experience changes of Fortune

There was quite a crowd of persons at the head of the stairs, for there being several King's ships as well as one or two merchantmen bound for the Indies, at anchor in the river, the town was more than usually full. We had pushed our way through the thickest part of the crowd and were passing before the row of little greengrocers' shops that stand between the bell-house and the stairs, when we came, quite suddenly, upon a couple of searchers. Bill and I saw them at the same moment and as I turned my face away, he shoved me up against the shops so that I nearly fell into a great basket of cherries.

"Good morrow, Master Hawke," said a voice from the back of the shop, "and glad to see you home again."

I turned a startled glance towards the speaker, whom I at once recognised as a man who had been used to buy fruit from my uncle.

"Come along for God's sake," exclaimed Bill, as I hastily returned the man's salutation. He passed his arm through mine, and, hurrying me past the shops, made for an archway in the front of the 'Christopher' tavern. Entering this, we passed through a narrow passage and presently came out into West Street, which we found to be filled with a crowd of sailors, watermen and pilots and blocked half-way down by a chariot.

"Now look at that!" exclaimed Bill, pointing at the unwieldy vehicle, that seemed to fill the whole width of the street – which indeed was little enough: "'tis like bringing a line-of-battleship into a canal. But she'll have to go out starn forrards, for there ain't no room to turn."

As we approached, I observed an elderly lady put her head out at the window of the chariot and call to the coachman to go on; which he, mindful of the difficulty of the return, was apparently unwilling to do. At length, urged by her commands, he touched his horses with the whip, on which they began to rear and curvet so that the people near them started back. It thus happened that a man backing hastily away from the horses, set his heels on my toes, whereupon I gave him a hearty shove, and this so angered him that he snatched off my hat and flung it under the chariot, and then made off amongst the crowd before either I or Bill could lay hold of him.

I stepped forward to recover my hat, and as I was about to dive under the chariot, I caught the eye of the lady within it; and a very bright eye it was, and fixed upon my face with such strange intentness that I paused for a moment full of surprise and confusion, before I rescued my hat from its dangerous situation. When I came out from under the vehicle with the hat in my hand, the lady's head was thrust out of the window, and, as I again glanced at her, I found her still regarding me with the most singular attention; and even amidst the embarrassment that her conduct caused me, I seemed to have some dim consciousness of having seen her face before.

Her interest in me had not escaped Bill's notice, for he now took me by the cuff and drew me away.

"Come, mate," said he, "here we are at the 'Mermaid'"; with which he entered a doorway and pulled me in after him; and, glancing round as I went in, I observed the lady craning out of the chariot, watching me with undiminished interest.

There were several persons in the hall, but without taking notice of any of them, Bill led the way upstairs closely followed by me. On the first landing we encountered a buxom young woman whom I immediately recognised by her likeness to Jacob Thorpe; and if any confirmation had been needed it would have been supplied by her reception of my companion; for, as soon as she saw him, she ran forward with a cry of surprise and bestowed on him a kiss that covered him with confusion.

"Look ye here, Biddy," said Bill, wiping his lips with the back of his hand, and turning his blushing face towards me, "this young gentleman is a friend of mine as is a-going for to ship aboard one of the packets tonight, and meanwhiles he wants for to lie snug, d'ye see."

"I know," replied Biddy, laughing and shaking her head at me. "He doesn't want to run up against the excise men, hey? Oh! you're a pretty lot, you sailors are! Well, he'd better stay in your chamber, Bill, and if he wants any victuals I can bring them up."

She ran up the stairs before us and threw open the door of a room on the top floor, bidding us enter.

It was a small chamber, lighted by a dormer window that looked out on the street, and was decently furnished with a four-post bedstead, a small table, a pair of rush-bottomed chairs and a folding washstand.

"This here is snug enough," said Bill, looking round with an approving smile, "though 'tis rather close quarters for you, Mr Roberts. And the next thing will be to send off that letter that you spoke about."

"I shall be grateful indeed," I replied, "if you will do me that service. But before the letter can be dispatched, it has to be written, and I have no writing materials."

"I will fetch you some, directly," said Biddy, "and find you a messenger too, if you wish it."

"One that won't chatter about the message," suggested Bill.

"Trust me to see to that," replied Biddy, smiling and looking excessively knowing. She then retired, followed by Bill, and I heard them descending the stairs together with quite extraordinary slowness.

Presently Bill returned with a shy grin on his face and a tray of writing materials in his hands.

"Biddy's brother, Tom, is to take your letter," said he, "so you may know that it will go safely; for Tom is a good lad, as keen as a weasel and as close as an oyster. Do you get your letter written, and when it is finished give it to Biddy. I shall now go and ask about the packets and try if I can get you a passage."

It smote me to the heart to think how I was wasting the poor fellow's holiday, and I said, penitently:

"You did not come to Gravesend to run on my errands, Bill."

"'Tis all one to me where I am," answered Bill, "and if I find a packet that will do, Biddy shall come out with me in the boat. That will be a change for her."

With that he departed, and as I looked out of the window, I saw him presently cross the road and walk away on the opposite side of the street, looking round and blowing kisses towards the house as he went.

I then drew one of the chairs up to the table and very deliberately cut myself a pen whilst I considered what I should say to my cousin. My intention had been to send a brief note, unsigned as a precaution, lest it should be intercepted. But since I now had a trusty messenger I thought I might allow myself a little indulgence and in the end I wrote as follows:

"*Friday, 25th July*, 1791.

"MY DEAREST PRUE, – 'Tis now (as the calendar tells me, though I can scarce give credit to its assurance) but three days since I bid you 'farewell.' Only three days, little cousin, that I have been without a sight of you; but yet it seems to me that, if the remainder of my life is to be made of such days, them may I bid fair to outrival the patriarch Methuselah, and in the end be as sick of my existence as the Wandering Jew. But I am not writing to complain of the hardness of my lot – at which indeed I would not repine if it did not seem to cut me off from you for ever – but to inform you as to my welfare; concerning which I may say that my health is excellent, and that I hope, this very night, to take effectual measures for exchanging my condition of a fugitive for that of an exile.

"Many adventures I have to relate, that would cause you no little entertainment in the reading; but these I must keep for another letter, since time presses and every word that I write further delays the messenger. But I have told you that which, I doubt not, you are principally concerned to know, and so will say no more but this: that if Fortune has treated me somewhat scurvily in making me to bear the burden of another man's iniquity, she has at least given me a very handsome set-off when she allows me to subscribe myself,

"Your Cousin,
"Robert."

When I had closed up and addressed this letter I proceeded to seal it with a great brass seal that was on the tray; which left on the wax a very lively image of a mermaid similar to that on the front of the house. I then rang the bell, and when the smiling Biddy responded to the summons, I gave the letter into her hands.

"You understand," said I, "that this is to be given into Miss Leigh's own hands, and that no other person is to see it or know of its existence."

"You might trust Tom with your life," said Biddy earnestly, "for he's the most prudent and faithful lad under the sun. Is he to bring you an answer?"

"That I shall leave to Miss Leigh to determine," I replied, "but she will probably send me a few lines to acknowledge my letter."

Biddy then departed with the missive, leaving me to beguile the time by looking out of the window at the people of the street below.

It was about six o'clock when I sent off the letter and I knew that I must wait for two or three hours before the messenger could return; nor did I expect to hear any news from Bill much sooner. Wherefore I set myself to dispose of the time with what patience I could command, and when I was tired of gazing out of the window I addressed myself to the perusal of a volume that I found on the mantelshelf, which proved to be the "Areopagitica" of John Milton; in which, I am bound to confess, I found but scanty entertainment.

About seven o'clock Biddy brought me a tray of victuals and a tankard of ale, and stayed awhile to gossip whilst I ate and drank; and

I had scarce finished my meal when we heard Bill coming up the stairs singing a stave of some sailor's ditty.

"You are soon back, Bill," said Biddy as he entered the room and beamed on us with his jovial smile. "How have you sped?"

"Right well, my lass," he answered cheerily, "for I pitched upon the very craft I would have chosen above all others. 'Tis a little French brig," he added turning to me, "bound for Dunkirk. She'll heave up her anchor tonight at high water, and, if this breeze holds, you'll be on French soil this time tomorrow. Her master is an old acquaintance of mine and he's willing to give you a passage for a couple of guineas."

"This is good news, indeed, Bill," I exclaimed, "and puts me in your debt more, I fear, than I shall ever be able to repay. Shall you be able to find the brig after dark?"

"Nothing easier," replied Bill, "for she lies nearly opposite, and not very far out from the shore, neither."

I was wonderfully encouraged by the successful issue of Bill's enterprise for it seemed now that, with Jacob's assistance, I should have little difficulty in reaching the vessel, and that a few hours might see me safe from pursuit. Already the dreadful incubus that had oppressed me for the last few days began to be lifted, and I seemed to breathe the air of freedom while yet I was shut up in the narrow chamber; and my spirits rose so that I supported, with only moderate impatience, the long delay in my messenger's return. He was, however, longer absent than I had expected, for Shorne is but four miles from the Town Quay and he had started at six o'clock; so that when the clock of St George's Church struck nine and he had still not returned I began to feel some anxiety.

Bill also appeared to be rather uneasy, and I think the same thought was in both our minds, for he came up to my room a few minutes after nine with a very anxious face.

"Tom's late," said he, "which aren't like him at all. I hopes as how he ain't got grabbed on the road; not as that's anyways likely. But, still, it's dark now and it might be safer to get aboard in case any mischance should have befallen him; and if he came in after you was aboard, the letter – if there was one – could be sent off to you. Jacob's a-waiting at the stairs now."

There was such obvious wisdom in Bill's advice that I assented at once, despite the deep disappointment that I felt at missing Prudence's reply; so Bill took up the candle and preceded me slowly down the stairs. But when we had reached the top of the last pair we met Tom coming up, very dusty and perspiring.

"I don't see what you've got to sweat about like that there," said Bill, holding the candle towards him and examining him critically, "'tis past nine o'clock."

"'Tain't my fault," protested Tom. "They was all gone to Rochester and I had to wait till they come back. The young lady was that glad to get the letter. Mr Leigh, he wanted to see it, he did, but she said she'd read it first; so she read it, and then she turned as red as a poppy, she did, haw! haw!"

"Wot are yer larfin at yer undecent young whelp?" asked Bill, much scandalised by this untimely levity on the part of his prospective brother-in-law.

"And when she'd read it," proceeded the unabashed Tom, "she said she'd tell him what was in it some other time, and that ud save his eyesight, and he said she was a baggage, and Mrs Leigh bid him mind his own affairs and he said she was a baggage too, and was old enough to know better, and then they all larfed and I larfed and Miss Leigh said I was to wait for an answer, and she went away to write it, and Mr Leigh he took me into the kitchen and give me a mug of ale as he said was fifteen year old and it got into my head so as I sat down on a stool that wasn't there and when Miss Leigh had give me the note, I walked into a cupboard a-thinking it was the back door and when I come to the stile by the Dover road – "

"Look ye here!" exclaimed Bill wrathfully, seizing him by the collar, "what d'ye mean by a-standin' there a-jawing away like some damned old woman? Give Mr Roberts his letter and take yourself off."

"I've got no letter for Mr Roberts," said Tom. "This here note is for 'Robert Hawke, Esq., at the 'Mermaid' in Gravesend.' Ain't he 'Robert Hawke, Esq.?" he inquired, pointing to me.

"Yes, he is," replied Bill; "So give him the letter. But you understand that he's Mr Roberts here, and you are not to know of any other name."

"Oh, I understand," rejoined Tom with a wink at me; "travelling *incog.*, eh? I know." He handed me the letter, for which I rewarded him with a florin, and departed, grinning.

"You'd better take the candle to read your letter by," said Bill setting down the light as he spoke. "I will wait for you outside in the alley."

He went down the stairs and out at the side door; and it seemed to me that he tripped on the threshold, for I heard him stumble forwards and utter an exclamation just as the door slammed to. But I gave no attention to the matter at the moment, being consumed with eagerness to read my letter; which I did by the light of the candle that Bill had set down on the stairs. It was addressed on the outside as Tom had said, and when I opened it, I read as follows:

"MY DEAREST ROBIN, – Your letter was more welcome than I can tell, for I have been tortured by anxiety since I learned you were not on the *Tally Ho* and I was truly rejoiced to get your news – the very best that you could send me – that you are well and safe.

"And now I shall give you some good news in exchange. You are free, dear Robin! Free to come home and walk abroad in the daylight. You need not go a-roaming after all, for the charge against you is withdrawn. So Mr Colville told my father this very morning – having ridden over for the purpose – and also informed him how, last evening, Godfrey Baker had confessed to the murder, and was to be sent for trial at the assizes. I had suspected Godfrey from the first, though I had no proof, for he was always wild and desperate and you know what terrible provocation he had. Indeed I am sorry for the poor fellow and so will you be when you recall the injuries that he suffered at Will Colville's hands.

"I have some other news for you, but these I will speak into your ear when we meet; and when you hear them, I make no doubt that you will be as astonished as

> "Your affectionate cousin,
> "Prudence."

"P.S. – We shall expect you home tonight, but if you are too fatigued, then tomorrow in the morning as early as you may. P.L."

When I had finished reading I stood for some moments with the letter in my hand, so overwhelmed with joy and relief that I was near upon bursting into tears and I must needs pause to recover myself before I could command my voice sufficiently to communicate my good fortune to Bill. At length, when the first storm of emotion had subsided, I ran lightly down the stairs, still holding the letter, and flinging open the door, stepped out into the alley.

As I came out of the door, I became aware of a crowd of men filling the alley, and at the same instant I received a blow on the head that, although somewhat deadened by my hat, sent me staggering forward, half stunned; and, before I could recover myself, I was seized from behind and flung to the ground, when some of the men held my arms and legs and pushed a handkerchief against my mouth, while others proceeded to pinion my limbs with cords.

"'Tain't no use for to struggle, brother," said a hoarse voice in my ear – for although still dazed by the blow, I was putting out all my strength to free myself from my captors; "you lie quiet and no one's a-going to hurt you."

"Ain't they, by God!" exclaimed another. "He's nearly broke my jaw. Here, let me come at him."

"What!" shouted the first man, "strike a man what's bound and helpless, would you, Jeff Rodman? I'll break your head if you lay a finger on him, that I will"; and somewhat to my relief, I saw my would-be assailant hustled away by two or three of the other men.

At this moment the handkerchief was removed from my mouth, and I immediately took the opportunity to protest against these unlawful proceedings.

"What the devil do you mean by this, you infernal ruffians?" I exclaimed furiously.

"Fair words, master, fair words," answered the man who held the handkerchief. "We're a-goin' for to take you along of us, we are, for to sarve the King, God bless him; and a proud man you ought to be 'nstead of abusing them wot's a-trying for to do you a sarvice. Now, lads, off we goes!"

Hereupon three of the men hoisted me up, and, as I was completely helpless, by reason of the lashings that confined my limbs, I could offer no resistance, beyond shouting for help; which I did with uncommon energy until the handkerchief was once more clapped over my mouth, and secured in its place with a piece of spunyarn.

My bearers now moved off down the alley, and, as our procession emerged into the street, there was a sudden clatter of retreating footsteps and warning voices of men and women shouting "the Press! the Press!" and when I was borne across the road, I had a momentary vision of Biddy, leaning out of a window and shaking her fist at the press-gang.

The sailors turned down a passage, nearly opposite to the 'Mermaid,' and when they had borne me to the end of this, they halted as a man bearing a lantern came forward.

"What have you got here, Mr Wilkin?" he asked, turning the light on to my face.

"A young fellow from the 'Mermaid,' sir," was the answer, "and a very likely lad he looks, too."

The officer examined my face attentively for a few moments and then turned to Wilkin.

"He'll do," said he. "Drop him into the boat."

The procession moved on again and I was lowered down a pair of stairs on to a wooden causeway, where my bearers proceeded to carry out, almost literally, the officer's orders; for they let me down so roughly into a large boat that lay alongside, that I was only saved from probable injury by falling upon a man who was lying on the bottom.

"Now what's a-doing?" exclaimed a familiar voice with unfamiliar savageness of accent; then, as the speaker recognised my helpless condition and caught the muffled sound of my mumbled apology, he added: "Why, burn me if it ain't another poor devil, and gagged too, by God! Here you kidnapping villains! Why don't you take the poor fellow's gag off? Don't you see you're a-choking of him?"

"You'd better mind your own affairs, my man, or you're like to get your jacket dusted," said the officer who had now stepped into the boat and was taking his seat in the stern.

"Shall I ungag the youngster, sir?" asked the sailor who had defended me in the alley, and whom the officer had addressed as Mr Wilkin, "he won't get no good by a-hollerin' now."

"Very well," replied the officer, "you can take his tompion out, and kick him if he shouts."

Accordingly the seaman cut the spunyarn and removed the handkerchief from my mouth; and as I drew a deep breath, he gme an admonitory punch in the ribs and said:

"You hear what the lieutenant says, young man."

"I hear," I replied; then turning my head towards the man against whose back I lay, I said:

"Is that you Bill?"

"What!" exclaimed Bill, "have they grabbed you too?"

"It seems very like it," I answered.

"Well, I'm darned!" exclaimed Bill, "they've made a pretty mistake this time, to be sure." Then raising his voice and addressing the lieutenant, he said: "Look ye, sir, this here young gentleman wot your men have took, ain't a seaman at all."

"We'll soon make him one," replied the lieutenant.

"But he's a gentleman of quality," protested Bill.

"Well, and what of that?" rejoined the officer, sourly, "d'ye suppose we want the King's navy filled up with ragamuffins like you?"

Bill was silent for a few moments, then screwing himself round with a superhuman effort, he whispered hoarsely into my ear:

"'Tis just as well for you, after all, though a sailor's life is a dog's life"; on which I suddenly remembered that he was still ignorant of the great change in my fortunes. The present occasion, however, was not one for the interchange of confidences, so, postponing my explanation to a more suitable one, I made no reply. Yet I could not but reflect how crossly things had turned out. But one short hour ago I should have welcomed this seizure as a most timely rescue. The floating prison, to which I was being hurried, would then have appeared as a veritable ark of salvation and I should have accepted thankfully as a supreme benefit that which I now recognised as a dreadful calamity.

Thus gloomily I meditated as the boat sped on its way, lighted by the moon that now stood high in the east. No one spoke, and the silence of the night was only broken by the rhythmical rumble of the oars and the slopping of the waves against the bows.

"Hadn't I better cast off the lashings, sir," asked Wilkin after we had been under way about ten minutes, "so as they can climb up the ship's side?"

"Very well," replied the lieutenant, "cast 'em off."

"Now young man," said Wilkin, commencing skilfully to unfasten the cords with which I was bound, "let the lashings go slack while I'm a-unhitching. So! there's yer legs free and now we'll get yer arms unlashed."

Very soon the bonds were all removed and I rose, stretching myself and rubbing the bruises that the cords had made.

"Set ye down on the thwart, youngster," said Wilkin; and as I took my seat, he commenced operations on Bill Muffin, who, as soon as he was released, rose and seated himself on the thwart by my side. I now perceived that there was a third captive in the boat, and, as Wilkin set to work to liberate him, I noticed that the seaman was having some trouble with the lashings.

"Turn over, can't yer!" exclaimed Wilkin in a tone of exasperation. "Don't yer see the knots is underneath? And how am I going to cast off if you keeps a-straining the lines like that there?"

To this appeal the man made no response by word or deed, so Wilkin, rather roughly, rolled him over and proceeded to unfasten the knots.

"Now get up and sit on the thwart," said Wilkin as he retired forward coiling up the lines as he went; but the man, instead of rising, turned over once more on to his side.

"Get up when you're told, you lazy beast!" roared the lieutenant.

"Beg pardon, sir," interposed Bill, "but he's as deaf as a post"; by which I gathered that the dimly-seem form was, as I had suspected, that of Jacob Thorpe.

"Deaf, is he?" growled the lieutenant; "well we've got a fine cure for that complaint in the navy."

He reached from behind him a stout rattan with which he fetched the prostrate and unconscious Jacob a thwack that rang out like the report of a pistol; and as the unfortunate waterman scrambled to his feet with a yell of agony, he aimed a second blow. But this never reached its mark, for Jacob very adroitly snatched the cane from the officer's hand, and, furious at the unprovoked brutality, slashed him heavily across the face. Then, before anyone could interfere, he leaped overboard.

For a few moments confusion reigned in the boat. The men had seen Jacob jump into the water but had received no orders, for the lieutenant was quite dazed by the blow; and so being at a loss what to do, they continued to pull at their oars. Very soon, however, the lieutenant recovered himself, when he stood up screeching with rage like an enfuriated elephant and roaring out orders to the men as he held the tiller hard over.

The boat was a large, ponderous craft pulling twelve oars, double-banked, and about as easy to manoeuvre as a Margate hoy. At the time Jacob jumped overboard we were rowing at no great distance from the shore (for we were stemming the tide) and were passing a fleet of the little Gravesend shrimp-smacks or bawleys; and, as our unwieldy boat slowly turned round, I could see Jacob, now a good distance off, striking out swiftly towards them.

"Round with her lively now!" exclaimed the lieutenant, "and a guinea to the man who pulls him aboard. By God! I'll have the rascal's back skinned properly, I promise you."

Before the boat was fairly round, however, I saw Jacob climbing into the little jolly-boat that lay astern of a bawley; in a moment he had cut the painter and shipped the sculls and was pulling away with the strength and skill of a trained waterman. Almost immediately we lost sight of him among the anchored craft, but, the boat being now turned sufficiently, the lieutenant bawled to the men to give way, encouraging them to the utmost exertion by promises, entreaties and horrid curses; and the great tub of a boat, urged forward by the twelve oars, moved off at a fair pace and plunging into the fleet of bawleys threaded the narrow passages between them with the agility of a hippopotamus in the Hampton Court maze.

At length we emerged from the fleet, and, for the first time, came in sight of the fugitive, who was at that moment making fast the painter of his boat to a post at the corner of the Town Quay. As he saw our boat approaching, he skipped lightly up the stone steps, at the top of which he paused to wave his hat and kiss his hand; then he turned and vanished up the High Street.

"'Tis no use, sir," said Wilkin; "he's gone right into the town."

"Who the devil asked for your opinion?" demanded the lieutenant angrily, but I noticed that he put the tiller over so that the boat made a sweep round on to her old course.

Nothing further happened during the journey excepting that the lieutenant swore continuously and mopped his face with a wet handkerchief. After a further ten minutes rowing we came alongside a small full-rigged ship, and when we had made fast, the lieutenant went up the side.

"Now, up you goes, my hearties," said Wilkin to Bill and me; and there being evidently no choice, we took hold of the side-ropes and ascended, followed by Wilkin and the boat's crew.

CHAPTER EIGHT

In which I am presented to my Cousin Percival

As we stepped on deck at the gangway, I halted and laid my hand on Wilkin's arm.

"I wish to see the commander of this ship," I said. "This impressment is irregular and illegal and I demand my immediate release."

"What is this?" inquired a midshipman who was pacing the deck.

"'Tis one of the pressed men, sir," replied Wilkin, "a-askin' for to see the commander."

"I have been illegally kidnapped, sir," said I, "and I desire to see the commander in order to claim my release."

The midshipman laughed with great apparent enjoyment.

"Illegally kidnapped!" he exclaimed. "Oh Lord! Why you've caught a regular sea-lawyer, Mr Wilkin. Well I suppose you'll stow him below and clap the bilboes on him. Illegally kidnapped! Well I'm damned!" and the young officer strolled away to impart this new and piquant jest to his messmates.

"Now you come along," said Wilkin gruffly, yet not unkindly, "and say what you've got to say below"; and with this he led me to the hatchway down which we descended to the dimly-lit gun deck, and from thence through a second hatchway, down into the dark and evil-smelling 'tween decks. As we neared the bottom of the ladder, my ears were greeted by a confused low growl of muttered conversation mingled with the snores and heavy breathing of sleepers; and the reek of stale spirits, together with the incredible foulness of the air made me catch my breath.

The gloomy, low-roofed cave was in total darkness save for the glimmer of the lanthorn that Wilkin had brought down from the deck above, by the light of which I could see that the whole space was filled with a mass of closely-packed hammocks, each sagging down with the weight of its occupant.

"You'll have to bend your back here, lad," said Wilkin, and suiting the action to the word, he stooped and led me under the long rows of hammocks until we reached a clear space right aft close to the rudder-trunk.

"I've got my orders you know," said Wilkin apologetically, as he produced a pair of leg irons, "but it's only for tonight. They'll be knocked off tomorrow. So I'll just bring you to your moorings and then we'll hear what you've got to say."

He fastened on the irons, to which operation I thought it best to submit without resistance, and passing a length of rope through the middle link, made it fast to a ringbolt on a stanchion.

"Now, then," said he, "what was it you was a-wishin' to say?"

"What I wanted to say is this," I replied, "that I am not a seaman and consequently not liable to impressment."

"Why as to that, d'ye see," rejoined Wilkin, "'tis true enough that you aren't a seaman; but as to not being liable to be pressed, why, d'ye see mate, you have been pressed."

"I mean not liable according to law."

"Law!" exclaimed Wilkin contemptuously, "What's the good of talking about law aboard ship? There ain't no law here excepting what the captain gives out."

"Well I shall demand my release from the captain," I replied. "I suppose I shall be allowed to see him?"

"I shall report your request and I make no doubt you'll be brought before him in the morning. And now, my lad," continued the sailor in a more serious tone, "you just listen to a word in season from a man what's old enough to be your father. When you come afore the captain, speak him fair! Speak him fair, lad, and keep your temper. Tell him who you are and ask permission to leave the ship, but speak civil and don't talk about no kidnapping nor law nor stuff of that sort. Maybe he'll let you go – I hope he will for your sake – but I doubt it, seeing as you're a likely lad; and if he won't, why you can't make him. And, remember, the captain of a ship of war is a king on his own deck with power of life and death, and answerable to no one. If you let your tongue wag before him he can have you brought to the gangway then and there – and by God! he'll do it too! He'll order you six dozen as soon as look at you, so I warn you. That's the sort of man Commander Hawke is."

"Hawke did you say his name was?" I asked eagerly.

"Aye," replied Wilkin, "Commander Percival Hawke of His Majesty's sloop-of-war *Asphodel*. D'ye know aught of him?"

I was on the point of disclosing my relationship to the commander, but suddenly reflecting that it would be wiser to see how things turned out before making any confidences, I refrained and answered:

"The name seemed familiar, but it may not be the same Hawke."

"Maybe not," Wilkin replied; "in any case, take my words to heart and don't put yourself in the wrong when you come before the captain."

With this last word of warning he departed, taking the lanthorn with him, and I was left crouching in the stygian darkness, and breathing with infinite disrelish the foul and reeking air.

It was a miserable position; and but for the single ray of hope that proceeded from the ungracious personality of my cousin, I could have wept aloud, in the bitterness of my heart, at the cruelty of fate; which seemed, indeed, to have pursued me with deliberate and intelligent malice, choosing for the infliction of this new misfortune, the very moment at which it would be most acutely felt.

About half an hour after Wilkin had departed, I observed a glimmer of light on the deck under the hammocks and presently a man came into view creeping along with bent back and casting the light of a lanthorn into every corner as though he were searching for something.

At length he spied me, and, advancing and straightening his back as he came out from beneath the hammocks, he held the lanthorn at arm's length and examined me narrowly.

"Why brother," says he, "this is a poor look-out for you to be tethered to a ring like a yard dog or a tame monkey. 'Tis the press I reckon, has brought you to this."

I answered that I had been taken by the press-gang that evening.

"'Tis the curse of the Service," he exclaimed, "is the press, and a disgrace to a country that calls itself free. Free! by the Lord! When a man can be dragged away from his home and put aboard ship like some poor devil of a blackamoor. Howsomever cursin' don't do no good. You'd best lie down and get a bit of sleep, but wait whilst I gets you something to rest your head on." He went away and presently reappeared carrying a couple of old boat cloaks, one of which he spread out on the deck, rolling up the other to form a pillow.

"There now," said he, "that's better than the oak plank to lie on, and now turn in and I wish you a quiet night and good luck in the morning."

I thanked the generous-hearted fellow very warmly and with a heart somewhat overflowing at this unexpected kindness from a stranger, but he hurried away on his rounds – for he was one of the ship's corporals, as I afterwards discovered – without listening or replying; so I settled myself upon the improvised bed and sought in sleep a temporary escape from my misfortunes. The long day, full of anxiety and bodily exertion had left me greatly fatigued, but the strange events that had followed one another with such startling rapidity, returned with a vividness that effectually banished sleep. Moreover, the future with its horrid uncertainties, rose before me and filled my brain with conjectures as to what my fate would be. The news that the ship in which I lay was commanded by my cousin had fallen upon me like a thunderbolt, and even now I viewed the circumstances with very mixed feelings. If it were a matter of Cousin Percival's good wishes, I knew that I might go to the galleys without a finger being raised to help me, for, as I have already mentioned, Percival had always, even from my childhood, regarded me with a hostility that he was at no pains to conceal, and that I found myself quite unable to understand.

It is true that, since my father was the elder son, and Percival's father the younger, my claim to the property and title of my uncle, Sir Thomas Hawke preceded his; but the chance of the succession falling in for either of us was so remote, seeing that Sir Thomas had sons of his own, that I had never taken any account of it. Yet this was the explanation of Percival's bitter enmity, and, ridiculous as it seemed, it was just now a matter to be gravely considered. My cousin was, as I knew, what is called a good hater, and I suspected he was none too scrupulous – as is the way of good haters. The question then was, what would he do? I felt no doubt as to what he would have done had the charge of murder still been hanging over me. But now there was but one thing that he could do, little as it might be to his taste. He must for the credit of the family, and his own sake, release me. His pride would not consent to his seeing upon his own deck a near kinsman hauling at the ropes or swabbing the planks, or to his knowing that a cousin of his swung his hammock and messed in the 'tween-decks with the common seamen. No! he had no choice but to set me ashore in the morning, and with this consoling reflection I began to doze.

I had not completely fallen asleep, however, when the loud chirruping of the boatswain's pipe sounded down the hatchway, and in an instant the whole of the 'tween-decks – hitherto silent but for an occasional snore – was filled with noise and bustle, as the occupants of the hammocks simultaneously turned out and scrambled up ladders. I sat up and looked about me in considerable perplexity. The 'tween-decks was now empty and it was evident that the boatswain's call had summoned all hands on deck. But what circumstances could render such a call necessary on board a vessel brought up in Gravesend anchorage and at near upon midnight?

Even as I was thus cogitating, the answer was borne to my ear in the rhythmical tramp of feet from the decks above. They were manning the capstan.

The significance of the sounds came on me with a pang of anxiety, and I sat listening with eager attention for what might follow.

Tramp, tramp, tramp, the feet of the sailors resounded on the planks overhead, while the great spindles that pierced the decks creaked and groaned with the tension of the cable. Presently these sounds ceased, and were succeeded by more irregular noises, with an occasional thump on the deck as though a heavy coil of rope had been flung down. Evidently the ship was getting under way; a fact that puzzled me not a little, for it must be, I thought, more than an hour yet to high water, and, at Gravesend, vessels were accustomed to weigh anchor on the top of the flood. Still, I reflected, a powerful ship might, with a fair wind, move down stream over the tide, and would thus more easily steer out of the crowded anchorage.

In a short time the steady tramp recommenced, and I judged that, having hove the cable short and set the sails, they were now heaving up the anchor. There could be no doubt that the vessel was leaving the anchorage, and the very serious and important question arose, whither was she bound? But as to her destination I could, of course, make no guess, but could only hope that she might bring up at the Nore, whence my return home would be easy. With this reflection I lay down again and continued to listen drowsily to sounds overhead. Presently they ceased, and, as the ship settled down once more into silence, I must have fallen asleep, for I have no recollection of having heard the men come down to their hammocks.

I was aroused by someone shaking me roughly by the shoulder, and, sitting up, I beheld Wilkin stooping over me.

"Come wake up, man," said he, "'tis past eight bells. I have brought you some breakfast, and as soon as you've stowed it away, I'll take you up to see the captain."

He took up from the deck a platter of beef and a pile of biscuit and handed them to me, together with a can of ale, requesting me to "forge ahead and not keep the captain waiting."

Nothing loath, I fell to upon the victuals, being ravenously hungry after my long sleep, and as I crunched up the stony biscuit, Wilkin regarded me with mingled envy and admiration.

"Aye, aye," he grumbled, "young teeth makes no trouble about hard tack; but 'tis different at my time o' life. Then 'tis the soft bread as suits best, but there ain't no soft bread to be had at sea. Aye, lad, a sailor's life is a dog's life, and a dog's teeth is what he wants for to tackle his vittles with."

I made no reply to these observations, my mouth being at the moment full of the despised ship's bread, but I continued to work my way through the provisions with the speed of hunger and impatience. When I had swallowed the last crumb and drained the can, I stood up and announced my readiness to go on deck.

"Right, lad," said Wilkin, "then 'tis off with the bilboes and up we goes."

He removed the irons from my ankles, and, directing me to follow him, ascended the ladders and stepped out on to the upper deck. As I came out suddenly into the open air and sunshine, I stood for some seconds blinking like an owl and unable to keep my eyes open; but I soon became accustomed to the bright light, and then I perceived two officers pacing the quarter-deck together. At the moment their backs were towards me, but when they turned at the end of their walk I examined their faces eagerly.

One of them was disfigured by a black eye and a purple weal across the cheek, by which I judged him to be the lieutenant who commanded the press-gang. In the other I recognised, without difficulty, my cousin Percival, although it was now some years since I had seen him.

As I was making these observations, Wilkin left me, and, running briskly up the steps on to the quarter-deck, touched his hat and made some communication to the captain. At the same moment my eye fell upon Bill Muffin standing on the opposite side of the deck in the custody of a couple of sailors; and I would have gone over and spoken to him, but an officer who was standing close by commanded me to keep my place. Then Wilkin, in response to an order from the captain, beckoned to the two sailors, who thereupon led Bill up on to the quarter-deck.

My comrade saluted the commander with a bold and cheerful air, apparently little cast down by his captivity, and I could see that he was being put through a somewhat lengthy cross-examination, and was making some kind of statement, for I observed the lieutenant making copious entries in a notebook.

When the examination was finished, Bill was conducted back to the main deck and Wilkin beckoned to me.

I must confess that the summons set my heart beating furiously, and that much of the confidence of the previous night had by this time evaporated. Nevertheless I ascended the steps with as resolute and confident a manner as I could assume, and, approaching the two officers, made a low bow.

My cousin was leaning negligently against the capstan with his hands thrust into his breeches pockets, and, although he stared at me with a lowering and sinister expression and spoke not a word, I saw at a glance that he recognised me. And something else I saw; for in the moment that I met his eye I recalled the face of the lady in the coach, and realised who she was. I had not seen her since I was a child, and had quite forgotten her. But as I looked in my cousin's face I remembered her well enough. She was his mother – my Aunt Anne.

"Who is this man, Wilkin?" he demanded gruffly.

"'Tis a young man from the 'Mermaid,' sir," replied Wilkin. "He was saying, sir, that seeing as how he aren't been brought up to the sea, he was hoping your honour would allow him to go about his business."

"Ha! Was he?" exclaimed Percival; then turning to me with an insolent stare he demanded:

"What is your name, fellow?"

"Robert Hawke," I replied.

"Say 'sir' when you speak to the captain," murmured Wilkin.

"Where do you live?" asked Percival.

"I live with my kinsman Mr Leigh at Shorne, near Gravesend."

"What is your occupation?"

"I am a gentleman; but I help my kinsman to look after his farm."

I answered these questions coolly and civilly, but I felt a flush of anger rising to my face at this barefaced and insolent pretence.

"You say that you have not been brought up to the sea," my cousin continued.

"I am not a seaman," I answered.

My cousin turned with a sly, wicked smile on his face towards the lieutenant.

"What think you of that, Wigmore?" he asked.

The lieutenant's countenance broke out into the most singular grin that I have ever seen, for the blow had deprived one side of his face of the power of movement, so that it remained as still as that of a dead man, while the other was covered with wrinkles and the mouth pulled all askew.

"A most fluent and ingenious liar, truly," said he.

"You are right," rejoined Percival; "a most barefaced and shameless liar. Now listen to me, fellow," he added, turning savagely upon me, "You have, perhaps, heard of a certain James Roberts, an ordinary seaman on board the Guineaman, *Charity*?"

"I have used the name of 'James Roberts'," I answered, "but my name is Robert Hawke, and my father – "

"Who the devil cares what your father was or which of your various names is the true one? You were an ordinary seaman on a Guinea trader, and have been impressed into His Majesty's service according to law. That will do, Wilkin; have his name entered in the ship's books, 'James Roberts' ordinary seaman."

He turned on his heel and walked away aft, followed by the lieutenant.

I sprang forward to renew my protests, but was held back firmly by Wilkin.

"Come, my lad," said he, "you see 'tis no use, and that he doesn't mean to let you go. 'Tis damned hard luck, I grant you, but you've got to put up with it, and if you are wise you'll make the best of a bad bargain. You are now one of the crew of this ship and I counsel you to see that there are no complaints against you, for the captain's a hard man and he don't seem more than ordinarily fond of you. I tell you, lad, that aboard this ship, what with the captain and Mr Wigmore, a seaman has got to keep his weather eye a-lifting if he wants to steer clear of the gangway and the grating."

There was such evident truth and good sense in this that I could only thank the old seaman for his advice, and assure him that, since I had failed to get my discharge, I would do my best to settle down contentedly in my new position.

"Spoken like a sensible lad," said he approvingly. "By the way, I reckon that was all gammon about your being an ordinary seaman?"

"Quite," I answered. "I was intending to take a voyage on board a Guineaman, but I have never been to sea in my life."

"Well, we'll soon make a seaman of you," said Wilkin, "and you'll be better off aboard of us, than you would on a stinking Guineaman. So the first thing to do is to put your name down in the purser's books and pass you into the slop-room, for you do look rather like a farmer in that there long-tailed coat."

This programme was speedily carried out, and when I returned to the deck a few minutes later I was fully dressed for the part I should now be called upon to play.

The first person I encountered as I came up the hatch-way was Bill Muffin, and, as his eye fell upon my new outfit, his features broadened into a grin.

"You're fresh from the rigger's hands, I see, Mr Roberts," he observed.

"Yes," I answered grimly, surveying my new garments with great disfavour; "it hasn't taken long to change the grub into the butterfly."

"Haw! haw!" laughed Bill, "that's a good 'un, that is; but 'tis t' other way about. 'Tis the butterfly has changed into a grub, Mr Roberts, sir. But there! Things aren't so bad as they seem; you're clear out of the country now and you're safer aboard a king's ship than you'd have been in the *Charity* with that psalm-singing porpoise."

"That's true so far, Bill," said I, "but you see I needn't have left the country at all. The man who committed the murder has given himself up and the charge against me is withdrawn."

"Where did you hear that?" asked Bill.

"Miss Leigh gave me the news in her letter, and she had it from Mr Colville, who issued the warrant."

"My eye!" exclaimed Bill. "If I had known this, I'd have pitched a very different yarn to those two swabs on the quarter-deck. I'm afraid, Mr Roberts, that it's me what has spiked your guns, though, God knows, I did it all for the best."

"Of course you did," said I hastily, for I could see that the honest fellow was reproaching himself with being the cause of my detention; "you acted like a staunch friend and a true comrade, as you always have, and as to spiking my guns, Bill, you can put that thought out of your mind, for I feel certain that, whatever you had said, the captain would never have let me go."

"I'm right glad to hear you say that, Mr Roberts," said Bill, grasping my hand with an air of profound relief, "for I wouldn't like to think that I had let you into this jail: and I'm glad, too, to hear that you're clear of that other job, for though accidents may happen to anyone, I never did think you'd done it."

"And now, Bill," said I, "we're shipmates, and Wilkin tells me we are in the same watch, so you must drop calling me Mr Roberts! On this ship I am James Roberts, a common seaman – Jim Roberts. I suppose they'll call me – so you must stow your politeness and do the same as the others."

"I quite understands, sir," said Bill.

"Not 'sir,' " said I. "Say Jim."

"Well then, Jim," responded Bill with an embarrassed grin.

"Whereabouts are we now?" I asked, looking over the bulwark at the wide stretch of calm water.

"A mile or two below Shoebury," he replied. "There's Sheppey over our starboard quarter, and beyond it, in the bight, is Whitstable – you can see the masts sticking up over the land. Many a time have Toby and I run the *Tally Ho* into Whitstable Harbour, or up the Swale to Faversham. But all that's past and gone now, Mr Roberts – Jim I means, sir, beggin' your pardon – and the Lord knows how long it may be afore I sniffs the mud of Faversham Creek again. Howsomever, 'tis no use a-grumbling, and she's a smart ship is this here *Asphodel*."

"She is large for a sloop isn't she?" I asked.

"Why, d'ye see, she ain't a sloop, properly speaking. She's what they calls a donkey frigate, but she's rated as a sloop because her commander *is* a commander. If he got his promotion tomorrow, she wouldn't be a sloop no longer; she'd be rated as a ship then."

At this moment Wilkin (whose rating I ascertained to be that of boatswain) approached with an air of friendly reproof.

"Come, come, my lads," said he, "this here won't do, a-lounging about the deck like a couple of sogers. You'll have Mr Parker after you. Did they teach you how to work an eye-splice aboard that Guineaman of yours?"

"Why I am afraid they rather neglected my education," I replied; "but I should be glad to learn all that I ought to know."

"That's the way to look at it, lad," rejoined Wilkin cheerily. "You've got to be a seaman, so you'd best be a good seaman. Now here's an end of rope; 'tain't much good but 'tis good enough to try a 'prentice hand on, and Muffin can show you how to work an eye-splice in it, can't ye, Bill?"

"Aye," replied Bill; "I think I can show him how to handle a marlinspike, and I'll trust him not to prove a dull scholar, neither."

He took the piece of rope, and, having possessed himself of a marlinspike, sat down on the slide of one of the carronades on the forecastle and proceeded to give me the first lesson in my new trade. Under his direction I managed to work a moderately neat eye-splice in the end, and he then cut the rope and showed me how to make a short splice; cut it again and made a long splice, and then went on to explain some of the commoner knots and bends. After this he took me to the fife rails and showed me how to belay and coil down, and then proceeded to explain the uses of the various running gear, taking each rope that led aloft, and making me follow it to its destination.

While this instruction was proceeding, the boatswain passed us several times with a nod and a word of encouragement, and I noticed that Mr Parker, the lieutenant of my watch, occasionally glanced towards us with evident approbation.

Meanwhile the ship crept slowly forward over the flood-tide with all her light sails set to catch the breeze that poured almost directly over her taffrail. As she crawled foot by foot over the calm water, we passed numerous merchant vessels anchored in the fairway, waiting for the ebb, unable to spread to the breeze a cloud of canvas like that which towered above our decks and overhung the water far on either side. But slowly as the *Asphodel* moved against the strong tide, the land continued to fall away towards the north, and when the ebb set in at about four bells in the afternoon watch, it had vanished below the sea horizon, and Reculver lay far away upon our starboard beam.

Since we entered the channels between the shoals in the mouth of the estuary, leadsman had been stationed in the lee chains, and here I received my initiation into the use of the hand lead: with which I was only moderately successful, for although I was soon able to whirl the lead expertly enough, I was not a little bewildered by the puzzling marks upon the line; and when it came to calling out the soundings, I tried in vain to imitate the musical sing-song in which the experienced mariner announces the result of the cast.

Soon after eight bells had sounded – that is about four o'clock – the silent ship suddenly awoke. We had now cleared the east end of Margate sand and were opening the North Foreland, and the order had been given to get in the studding-sails and booms, preparatory to altering the ship's course to the south. The shrill whistle of the boatswain's pipe sent all the men to their stations, and, in a moment, the silence that had hung over the ship all day was succeeded by a roar of bustle and movement. Troops of sailors scampered up the shrouds and lay out on the yards, while those on deck cast off or hauled upon the various ropes connected with the light sails, so that, in a space of time that seemed incredibly short, the great wings that had spread out on either side of the vessel, had been gathered in and stowed away, the booms rigged in and the ship reduced to her plain canvas, when the braces were manned and a course set nearly due south.

Slowly the green uplands and yellow cornfields of Thanet rose out of the summer sea, and the chalk cliffs – here lighted by the sun until they gleamed a rosy yellow through the thin haze, there wrapped in shadow, blue and mysterious – drew near, slipped past, and presently sank on our quarter. The Goodwin Sands, as yet covered, but marked by lines of broken water, were left on our larboard hand, and we swept down the Gull Stream with bowlines taut, and a favouring tide urging us forward, until, as the sun was setting red behind the low land by Sandwich, the *Asphodel* joined the great assembly of vessels that rode in the Downs, and let go her anchor opposite Deal Castle.

CHAPTER NINE

In which I discover a New Enemy

As I lay that night in my hammock while the 'tween-decks resounded with the snores of my companions, it was natural that I should review the strange and disturbing events of the day. In truth they afforded me no little food for speculation, and the more I considered them, the less possible did it appear to regard them as the result of accident or chance. As I reconstructed them and arranged them in their proper order of succession, a very evident chain of connection became apparent, so that what had at first seemed to be a purely fortuitous series of events, now resolved itself into a carefully conceived and well-executed plan.

First, I recalled the glance of astonished recognition that my aunt had bestowed upon me from the coach, and her manifest eagerness to ascertain my destination. I remembered how, even at the moment when I was entering the door of the 'Mermaid,' she had craned from the coach window to watch me. Then the press-gang, lying in wait for me – a landsman – at the side-door, instead of ransacking the 'Three Daws,' 'The Privateer' or the 'Pope's Head' (in any of which a good haul of seafaring men could have been obtained), strongly suggested some private motive, while the cross-examination of Bill Muffin was obviously designed to anticipate and defeat my claim to be released, and to fix on me a false name and identity.

There could be no doubt that it was a plot to get me out of England, but what could be the object? Could it be that I had misjudged my cousin? That he and my aunt were ignorant of the change in my circumstances, and, believing me still to be a fugitive from justice, had taken these measures to ensure my safety? I would have gladly thought so, for no man wishes to think his kinsman a scoundrel; but, apart from my previous knowledge of Percival's character, his present conduct lent little colour to such a belief.

No, it was clear that there was a plot against me, and that Percival was at the bottom of it, but his motive I was unable to fathom – for my removal from the country would in no wise help him to the coveted inheritance.

It was a mystery, and so I must leave it until time should furnish the solution. Meanwhile my identity was known to no one on board but my cousin and – as I suspected – the first lieutenant; for I had no doubt that Mr Wigmore was a party to the plot, and, to some extent at least, in his commander's confidence. More than once I had been tempted to let Bill or the boatswain into my secret, and during the interview with my cousin I was at one time on the point of proclaiming our relationship; but prudence had kept me silent on each occasion, and I was now glad to think that I had kept my own counsel and refrained from making a statement that Percival would certainly have contradicted, and that no one would have believed; by which I should have become an object of ridicule, and a fair mark for persecution on the part of the officers.

We remained at anchor in the Downs for a week, but whether we were waiting for orders or were detained by the south-westerly wind, I could not judge. The roadstead was, however, very full, owing to the long prevalence of westerly winds; there being some three hundred sail brought up, including three ships of the line, a frigate and a corvette. Each day added to the numbers of the wind-bound fleet, for with every ebb-tide a fresh instalment of outward-bound vessels would arrive by the Gull Stream or round the South Sand Head, until the anchored multitude extended from beyond Walmer into the Small Downs.

At about nine o'clock in the morning of the sixth day of our stay in the Downs, I was seated astride a carronade on the forecastle, looking rather wistfully shoreward, and watching the Dealmen as they steered their long, powerful boats in and out among the anchored craft, bearing stores or provisions from the shore, taking off passengers or carrying messages or letters. I had been hoping for an opportunity to send a letter to Prudence, that she might at least know what had become of me, and perhaps take steps to ensure my being set at liberty; but, on making inquiries, I was astonished to learn that no communication with the shore was to be permitted. I had endeavoured, cautiously, to find out if this order could be evaded and a letter sent by one of the shore-boats, but had soon been convinced that the thing was impossible; for so strictly was the order enforced, that all bum-boats were warned off before they could come alongside, while boats bearing messages from the shore were kept under strict observation by an officer until they had cast off and were clear of the ship. These unusual orders had occasioned much surprise on board, and innumerable conjectures were made as to their object. For my part I had no doubt on the subject; my worthy cousin, having been at so much pains to get me into his clutches, did not intend that my whereabouts should be known until I was beyond the chance of rescue.

It will, therefore, be easily understood that, as I sat gazing across the anchorage at the land, the spectacle of the sturdy luggers and lean-bodied galleys bearing shoreward their freights of passengers and bags of letter was, to the last degree, tantalising, and induced in me such a feeling of despondency that I could almost have flung myself into the sea and taken the slender chance of reaching the shore.

Suddenly I was aroused from my gloomy reflections by a shout from Bill Muffin, who was standing on the opposite side of the deck, and as I turned my head to look at him, he smote his thigh and burst into a roar of laughter.

"Here's a sight for sore eyes, Jim," he called out to me. "My heart! come and look at this."

I jumped down from the gun and ran across the deck to where he was standing, and, following the direction of his gaze, perceived a small ship crawling into the roadstead on the last of the ebb.

"Aren't she a clipper, Jim?" chuckled Bill wiping his eyes. "Don't she cut through the water like a razor? Oh, my eye!" and he was again overcome with mirth.

"She is certainly an ungainly-looking craft," I replied, not quite clear, however, as to the cause of my companion's merriment, for there were many vessels around of even more uncouth appearance. "I suspect she wouldn't make much of it with the tide the other way."

"You're about right there," said Bill; "but take another look at her and tell me what you see."

I examined the stranger afresh as she slowly drew nearer, and suddenly my eye fell upon the group of painted figures under her high-pitched bowsprit.

"Why 'tis the *Charity*!" I exclaimed.

"To be sure it is," answered Bill. "The old man hasn't took long a-getting a new mate, for all he was so mighty partickler. Well, I hopes as he's a godly man and reads his Bible reglar; he'll want to when he gets to sea in that precious old bucket."

We both watched with absorbing interest as the clumsy little ship slowly drew nearer, and I think we both drew some consolation for our captivity from a comparison of her squab unshapely hull and meagre spars with those of the fine ship on whose deck we stood. The last of the ebb had by this time run out, but the *Charity* still crept on through the slack water until she was so near that we could recognise the unwieldy form of her master, and Mr Wigmore sang out to her, through the speaking trumpet, to leave room for the *Asphodel* to swing.

The whole of that day and the next the *Charity* lay within a cable's length of us, and we could see Mr Murking pacing the poop in company with a small thin man whom we took to be the new mate. The breeze continued from the south-west, and the crowd of shipping was augmented by each succeeding tide.

When I came on deck soon after daybreak on the eighth day there were evident signs of a change in the weather. It was dead calm, and the water, reflecting the hue of the cloudless sky, was like a sheet of pale blue satin. The sea horizon was hidden in a rosy haze and the land loomed indistinctly as though seen through a veil of delicate gauze. These signs were not noted by me alone, for already the anchorage was wide awake and full of activity and bustle. On all the ships, far and near, the yards were covered with men and draped with festoons of the loosened canvas, and from every part of the roadstead came the musical clink of capstan-pawls, telling of cables being hove short, and the creak of block and parrel as sails were mast-headed and sheeted home. In less than an hour after sunrise, the preparations were complete: the men vanished from the rigging, the sounds of labour died away, and silence once more settled down upon the anchorage.

There was something very solemn and impressive as well as exquisitely beautiful in the spectacle which the Downs now presented as the great multitude of ships lay, with sails drooping and motionless and anchors apeak, waiting silently for the coming of the breeze; those that lay to the eastward, between us and the sun, standing out in dark grey, sharp silhouette against the sky, while those to the west and south, whose canvas was lighted by the sunshine, gleamed through the hazy air, a warm and luminous yellow.

So they remained for near upon an hour, silent, motionless and expectant.

Then came the first harbingers of the promised breeze advancing stealthily out of the north-east. First, along the pale blue, glassy surface, in which the waiting ships were pictured in shimmering reflections, soft airs and tiny cat's-paws began to steal, streaking it with lines of vivid blue that darted forward, spread out hither and thither and vanished suddenly, as though invisible fingers were playing daintily over the quiet sea. Then the lighter sails began to lift or press against the masts; the streaks of blue grew wider and ran together; the trembling reflections broke up and melted away; and as little ripples began to clamour at our waterline, the sleeping ocean awoke to the whisper of the morning breeze.

Almost immediately there was an answering movement in the fleet, for time was precious – the wind was of the lightest, and the tide was more than half-run out. One by one the vessels to leeward, which had room to manoeuvre, were seen to heave up their anchors, pay off, and move away southward, leaving space for the others to get under way; and so rapidly did the movement spread that in half an hour the entire fleet, with the exception of the *Asphodel* and a two-decker, had weighed and was in motion. It was a glorious procession, a water-pageant on a scale that I had never dreamed of, made up of near upon three hundred and fifty sail of every rig and size, from the majestic ship of the line to the little jackass schooner. I watched them with unflagging interest and pleasure as they dwindled slowly in the distance, until the last of them – a Dutch galliot – had rounded Hope Point and the roadstead was left empty and bare.

The *Charity* had been among the first to get under way, and I had noticed Murking, despite his unwieldy figure, taking an active part in the preparations; and I could not but observe that his ship, clumsy and lubberly as she was in build and rig, was handled as smartly as any vessel in the fleet.

About three o'clock in the afternoon a gallery-punt was seen approaching the ship, and, as she lowered her sail and swept alongside at the gangway, I saw my cousin seize the man ropes and step lightly up the side.

He had hardly reached the deck before the order was given to heave short and loose the sails, whereupon, in response to the boatswain's call, the men came tumbling up from below to take their places at their stations.

I had made up my mind not to be behindhand in the performance of any duties that fell to my lot – for reflection had convinced me that if I would make my life endurable in my new circumstances, I must follow the advice of Wilkin to the letter – so now, when I saw a part of the crew busily engaged in passing the messenger, I hastened to the rack and lifted out a capstan-bar, which I was just fitting into its hole when the boatswain came by and touched me on the shoulder.

"Up with ye, lad," said he, "and help loose the fore-royal. Best make your first trip aloft in calm water and fine weather."

Now, as I had never before ascended a vessel's rigging, it was natural that I should experience a little nervousness on being suddenly ordered to climb to the summit of the lofty mast and lie out on the yard that, seen from the deck, appeared to soar in the very clouds. However, I was strong and active and the thing had to be done, so, having shipped the bar and slipped in the safety pin, I sprang into the rigging and began to mount aloft. I ran nimbly enough up the lower shrouds, and though, when I reached the cat-harpings, I cast a wistful glance at the lubber's hole, I laid hold, manfully, of the futtock-shrouds, undismayed by their fearful overhang, and drew myself into the top. Encouraged by my success, I started up the topmast rigging with more confidence, finding the ascent easier than I had expected, and at length after what seemed an interminable climb, I arrived, a good deal out of breath, at the royal yard on which several men were already busy casting off the gaskets.

I took my place at the slings, letting myself down on to the foot-ropes with a degree of care that set the sailors on the broad grin, and proceeded to untie the few gaskets that were within my reach, and, as the sail now hung loose, I crawled gingerly back into the rigging and was preparing to descend the shrouds, when one of the men hailed me.

"Hallo, brother!" he sang out, "that aren't the way to go down. You follow me. So," and grasping a backstay, he coiled his legs round it and away he went like an arrow. I was not long in following his example and in less than a minute was down on the deck; and though my hands were raw from the friction of the rough rope, I felt no little satisfaction at having fairly mastered the rudiments of my new calling.

Meanwhile the men tramped round the capstan to the cheerful squeak of a fiddle, and, as the sails were now loose, orders were given to sheet home as soon as the cable was hove short. In a very few minutes these orders had been carried out, the anchor was weighed, the sails sheeted home, the yards trimmed, and the *Asphodel* began to glide down the roadstead on the first of the ebb-tide. As soon as she was fairly under way, the order was passed to set studding-sails, and once more I found myself climbing the rigging; but this time my confidence had so much increased that I lingered a few moments after the other hands had gone down, to take a look round from my lofty station and note the immense expanse of sea and land that was visible, and the absurdly diminutive aspect of the ship beneath me.

Under the press of canvas that we now carried, we slipped along at a good pace, despite the lightness of the breeze, and by the time we were abreast of Folkestone we began to overtake the vessels which had sailed out of the Downs, and had been delayed by the intervening flood-tide. Opposite Sandgate we passed the *Charity*, staggering forward with every rag of canvas set, and a line of foam across her square, clumsy bows; and this was the last I saw of her, for, having been set to work under the direction of the sail-maker to assist one of his mates in some repairs on a spare stay-sail, my hands were full for the next two hours, and when I at length put my head over the rail for a last look at my old acquaintance, she had vanished astern.

For the next two days the *Asphodel* held on her course down Channel keeping some ten or fifteen miles off the land, but on the third day, as we came into the chops of the Channel she bore away more to the south, and although it was known that we were abreast of Cornwall, no land was in sight. On this day we met no less than three French ships of war, and I could not but feel amused at the expressions of regret on the part of our men that we should have to let them pass with no better salutation than a dip of the ensign. By sunset we were clear of the Land's End and were heading south-west by west out into the Atlantic.

It would be tedious if I were to recount the incidents of this voyage from day to day. No doubt, in time of war, the life of a seaman on a king's ship is one of unceasing excitement and adventure; then every sail that appears on the horizon is a possible enemy, and is eagerly examined by everyone on board, from the captain to the powder-boy; for, at any moment, the quiet routine or ordinary duty may be exchanged for the furious excitement of battle; but at the time of which I am writing, England was at peace with all the world, although war clouds were gathering darkly enough on her horizon, and the crew of the sloop-of-war could look forward to nothing more stirring than a gale of wind; and even this excitement was for a time, withheld, for the north-easter continued and followed us for more than a week, during which time we held on our course before it without once having to trim the yards.

One circumstance, however, occurred about this time, which was fraught with the most momentous consequences to me – consequences that I little foresaw at the time. It arose out of a quarrel – or rather a series of quarrels – with one of my shipmates, a certain Jeffrey Rodman, a man whose fierce and morose disposition had made him far from a favourite on board. Rodman had been a member of the press-gang which captured me, and, unfortunately for him, had come in the way of my fist, catching a buffet that had gone near to breaking his jaw; and it now appeared that the blow had loosened several of his teeth, a fact of which he was daily reminded when he made his attack upon the hard ship's bread.

Now I had not been on board many days before I was made aware that Rodman entertained the most vindictive feelings towards me. From several of my shipmates I received friendly hints and warnings, and Bill Muffin especially begged me to give the surly ruffian as wide a berth as possible.

However, nothing happened for the first fortnight beyond the petty annoyances and incivilities to which he had subjected me from the first; but on the fourteenth day out – by which time we were well south of the Western Islands – we came into actual collision.

My watch was on deck, the starboard watch – to which Rodman belonged – being below at dinner, and as there was little to do (for we had now picked up the north-east trade wind and were bowling along before it with studding-sails out on both sides) I obtained permission to go below to turn out my kit. As I passed along the 'tween-decks, where the men of the starboard watch were sitting round the little mess-tables, I noticed Rodman hammering a biscuit into small fragments with the haft of his knife, while his mess-mates encouraged him with ironical jests. He appeared to be not a little out of humour at the coarse wit of which he was being made the butt, for as he glared round the circle of grinning seamen he discharged volleys of curses and threats, at which they scoffed the louder. I was passing the berth as unobtrusively as possible when one of the seamen spied me and proceeded to improve the occasion.

"Why, here he is!" he shouted; "here's the jolly farmer's boy what knocks out the pore sailor's grinders so as he can't chew his rations. I'll tell you what, mate," he added, "if you're a Christian man, you'll swop your duff and pea-soup for pore old Jeff's biscuit, for he's a-wastin' away afore our very eyes."

"I'm truly sorry, mates, for what happened in that scuffle," said I, which was no more than the truth, for the ship's provisions were bad enough to a man with the strongest of teeth, "but Jeff knows 'twas an accident, and I am sure he bears no malice."

"Doesn't he, by God!" exclaimed Rodman, leaping up and seizing a hook-pot from the table. "If that there was an accident, why then, you blasted farmer, here goes another," and with that he sent the hook-pot flying at my head.

I ducked in time to avoid the missile, but before I could recover myself, he rushed at me and bore me to the deck, where we sprawled together, struggling and pommelling one another, until Rodman, who had taken me somewhat at a disadvantage, managed to plant his knee on my chest and grip me with both hands by the throat; and there is no doubt that he would have strangled me there and then had it not been for a sergeant of marines who at this moment happened to be passing, and who fell to belabouring my assailant on the head with his supple-jack with such goodwill that he was glad to let go his hold to protect his crown.

As I scrambled to my feet, giddy and breathless, Rodman suddenly darted away from the sergeant, and snatching up his knife, made another rush at me; but this time I was ready for him, and, avoiding the blade, struck him fairly between the eyes and sent him staggering backward.

"Drop that knife, you blackguard!" exclaimed the sergeant, advancing with his supple-jack raised; but Rodman, who was now mad with fury, endeavoured to push past him to get at me, and in the scuffle that ensued, his knife ripped up the marine's sleeve and drew blood from his arm. This was too serious an affair to be disposed of by a summary beating, so Rodman, having been disarmed, was led away and put in irons, and his name entered on the report of the master-at-arms.

The end of, or rather I should say the sequel to this miserable business — for it was by no means the end of the affair — occurred next morning, when, about an hour before noon, the order was passed to muster all hands aft "to witness punishment."

I must confess that, as I took my way aft to join my shipmates on the lee side by the break of the quarter-deck, my knees trembled and my heart beat as though I were myself the culprit. This was the first ceremony of the kind that had taken place since I came on board, for, with due respect to Mr Wilkin, the *Asphodel* was not a flogging ship; unscrupulous villain as my cousin was, and cruel when angered, he was not one of those coarse and savage brutes who flog the men for every trivial fault, nor was the crew such a collection of rogues, vagabonds and jail sweepings as formed the ordinary company of a king's ship a few years later. It has therefore happened that, up to this time, no offences had been committed on board except such as could be met by the stoppage of beer or wine or a sound drubbing with the boatswain's starter.

When the whole of the ship's company was assembled and the marines drawn up at the quarter-deck rail, the captain read out the name of Jeffrey Rodman with the nature of his offence, and the prisoner was brought forward.

"How did this happen, Mr Wigmore?" asked the captain, turning to the first lieutenant. "What induced the man to assault the sergeant?"

"I believe, sir, he was fighting with another man and the sergeant interposed."

"Who is the other man?" inquired the captain.

The sergeant pointed me out, and I was directed to step forward.

"What is your name, fellow?" the captain demanded.

"James Roberts, sir," I answered.

The ghost of a smile flitted over my cousin's face as I made this reply, but, recollecting himself instantly, he looked me sternly in the face and said:

"Your name does not appear in the report, although it appears that you were equally to blame with the other man. You were both fighting, and, if I may judge by the appearance of Rodman's face, he had the worst of it.

"He will now take the punishment while you go scot-free with the satisfaction of having brought your shipmate to the gangway. But you may not come off so well next time; for, understand, I will have no brawling on board my ship. That will do." He whipped off his hat, and as everyone present followed suit, he read out the section of the Articles of War relating to the prisoner's offence. Rodman was then asked if he had anything to say, and on his replying in the negative, he was made to strip to his trousers and his wrists were seized up to the grating.

I need not describe in detail the horrid scene that followed – indeed I should not be able, for although I could not close my ears to the dreadful thud of the cat and the gasping cries that escaped the poor devil as each blow fell, I kept my eyes turned away, and only looked once as the seizings were being cast off. Two dozen lashes only had been delivered – a light punishment in those days when two or three hundred was a not uncommon sentence – but the man's back was purple, and bleeding from the neck to the waist, and as he was led away, white-faced and breathless, he trembled as though shaken by a fit of ague. Coming abreast of me, he stopped and shook his fist in my face.

"You white-livered carrion," he exclaimed in a hoarse, shaking voice, "you have had your turn; the next is mine, and by God you'll pay the full price for this."

"Silence, there!" shouted the captain angrily; but when I looked at him I could not help thinking I detected on his face something uncommonly like a smirk of satisfaction.

The events that have just been related gave me, when I had time to consider them in the brief and broken leisure of my watch below, abundant cause for uneasiness. As to Rodman, I knew him to be one of those desperate and ferocious ruffians who will allow no risk to deter them from the pursuit of their vengeance, and that, so long as I remained in the same ship with him, my life would never be safe from one hour to another. But my cousin's conduct gave even more food for thought, for, young and simple as I was, I could not fail to see behind it a definite intention and purpose. It was quite true that, in the Articles of War, brawling on board ship was set forth as a serious offence, and my cousin, in his speech to me, had not exaggerated or gone beyond the facts; but the real significance of that speech lay in the manner in which the burden of the offence was laid upon me, by which I was made to appear as a common sneak, leading my comrade into trouble while keeping out of danger myself, and Rodman was shown as an injured man, bearing the whole punishment of our joint misdoing. The meaning of this was that my cousin was playing a deeper game than I had supposed, and I now began to understand how it was that I had enjoyed such immunity from persecution by the captain and his creature, the first lieutenant. Evidently it was no part of Percival's plan to appear in connection with any mischance that might befall me; but if it should happen that I was stabbed or knocked on the head by a shipmate, his purpose would be very completely served, and I thought he perceived in Jeff Rodman a most efficient instrument to carry out his designs.

Here, then, was something to occupy my thoughts when my watch was sent below for its four hours of rest, and the dark 'tween-decks was filled with the murmur of sleeping shipmates. I was beset by perils, and those of the most alarming kind, for no one could tell from what quarter they were to be expected, and no foresight would enable me to avoid them.

CHAPTER TEN

In which I have a Narrow Escape

For several days after the painful incident of Rodman's punishment, nothing occurred to give colour to my apprehensions. But Rodman himself was in the sick bay, his back having become so inflamed that he was rendered unfit for duty so that the apparently peaceful course of events was the less reassuring. He made his reappearance on the sixth day after the flogging – when we were twenty days out – and his manner on that occasion made it clear that he had not developed any more benevolent feelings towards me during his retirement; for, as he passed me at the fore-hatch, when the hands were piped down for dinner, he snarled in my face and showed his teeth as a savage dog might have done.

That same day, in the afternoon watch, I got the first hint of his intentions. We were bowling along with the trade wind a couple of points free and all plain sail set, when the captain ordered the hands to be set to drill at making and shortening sail. Instantly the men ran to their stations, and when the order was given to strip the ship down to reefed topsails, the top men scampered aloft and lay out on the yards with such speed that the great expanses of canvas vanished as if by magic. Again sail was set and again the order given to reef and furl until the manoeuvre had been executed half a dozen times, when the order was passed to rig out studding-sail booms and set the studding-sails. All this time I was stationed near the foot of the foremast hauling on or letting to the various ropes that work the sails, while Rodman's station aloft was on the topgallant yard.

I had, however, been kept so busy handling the ropes that I had not observed him, and it was during the pause that preceded this last order that I saw him for the first time. He was standing amongst his mates with his back to me, and I noticed a curious bulging under his jacket in the small of his back which he seemed, by his over-erect attitude, to be endeavouring to conceal. Connecting this with his recent sojourn in the sick bay, I supposed it to be some dressing that the surgeon had applied to his back, and so dismissed the matter from my mind. At this moment the order that I have mentioned was given, and the men sprang into the rigging, while I cast the halyard of the starboard topgallant studding-sail off its pin ready for hoisting. I was standing a few feet from the mast with the rope in my hand when, just as the word was given to hoist, some object whizzed past my head and struck the deck beside me with a crash that sent the hands hopping away in all directions.

"What was that?" shouted Mr Wigmore, as the men backed away from the mast and stared aloft.

"'Tis a block, sir," said one of the boatswain's mates, who had picked it up and was examining it curiously. "Seems to be a jewel-block," and he stared up at the yards with a puzzled expression.

"Let's see it," said Wilkin, who had hurried up on hearing the crash, and now took the damaged block in his hand. "Yes, sir, 'tis a jewel-block sure enough," and he, too, backed away and gazed up from one yard to another.

"Nonsense," said Mr Wigmore; "there's no jewel block carried away. You can see that all the stu'n-sails are standing."

"Why that's true, sir," answered Wilkin, "and a most uncommon queer start is this here. But a jewel-block it is, sir, as you can see for yourself," and he passed the article in question to the lieutenant, who examined it with a puzzled frown.

"Muster the men who were on the yards when it fell," said he, "and just run aloft and have a look round. It can't have dropped from the clouds."

The foretopmen, who had by this time reached the deck, were drawn up in line while the boatswain ran up aloft, and the lieutenant proceeded to question them.

"Did anyone see this block fall?" he demanded, running his eye down the line.

"I see it, sir," said the captain of the foretop, a mahogany-faced elderly man with a queue like a boatswain's colt, pulling his forelock as he spoke.

"Where were you?" asked the lieutenant.

"On the topsail-yard, sir," replied the seaman, "and I see it come a-flyin' past like one of these here thunderbolts and – "

"Like your grandmother!" interrupted Mr Wigmore, irritably. "Where did it seem to come from?"

"Looked as how it come from aloft, sir," replied the sailor.

"From aloft!" roared the lieutenant, "of course it came from aloft you confounded idiot! Where the devil else should it come from? No one supposed it came up out of the hold. Did anyone else see it?"

None of the others knew anything about it, and as the boatswain presently returned from his inspection with the report that nothing was carried away and no ropes were adrift, the matter became more mysterious than ever.

"Some of you must know how it came to drop down," said Mr Wigmore, looking at the men sullenly, "and the rest of you are fools. What do you think, Mr Wilkin?"

"It must have come from somewhere, sir," answered the boatswain.

"That's what I thought, myself," rejoined the lieutenant sourly. "I am glad you agree with me, but the question is where. Did any of the men on deck see it fall? Did you, Roberts?"

"I saw it strike the deck, sir," I answered, "but I didn't see where it came from."

"Well," said the lieutenant, "if Jackson saw it pass the topsail-yard, it must have dropped from the topgallant or royal. Let the master-at-arms enter the names of the men who were on those yards in his report." With this he walked away aft, and the drill was resumed.

As the men returned to their stations I kept a sharp eye upon Rodman who, I noticed, rather avoided my vicinity. Presently, however, he passed quite near me but without looking in my direction, and my eye instantly sought the protuberance that I had noticed under the back of his jacket.

It was gone; and to me, at least, the mystery of the falling block was solved.

On the following morning at eleven o'clock, the hands were piped aft, and the captain read out the names from the report, and inquired into the facts relating to the accident; but no fresh evidence was brought forward — for I did not consider it prudent to disclose what I knew — and the case was settled by stopping the wine allowance of all the men whose names had been read out.

At this moment the look-out in the foretop hailed the deck with the cry. "Sail-ho!"

Mr Wigmore walked forward, and as he reached the foot of the foremast, sung out:

"Foretop there! Where away is the sail, my man?"

"On the lee bow, sir," was the reply.

"What is she like?" asked the lieutenant.

"I haven't rose her hull yet, sir," answered the man, "but she looks like a ship a-going close-hauled on the larboard tack."

"Run up on to the royal yard and see if you can make her out," said Mr Wigmore.

The man ran up the rigging, and as he reached the yard he sang out:

"There's two of 'em, sir, a ship and a schooner, both a-carryin' on on the larboard tack."

"Kindly take the glass aloft, Mr Wigmore, and have a look at them yourself," said the captain, who had come forward to hear the report of the look-out.

The lieutenant took the telescope and mounted to the royal yard, where he sat for some minutes examining the distant vessels.

"What do you make out, Mr Wigmore," shouted the captain.

"The ship is a merchantman — British I should say — and the schooner looks as if she were chasing her."

"Ha!" the captain gave a grunt of satisfaction, and stood looking up as the lieutenant sedately climbed down the rigging.

"What do you make of the schooner?" asked the captain as Mr Wigmore stepped down on deck.

"She's some distance astern of the ship and to leeward of her, but she is evidently a faster vessel and looks to me like a foreigner – French or Spanish."

"Well, get all the stu'n-sails set, Mr Wigmore," said the captain, "and let a man be stationed on the fore-royal yard to report."

The men sprang aloft at the order, as full of eagerness and glee as a parcel of schoolboys, for in such a voyage as this any small excitement that promises to break the deadly monotony of the daily routine, is welcomed as a heaven-sent boon, and the booms slid out and the sails mounted almost before the sound of the order had died away. The look-out sat on his lofty perch with eyes fixed on the horizon, and the hammock nettings were lined with rows of eager faces all turned in the same direction.

In half an hour the ship had risen and showed her hull fairly above the horizon almost dead ahead, and a tiny speck on the rim of the ocean indicated the position of the schooner, broad on our lee bow. We were now near the heart of the trade wind, which sang softly through the rigging and rumbled in the great hollows of the sails, and the sloop bowled along swiftly before it with an easy swing and a gentle roll as the big round billows passed, one after another, under her weather quarter.

The ship which we were approaching was sailing close-hauled, her course being nearly at right angles to ours, so that she presently began to draw away on to our weather bow.

"Shall I fire a gun, sir?" I heard Mr Wigmore call out; but at that moment the look-out hailed the deck.

"The schooner's wore, sir, and she's off to leeward."

All eyes were turned towards the distant sail, but, a few seconds later, the ship was seen to come up into the wind, and brace up on the starboard tack, shaping a course that would bring her right across our bows.

"Aye, aye, sir," responded the look-out, and by way of giving himself a little extra altitude, he stood up on the yard with his back against the mast and one arm passed round the head of a shroud.

The two ships now rapidly approached until they were but half a mile apart, when the stranger clewed up her courses, let fly her topgallant sheets and laid her main topsail aback. A moment later, a boat shot from behind her stern and pulled forward to meet us.

"Shorten sail and heave the ship to, Mr Wigmore," said the captain; "but don't strike off more than is necessary."

The sloop was brought to and sidesmen stationed at the gangway to hand the man-ropes, by which time the boat was close alongside, and we could see a stout red-faced man in the stern who bobbed forward at each stroke of the oars, and stared up at the sloop-of-war with an expression of eager curiosity. When the man-ropes were handed to him he seized them and was up the side in a twinkling and stood in the gangway with his glazed hat in his hand, bowing profoundly to the officers who had come forward to meet him.

"Your good ship, sir," said he, addressing the captain, "appeared in the very nick of time. That rascally picaroon was coming up hand over hand."

"I am rejoiced, sir," replied the captain, "that we came up so opportunely. I shall trouble you for a few particulars, and I am sure you will pardon me if I ask you to be brief."

"I won't detain you, sir," said the stranger; "not I; God forbid!"

"Then if you will accompany me to my cabin, we can dispatch our business without delay," and the captain – to the profound regret of all hands – retired from the quarter-deck, followed by Mr Wigmore and the stranger.

They were not long absent, and, when they reappeared, the captain was rubbing his hands with a satisfied air, the stranger was wiping his mouth, and Mr Wigmore was glancing over a paper that he held in his hand.

"I trust you will finish your voyage in safety, now," said the captain, as our visitor dropped down into his boat, and prepared to push off.

"I thank you, sir," was the answer, "and, for my part, I hope you will sink that accursed schooner and send her company of cut-throats to the bottom."

"I hope so," rejoined the captain with a farewell flourish of his hat. "Make sail, Mr Wigmore. Aloft, there! Do you see the schooner?"

"No, sir," replied the look-out. "She's just sunk to the sou'-west."

"Hum!" grunted Percival. "A stern chase is a long chase, but we ought to be able to overhaul a schooner going free. Pile everything on to her, Mr Wigmore."

The *Asphodel* was put dead before the wind, and, with all her light sails swelling out aloft and overhanging the water on either side, she staggered along with a roaring at her bows and a long white wake astern, while the merchantman grew small in the distance. An extra look-out was posted at the main-royal and the boatswain himself went aloft to sweep the horizon with a telescope.

All hands were now piped to dinner, and, as the men sat round their little tables in the berths between the guns, the prospects of the chase were eagerly discussed by the respective messes. Very soon news from the cabin began to filter in the gun-deck, for the captain's steward and the sentinel at the cabin door, had between them, managed to glean enough scraps of conversation to build up the merchant skipper's story. Briefly stated it was as follows:

Three days previously our friend the *Susan* of Bristol, homeward-bound from Monte Video, had fallen in with the schooner which at the time was proceeding south under easy sail; but immediately after she was sighted the strange vessel set all her plain canvas and bore up to the north-west in pursuit. On this the master of the *Susan* put his ship a few points off the wind and set studding-sails, hoping thus to get the advantage over a fore-and-aft rigged vessel. But the schooner crowded on a quantity of light sails and soon showed that she was much faster off the wind than schooners usually are. However, the *Susan* held on, the stranger overhauling her very slowly, and, as night was approaching, there seemed some chance of escape.

Suddenly the schooner was seen to luff up as if giving up the chase, and then, for the first time, the people of the *Susan* perceived another sail on the horizon. The master ran aloft with a glass, and from the foretop he could make out the vessel to be a jackass barque, which he recognised as the *Morning Star* of Poole, which had sailed out of Monte Video a week before the *Susan*.

Night came on shortly, and, when the darkness fell, the schooner was seen to be approaching the barque, which had not altered her course.

As soon as she was concealed by the darkness the *Susan* was put on her proper course, but the breeze fell light and they made little headway. About midnight the people on board observed, reflected on the clouds to windward, the red glare of a ship on fire below the horizon. The master made every effort to reach the distressed vessel (which all hands suspected to be the *Morning Star*) but she lay so far to windward and the breeze continued so light, that it was not until the following morning that they reached her vicinity. A look-0out from the mast-head then observed a dismasted and water-logged vessel, and, as soon as the *Susan* was near enough, the master and mate put off in a boat to examine her.

The hulk was that of the *Morning Star*, lying with her decks awash, and littered with the charred remains of her spars. With some difficulty they got on board, and, on entering the round-house, found it gutted and partially burned. There were splashes of blood on the bulkheads, and the bodies of the master and two mates were washing about in the water on the deck. A very little examination showed that they had all been murdered, for the corpses were covered with knife wounds and it was seen that all the lockers had been broken open and everything of value carried away. It was evident that the pirates when they had murdered the crew and quitted the ship had scuttled her and set her on fire; and had it not been for the buoyant nature of the cargo, all evidence of the crime would have been destroyed by her sinking.

The *Susan* held on her course the whole of that day without incident; but on the following morning – which was the day of which I am now writing – about nine o'clock, the look-out aloft reported a schooner down to leeward, lying to under a single topsail and trysail. The master immediately ran aloft with a telescope, but by the time he had reached the cross-trees she had set mainsail and head-sails and was crowding on the rest of her canvas with a speed that gave an unpleasant hint as to the number of hands on board. She at once made sail in chase of the *Susan*, but, being so far to leeward, had only gained slowly. About eleven o'clock the *Asphodel* was sighted to windward, but the schooner held on, not having yet seen the man-of-war. Presently, however, the new arrival was observed by the pirates and her formidable character evidently made out, for the schooner suddenly wore and made off to leeward, piling on all the sail she could set.

Such was the story that circulated on the gun-deck during the cheerful dinner-hour, and a mighty commotion it created; so that when the notes of a fife playing, "Why should we quarrel for riches?" came down from the main deck to announce that the wine tub was manned (and carrying my thoughts back to East Tilbury and the sweet, peaceful life of my Kentish home) there was little inclination to linger over the delights of "Miss Taylor" – as the strong white wine was facetiously nicknamed – but the black-jacks were speedily emptied, with many a jovial toast of "destruction to the bloody picaroons," and all hands trooped up on the main deck to gaze out once more over the hammock-nettings.

Just as I stepped out of the hatchway, the look-out on the main-royal hailed the deck:

"Sail-ho! Sail broad on the larboard bow."

"Take the glass aloft, Mr Wilkin," the captain sang out, "and see if it is the schooner."

The boatswain was soon at the masthead with his glass directed at the sail; after a short inspection of the stranger, he called down:

"'Tis the schooner, sir, fair smothered in canvas and bearing away south-east. In another quarter of an hour we'd a' lost her."

The sloop's head was put to south-east, and some of the lighter canvas taken in, but so much was left set that the ship heeled over sharply and the upper masts bent like canes, while the weather rigging groaned and creaked in a way that made the boatswain's mates stare aloft in dismay. But with all this it was upwards of an hour before the strange sail was visible from the deck, and the afternoon was on the wane when her hull came in sight above the horizon.

"She must have the devil hisself aboard of her, must that there craft," said one of the old hands. "I' never see the schooner afore as could show her heels like this here a-goin' free."

"She's foreign built, that's what she is," said Bill Muffin. "I've sailed into some of the Mediterranean ports myself and I've seen the craft what they builds there, xebecs and feluccas and what not. They're meant to go through the water them craft are, and they builds 'em accordin'. Uncommon beamy they are, so as to stand up agin a press of sail, but wonderful fine below the waterline, and as sharp as a knife."

"Well, well," returned the old seaman, "every nation has its own fashions. I grant you the foreigners can turn out a prettier model than you'll see launched from our own shipyards. But it ain't the ship what matters mate, 'tis the sailors; and there I reckon as Old England can wallop the best of 'em."

"You're about right there, brother," replied Bill; "all's accordin' to nature and every man to his own job, and the one what's a-going to run wants the cleanest pair of heels."

The hands were now piped down to supper, and when the evening meal had been dispatched, the drummers beat the usual call to quarters. This was part of the daily routine, but on this occasion, with a chase in sight, the preparation and inspection was more than usually rigorous, the captain himself accompanying the first lieutenant round the decks to see that all was in order and ready for action; so that all hands were kept busy till it was time to pipe down the hammocks and set the watch. It had now been dark for more than an hour – for we were drawing near to the equinoctial line – but the moon was well above the horizon and the schooner was plainly visible on our lee bow. Now and again some flying cloud shut out the light for a few minutes at a time, but when it passed, the fugitive hove in sight again, holding on to her course to the south-east.

As soon as eight bells was struck, the starboard watch, to which I belonged, went below and turned in, determined to get what rest they could before all hands were called to quarters; and they were joined by a part of the larboard watch who were allowed to come down to their hammocks until they should be wanted on deck.

About seven bells – or half-past eleven – I was roused by the sound of the drum beating to quarters, and, dropping out of my hammock, I slipped on my jacket as I joined the crowd that was pouring up the ladders. When I reached my station on the forecastle, I perceived that we were now within a mile of the schooner, which lay directly to leeward and was sailing on a course parallel with ours, a few points off the wind. The chase appeared to be as good as over, for having come abreast of the fugitive, the sloop could now gradually edge down until she was alongside. The schooner was, in fact, quite at our mercy, for if she came up closer to the wind, she would only close on us the sooner, while if she put up her helm and ran before it, she would be on her worst point of sailing and would be rapidly overtaken.

"We'll be aboard of her in a hour," I heard one of the boatswain's mates say. "We're a-travelling faster than her and we've got the weather gauge."

"Aye," agreed the other, "her glass is run out, I reckon. D'ye think the captain'll sink 'em all or send 'em aloft to the yard-arms?"

"I dunno," answered the first speaker. "Maybe he'll ship the whole crew of 'em off to the West Indies to take their trial."

The conversation was here interrupted by the arrival of the gunner's mates carrying the match tubs, which they proceeded to place in position between the carronades, and they had but just cleared the guns ready for firing when a dense bank of cloud swept across the face of the moon, and in an instant the sea was wrapped in impenetrable darkness.

"Keep an eye on the chase there forward," shouted Mr Wigmore. "Do any of you see the schooner?"

"No, sir," answered one of the men. "'Tis as dark as a miser's pocket. We wouldn't see her if she was alongside."

"Silence, there, and keep a bright look-out," rejoined the lieutenant, a little inconsistently as I thought, and we heard him stumping aft cursing volubly, although he was invisible in the pitchy darkness.

The ship remained wrapped in silence save for the washing of water under her bows and the murmur of the wind in her sails while all hands peered into the gloom or gazed up at the flying cloud. In a few minutes a fringe of pale gold appeared at its windward edge, and then the moon sailed out into the dark blue sky, lighting up our decks and revealing the schooner dead to leeward, holding on her course, but perceptibly nearer.

"Give her the broadside, Mr Wigmore," I heard the captain call out, and a few seconds afterwards a sheet of flame burst out of the ship's side with a rolling thunderous crash that shook the whole fabric. A great pall of smoke rose to leeward, rolling away down the wind between us and the schooner, and, for the time, completely concealing her from our view. When she came into sight again, as the smoke blew past her, it was evident that she had taken our hint with great promptitude, for she was now going dead before the wind with her mainsail and trysail goose-winged, and large studding-sails out on both sides. Her course was now nearly at right angles to ours, and in the interval we had passed her, so that she now bore on our starboard quarter.

The *Asphodel* was instantly put before the wind and the hands rushed aloft to set the remaining studding-sails while the officers paced the deck with feverish strides. The schooner had so far attained her object, for it was now impossible to bring the broadside guns to bear on her, but it was evident that, despite her great press of sail, we were gaining on her rapidly on the new course.

"The gunner reports that the starboard-bow gun could be brought to bear," the second lieutenant called out. "Shall we give her a shot, sir?"

"No, no," replied the captain. "Let us get alongside; we should only give her a chance to dodge in the smoke."

The schooner soon began to loom up larger as we diminished the space between the two vessels, so that we could make out more of her character – her great beam, her low free-board and the immense expanse of canvas that she spread. But it was now observed, also, that a large mass of cloud was creeping across the sky and threatened very shortly to obscure the moon. All eyes were turned anxiously towards it as it drew nearer and nearer, and when, at length, its leeward edge broke out into a luminous fringe, the captain called out sharply to the hands in the forecastle:

"Forward, there, don't lose sight of the schooner."

This was all very well, but when the dense black shroud drew over the moon and extinguished its beams, the darkness became profound, and the schooner vanished as though she had never been.

"This is damned unlucky," exclaimed Mr Wigmore, running on to the forecastle with a night-glass and pointing it into the black obscurity, "where the devil is she? Here, Mr Wilkin, take the glass and see if you can make her out."

Now a night-glass is an excellent invention and will make the most of a very dim light, but the glass was never made that would enable a man to see in utter darkness; and this the boatswain duly realised, for, after peering through the instrument for more than a minute, he handed it back to the lieutenant.

"'Tis no use, sir," said he; "'tis like searchin' for a pin on the orlop deck. We must wait till the moon comes out again."

Once more the ship subsided into a tense silence, broken only by the sounds of wind and water and the curses of the officers as they impatiently stamped up and down the decks. The last streak of moonlight had faded from the horizon and the ship rushed forward into the black void, her own decks wrapped in total darkness save where, at long intervals, the dull glimmer of a horn battle lanthorn made the obscurity seem even more profound.

The bank of cloud was more than a quarter of an hour in passing, during which time the whole ship's company was kept on the very tiptoe of expectation and suspense. At length the pale light appeared dimly through a thinner portion near the edge, and the night-glasses were once more pointed into the gloom ahead.

"Does anyone on the forecastle see the schooner?" shouted the captain.

There was a brief interval of silence and then one of the men sang out:

"There she is, sir, over the starboard quarter"; and the moon, at that moment, bursting out from the edge of the cloud, revealed the schooner a good two miles distant, going full and by on the starboard tack.

"Bring the ship by the wind, Mr Wigmore," exclaimed the captain; and, as the lieutenant bawled out his orders through the speaking-trumpet, the hands flew aloft to get in the studding-sails.

"We've lost her," said Bill Muffin, who had been called up from the gun-deck with the other hands to work the ship, and now stood near me at the weather fore-brace. "That schooner's like the handle of my grandmother's teapot, she's off."

"Gammon!" exclaimed one of the seamen. "We're faster than what she is, even by the wind. We'll overhaul her yet, never you fear."

"We could overhaul her right enough," answered Bill, "if she'd let us, but she won't. I've sailed in schooners, and I knows their ways. She can go a full point nearer the wind than what we can and she can go about a dozen times to our once as you'll see."

In a couple of minutes the ship was brought by the wind on the starboard tack nearly in the wake of the schooner; but hardly had the ropes been coiled down, before the stranger was seen to shoot up into the wind and fill on the larboard tack, heading so as to pass us about a mile to windward.

"What did I tell you?" chuckled Bill. "We can't spin round like that. She's off to windward, I tell you."

This was evidently the captain's opinion, for he immediately gave the order to 'bout ship; and the justice of Bill's observations now became apparent as the complicated evolutions necessary for tacking a ship were carried out; and the sloop-of-war was still head to wind with her head-sails shaking and her forward square-sails aback, when the schooner once more flew up into the wind and was off on the other tack.

"She's gone about," shouted a dozen voices at once.

"Never mind," roared the captain. "Mainsail haul and be damned to her or we shall have the ship in irons."

The *Asphodel* now paid off slowly and the two vessels began to recede rapidly on opposite tacks.

"This here won't do," grumbled a boatswain's mate. "'Tis a-cloudin' up and we'll be losin' sight of her."

"Ready about." The order discharged along the deck from the lieutenant's speaking-trumpet sent all hands to their stations, and once more the evolution was performed. But no sooner had the ship filled on the starboard tack, than round came the schooner on to the larboard, to the intense amusement of Bill Muffin, whose *esprit de corps* as a man-of-war's man was being fast overpowered by his professional enthusiasm as a fore-and-aft sailor.

"Ho! ho! my eye!" he exclaimed, but stopped suddenly as Mr Wigmore strode up angrily.

"Who was that laughing on the forecastle?" he demanded fiercely. "Hey, who was it, you?" This was addressed to Bill.

"Seemed as how the voice come from somewhere in the head," answered my guileless shipmate, "but I didn't see who it was."

"There'll be a voice coming from the gangway if I hear any more laughing," said Mr Wigmore, and he stumped aft muttering and shaking his speaking-trumpet.

The schooner was now seen crossing us about two miles to windward, and the order was again given to bout ship; and again, as the *Asphodel* filled on the larboard tack, the schooner went about and filled on the starboard; and it became increasingly evident that with each change of tack, the distance between the two vessels increased. Yet it was impossible for the captain of the sloop-of-war to do what he would no doubt have done by daylight, viz., to make long boards on each tack so as to get the advantage of his vessel's greater speed and avoid the delay of going about so frequently. Had he done so the schooner would have run out of sight at once on the opposite tack, and probably vanished for good.

As it was the schooner steadily increased her distance to windward, while the sky clouded over more and more, and frequently hid her from view. At length, after standing on the starboard tack a little longer than usual, the captain hailed the forecastle:

"Forward, there, where away is the schooner?"

"I see her over the quarter, sir, a minute ago," said Wilkin, "but I don't see her now."

"Ready about!" exclaimed the captain. "We must keep her in sight or she'll give us the slip."

Once more the vessel was put about and filled on the opposite tack and a look-out stationed in each top. But the time passed and no sign of the schooner appeared, and presently it became evident that she had gone about unseen and crossed us in the dark, unless she were actually out-sailing us, which was most improbable. After holding on for over an hour all doubt as to her having escaped was at an end, and though the ship was still kept on a bowline, the guns were secured, and the watch below piped down to their hammocks.

CHAPTER ELEVEN

In which we approach a Strange Island

When our watch was piped up on the following morning at half-past seven, the ship was still on the same course, heading about south-east, but the breeze was now much lighter, for we were sailing out of the trade wind into the equatorial calms. Light as the breeze was, however, it was enough to keep the sails sleeping, as the mariner expresses it, and the ship continued her stately progress across the blue ocean, curtseying gently as the water whitened under her stem and streamed away aft into her wake.

So we sailed on all that day and the next, never quite losing the breeze, though the airs grew lighter and the heat became so great in the middle of the day that the pitch in the deck seams liquefied and stuck to the soles of our shoes. On the third day – which was the twenty-ninth of August, the twenty-sixth day out from the Downs – the observation at eight bells showed that we were crossing the line, and after dinner an allowance of spirits was served out and the hands turned up to skylark and amuse themselves. The decks were soon cleared, the fiddler perched on the capstan and the sailors proceeded to dance with a mixture of high spirits and solemnity that was highly diverting. The older hands, in particular, took the whole affair very seriously and it was most comical to see the sedate sergeant of marine's coming down the middle in company with a gunner's yeoman while the fiddler sawed away to the tune of "Drops of

Brandy," and the other dancers gravely pointed their toes and stuck their arms akimbo.

When the men were tired of dancing they fell to playing various games, most of them of a rather rough and boisterous character, and it was at this point that the first discordant note was struck. One of the men had produced a pack of cards, although these were ordinarily forbidden articles on board ship, and had gathered a part of his shipmates to play able-whackets – a foolish kind of marine forfeits in which the losing player has to receive so many blows on the palm of the hand with a knotted handkerchief. I had taken my seat in the ring which was formed by the players before I noticed that Rodman was one of them, when I would have risen and gone away but the man next to me caught hold of my sleeve.

"What's amiss, brother?" said he. "Is it old Jeff that you don't like the looks of? Why old Jeff's as mild as a lamb he is. He wouldn't hurt nobody."

At this there was a general laugh, for Rodman's savage temper was notorious, and had caused him to be turned out of more than one mess. But I could see there was no retreating, for the prospect of a rougher element being added to the play gave an extra piquancy to the silly game, and the men were determined to see Rodman pitted against me.

It was not long before they had their desire, for a newcomer like myself easily falls into the traps that are set for him. In the second round I was adjudged to receive two whackets from each player and accordingly held out my hand. Now a stroke from a twisted handkerchief is no very serious matter to a man whose palms are hardened by handling ropes, and the whackets that I received caused nothing more than an uncomfortable smart until it came to Rodman's turn. I had noticed him put his handkerchief in his pocket just before, and I now observed that he drew one out of a different pocket, which made me somewhat suspicious. I had no choice, however, but to hold out my hand, which I did, and received a blow that made me cry out with pain, whereupon my shipmates broke out into shouts of laughter.

"That's one for Jeff," chuckled the man at my side. "You've got to grin and bear it, Jim, and then when your turn comes, you can make old Jeff holler. Out with your flippers for number two."

I held out my hand again, close to the deck, and, as Rodman brought the handkerchief down with all his strength, I drew back suddenly and let the blow fall on the planks. As the knotted end stuck the deck, it gave out a sharp sound that confirmed me in my suspicions, and with a quick snatch I whisked the handkerchief out of Rodman's hand.

When he saw that he was detected, the ruffian scrambled forward with a furious oath, but was immediately collared and held down, kicking and struggling, by two of the seamen, while the others gathered round me to watch while I examined the handkerchief.

"That there knot sounded uncommon hard, Jeff," remarked one of the men. "Just you untie him and let's see what's inside."

I accordingly unfastened the knot; when, as I had expected, out fell a pistol ball.

"Well I'm jiggered!" exclaimed old Jackson, the captain of the maintop, "of all the darned scurvy tricks for to play upon a shipmate! Here," he cried indignantly, "pass that handkercher to me, and the ball too. We'll show him how to play whackets to a new tune."

He replaced the ball, and, when he had tied the knot securely, the blaspheming Rodman was laid prone on the deck with two men sitting astride on him. Then each of the players in turn took the handkerchief and bestowed two well-directed and vigorous thwacks on such part of the victim as offered the best mark, and, by the time this proceeding was finished, Rodman was fairly foaming at the mouth with rage.

As soon as he was released, he rushed to the pin-rack and pulled out a belaying-pin, with which he was in the act of charging at his tormentors when a ship's corporal interposed and gave him a cut with his rattan that speedily brought him to his senses.

At this moment the pipes of the boatswain's mates sounded the call for supper, and as we all dispersed to our respective messes, the unpleasant episode was brought to an end.

For a week after this the ship sailed on without incident, sometimes running before a favouring breeze, and sometimes going close-hauled, but never actually becalmed. On the afternoon of the third day we met the first of the south-east trade wind; three days later the island of Ascension rose from the horizon to the south-east, and at noon on the following day we brought up in the anchorage, where we found two other king's ships riding at single anchor. Many of our crew had indulged hopes of being allowed to go ashore, in which, however, they were disappointed; but although no shore leave was granted, permission was given for the men to visit the other ships, and, as one of the latter, a frigate, was leaving shortly for England, it was announced that a bag would be made up for any men who wished to send home letters.

"Now'll be the time to rouse up your friends, Jim," said Bill to me when this order was made known. "Tell 'em to go to the Lord High Admiral or the King, and kick up a rumpus. They'll soon have you out of this, for, d'ye see, there ain't no war for to excuse this here pressing job."

This had been my intention, but when I considered my cousin's conduct, I had little doubt that the letters would be looked over, and that one written by me would have but a poor chance of reaching its destination.

I therefore resolved that my letter to Prudence should go enclosed in one belonging to some other man, while, to disarm suspicion, I would send a letter to Mr Leigh in the ship's bag.

An excellent opportunity for carrying out this scheme occurred on the second day after our arrival when I obtained permission to join a party of liberty men who were going to visit the line-of-battleship. Here, I found, a bag was also being made up to send home by the frigate, and, as very few of the men could write, I tendered my services as scribe. This offer was eagerly accepted and I was soon seated at a mess-table on the upper gun deck, surrounded by a group of shy and grinning seamen each with his sheet of paper in his hand.

"Now," said I when I had trimmed my pen, "who is first?"

"I'm first," answered a great burly fellow, laying down a sheet of paper and spreading it out with his brown hairy paw. "We've took our turns with the dice and I come out first."

"Very well," said I. "What am I to say?"

"Why d'ye see," said the sailor, smoothing his hair down on to his forehead and looking round with ludicrous dismay at the circle of faces, all on the broad grin, "my name is Joe Crabtree, that's what my name is, and her name is Poll."

"Mary," I suggested.

"Maybe you're right, mate, but Poll is what she's called."

"Very well," said I, " 'Dear Poll' now what am I to say to her?"

"Why," answered Joe in increasing confusion, "you can tell her as how we've been in the West Indies where the rum comes from and damned hot it was; and you can say as the ship's provisions ain't good for nought, for the bread is that lively as you has to chevy the biscuits round the deck – "

"She won't believe that," interrupted another sailor.

"She wouldn't if you told her," retorted Joe, "but she knows me and respecks me."

I set down the statement of the veracious and respectable Joseph and then asked:

"What else shall I say?"

"Why that's all, mate – exceptin' as you might mention," – here he leered shyly at his delighted shipmates – "you might mention as I loves her like blazes; also you might tell her that when I comes home, if I hears as she's been a-cruisin' about with any other chaps I'll fetch her a lift with a rope's end as'll make her hop."

A roar of applause greeted this conclusion, which I set down as well as I could, while I controlled my mirth until I was on the point of suffocation.

"What is her name?" I asked, when the letter was finished, and I proceeded to add the address.

"Poll, I tells you, mate," was the answer.

"Yes, but her other name?" I persisted.

"Her other name," repeated Joe, smoothing his hair in great perplexity. "Why I don't know as I ever heard tell of it. Poll is what she's called, and Poll is her name."

"Well, where does she live?" I asked.

"Sheerness, Blue Town," replied Joe promptly.

"Yes, but what street and number?" I asked.

"Damned if I know," replied Joe, "but that ain't no matter; everybody knows Poll. Why, bless your heart, mate," he continued earnestly, "you couldn't mistake her nohow. She's got a figure fit for to put on the head of a West Indie trader, and besides that she's got a swivel eye – starboard side as far as I remembers."

With this somewhat imperfect address, the letter was closed up and sealed with the impression of a sail palm, and then the next man came forward for his turn.

By the time I had worked my way through the crowd of applicants it was getting towards the hour for our return to the sloop, and I had to beg the last of my clients to be as brief as possible.

"Right, brother," said he. "'Tis my old mother as I wants to send a word to, and there ain't no call to be long-winded about it."

He gave me a short message stating that he was well and happy and when I had written it down, I asked for the address.

"Mrs Royle, Snodland, Kent," said he.

"Snodland!" I exclaimed. "Why that is close to my home. You know Shorne, I expect."

"I've good reason to," he answered with a grin, "for 'twas Shorne wood as sent me to sea."

"Indeed," said I, "how was that?"

"Why," he replied, "'twas a matter of brace of pheasants and a meddlesome swab of a gamekeeper. So they claps me into Maidstone Gaol and when this here ship was a-fittin' out at Chatham, they puts me aboard of her, and here I am."

"Do you think," I asked, "if I were to put a letter of my own in with yours, that your mother would have it delivered?"

"Why of course she would," he answered, "and proud to be of service to you."

Accordingly I added a few words of instruction and slipped into the enclosure the long letter which I had written to Prudence and had carried about with me in readiness for an opportunity to dispatch it. When the missive was closed up, sealed, and dropped into the ship's bag, my heart was lighter than it had been since I left England, for, though I had no doubt that my little cousin must have learned from the people at the 'Mermaid' of the manner in which I had been spirited away, yet it was a consolation to tell her in my own words of all that had befallen me, and to send her a greeting from this faraway island in mid-ocean.

When I was once more back on board the sloop, I wrote a letter to Mr Leigh, brief and dry in character, as I felt little doubt that it would be intercepted; which turned out to be the case, for whereas Prudence received her letter in due course, the one sent to Mr Leigh was never heard of again.

The day before we sailed from Ascension a ten-gun brig came in and dropped anchor a short distance from us. Shortly afterwards the order was given to man the gig, of which I had been told off as one of the crew, and as soon as the captain had taken his place in the stern, we pulled off to the brig.

Here, as we were waiting on the gun-deck, while our captain was conferring with the lieutenant in command, we gathered from the brig's people some news that caused us considerable excitement. It appeared that the *Puffin*, as the brig was named, had been cruising for some months off the South American coast and had heard many complaints of the piccaroons who lurked in those seas from the River Plate to the West Indies, and especially of a large schooner, the crew of which was said to have plundered and burned a number of merchantmen. The *Puffin* had fallen in with this schooner no less than three times, but on each occasion the pirate had escaped without difficulty owing to her superior sailing qualities. The last meeting had occurred only four days previously, when the *Puffin* encountered the schooner sailing in a southerly direction under a great press of canvas. The brig immediately gave chase, but the schooner, having shifted her course a few points nearer the wind, left the *Puffin* astern so rapidly that the pursuit was abandoned. At the time of the meeting, there was no sail in sight to account for the quantity of canvas that the schooner was spreading, and the brig's people supposed that the pirate was either bound for a rendezvous or had information that a valuable prize was sailing from one of the southern ports.

It was evident that the captain had received similar information, for, shortly after our return to the *Asphodel*, orders were given to see all clear for getting under way on the following morning at daybreak.

In accordance with these orders, the hands were piped up while the stars were yet twinkling aloft, and the glow of the coming day had hardly begun to show in the eastern sky; and by the time the first streaks of sunlight came slanting over the horizon, the sails were set, and the ship was standing out to sea.

The course set was about south-west, and as we were now in the heart of the south-east trade wind, we bowled along merrily with braced-up yards and bowlines taut, and a long, white wake streaming away astern. All was excitement and exhilaration on board, for the men were pretty well in the commander's confidence, and although there was a regular look-out constantly stationed at the fore-royal, a keen desire was shown by the men for such jobs as greasing the upper masts and rigging, and overhauling the running gear aloft.

The eager look-out, however, was rewarded by nothing more exciting than an occasional glimpse of some merchant vessel, and the ship settled down into the usual routine of hard work and scanty rest. The monotony of the run was broken for me by an event which, though it was but one of the trivial disagreeable occurrences common on ship-board, I mention because it was not without consequences of moment to me.

One night – it was, I think, the sixth out from Ascension – I had turned into my hammock, and was just sinking into the first delicious doze of a tired man, when I became aware of a soft grating sound near my head, as though a rat were nibbling at some part of the hammock. I listened drowsily for a few seconds, and then, becoming suddenly wide awake, I raised myself on my elbow; and at that moment part of the fastening of the hammock parted with a snap.

In an instant I had bounded out on to the deck and was just in time to hear someone run off under the hammocks and hastily ascend the ladder. I followed as quickly as I could in the crouching position that was necessary to creep under the crowded hammocks, which sagged down with the weight of their occupants, and at the top of the ladder ran into the arms of a ship's corporal.

"What are you doing up here?" he demanded. "Isn't it your watch below?"

"Yes," I answered, "but I came to see who that was that ran up the ladder just now."

"And what concern is that of yourn, mate?" he asked.

"Why," I replied, "someone has been tampering with my hammock clews, and I suspect it was the man who went up the ladder."

"Ho!" said the corporal; "here, just wait whilst I fetches a glim and we'll have a look at that there hammock."

He went away and returned presently carrying a battle lanthorn, and we descended into the 'tween-decks.

When I had found my hammock he turned the dim light of the lanthorn on to the head clews and uttered a grunt.

"'Tis well for you, Roberts," said he, "as you woke when you did or you wouldn't never have woke at all. Jest look at them knittles! If they'd parted whilst you was asleep, you'd have broke your neck or stove in your skull as sure as you're a living sinner."

I looked at the knittles, or small cords of which the clews of a hammock are made up, and by the light of the lanthorn I could see that a number of them had been half cut through. Had I been asleep the remainder would have been nicked in the same manner and would have parted, one by one, until there was not enough to bear my weight, when I should have been thrown down on to my head and most probably killed on the spot.

"Who played you this rascally trick, think you?" asked the corporal.

"I did not see the man," I answered, although I had little doubt as to his identity.

"Well I did," said the corporal, "and down in the report he goes, the darned swab, and do you knot up them knittles sharp now and turn in again."

I secured the clews as well as I could while the corporal held the lanthorn, and then, having thanked him for his assistance, I turned in, taking the precaution to change my pillow over to the sound end of the hammock.

At eleven o'clock on the following morning, the hands were piped aft to witness punishment, and when the grating had been rigged and the boatswain's mate had taken the cat out of the bag, the prisoner was brought forward.

It was, as I had expected, Jeffrey Rodman, and as he stood before the captain, sullen, but evidently filled with dread of the impending punishment, and I caught the look of terrified hate that he cast on me, I felt in my mind, a sensation of mingled commiseration and disgust.

"Have you anything to say?" the captain asked him when the section of the Articles of War had been read.

"I never done it, sir," answered Rodman.

"Who saw him do it?" the captain inquired, turning to the master-at-arms.

"No one did, sir," was the answer; "but the ship's corporal saw him come up the hatch directly after the clews were cut and 'tis known that he bears a grudge against Roberts – the man who was sleeping in the hammock."

"Is that all?" asked the captain.

"That's all, sir," the master-at-arms replied.

"What were you doing down in the 'tween-decks, Rodman?" demanded the captain.

"I got permission to fetch a neckerchief from my hammock, sir."

"Where do you sling your hammock?"

"'Tis the sixth one forrard of Roberts, sir," replied Rodman.

"Humph," said the captain; and then to my intense relief, as well as Rodman's, he continued after a pause:

"There is not enough proof to justify the infliction of punishment. You will be released," he added, addressing the prisoner, "but let me give you a warning. I'll have no malice or ill-blood among my crew, and if you are caught paying off any grudges against your shipmates, you may look to get a bloody shirt for your pains, so have a care."

On this the grating was unrigged and the hands piped forward to resume their routine duty.

About three o'clock in the afternoon Mr Wigmore came forward with his speaking-trumpet and hailed the look-out:

"Aloft, there! Do you see any sign of land ahead?"

"Nary a sign, sir," was the reply, after an earnest gaze at the horizon.

"Keep a bright look-out," shouted the lieutenant as he tucked the trumpet under his arm and returned to the quarter-deck.

The inquiry was repeated several times during the afternoon, eliciting always the same reply, and once the lieutenant himself went aloft and scanned the horizon with a glass. But even this scrutiny was apparently without result, for he presently descended with a dissatisfied air and proceeded to examine the board on which the rate of sailing was recorded.

About five o'clock, however, all hands were roused by a loud hail from the fore-royal:

"Land-ho! Land on the larboard bow."

"Heave the log," exclaimed Mr Wigmore; and, having taken a long look at the compass in the binnacle, he once more ascended the rigging.

The ship was going at about eight knots with a moderate breeze blowing from north-north-east – for we had run out of the trades the day before and had picked up this breeze in the evening – so that we might reckon to have the land aboard during the night if we stood on as we were sailing. As this prospect was not greatly relished either by the officers or men, it may be supposed that the reports of the look-out in answer to inquiries from the deck were listened to with uncommon attention. By six o'clock the land was clearly visible from the fore-top, although it was not yet in sight from the deck, and as it was seen to lie pretty broad on the larboard bow, the ship's course was altered a couple of points to starboard to allow for leeway, and she stood on under all plain sail.

Soon after this the daylight faded, and the crew gathered in little parties about the dark decks earnestly discussing the position and cross-examining the men who had been relieved from the look-out aloft.

"What did this here land look like, Bill?" one seaman asked. "Is it the coast of South America think ye?"

"Lord love ye, no, mate," answered the other. "'Twas two small islands with peaks on 'em, like the Desertas or the Salvages."

"I'll tell you what it is," said another. "These is some of them there desert islands with no one aboard of 'em what I've heerd about in these seas, where the pirates puts in to refit and share out the swag – what they calls a rondy voo."

"Ned's right, you may take your davy," said the man who had been on the look-out. "It's a rondy voo, right enough. I heerd 'em say aboard the gun-brig that the schooner had gone off to a rondy voo, but I didn't know at the time as that was a name for one of these here hislands."

"'Tis French, d'ye see, mate," said Ned with a superior and even slightly pompous air, "and means in their lingo, a island what nobody don't live on."

"Do it now?" rejoined Bill, regarding his shipmate admiringly; "that's what it is to be a scholar. Now when I heerd 'em say as the pirate had gone off for a rondy voo, I thought they meant some kind of foreign trader."

The pipes of the boatswain's mates broke in upon the conversation at this point, and the men trooped down to their mess berths where, when the beef and biscuit had been disposed of and the tin cups filled from the black-jacks, the subject was revived, and considered in all its bearings.

It was my watch on deck from midnight to four o'clock – the middle watch as it is called – and during this time the ship continued to forge ahead with the steady breeze pouring into her sails and the seas churning noisily under her lee-bow. It was evident that, though there was little work to be done and few orders were given, a watchful care was being exercised by the officers, for not only was the lieutenant of the watch continually prying into the darkness ahead and to leeward with a night-glass, but several times I saw Mr Wigmore himself come out on the deck to make sure that all was well. Nothing, however, was to be seen through the blackness of the night, nor even when, at about three o'clock, the moon rose, red and spectral, from the eastern horizon, and I was not sorry when the time came to rouse up the "larbowlines" and go below to my hammock.

When I came on deck at eight o'clock the scene was changed indeed. The sun was shining, the white clouds were flying, and the ship was heading due east with a moderate breeze from the north. Right ahead, at a distance of not more than five miles, was a small island rising sheer from the ocean and standing grey and flat against the morning sun like a mass of dense cloud.

Its aspect, even at this distance, was strange and forbidding, for it rose in a multitude of spires and pinnacles and flung aloft a range of tall peaks which were all rugged and shattered as though they were but the ruins of decayed mountains; and above them great wreaths of cloud whirled and twisted in the sky like masses of colossal drapery blowing hither and thither in the wind. All along the foot of the island we could see a snowy line of surf which, as we came nearer, was seen to leap, in places, in great jets and clouds of spray, while there was borne to our ears the sullen, hollow growl that told of the weight of water that was flung upon that iron-bound coast.

The men crowded along the bulwarks, peering over the hammock-nettings with something of awe in their faces as the uncouth mass of rock drew nearer, and all a seaman's dislike of a surf-bound coast appeared in the comments that were passed on the leaping waters and the flying spray.

The island terminated northward in a long promontory crowned by a jagged, conical peak, and, as we approached, the ship was brought nearer to the wind so as to clear this by about a mile, and we sailed for a time nearly parallel to the north-west shore. When we were within a mile and a half of the land, an immense cloud of seabirds rose into the sky, looking in the distance like a mass of dark smoke, and presently a prodigious multitude of them bore down upon the ship and came circling around the masts, surrounding the vessel with a most infernal clamour of screams and unearthly cries; and so fearless were they that they actually lighted on the hammock-nettings and ran about the deck, screaming aloud and threatening the sailors with gaping beaks.

I could see that our men – who were as superstitious as most sailors are – by no means relished the unnatural behaviour of these birds (which indeed were as strange and uncouth in their appearance as in their manners), and kicked and struck savagely at them as they ran amongst our feet or whirled bewilderingly around our heads; nor did this reception seem to increase their liking for the land we were approaching, for more than one man remarked that this must be a God-forsaken place indeed, if the very birds did not understand what manner of creatures men were, and expressed the earnest hope that the captain would give it as wide a berth as possible.

The men were so engrossed with the swarms of boobies and gannets that were flopping around them that little attention was paid to anything else.

Suddenly one of the foretop men uttered a loud shout and every face was turned in the direction in which he was pointing. The ship was just passing the promontory and opening the north side of the island; and there, not more than three-quarters of a mile away, was a large schooner creeping lazily towards us under topsail and trysail, parallel to the shore and less than a mile distant from it.

CHAPTER TWELVE

In which the Pirate shows his Wit and his Heels

There were evidently sharp eyes on board the schooner, for we had hardly cleared the promontory when she flew up into the wind and went about. For a moment we thought she was going to creep out to sea close-hauled, a course that would very soon have brought her alongside; but the danger of doing this was clearly perceived by her people, for she fell off the wind and began to run parallel to the shore, setting her sails as she went.

The north shore of the island, which we had now opened, was a long, straight stretch, trending away south-east for about five miles, and, as the vessels now stood, the schooner was on our lee bow, and between us and the shore. She had soon set all plain sail, but, rather to our surprise, showed no studding-sails although the wind was about four points free, whereas our studding-sails had been run up within a minute after we had sighted her, and we were now coming up with her hand over hand.

"Mother of Moses!" exclaimed Michael Rafferty, one of our foretop men, rubbing his hands with glee, "'tis our old friend jolly Roger. Faith! But he's between the divil and the deep sea this time. He can swallow our pills or go ashore as he pleases, and an elegant choice it is, sure."

"You're right and that's the fact," said Bill who was watching, not without regret as I suspected, the precarious situation of the schooner. "Nothing can save that craft now, jammed right up agin a lee shore."

The pirate's case, indeed, appeared hopeless, and when the drum beat to quarters, and the order was given to clear the guns for action, it seemed that the last act in the drama was about to be played.

Meanwhile we had drawn up to within a quarter of a mile of the schooner, which, oddly enough, instead of creeping out seaward, had closed in with the land and was now barely half a mile from the shore. We were now so near that we could make out the handsome gingerbread work on her stern, and could see the flowerpots on the little balconies outside the stern windows, at one of which a man was visible inspecting us through a glass. All hands were on the very tiptoe of expectation; grappling irons were got ready to claw hold of her rigging as we came alongside; cutlasses, pistols and boarding pikes were served out in readiness for a rush on to her decks, and the sprit-sail yard was brought fore and aft so as to be clear for lying alongside.

Suddenly, without a moment's warning, the schooner luffed sharp up and headed so as to run right across our bows.

A cry of dismay rose from our men, for it seemed that we must crash right into the pirate and that with a shock that must inevitably bring the whole fabric of our masts and spars rattling down upon our heads.

"Hard down with the helm!" roared the captain. "Back main and mizzen topsails! Quick, for your lives, men!" and the hands, keenly alive to the danger, flew to the braces and clew garnets, and had the mainsail clewed up and the great yards swung round in a twinkling. For a few awful seconds the helm had no effect, though the speed of the ship was immediately slackened. But not soon enough; for, just as she began to turn, the schooner darted across her bows and the tip of our flying jibboom was caught by her main shrouds.

For an instant the long, slender spar bent like a cane. Then with a loud snap, the jibboom broke off a few feet beyond the cap, and an instant later a splintering and clattering aloft sent the men scurrying off the forecastle, and the wreck of the topgallant-mast – snapped off at the cap by the jerk – was seen dangling by its rigging over the topsail, which it had already split from head to foot.

In the hideous confusion that followed, the stern of the schooner was seen for a few seconds close aboard our weather bow, but, as the ship swung round, the fugitive was again brought dead ahead, and not a single shot could be fired at her.

The whole thing had happened so quickly that our men stood staring at one another in speechless surprise and bewilderment, gaping foolishly over the larboard bow at the retreating schooner who had trimmed her sails, and was standing out to sea close-hauled on the larboard tack. But not for long did they stand silent; for, as they perceived that the ship lay with her shattered jibboom steadily pointing in the wind's eye, an ominous cry arose.

"By God, the ship's in irons!"

It was only too true. With her way deadened by the backed sails, she had swung round assisted by the shove that the schooner had given to her jibboom, and now lay motionless, head to wind and for the moment quite out of control.

She was in irons on a lee shore! And what a lee shore! It needed not the terrified landward glances of the seamen to emphasise its horrors, for there it stood, its frowning cliffs but half a mile away with the tall plumes of spray shooting up for more than a hundred feet, and the hollow growl of the breakers booming forth at once a warning and a menace.

In a moment the pirate was forgotten and all eyes were turned to the quarter-deck, and from thence to the shore towards which the ship was beginning to drive, impelled not only by the wind but also by the send of the long swell.

I could see the captain standing on the quarter-deck, quite calm, though evidently fully alive to the situation, for he glanced sharply aloft and then peered intently into the binnacle as though to discover if the ship showed any signs of paying off. After waiting for more than a minute he looked up and sang out:

"Square the maintop-sail, brace the head yards over and hold the helm hard down; and let some hands go aloft to clear away the wreckage."

The braces were manned with a right good will, for the men were almost in a state of panic, and the task of clearing away the raffle aloft came as quite a pleasant distraction. The vessel soon began to feel the pressure of the sails in their new trim and very slowly commenced to pay off, although she gathered stern-way at a rate that filled all hands with dismay. For a few minutes her fate hung in the balance, and it seemed doubtful if she would not be in the breakers before she had brought the wind abeam. All eyes were turned shoreward as though fascinated by the towering cliffs and their fringe of black and jagged rocks, from which was borne to our ears the thunderous roar of the surf – all eyes but those of the captain, who stood watchful and calm as the ship slowly turned away from the wind.

At last, when the vessel seemed to be driving landward beyond all hope, the welcome orders rang along the deck:

"Mainsail haul! Head braces! Of all, haul!" and with a simultaneous rush, the men tailed on to the ropes and the great yards swung round like dog-vanes in a squall.

Even now the danger was not over, for, though the sails were full and drawing, it was a full minute before the ship began to move forward, and all this time she was drifting towards the shore. At length, however, she appeared to draw slowly ahead and as the wind was not dead on shore, she soon began to creep away from the land.

"Well, Jim," said Bill Muffin, taking off his hat to mop his forehead, "we'll sling our hammocks in the 'tween-decks tonight arter all. But that there was a close shave; and, Lord bless us, what lubberly craft these here square-riggers is to be sure. Did ye see the way the schooner nipped round?"

"See her!" exclaimed one of the sailors, shaking his fist at the distant pirate. "Aye! And I hopes to see her again and to stick my pike into that darned picaroon what commands her, with his cursed artful dodges, a-ticin' us in shore and then a-disablin' of us."

"If he done that a-purpose," said Bill solemnly, "he ought to be a Lord High Admiral."

"He'll be high enough if we gets hold of him," growled the other, "for he'll swing from our yard-arm."

"We've got to catch him first," chuckled Bill, "and that's easier said than done, seeing the start he's got to wind'ard."

There was a good deal of truth in this, for the schooner, as soon as she was out of gun-shot, had gone about on the starboard tack and was now reaching away to the north-west, parallel to the shore, a course that we were unable to follow at present, as it would have brought the island, once more, close under our lee.

As soon as we were clear of the south-eastern point of the land and had the open sea to leeward, the tattered topsail was unbent and replaced by a new one. Then sail was made and we stretched out to the north-east to get an offing that would enable us to clear the projecting northern promontory. In our partially disabled condition, this occupied nearly half an hour – for the loss of the jibs compelled us to reduce the after-sail – and by the time the ship was put about to give chase, the schooner was hull down on the north-western horizon.

All this time the carpenter and his mates were busy getting ready the new spars, while the boatswain and his mates were equally busy with the rigging, with the result that, before the hands were piped down to dinner, the new jibbooms were run out, the topgallant-mast sent aloft, the rigging set up, the yards swung and the ship covered with her full spread of canvas.

The chase, however, promised to be a long one, for, by this time, the schooner's upper sails only were visible from the deck, so that she had a good twelve miles start, and this, together with the fact that she sailed nearly two points nearer the wind than we did, made it probable that we should not come within striking distance before dark.

It may well be supposed that all our people, from the captain downward, were on their mettle and eager to retrieve the honour of their ship after having been so completely out-manoeuvred on two separate occasions, and now that the sloop was once more in trim, every kite that could be flown was crowded on, if by chance another half-knot could be added to her speed. Moreover, the captain, very wisely, made no attempt to sail in the wind's eye, but kept every sail full and drawing, knowing well that his only chance lay in getting within hail before dark, even though he were to leeward of the chase. The schooner, on the other hand, adopted the opposite tactics and lay as close to the wind as she could steer, with the result that by six o'clock we had drawn up nearly abreast of her, though she was a good five miles to windward of us.

At this juncture she went about and steered north-east on the larboard tack, and as soon as she had well passed us, the *Asphodel* was put about on a parallel course.

We had not been sailing on this tack more than a quarter of an hour when there appeared indications that fortune was at last about to favour us; for, as the sun declined in the west, the breeze began rapidly to fail, and in a short time it had fallen to a flat calm. It was clear that this was no merely local phenomenon, for a look-out in the foretop who was watching the schooner through a glass, reported that her sails were hanging up and down and that already she had put out a couple of large boats with a tow-rope and was endeavouring to escape by means of these and a number of long sweeps worked from the deck.

"Get the boats launched, Mr Wigmore," shouted the captain as soon as he received the report, "and see that each is supplied with a compass and night-glass. You'll get near enough not to miss her before it falls dark."

No sooner was this order heard than there arose a roar of bustle and excitement. The boatswain's pipe sounded "all hands"; the men came tumbling up the hatches to run to their stations at the davit tackles; and as the great boats descended into the water, the arm chests were flung open and cutlasses and pistols spread on the deck ready to serve out to the boats' crews.

I could not but feel some surprise at the eagerness of the men to be employed on this duty; but I suppose the deadly monotony of ship-board life made them – thoughtless and happy-go-lucky as most of them were – welcome any kind of excitement or distraction. But, in truth, the expedition was a most hazardous one, for the schooner was probably heavily armed and we had already had abundant proof of the skill, courage and resource of her commander. Nevertheless, as I watched the three great boats with their freights of sailors and marines, pull away from the ship, I was conscious of a feeling of disappointment that I was not one of the party.

The expedition was a very powerful one, for the big launch carried over eighty men and moved forward but sluggishly in spite of her sixteen oars; while the pinnace and the cutter carried nearly fifty men apiece and each pulled twelve oars. The three moved off in a line led by the launch, in the stern of which sat the first lieutenant, and, as they crept away towards the distant pirate, the men who were left followed them wistfully with their eyes.

I was standing close by the main rigging, watching the receding boats and wondering how my friend Bill (who was in the cutter) would fare in the approaching conflict, when I noticed the captain standing just abaft the rigging following the boats attentively through his glass. I was about to move further forward when he suddenly lowered the telescope and beckoned to me.

I approached him and saluted.

"Have you learnt how to pull on oar yet, my man?" he asked.

I replied that I had.

"Well I want a message taken to Mr Wigmore. What is that fellow's name?" and he pointed to Rodman, who was standing close by.

"Rodman, sir," I answered.

"Come here, Rodman," he called out, and as the latter came forward and touched his forelock, the captain continued: "I want you and this man to carry a note to Mr Wigmore. You will take the dinghy and the pair of you ought to be able to overtake the launch before she reaches the schooner. I can't spare any more hands. Get the dinghy lowered, there!" he sang out, and then retired to his cabin to write the note.

By the time the dinghy had been down and brought alongside at the gangway, he reappeared and handed the note down to me.

"Now, off with you!" he said, "and put your backs into it; the launch is not more than half-way there yet."

Rodman and I took our places on the midship thwarts (for the boat was fitted for four rowers), he taking the forward oar and managing the steering; and, having pushed off, we settled down to pull with a will. There did not seem to be the faintest chance of our urging the heavy boat forward fast enough to overtake the launch, but we had our orders, and were, no doubt, being closely followed by the captain's telescope. Moreover since we were unprovided with either compass or night-glass, I, at least, was anxious to get within hail of the other boats as soon as possible.

It was a mystery to me why the captain should have sent only two men with this boat if the matter was so urgent, short-handed as the expedition had left him; and I most heartily wished that some other companion had been chosen to accompany me. Indeed, it was just beginning to dawn on me that my cousin had made the choice with deliberate malice when my cogitations were disturbed by a volley of curses from Rodman.

"Come, stir yourself, you dirty clodhopper," he shouted, "am I to do all the work and drag a great hulkin' chaw-bacon along as well?"

As I was already pulling as hard as was possible without throwing the boat out of her course, I made no reply to this.

"D'ye hear me, hawfinch?" Rodman continued after a pause. "You seem to think as you're a-sittin' on a gate a-chewin' turnips; but you ain't; you just heave at that oar, and put some beef into it or I'll learn you."

I still made no reply, and we rowed on in silence for some minutes.

"Struck dumb, are you?" said Rodman presently. "You can jaw fast enough when it's the ship's corporal, can't you? Answer me, you fat-headed, muck-raking bumpkin, or I'll skin your back."

Having passed these delicate compliments, he rested on his oar, as though listening for my answer.

"Look ye, Rodman," said I, addressing him over my shoulder, "we can find some better time and place than this to settle our differences. You can see that it is getting dark rapidly, and that we are little more than halfway to the schooner. In another minute we shall not be able to see either her or the ship, and if we miss them, our lives are not worth a groat."

"Oh, all right," replied Rodman, calmly taking in his oar, "if you ain't a-goin' to row, we may as well take things easy."

He stepped over the thwart past me, and, sitting down in the stern-sheets, opened the locker and peeped in.

"What are you after now?" I demanded, taking in my oar also.

"This here's what I'm after," he replied, drawing an anker, or small keg, from the locker and pulling out the spile. "That's rum, that is," he added, after sniffing at the hole; and then, applying it to his mouth, he took a long draught of the spirit.

"Come, Rodman," said I coaxingly, "this won't do. We must pick up the boats or we shall get lost. Take your oar, man, and stop this fooling."

By way of reply Rodman took another long pull at the anker, and, having carefully replaced the spile, sat down on the stern seat and grinned at me.

At this moment the boom of a gun came across the sea, and, looking up in the direction whence the sound seemed to proceed, I observed with alarm that the ship was already hidden by the darkness. At the same time I became aware of a cool draught of air blowing across the boat and carrying with it thin, gauzy streamers of mist.

"Do you hear that?" I exclaimed. "The captain is recalling the boats and there is a bank of fog blowing down on us. Back to your oar if you value your life!"

"Who are you a-orderin' about?" Rodman demanded fiercely. "You mind your pigs and your cabbages and don't come a-waggin' of your jaw at a able seaman. And don't you come near me," he added, as I stepped over the thwart into the stern-sheets, "or I'll make your face look like one of your own beetroots."

He stood up and aimed a blow at me as he spoke, whereupon, being now thoroughly out of patience, I grabbed him by the collar, and, shoving him down across the thwart, snatched up a stretcher with which I belaboured him until he roared with rage and pain.

When I let go, he scrambled over the thwart in a mighty hurry and bundled into the fore part of the boat where he stood and gibbered at me; then, snatching up an oar, he aimed a tremendous blow at my head. This I avoided without difficulty, and, hastily arming myself with an oar, likewise returned the compliment in the same manner, but with more effect. He soon found that he had no chance at this sport, for I had had some reputation as a player at the quarter-staff, so after I had dealt him one or two sounding cracks on the crown, he flung down his oar and cried for quarter.

"Now get your oar out and pull," said I, "or I'll beat you into a jelly."

He obeyed without a word, and as he seated himself I ran out my oar, standing up and facing him, and took a stroke.

"Oh! play fair, Jim," he protested. "Sit down and row properly or we shan't make no headway."

But I had no intention of sitting with my back to him after what had passed, and I told him so, plainly.

"Well I ain't a-goin' to pull like this here," he growled. "I tell you what," he added suddenly; "let's hoist the sail. There's good little breeze and that'll drive us along faster than we could row."

There was some reason in this suggestion, and, as our position was momentarily becoming more serious, I agreed.

"Right, mate," said Rodman, cheerfully, "you ship the rudder and I'll step the mast."

I took up the rudder, and, kneeling on the transom, slipped it on to its pintles. At the moment that it dropped into its place, I heard a sound behind me, and looking quickly over my shoulder, saw Rodman with an oar poised, ready to thrust at me. I sprang to my feet, but as I rose, the blade of the oar struck me under the arm, and though I clutched at it, the force with which it was thrust sent me flying over the boat's stern.

Down I plumped into the water, still holding on to the oar which Rodman had flung from him, and when I rose, gasping and coughing, and shook the water from my eyes, the boat was a dozen feet away.

I struck out frantically with one hand, holding on to the oar with the other, but the breeze carried the boat away from me faster than I could follow, and already Rodman had shipped another oar and pulled several strokes.

"You are not going to leave me adrift, are you?" I called out. "For God's sake, Rodman, put back and let me come aboard. Surely you wouldn't murder a shipmate in cold blood!"

The vindictive scoundrel made no reply to this appeal, but, calmly putting out a second oar, pulled away in a leisurely fashion until there was a space of twenty yards between us.

Then he unshipped his oars and stepped the mast; and, as the boat slowly faded away into the misty darkness, I heard the halyard run through the sheave and saw the dark shape of the sail look up for an instant before it vanished.

My condition was now a parlous one indeed. Here was no highway of shipping like that into which I had been cast when I went overboard in the Thames, but a vast ocean on which frequently no sail was visible for days at a time. As I clutched at the oar, and stared into the gloom around, my heart was filled with despair; the dreadful prospect of dying from thirst and exhaustion seemed only less remote than that of being snapped up by the sharks that infest these seas. The latter contingency, however, as the more immediate one, kept me in a state of horrible expectation, and, as the swell lifted me and the water surged past, I fancied every moment that I felt the snout of one of these hideous monsters against my limbs or body.

I had been in the water about twenty minutes – although it seemed to me as if hours had passed since I was thrust out of the boat – when, apparently in response to the guns which the frigate had been firing at intervals, a musket-shot rang out loudly, and as I raised myself and listened, I could made out the rhythmical rumble of oars.

I lifted myself, by means of the oar, as far above the surface as I could, and, putting one hand to my mouth, shouted with all the strength of my lungs. There was no reply, but the rumble and creak of the oars continued audible and seemed to grow nearer.

After a few moments I hailed again.

"Boat ahoy!"

This time my shout was heard, for the sound of the oars ceased abruptly and a voice came out of the darkness faintly, and evidently from a considerable distance.

"Hallo, there! Who are you?"

"Man overboard!" I roared; and almost immediately the sound of the oars recommenced.

After a few minutes, in which the boats had drawn perceptibly nearer – as I judged by the increasing distinctness with which I could hear the rowers – the voice hailed me again and I could recognise it, now, as Mr Wigmore's:

"Man overboard, ahoy!"

"Hallo, sir," I returned.

"Do you see us yet?" asked the lieutenant.

"No, sir," I answered.

A few minutes more elapsed, the sounds waxing louder every moment, and then of a sudden a glimmer of light appeared through the fog.

It was a welcome apparition, for, though I had not been in the water more than half an hour, I was already beginning to feel the effects of the immersion, and the fatigue of holding on to the incessantly-moving oar.

The luminous smudge on the fog rapidly brightened, and soon resolved itself into a lanthorn, by the light of which I could see the men crowded together near it, and could catch an occasional gleam from the wet oars.

"Whereabouts are you?" the lieutenant sang out.

"Here I am, sir, on your larboard bow," I answered.

The boat swung round until it was end on, and bore down on me.

"I sees him, sir," one of the men in the bow called out. "We're nearly a-top of him."

"Way'nough," shouted Mr Wigmore; and as the rowers held their oars above the water, the great boat swept up to me. The lanthorn glared in my face for an instant; I felt several powerful hands grasp my clothing, and then I was hauled up, dripping and breathless, and carefully seated on a thwart.

"Why, it's Jim Roberts!" exclaimed one of the seamen, scrutinising my face by the light of the lanthorn.

"Never mind who it is," said Mr Wigmore. "Pass that lanthorn aft. There are no more overboard, are there?"

"No, sir," I answered.

"Give way, then," said he; and as the men once more bent to their oars he held the lanthorn to the compass and put the boat on her course again.

The boom of a gun from the frigate came across the water at intervals of a few minutes, and though it was difficult to judge the direction from which the sound came, the successive reports appeared louder as we proceeded.

"Do any of you see the ship?" asked Mr Wigmore after we had been rowing for about half an hour.

"No sign of her yet, sir," was the reply from the bow; but a few seconds later a flash of light was seen through an opening in the fog, and was quickly followed by a loud report. The lieutenant immediately took the bearing of the place where the flash had been seen, and, having put the boat on the indicated course, he ordered a musket to be fired.

We pulled on for another ten minutes and then, quite suddenly, the form of the ship looked up before us, dim and gigantic in the mist; and as we swept alongside, I saw for the first time that the other two boats were connected with the launch by a long tow-line.

When the men had been mustered on deck the lieutenant reported the incidents of the expedition; which did not take long, for it appeared that the breeze had caught the schooner before the recall gun was fired and she had hoisted in her boats and slipped away as the mist closed in.

"We picked up a man holding on to an oar, as we returned," Mr Wigmore continued, "but I have not obtained any particulars from him."

Where is he?" asked the captain, in evident surprise.

"This is the man!" said the lieutenant, beckoning to me; and as I stepped forward and touched my forehead, my cousin greeted me with a stare of astonishment and displeasure.

"Why, how did you get overboard?" he demanded.

I gave a brief account of what occurred in the boat, to which he listened with an air of sullen incredulity.

"This is all very well," said he, when I had finished, "but I should like to hear the other man's account of the affair.

"Fire another gun, Mr Wigmore," he added, "and have a lanthorn shown from either gangway. We can't hang about here or the schooner will slip through our fingers again."

Nevertheless the ship remained hove-to for another quarter of an hour and a gun was fired every five minutes, the captain, meanwhile, pacing the quarter-deck with every sign of impatience and vexation.

At length, as there was still no sign of the dinghy, I heard him call out to the lieutenant:

"Was that boat provisioned, Mr Wigmore?"

"Yes, sir," was the reply. "She had provisions and water enough to last four men for a week."

"Then in that case we'll make sail at once," rejoined the captain, and the main-yard was accordingly swung, and the ship put on a course towards the supposed position of the schooner.

CHAPTER THIRTEEN

In which I am Marooned

It was my watch on deck at daybreak on the following morning, and great was the expectation on board as the first glimmer of dawn appeared in the sky.

All night a light breeze from the north-east had kept us moving, and, as we had kept on a single tack all the time, it was now possible that we might be close on the heels of the schooner; or, on the other hand, we might have been sailing in a contrary direction, and now be a good hundred miles distant from her.

Hence the coming of the day was waited for impatiently by everyone who was stirring on the ship, and, long before the light of the dawn was actually visible, an experienced look-out was already sweeping the horizon – or as much of it as could be made out – with a night-glass.

At length the rosy flush in the upper sky crept down until the rim of the sea stood dark and sharp against it; and then it could be seen that we had this part of the ocean to ourselves; for all around, the line of the horizon ran unbroken by a single speck, and clear as the edge of a compass-dial.

Soon after the sun had risen it fell flat calm, and so continued until nearly noon; leaving the ship rolling foolishly on the long swell, with a rhythmical creak of her rigging, and her sails now filling and now backing against the masts with the meaningless flop that is so irritating to the seamen's ears.

All the morning the captain and Mr Wigmore paced the quarter-deck in earnest conversation, and the result of their consultation – as we supposed it to be – appeared when, shortly before eight bells, a light breeze sprang up from the old quarter, for the ship's head was then turned south-south-east, or in a direction nearly opposite to that in which she had been sailing in the night.

"Darned if I don't believe we're a-puttin' back to that cursed island," exclaimed one of the seamen, as the ship was set on to her new course.

"Not us," said another with deep conviction; "the cap'n'll have had enough of islands to last him for many a day."

But it appeared that the first man was right, for towards evening the look-out reported that the island was visible nearly dead ahead, and that a couple of small islets could be seen on the starboard bow.

As soon as this report had been verified with the aid of a telescope, sail was reduced until the ship was under maintopsail and foresail only, which gave her a speed of about four knots, and in this trim she remained through the night.

When I came on deck at half-past seven on the following morning, the island was clearly visible at a distance of about fifteen miles. The breeze, however, was rapidly dying away, and the ship, although now under all plain sail, was moving forward but sluggishly. Presently it fell flat calm, and our experience of the preceding morning was repeated. Little flaws of wind came and went, filling the sails for a few minutes and then leaving them once more, drooping and idle, so that by noon we had crept forward but a dozen miles or so.

At length, about one o'clock, a steady breeze sprang up from the north-north-east, before which we soon began pretty rapidly to approach the land, and by four in the afternoon its rugged, threatening shore was but a mile or two away.

We coasted down the north shore, maintaining a respectful distance from the land, keeping the lead going constantly, until we had cleared the eastern extremity, when the ship's head was turned southwards, and we sailed past a shallow bay filled with a mass of black rock, over which the sea was breaking in a sheet of foam. Passing the southern horn of the bay we opened the south shore, which appeared more precipitous and forbidding even than the north, for here the towering peaks and lofty cliffs ran out into bold and frowning headlands, and numbers of detached rocky islets stood off the land like sentinels.

As we turned westward to sail along the south shore, we observed a wide and deep bay enclosed between two jutting promontories, and at once all eyes were attracted to an object that lay near the middle of the bight. It was the wreck of a large ship which had been driven by the roaring surf up on to the strip of sandy beach, and now lay, canted over on its bilge, with the daylight peeping between its skeleton timbers – an eloquent picture of desolation and decay.

Creeping along parallel to the south shore, we were in the lee of the island, now becalmed by the huge peaks that shot their splintered pinnacles into the sky, and now struck by squalls and gusts of wind that poured down the deep ravines. Near the western end of this side of the island a snowy streak on the dark face of the cliff showed where some rivulet cast its waters down the precipice into the sea below, and at this I noticed the officers gazing through their telescopes with uncommon interest.

When we rounded the high bluff in which this shore ended, and opened the west side of the island, a very curious sight met our eyes. A short distance from the land was a small but lofty islet rising sheer from the sea, with cliffs of dazzling whiteness, as though composed of chalk, and a summit capped with a mass of verdure. Around the islet in a dim, moving cloud, circled the screaming seabirds in myriads beyond imagination or belief, conveying, by their very multitude, the most impressive sense of solitude.

Nearly opposite the islet there shot aloft from the cliffs an immense pillar of rock, so regular and cylindrical in shape as to appear like a column from some Titanic building. In height it must have been near upon a thousand feet, for, as the eye travelled up its towering sides, the sea-birds dwindled until, long before its green summit was reached, they had become too small to be distinguished.

By the time we had cleared the northern point, and thus made the complete circuit of the island, the light was beginning to fail. The deep-sea-lead was hove, and, as it showed too great a depth for anchoring, the ship bore off once more towards the south-west of the island where sail was reduced, and the frigate hove-to for the night.

At daybreak on the following morning – it being then my watch on deck – there were evident signs that something unusual was afoot, for, as soon as there was light enough to make out the position of the island, sail was made in the direction of the eastern extremity. Presently it became known that a shore party was to be formed, for Mr Wigmore came round the decks with the boatswain to select the men for this duty; and, much to my delight and surprise, I was amongst those chosen.

"Let these men get their breakfasts at once, Mr Wilkin," said the lieutenant, "and have the pinnace cleared for lowering."

Accordingly we joyfully abandoned the holystones, with which we had been at work on the deck, to our envious shipmates, and retired to the gun-deck for our morning meal.

By the time we returned to the spar-deck the ship was within four miles of the land, and orders were just being given to heave her to. A number of picks and shovels and some hoisting tackles had been brought up from below, and when these had been deposited in the pinnace, orders were given to lower her. This was very quickly done, for the crew were as eager to be off as a party of schoolboys on a holiday jaunt, and as the boat came alongside the gangway, the captain, Mr Wigmore, and the boatswain stepped down into her.

"You had better take charge, Mr Wilkin, as you know the way in," said the captain, as we shoved off and shipped our oars. "The landing should be pretty easy on a calm day like this."

"That don't always follow, sir," replied Wilkin, taking hold of the tiller. "'Tis a contrairy place, is this, sir, and the surf is often worst when 'tis calm and quiet outside."

Impelled by the twelve oars, the boat swept forward rapidly, and we soon had an opportunity of verifying the boatswain's statement; for, as we drew nearer, we could see no less than three lines of breakers, each flinging great jets of spray high into the air, and separated from the others by a wide space of broken water. The barrier looked formidable enough even from seaward, and we had the consolation of knowing that a surf, viewed from the rear, never shows as bad as it really is.

"Will it be safer to back in, think you, Mr Wilkin?" asked the captain, as he looked with great disfavour at the expanse of seething water ahead.

"I think not, sir," answered the boatswain. "'Tis a wide surf and too heavy to stand up against. We shall have to watch our chance and run in before we are overtook."

When we had arrived within five hundred yards of the outer line of breakers, we were ordered to rest on our oars while Wilkin unshipped the rudder and replaced it by an oar secured in a grommet of rope which was made fast to the stern.

"Now, men," said he, standing up and grasping the loom of the steer-oar, "listen to what I'm a-goin' to say. When we gets into the surf, don't go a-starin' at the breakers, but attend to my orders and keep cool. Let the man in the bow – you, Watson, I means – see the painter coiled down and take charge of it. When I gives the word 'overboard' you all pitches your oars into the sea and jumps overboard. The four forrard men helps Watson to carry the painter up the beach, and haul on it for all you're worth, and the rest of you hangs on to the gunnel to steady the boat, and helps haul her ashore. Now you knows what you've got to do; give way!"

We bent to our oars once more and urged the boat forward towards the roaring surf, while the boatswain glanced anxiously first ahead and then astern, watching the backs of the combers and the great billows that rolled in after us. About fifty yards from the edge of the expanse of broken water, Wilkin gave the command to cease pulling.

We lifted our oars and remained motionless, staring wide-eyed – notwithstanding the boatswain's orders – at the oncoming swell.

Each giant roller, as it swept towards us with a motion at once swift and unspeakably majestic, reared aloft its tremendous mass, with steep face and quivering crest, like a moving mountain of clear, transparent green. For a moment it towered above us as though we must be overwhelmed in an instant; then we soared breathlessly upward, remained for a moment poised, as it seemed, high above the ocean's surface, and once more sank into the trough, while from behind us came the deep thunderous boom of the bursting wave.

We remained thus for several minutes, dazed by the uproar of the surf and the violent motion of the boat, and turning our startled gaze from the approaching billows to the watchful face of the boatswain, and back again.

Now and again we backed a stroke or two, as the send of the swell drove us towards the breakers, and then, at a word, relapsed into motionless expectancy.

Suddenly, while our ears were yet stunned by the crash of the breaker behind us, the boatswain looked sharply over his shoulder at the sea astern, where, for the moment, no advancing billow appeared; then, facing us, he roared:

"Give way! Pull, men! Pull for your lives!"

We needed no second bidding nor any urging to put out our utmost strength. The good ash oars bent like wands, and the heavy boat rushed forward into the yeasty ruins of the last breaker.

But, swiftly as we went, we were still in the midst of the broken water when the shape of a great roller arose astern and followed yet more swiftly, rearing itself higher and still higher as it approached, until it was little more than a dozen fathoms away, when it burst with a roar and sent an avalanche of snowy foam rushing after us.

"Hoist your oars clear!" shouted the boatswain, and at that moment the mass of foam struck the stern, enveloping us in a cloud of spray. The boat darted forward with such speed that, before the force of the wave was spent, we were close on the second line of breakers. Another great wave appeared astern, and charging down on us, flung our stern high into the air, rolled under us, turned over, and broke just ahead.

"Give way!" roared the boatswain, and once more we bent to our oars, although here the seething water seemed to offer but little resistance to the blades. Nevertheless, before the next wave broke we had passed inside the line, and a momentary lull in the surf enabled us to dash through the last row of breakers.

"Overboard!" shouted Wilkin, and, as the forefoot bumped on the sand, all the oars were flung into the sea and the men vaulted over the gunwales. The bowmen, carrying the painter, waded into the shallows and hauled on the rope as the undertow rushed past, while the rest of us clung to the gunwales and struggled to keep the boat from being drawn back into the surf. Then another wave thundered in towards the beach, smothering us with spray as it struck full on the stern; the boat lifted and moved forward, directed by the pull on the painter, and before the undertow swept back, we had fairly run her up on the sand beyond the reach of the breakers.

"I must compliment you, Mr Wilkin," said the captain as he stepped out of the boat and shook the water from the brim of his hat. "You brought us ashore in gallant style, and I only hope we may get off with similar success. Now men," he added, turning to us seamen who stood on the shore gaping around us, "I will give you your instructions. We have landed, as you have probably guessed, to look for traces of those piratical rascals who, beyond doubt, made this their haunt. You three," indicating me and two other men, "will remain in charge of the boat, and should any change in the weather, or anything else of importance occur, you will fire a musket. The rest of you will go off in parties of three and will keep a sharp look-out for any buildings or other evidences of the island having been lately visited. Each party will take a musket and will fire it if it should be necessary to summon assistance, and under no other circumstances. Mr Wilkin, you will accompany Mr Wigmore and me, and will please bring a musket. And now, before you go off, I must give you all a warning: at any moment the sea may rise so that it will be impossible to put off from the shore, or a sail may be sighted, rendering it necessary for us to return at once to the ship. Consequently, if you hear a musket fired, you must make your way with all speed back to the boat, for I warn you I shall not hang about, with a rising surf, waiting for laggards, but shall put off as soon as a sufficient crew is assembled and leave any loiterers to their fate. Now, you understand me; keep a bright look-out for what we are in search of, don't stray away too far, pay no attention to the goats or hogs that you may see, and listen for the recall gun."

With these injunctions he walked away, in company with the lieutenant and followed by the boatswain, and the three disappeared into a rocky valley overhung by a lofty, conical hill.

The three of us who remained in charge of the boat witnessed, with no little envy and disappointment, the departure of our more fortunate shipmates as they set off on their adventurous missions; and when the last party vanished into a rocky gorge and the sound of their voices and laughter died away in the distance, my shipmates broke out into open complaints.

"Here's a pretty go," grumbled Watson, who was one of the unfortunates, "arter all our trouble and a-pullin' of our blessed arms off, to be stuck here like some darned Jack-o'-the-causeway a-holdin' on to a boat's painter."

"Reglar do I calls, it," agreed the other, carving a quid from a cake of tobacco and popping it into his mouth. "Goats and hogs, didn't he say," he continued, when he had settled the quid comfortably into his cheek, "and no one wasn't to take no notice of 'em, hey? Well I reckon I'd have had a rap at 'em if I'd come across any and let the pirates go hang. What do you suppose *she* was, Bill?" he pointed as he spoke at the wreck, which lay about a quarter of a mile to the west.

"Foreigner, most like," answered Watson. "She's an old ship too; my eye, look at her poop! Them people didn't mean for to get no nearer the water than they could help."

"It is odd," said I, "that she should have drifted so high on the beach and not have got broken up more."

"Why that's where it is," replied Watson. "She must have been light, d'ye see, or she'd have took the ground further out and gone to pieces. Most likely she drove ashore starn first, a-draggin' her anchors, and got worked up further and further by the seas a-breakin' in. You can see as the bows is all smashed up and carried away, and then d'ye see the eddies from the undertow a-runnin' past her have thrown up a sandbank just ahead, and that's why she don't break up no more. That bank's a sort of breakwater, as you might say."

We all gazed at the wreck while Watson was speaking, and a very singular spectacle she presented. Her high, peaked stern had worked right up on to the beach, and was so little damaged that many of the cabin windows still had their glass unbroken. Forward, indeed, she was a mere skeleton, her timbers standing up, bare and jagged, like a row of decayed piles; but the sandbank had, as Watson had said, enclosed her within a kind of breakwater, so that she was now almost completely protected from the surf. The seabirds had evidently, long since, taken possession of her, for we could see them circling around her in myriads, and to them was owing the most strange and unnatural feature in her appearance, for she was all over of a dazzling whiteness as though she had been carved out of chalk.

My two companions, after gazing about for some time and taking in what there was to be seen without straying away from the boat proceeded to scratch out, on the smooth sand, a kind of primitive draughtboard, and having picked up a number of pebbles of different colours to use as "men," they settled down to pass the time by playing for next day's wine allowance, while I paced up and down at a little distance, enjoying the unwonted luxury of quiet, uninterrupted reflection.

In this way a couple of hours passed in which we neither heard nor saw any sign of our shipmates, and, excepting for the presence of the frigate lying hove-to away to the south-east, we might have been a party of castaways.

At length, as I saw a figure emerge from the ravine into which the captain had disappeared.

As it came more clearly into view, I saw that it was the boatswain, and I noticed that he was not carrying the musket that he had taken with him. He advanced at a rapid pace, and as he came within earshot, he hailed in his strong penetrating voice:

"Hallo there, Roberts! The cap'n wants you. Get out one of them coils of rope and a pick and shovel and come along."

"Aye, aye, sir," I sang out cheerfully, glad enough to get a chance of seeing some of the sights of the island; and tumbling into the boat I threw out the tools and a coil of stout rope on to the sand.

"Hallo, mate," exclaimed Watson, jumping up and staring from me to the boatswain; "pick and shovel and rope, hey? They've found something, Jim, I'll wager. You'll be off for Tom Tiddler's ground a–diggin' for gold and silver. Lord! I wish he'd sent for me."

I slung the tools over my shoulder, and, catching up the rope, started off at a run.

"That's the style, lad," said Wilkin, as I came up; "don't keep the cap'n waiting. Keep close behind me and be careful how you go, for 'tis darned rough ground and that's the fact."

"Did the captain ask for me?" I inquired.

"Aye, that he did," was the answer, "so you're not in his bad books no more. 'Send young Roberts,' says he. 'He seems a steady lad,' he says, 'and has his wits about him,' he says, 'and so we shan't have to stand by and watch him dig,' he says, 'a-wastin' out time when we might be a-searchin' elsewhere,' he says."

The worthy boatswain seemed genuinely rejoiced at my good fortune, and I could not do less than express myself as highly gratified; but the ground was too rough to allow of much conversation, although I noticed on the rotten, crumbling rock the impressions of a number of feet, showing that we were by no means the first travellers along the gorge.

We stumbled on for upwards of half an hour, clambering among great masses of rock and scrambling up and down gullies, until we reached a more level expanse covered with white sand. Following the track of footprints across this we entered another narrow ravine, and we had not gone far along it when, on turning a boulder of rock, we came suddenly upon the captain and Mr Wigmore.

Both officers looked up at the sound of our footsteps, and Wilkin, touching his hat, announced (somewhat unnecessarily):

"Here he is, sir,"

"Come here, Roberts," said the captain, beckoning to me and stepping a few paces forward, "Here is a pit which has been sunk, no doubt, by the pirates. I want you to go down and examine the bottom so that we may see whether anything has been buried, or whether the pit was only prepared in readiness for hiding their booty. You are to dig about three feet down in several places, when you will be able to judge if the ground has been disturbed or not. You need not hoist out the earth that you turn up, but when you have finished in one place, if you find nothing, shovel the earth back into the hole. Now, down with you and get to work briskly, for our time is short. If you find anything, go down to the boat and report it; if not, work away till you are recalled. And meantime," he added, turning to his companions, "we will move on and see if we can make any further discoveries."

With this he walked away up the ravine, followed by the lieutenant and the boatswain, and I addressed myself to my task.

The pit into which I was about to descend was roughly circular, and about eight feet wide by twelve deep. The sides were perpendicular, and, owing to the rock being here firmer and less crumbling than most of that which I had met with, they had been cut pretty smooth, and were unsupported by shores or boarding.

A few yards away from the pit was a group of small trees – all of them dead and covered with bare patches where the bark had scaled off – and to one of these I determined to secure my rope; so taking the end from the coil I passed it twice round the tree, and, having secured it with two half-hitches, I gave it a hearty tug to make sure that it was firm. Then I hitched the pick and shovel on to the other end of the rope, and when I had lowered them into the pit I let myself down after them.

The floor of the pit was covered with a mass of loose earth and fragments of rock, and, before commencing to dig, I raked this over carefully in case anything should be hidden in it; nor was my search without result, for presently my shovel struck some hard object, and on my picking it out of the rubbish, it proved to be a small tinderbox.

Finding nothing more I shovelled the earth to one side of the pit and began to dig in the centre of the floor space. I had excavated a hole about a couple of feet deep and was pausing a moment to get my breath, when I heard footsteps approaching, and a moment later my cousin appeared at the edge of the pit, looking down at me.

"Have you found anything, my man?" he asked.

"Only this," I answered, holding up the tinder-box.

"Well put it in your pocket and we'll look at it later," said he. "What is the ground like?"

"It doesn't seem to have been disturbed," I answered. "It seems to be the native rock."

"Never mind," he rejoined with a faint, cynical grin, "dig away. When you have finished with that hole, fill it up and dig another. And listen for the recall gun, mind. Hurry down to the beach directly you hear it or you may lose the number of your mess."

With this parting injunction he turned away, and I resumed my labour.

I carried the first hole down to a depth of nearly four feet, when, feeling sure by the way in which the rock broke under the pick, that the ground was quite undisturbed, I filled it up again, after probing the sides in all directions, and commenced to dig in a fresh place. It was hard and exhausting labour driving the pick into the solid rock and shovelling out the heavy fragments, and the heat made me perspire so profusely that I presently began to be tormented by thirst. However, there was no water at hand so I was fain to toil on in the hope that I should shortly be relieved, or at least given some refreshment.

I had excavated the second hole to nearly the depth of the first, and was pausing to wipe the sweat from my forehead, when my ear caught the sound of a distant report.

It was the recall gun.

I instantly dropped the pick, and, straightening myself, heaved a sigh of relief. In half an hour at the most I should be back in the boat, and I knew there were two breakers of water on board of her. Catching up the pick and shovel, I flung them, one after the other, over the edge of the pit, and, grasping the rope firmly with both hands, planted my feet against the rock and hoisted myself off the ground. Suddenly something gave, and in an instant I was lying on my back among the loose earth, while the end of the rope came tumbling down on top of me.

For a moment I was so dazed by the suddenness with which the thing had happened that I did not realise the dreadful nature of the catastrophe; but as my glance fell on the rope lying in a heap on the

172

ground, and I looked up at the smooth, perpendicular walls, the full horror dawned upon me, and I felt my skin break out into a cold sweat.

The report of a second gun which reached my ear, and then those of several muskets fired in a volley, served only to make my deadly peril more apparent. The boat would certainly put off before I could reach her, but this was, after all, a small matter, if only I could escape from this hideous trap.

But should I ever escape?

A glance at the smooth sides of the pit, barely offering foothold for a fly, plunged me in despair; and the burning thirst that already tortured me gave a dreadful hint of the agony that was in store for me if I should fail in my attempts to climb out of this terrible *oubliette*.

If I had only had the forethought to haul up the pick and shovel after me, instead of flinging them up first, the slipping of the rope would have mattered less, for I could have dug my way out in time, whereas now I was like a rat in a trap.

But how came the rope to give way? It had not broken, for there was the end with its whipping of spunyarn. Then could my knot have slipped? No, it was impossible, and I rejected the idea instantly. Two round turns with two half-hitches would have been more than enough to take a strain that would have broken the rope. Then what was the explanation? And when I asked myself this question I thought of my cousin's return to the pit. He was then evidently alone, and I recalled the cynical smile on his face as he told me to go on digging.

It was he who had done this thing. Fate had delivered me into his hand, and he had taken this shocking means to put me for ever out of his way.

The storm of anger that arose in me, as I realised my cousin's horrid treachery, did me good, and braced me up for a resolute effort to save my life.

The walls, as I have said, were about twelve feet high, smooth and perpendicular and quite unscalable. But the rock, although solid and firm, was not hard, being, in fact, somewhat softer than chalk; and I had my knife, a good, strong implement, the gift of Bill Muffin, who had bought it out of the purser's stores and carved my name, "Jim" on the haft in large, sprawling letters. I remembered having, as a boy, cut footholds on the side of a chalk-pit near Shorne, and what I then did for sport I could surely do now to save myself from a terrible and lingering death.

I drew the weapon from its sheath and commenced to cut a foothold about three feet from the ground. As I had hoped the blade cut away the rock without difficulty, and I soon had the first step completed and began on the next.

After the first two recesses had been cut out the work became more difficult, for I had to cling on by one hand and foot, in a very fatiguing position, while I dug out the next hole above; but I persevered, dropping down from time to time to rest my strained fingers, until I had carried the steps half-way up the wall.

At this point a serious mishap befell me; for I was digging away vigorously with my arm above my head, when my foot slipped and I fell to the ground, and the knife, engaged in the cavity, broke off about three inches from the handle.

After this the labour became much greater, and the progress proportionately slower, while the prolonged exertion was making me feel weak and faint.

Still I worked away with the fear of death to spur me on, until at last, on putting my fingers into the cavity that I had just made, I drew myself up high enough to reach the top of the pit with the other hand. Holding on to the knife with my teeth I made a last effort, and crawling over the brink sat down upon the ground under the tree.

But I only rested a few moments. There was even now the possibility that the boat might be within sight of the shore, and if I were seen on the beach surely even that treacherous villain, Percival, would, for decency's sake, put back and fetch me. Without further reflection I stuck the broken knife into its sheath and set off over the scattered rocks, across the sandy level, and down the gorge as fast as I could run on that broken and dangerous surface. One after another of the landmarks that I had passed with the boatswain came into sight and was left behind, and in less than half an hour after leaving the pit

I saw the sea at the end of the ravine. In terrible suspense I redoubled my pace, stumbling desperately over the rugged, crumbling rocks, and leaping across gullies, until at last I rushed out on the beach.

A single glance confirmed my worst fears. The boat was gone; and as I ran despairingly up to the place where she had been, and where the furrow in the sand that her keel had made was yet visible, my eye fell upon a water-breaker with a pannikin on top of it, and a bag of biscuit by its side, and I felt that I was indeed abandoned. Eagerly I scanned the expanse of sea that was visible from the bay, but not only had the boat vanished, but the frigate herself had disappeared behind one of the headlands.

CHAPTER FOURTEEN

In which I explore my New Territory

When I had swept my eyes round the vacant horizon and realised that I was left alone to the dreadful solitude of this desolate and forgotten island, I stood for a while as one in a dream. It was true that events had but fallen out as I had expected. The last volley had sent its warning echoing among the rocks, and the ensuing silence had told plainly enough of the departure of the boat; but yet in my heart there had still flickered some feeble flame of hope of which I was hardly conscious, so that the terrible reality fell upon me with an overwhelming shock, and I gazed round the deserted bay, still half incredulous.

There lay the wreck, pallid and spectral – a veritable *memento mori* to the castaway mariner – with its attendant cloud of seabirds circling around it with melancholy cries, like sad-voiced sirens mourning over the grave of their victims.

And there, too, full of dreadful significance, was the little hoard of provisions and the breaker of water, left as a parting dole to remind me of the thirst and starvation that looked ahead. As my eye fell on them again, I became, of a sudden, conscious of my parched and famished condition. Drawing out the plug from the bunghole of the breaker I filled the pannikin with water and drained it at a draught; after which, though the water was lukewarm from lying on the beach in the burning sun, and musty from long storage, I felt so much refreshed that my appetite revived, and seating myself on the breaker I cracked a biscuit on my knee and began to eat.

There is, according to the universal agreement of persons of judgment, nothing that effects a more radical alteration in a man's outlook on life than a good meal. It is true that diversity of opinion may exist in respect of what constitutes a good meal, and that those who pique themselves on a nice discernment in such matters might not consider the conditions as being met by a draught of stale and tepid ship's water and a handful of musty biscuit. But, however this may be, when I had eaten half a dozen biscuits — not despising even that stony portion of them, scornfully designated "the reefer's nut" — and once more drained the pannikin, my spirits revived so far that I was able to view my condition almost with cheerfulness.

It now occurred to me that, as the day was advancing, it would be well to explore my new territory, and also to ascertain whether the frigate was still in sight. With the latter object I determined to make for the north side of the island, seeing that the ship was nowhere visible to the southward, so having stuffed into my pockets as many biscuits as they would hold and slung the pannikin on to my belt, I started to retrace my steps along the ravine.

As I walked at a leisurely pace along the now familiar track, I reviewed the events of the day with mingled astonishment and indignation at my cousin's incredible perfidy and wickedness. Had this expedition been nothing more than a device on his part to get rid of me? That was hardly probable, since he could not have been aware of the existence of the pit. And yet it was a suspicious fact that he should have selected me — the least experienced seaman on board — as a member of the boat's crew. But, whether the plan was preconceived or not, one thing was certain; he had deliberately unhitched the rope with the intention of consigning me to a lingering and terrible death.

Meditating thus, I reached the pit and halted for a moment on the brink to look down into what had so nearly been my grave.

The broken knife-blade lay on the earth directly under where I was standing, and I regretted that I had not had the prudence to put it into my pocket, for the fragment of steel that remained attached to the haft was not more than three inches long.

However, I could not muster up courage to descend into the pit, so, mentally noting that I could fetch the blade at any time if I should need it, I moved away.

The track made by the two officers and the boatswain was quite distinct in the crumbling debris of the rock, and, as Wilkin had been in the island before, I determined to follow it; indeed there was not much choice, for, on either side, the rock rose much too steeply for climbing to be practicable, and even the bottom of the gorge made a sharp ascent, up which I scrambled with some difficulty.

The precipitous sides of the ravine were covered with trees similar to those that I had seen by the pit; and, like them, these were all dead, and seemed to be undergoing a kind of dry decay, for, in many cases, the bark had fallen off, leaving the bare wood exposed. These leafless skeletons imparted to the sombre landscape a very dismal and gloomy character, which was not a little increased by the circumstance that many of the naked branches were occupied by the nests of seabirds.

Toiling on up the steep and rugged ascent, I presently reached the summit of the ravine between two conical peaks of bare, splintered rock, each of which towered above me for over a thousand feet. From this point the ground fell away in a steep and broken surface to the north shore, and the wide expanse of the ocean lay before me.

And now the recall of the boat was, to some extent, explained, for, directly opposite the island, the frigate could be seen with all sail crowded on in chase of a vessel – apparently a brig – whose white sails appeared as a tiny spot on the extreme verge of the horizon. Both vessels were sailing close-hauled to the north-west, and as the brig was a long distance to windward, I knew that the return of the frigate was not to be looked for on that day, even if – as I greatly doubted – the captain had any intention of returning at all.

Dismissing, therefore, all thoughts of rescue from my mind, I commenced, with infinite caution and care, to descend the long slope towards the shore; and an excessively arduous and dangerous climb I found it; for, owing to the rotten, crumbling nature of the rock, the foothold was most uncertain and treacherous. One moment my foot would sink ankle deep into an apparently firm surface, and the next a great mass would detach itself bodily and go bounding down the slope, nearly carrying me with it; and on two occasions large overhanging fragments split away above me and came thundering down towards me with an avalanche of dust and stones which I barely managed to escape.

At length I reached the foot of the rocks and paused to look about me while I beat the red dust out of my clothes and wiped it from my hands.

Despite the brilliant afternoon sunshine, the warm blue sky with its flying clouds and the sparkle of the ocean, the scene was one of utter desolation. Behind, the bare, forbidding rocks rose in chaotic ruin, mass piled on mass away to the inhospitable peaks, whose splintered forms towered aloft like the monuments to a life extinct and forgotten. Seaward, the great ocean swell came rolling in unceasingly, flinging its ponderous burden upon the jagged ridges of lava until the earth trembled with the thunder of its impact and the air was filled with chill, rainbow-tinted spray.

Strewn along the shore in strange profusion, were the relics of many a bygone disaster. Here a cask, ancient and waterlogged, with a half-erased inscription graved in its head, rested at high-water mark where the waves had driven it long since; there a sodden crate or decaying basket lay amidst a tangle of rotten cordage. Planks and shattered timbers were scattered on every hand, with here and there a spar or fragment of a mast; and all dead and mouldering away, each swathed in its funeral shroud of green sea-grass or white with encrusting barnacles.

It was, in truth, a melancholy prospect, and, as I turned from one to another relic of marine mortality, I had a feeling as of one walking in some neglected churchyard among the remains of the forgotten dead; though, for all their sad suggestions of misfortune, these pathetic remnants were not without some glimmer of comfort: there would, at any rate, be no lack of fuel on this desolate shore.

Meditating rather gloomily upon the ocean tragedies mutely recorded by these objects, I turned my face westward and began to pick my way along the rocky beach, stooping from time to time to examine, with a sailor's curiosity, such pieces of driftwood or other remains as bore any marks that gave a clue to their origin. In this way I wandered on for a couple of miles, when, to my great satisfaction, I came suddenly upon a small stream whose limpid water babbled noisily over its shingly bed as it ran out towards the little bar at its mouth. I was greatly cheered by this discovery, for here, at least, was the means of supplying the first necessity of life; and as I filled my pannikin and drank a deep draught of the clear, cool water, I reflected that it should go hard if I could not keep soul and body together with the aid of this stream, seeing that the island abounded with seabirds and their eggs.

When I had rested a while and drunk another pannikin of water, I took off my shoes and stockings and began to wade up the stream, noting with pleasure that the banks were clothed, not only with fresh green grass, but also with great quantities of a kind of bean, which I judged was probably good to eat, as most beans are said to be; and I had not walked above a couple of hundred yards up the bed of the river, when I came in sight of an object so unexpected that I could hardly believe my eyes.

It was a house – or rather I should say, a small hut, very ruinous and tumbledown, but undoubtedly a human habitation, and I hailed its presence with the utmost joy and relief, since I had understood the island to be quite uninhabited. But when I scrambled up the bank on which it stood and approached to examine it, its aspect struck me with a chill of disappointment; for it was the merest ruin and had evidently been long since abandoned. The roof had fallen in and lay, a decaying mass, upon the floor; the rough stone walls were overgrown with the climbing bean-plants, and what had been its single room was choked with vegetation.

Turning away from the gaping doorway, I looked around for other traces of human occupation. Across the river I could now see a level terrace on which were several other huts, and though, even from this distance, their appearance was not encouraging, I crossed the stream and walked towards them. But a nearer view only confirmed my misgivings; they were all, like the one I had just seen, mere ancient ruins, roofless and decaying with the walls alone standing, and these so thickly mantled by the luxuriant creeper that the stone was only here and there visible.

Profoundly depressed by the unearthly silence and stillness of the deserted hamlet, I sat down on the terrace to put on my stockings and shoes, speculating pensively on the history of this strange settlement, and wondering what manner of men had dwelt in it, and how it had come to be abandoned. It seemed as if some curse hung over this forbidding land, so that nothing could live or flourish on it, but all must turn to dust and ashes under its malignant influence. The decaying ship in the bay, the mouldering jetsam on the beach, and these crumbling cottages – once busy with human life and glad with the voices of men and the laughter of children – were so many emblems of mortality, and gave to the place the air of a charnel-house. The very trees were dead and falling into dust, and even the mountains were not as other mountains, but seemed to be ruinous and on the verge of dissolution.

And now, as if in sympathy with these gloomy reflections, the declining sun dipped suddenly behind the peaks to the west, and instantly, upon the whole landscape, fell the sombre shadow of approaching night. The clouds that sailed across the sky were, indeed, still warm with sunlight, but here, in the shadow of the mountains, the heat of the tropic day passed at a step into the chill of evening.

I rose with a slight shiver and began to saunter dejectedly along the terrace, glancing around with incurious eyes, and considering how and where I should pass the night. Scattered here and there upon the ground were fragments of rude pottery – the sole traces of man that were to be seen. One of these I picked up, and, having idly examined it, was about to fling it into the doorway of a hut that I was passing, when my eye caught something inside the ruin, at the sight of which I stopped, with the potsherd poised in my hand, as though petrified.

A man was lying, apparently asleep, among the herbage that choked the interior of the ruin.

There was little of him to be seen but his feet, which were just within the doorway; but I noted that he wore a pair of stout shoes, and I also observed on the ground, close by his feet, a small keg or anker such as spirits are kept in.

Recovering, after a few moments, from my astonishment, I hailed the man with a loud and cheerful halloo! and stepped up to the doorway of the hut.

He had apparently not heard me, for he made no movement; so, perceiving by his white duck trousers that he was a sailor, I hailed again.

"Come, shipmate!" I sang out, "wake up and give a castaway brother a word of welcome."

The man still remained immovable; and now, with an uneasy suspicion, I drew a step or two closer.

It was one of our own men, as I could see by such of his clothing as was visible; which was identical with my own, and had evidently come from the *Asphodel's* slop-room. Hesitatingly, and with growing dread, I stooped to draw aside the plants, that I might set my doubts at rest; but when, at length, the herbage parted, I sprang back with a gasp of incredulous horror; for the face that I looked upon was that of a bare and grinning skull.

It was frightful and beyond all belief. Not a dozen hours had passed since we landed on the island, and yet, in that brief space of time, this robust seaman had wasted to a skeleton. It was impossible! No natural decay could consume a body in twelve hours. And now, when I looked again at the dreadful thing, a certain gory raggedness in its aspect seemed to suggest an explanation, which was strengthened by the existence, close to the corpse, of a hole in the ground like the burrow of some great species of rat; and, even as I was noting this, a muffled rustling from within the body, and a heaving of the clothing, gave horrid confirmation.

And yet, even so, it seemed incredible that so short a time should have sufficed to work so dreadful a change. As I was thus reflecting, my eye, once more, fell upon the anker lying at the dead man's feet, and immediately another thought flashed into my mind.

Could it be Rodman?

Incredible as the thing appeared at first sight, it was not really so unlikely, for, at the time of his disappearance, the island lay directly to leeward, and his light boat would naturally have been carried towards it, arriving at its shores, probably, about daybreak. It was true that the dinghy could never have crossed the surf, but then Rodman might have swum ashore and left the boat to its fate.

And then there was the anker. I was quite sure that none of our men had brought it, for no such thing would have been permitted; besides I had seen them all start from the boat.

Once more I bent over the repulsive remains to see if I could find any clue to the identity of the body. The clothes were like those of most of our people – purser's slops of a uniform pattern; but under the edge of the jacket the haft of a knife projected, and, remembering that seamen commonly cut some identifying marks on the handle, I drew the knife from its sheath. It was a common seaman's knife, precisely similar to my own, and, evidently like it, bought out of the purser's stores; but on one side of the wooden haft, deeply cut in, were the letters J.R.

There was then no doubt that these poor remains were those of my old enemy, Jeffrey Rodman. Strange irony of fate! That I whom he had last looked upon as a dying man, consigned to an ocean grave by his own act, should now be standing beside his corpse. But there was little occasion for me to exult, even had I been so minded, for who could say if a few short hours might not see me reduced to a miserable heap of dry bones, even as he was.

I looked at the grim face, with its empty eye-sockets and grinning jaws, and, as I recalled the various emblems of mortality that this gloomy island had presented to my view, there came into my mind some verses that were cut upon an old headstone in Shorne Churchyard:

> "Behold me now as ye pass by,
> As ye be now, so once was I;
> As I am now, so much ye be,
> Therefore prepare to follow me."

Many a time, as a lad, had I read these lines – inscribed beneath a grotesque *memento mori* – and reflected on the malicious satisfaction that they expressed in the misfortunes and bereavements of others; but never had their truth been borne home to me as it was now, when I seemed to be face to face with a ghastly adumbration of my own fate.

I was about to return the knife to its sheath when, remembering the condition of my own, I determined to make an exchange, little as I relished the idea of taking anything from the dead man; so, drawing out the broken blade, I flung it down beside the body and slipped Rodman's knife into my own sheath.

The anker next engaged my attention, for, though I was no toper, the fatigues and miseries that I had endured, made me feel that an allowance of spirit would be not a little acceptable. I caught up the little barrel and shook it, and was well satisfied to find that it was still more than half full.

I was about to leave the hut with my prize when it occurred to me that I had often seen Rodman smoking tobacco in the galley. I had been little accustomed to this indulgence myself, but had often heard it said that the taking of tobacco tended to induce a peaceful and contented frame of mind (not that it seemed to have any such effect on Rodman); and as I had, just now, great need of some aid to peace and contentment, I determined to examine the dead man's pockets in case he should have carried with him the materials for his favourite indulgence.

Setting down the anker, I stooped and passed my hand over the outside of the jacket pocket, but withdrew it with a start, as I felt something move underneath. But I had distinguished some hard object through the cloth, so, gathering fresh courage – though my nerves were by this, all of a tingle – I slipped my hand inside and drew forth a good-sized lump of tobacco. There was no pipe, however, and I was just considering if I could muster courage enough to search the pocket on which the body was lying, when a slight rustle in the further corner of the hut made me look up.

In a moment my limbs stiffened with horror as though I had been turned into stone; my skin broke out into chilly sweat and my hair stirred like the fur of a frightened cat. For there in that obscure corner, watching me with a malignant smile, was a face – a great, yellow, bloated face, fantastically hideous beyond belief – a face with a huge, swollen jowl, and high peaked forehead, with frightful, staring, protruding eyes, fixed in an outward squint; and the whole countenance set in an unchanging grin that was most devilish and inhuman. It stared out at me from a mass of herbage and seemed to be but an inch or two from the ground, as if it had risen out of a hole in the earth to watch me. As I gazed at it, holding my breath in the extremity of horror, it seemed to me to be the face of Murking – pious, villainous Enoch Murking – dead and damned, and rising from his grave to curse me once again.

"God!" I gasped, "am I going mad in this horrible place?"

I rose from my stooping posture over the corpse, and as I moved, the face moved, wagging slowly at first, from side to side, and then sliding in an astounding fashion, along the surface of the ground until it came out on to an open space on the floor of the hut.

And then I laughed aloud – a wild hysterical laugh, shaken by the tremors of my previous terror: for the thing was nothing more than a great land-crab, hideous and loathsome indeed, but in nowise supernatural.

Reassuring as this discovery was, however, there was yet in the aspect of the great beast something very revolting and even disconcerting; for he crept across the hut towards me with an air of stealthy confidence that seemed sinister and unnatural, holding his massive pincers aloft and never ceasing to stare at me with his squinting eyes, nor relaxing that strange diabolical smile.

Chancing to turn my eyes towards the dead man, I perceived a second hideous face looking at me from the mouth of the burrow by his side, and, as I looked, it advanced and was instantly followed by another; and when I glanced back at my first visitor, behold! He had been joined by three more, the whole assemblage creeping towards me in a slow procession, like a troop of hobgoblins. Their stealthy manner and utter fearlessness filled me with dismay, and I felt all my dread and horror returning. Snatching up the anker, I turned to fly from the hut, and, when I found the doorway guarded by another group of the goblin-like shapes, an exclamation of terror burst from me as, leaping over them, I fled down the terrace.

The last glow of the sunset was now fading from the clouds, and, though the daylight was not yet extinct, the cheerless hillside was fast growing shadowy and dim. And everywhere, on the terrace, on the beach, and on the crumbling rocks above, multitudes of moving objects could be seen in the waning light, while, near at hand the elfin forms continually arose out of the earth as if by magic.

At the margin of the brook I paused to fill my pannikin and sat down on the bank to drink; but hardly had I drained the vessel when a shrewd nip in my back caused me to leap to my feet with a cry; and when I saw a great crab standing behind me and several others advancing with uplifted claws, I ran down the bank and splashed through the water.

I now began, as I retraced my steps along the shore, to consider again very earnestly where and how I should pass the night. The whole island seemed to swarm with these repulsive monsters, and it was very evident that if I lay down to sleep I had but a poor chance of ever arising, for they would undoubtedly devour me alive. On the other hand, should I decide to walk about through the long tropic night until the returning day sent them back to their burrows, there was the danger that, fatigued as I was, I might drop asleep as I stood. And what would happen then I could judge well enough, for I had but to stand still for a minute to find myself surrounded by a circle of goblin forms, each menacing me with his pincers, and each bloated, yellow face fixed in the same inscrutable, devilish smile.

In truth I was almost in a state of panic and at my wit's end for some means of safety for the night. Mechanically I scrambled on over the rocks by the way I had come, a little encouraged by the red disc of the rising moon which came sailing over the peaks to the eastward, until I came to the mouth of a gorge. This I took to be the one by which I had reached the north shore, and led instinctively towards the bay in which we had landed. I entered it and turned my face southward. I had not proceeded far before I realised that this ravine was not the one along which I had travelled earlier in the day, for it presently opened out into a narrow valley which I did not recognise. Still, as it seemed to trend towards the south shore, and as, moreover, I had no very definite object in view, I continued on my way, hoping to find some shelter in which I should be secure from the attacks of the crabs.

As I went on, climbing painfully over the rocky spurs that intersected the ravine, the scenery became more and more gloomy and appalling. On the one hand a giant peak reared itself, black and threatening, against the moonlit sky, while on the other the rocks rose in a confusion of shattered masses like the ruins of some cyclopean building. Farther on, where the gorge widened out somewhat, I entered a valley of unspeakably repulsive aspect, for here the sides were clothed with a forest of dead trees which looked most dismal and ghostly as the moonlight struck their skeleton branches. Every tree was crowded with the nests of seabirds, and the ground was so thickly strewn with the putrid remains of their feasts that the stench was almost intolerable; and on all sides countless swarms of land-crabs were gorging themselves with the stinking offal like troops of filthy ghouls.

Through this loathsome valley I hurried as best I could, and, having clambered to what seemed to be the summit of the pass, commenced a steep descent.

Presently the valley closed in to a narrow passage between two sheer precipices and turned sharply to the left; then, quite suddenly, it opened out, and the wide expanse of the bay spread out before me.

Down on the shore I could see the water breaker, and, as I had expected, a swarm of crabs gathered round the biscuit bag busily devouring my slender store of provisions. I ran furiously down the beach, and, my fear of the hideous brutes quite overcome by rage, I kicked their great bloated bodies right and left, and, snatching up the bag, bore it away.

As I looked back I could see the crabs, quite unmoved by my assault, calmly picking up the remains of the biscuit or gathering round their wounded comrades, and deliberately pulling them to pieces and devouring them; but all the while starting at me with their squinting eyes and maintaining the same fixed, mocking smile.

It seemed that I was little better off here than on the north shore, except that I was farther away from that grim and silent figure in the hut. It was a cheerless prospect, that of wandering up and down the beach through the long hours of the night when already I was spent with fatigue.

I glanced round the bay, disgusted with its haunted solitude and heedless of the beauty of its shining sands, the silvery wake on the sea and the untiring surf. In the cold moonlight the wreck appeared even more wan and spectral than by day, for now no touch of life or colour relieved its pallid lights and inky shadows. Yet as I looked at it, the thought came into my mind that perhaps in its deserted fabric I might find a haven of refuge from the loathsome vermin that swarmed upon the land. The tide was out and the afterpart of the vessel was now high and dry upon a bank of sand that had silted up around it, which was separated from the beach only by a little stretch of shallow water. And as I drew nearer, I could see a couple of ropes hanging from the stern gallery, by which, no doubt, the crew had let themselves down when the vessel drove ashore.

My mind was made up. If I had to sleep in the open gallery I should, at least, be secure from the crabs; and, as to the birds, I did not view them with any alarm.

My course of action thus settled, I waded out through the shallows on to the sandbank at the vessel's quarters. As I stood in the shadow and looked up at the structure that towered above me, the old ship loomed up in the unexpected magnitude that a vessel always assumes out of her native element.

There were, as I have said, two ropes hanging from the gallery – both, no doubt, old and rotten; but rotten indeed they must be if they were not, together, capable of sustaining the weight of one man. To the smaller of them – for one was a nine-inch cable – I made fast the anker and biscuit-bag, and then, taking them both in my hands, I began to swarm up, a task of no little difficulty since they were sodden and slippery from the filth of the birds.

At length I swung myself over the rail into the gallery, the floor of which was cleaner than I had expected, owing to the slope caused by the heel of the vessel. I next drew up the anker and the bag, and, detaching them from the rope, laid them down whilst I examined my new quarters.

A glance through one of the broken windows gave little encouragement, for the great cabin had been long ago taken possession of by the birds; and, as the moonlight streamed in through the shattered skylight, it revealed a scene of the most utter desolation.

The centre table was packed with the nests of gannets and boobies, over the sides of which the birds, disturbed by the noise of my arrival, peered uneasily with complaining cries. The side lockers and most of the floor were similarly occupied, and everything, from the swinging lamp and panelled walls to the solitary chair and the ruined harpsichord by the forward bulkhead, was swathed in a uniform coat of white, while the floor was buried under a heap of fish-bones and offal, the stench of which poured out in a sickening stream even through the small shattered pane to which my eye was applied.

There was evidently no resting-place for me in the great cabin, so I proceeded to explore further. At each end of the stern-gallery was a small door leading into the quarter-gallery; of these I selected the one at the higher end, judging that side of the ship to be the drier. The door was not shut fast, although the narrow chink of its opening was not sufficient to admit even a petrel, and when I pulled it open I was delighted to find the quarter gallery quite dry and clean; for, by some strange chance, the skew windows that lighted it had all remained unbroken.

Hereupon my spirits rose amazingly – so inconstant and unreasonable a creature is man – for though I was now in no better plight than when I had stood on the deserted beach in the morning, yet, being relieved of the added horror of the crabs, I seemed to have obtained a positive benefit; and it was with quite a cheerful air that I fetched in the anker and biscuit-bag and closed the door. Even if the wreck offered no better lodging than this, I had at least a clean, dry apartment in which I could sleep, secure from intrusion; but I decided, before settling down for the night, to explore a little further.

The quarter-gallery was quite light, for the moon shone full on the large windows which, despite the filth with which they were encrusted, transmitted a great part of her rays, and I was able to see that, besides the door by which I had entered, there were two others, one at the after-end and one forward. The former of these I opened, but quickly shut it again, for it gave entrance to the great cabin and let in a gust of stinking air that was like to choke me. Then I tried the forward door and found that it opened into a sleeping berth which was much darker than the quarter-gallery, being lighted only by one small scuttle, through which a narrow beam of moonlight poured on to the deck.

When my eyes had become somewhat accustomed to the dim light, I was able to make out some of the objects that the little cabin contained. It was in a state of great disorder, having, doubtless, been rummaged hastily when the ship was abandoned, and the deck was littered with the contents of lockers and drawers that had been hurriedly turned out. A bunk, or fixed bed, occupied one side and at the forward end was a good-sized table or desk, on which were two candlesticks with half-consumed candles in them. By these I was reminded of the tinderbox in my pocket, and I determined to obtain a light, if possible.

This I found to be by no means an easy matter, for the tinder, as may be supposed, was none of the driest; but, after a good ten minutes of anxious blowing and nursing the feeble spark, I had the satisfaction of seeing one of the candles fairly alight.

And now I was able to see what manner of place I was in. It had clearly been the master's berth, for a great watch slung in gimbals rested on the table, and a number of rolled-up charts projected from a rack above. The bed had not been disturbed, and, though it looked a thought mouldy and damp, was far beyond my hopes. As to the various articles strewn about the deck, I gave them no attention at present, excepting a tobacco-pipe of curious workmanship, with a silver bowl and a mouthpiece of mother-o'pearl; which I took possession of for present use.

It was now clear that the lodgings would suit me, at any rate for the present, and I set about making my preparations for the night. First, I set the outer door of the gallery an inch or so ajar, in order that some air might find its way in. Then I carried my provisions into the berth, and, having poured into the pannikin a liberal allowance of rum, made a very cheerful and hearty supper of biscuit; and when I had eaten my fill and drained the pannikin, I felt that I cared not a snap of the fingers for all the crabs on the island, with the skeleton thrown in, so long as they were at a suitable distance.

As an appropriate conclusion to these convivial proceedings, I cut some shavings from Rodman's tobacco and filled the pipe; and, having lit it at the candle I reclined luxuriously on the bed and smoked until the little cabin was dim with the fragrant fumes.

Presently my enjoyment began to diminish, as the unaccustomed indulgence, combined with the rum, made me somewhat giddy; whereupon I laid the pipe carefully upon the table, blew out the candle, and having put off my shoes, turned into bed.

For some time I lay gazing at the beam of moonlight that streamed in through the scuttle, and listening to the hollow boom of the surf, while I turned over, rather vaguely, the strange and disturbing events of the day. Gradually my thoughts grew more vague and wandering and began to mingle with fragments of dreams until, at length, I sank into a heavy sleep in which my past perils were forgotten and my present miseries ceased to exist.

CHAPTER FIFTEEN

In which I find a Key to unlock my Prison

When I opened my eyes, the beam of pallid moonlight had given place to a streak of sunshine which threw, upon the partition opposite the bunk, a circle of brightness, by the rosy colour and high position of which I could tell that the sun was but just risen.

I was in no hurry to follow his example, for my fatigues of the previous day made it very pleasant to lie idly in this haven of security, and let my thoughts ramble over the events that had recently happened, or speculate as to what the future held in store for me.

The existence of this refuge with its simple comforts altered the aspect of my exile to an amazing extent; and since the discovery of the river secured an ample supply of water, while the multitudes of birds assured me a sufficiency of food, unpalatable though it might be, I could consider my future movements at my leisure, undisturbed by the fear of starvation.

As to what those movements were to be, I had at present no idea. Sometime I must make my escape from this solitary place, but, now that I was so well lodged, the matter did not appear so urgent; for though a sociable lad and fond of the companionship of my fellow-creatures, I was not so terrified of my own society as many young men seem to be. Still, I did not propose to spend my days in this wilderness, cut off from all sights and sounds of humanity, and some means must be devised for transporting me back to my country and kinsfolk.

Many plans floated indistinctly through my brain as I lay and followed with my eyes the patch of sunlight creeping down the partition as the sun rose. I might make a fire upon a headland as a signal to some passing ship, or I might build a raft of driftwood, and put out to sea, or the pirates might revisit the island – nothing was more probable; but I decided to give them a wide berth in any case, for it was pretty certain that, if I fell into their hands, they would either knock me on the head at once, or press me on board their vessel and so set me on a fair course to the gallows.

Then again, the *Asphodel* might return and give me a chance of rejoining; but this also I viewed with little favour, after the very broad hint that I had received as to my worthy cousin's intentions towards me; especially as I might, with some show of reason, be regarded as a deserter.

My thoughts next turned to Rodman. How had he managed to get ashore? He had not landed in the bay, or the wreck of his boat would surely have been cast up on the beach. Nor had he swum ashore through such a surf as beat into the bay, for not only had he his hat and the anker – which might have drifted ashore after him – but he wore his shoes, in which it would be almost impossible to swim through the breakers; and, now that I recalled the fact, his knife had been quite free from rust, as I confirmed by drawing it out and examining it.

Could it then be possible that Rodman had chanced upon some more sheltered landing-place, the existence of which was unknown to the boatswain? The facts seemed to point to that conclusion, and, if it were correct, I might possibly find the remains of the boat and get possession of the store of biscuit that I remembered having seen in the stern locker.

Stimulated by the idea of replenishing my waning stock of provisions I sat up, and, throwing my legs over the side of the bunk, slipped on my shoes. The patch of sunlight had reached the deck by this time, and the loud flutterings and rustlings from the great cabin, which had been going on since I woke, were now dying away as the birds, one after another, sallied forth to their fishing grounds. The day was fairly awake and it was time for me to set out on my journey of exploration.

Having filled my pockets with biscuit and taken the pannikin, I passed out through the quarter-gallery on to the stern walk. The tide was running out, but the sandbank was not yet uncovered, so I decided to take off my clothes and wade ashore. Accordingly I removed my clothing, and, having tied it up into a bundle with a piece of line that I found in the berth, I made it fast to the smaller of the two ropes so that, when lowered, it would be clear of the water but yet within reach. Then I slipped down the cable, and, unfastening the bundle, set it on my head and waded to the beach.

The cool water was so pleasant that I laid my bundle on the sand and plunged in again, amusing myself for some time by swimming about in the quiet shallows between the sandbank and the beach; and when I was tired of this sport, I ran up and down the smooth sand and dried myself in the sun, after which I dressed, and filling the pannikin with water from the breaker made a good breakfast. I now looked about to see if it was possible to make my way along the south shore to the westward – the most likely direction in which to look for another landing-place – but the bay was shut in there by a rocky headland of great height, and evidently quite inaccessible. The only way, in fact, out of the bay, appeared to be by one or other of the ravines along which I had travelled; so, having taken another drink of water, I slung the pannikin to my belt and set off along the nearest one – that by which I had come on the previous night.

By the cheerful light of the morning the gorge bore a very different aspect from that of the night before, and, if the offal that the birds had scattered around was none the sweeter for having the hot sun shining down on it, the valley was purged of the loathsome ghouls that feasted there after dark.

Most of the full-grown birds were absent from their nests, doubtless fishing round the coast, and the young ones – uncouth, overgrown fledglings – raised their fluffy white bodies and stared at me with foolish curiosity as I passed, showing no fear or consciousness of danger even when I approached within a couple of feet. It was clear that, if I should be driven to adopt a diet of young seabirds, the furnishing of my larder would present few difficulties.

This morning, however, I had other business on hand and could not spare the time for making fires and cooking; so, noting the abundant supply of food with a view to future contingencies, I hurried on towards the north shore.

When I came in sight of the sea I was interested to observe that two vessels were visible, one a fine ship which, for a moment, I mistook for the frigate, and the other a small barque. They were both too far away for their people to see the smoke of such a fire as I could make without preparation, but I was greatly encouraged by their presence, which, together with that of the brig that I had seen the day before, seemed to show that the sea hereabouts was less deserted than I had supposed.

I did not loiter on the shore today, but made my way, as well as I could over the rocks, towards the west; but I stopped once to secure what turned out afterwards to be a treasure indeed – a high-shouldered Geneva bottle holding about a quart. This I picked up with great exultation, and, taking a length of weed-covered rope that was lying on the beach, I unlaid and cut off one of the strands, from which I made a secure sling by which I could carry the bottle from my shoulder. Then, having fitted it with a stopper, cut from a piece of driftwood, I went on my way rejoicing.

Shortly afterwards I came to the stream, where I rinsed out the bottle and filled it with water, and, when I had drunk a deep draught, climbed up the bank and proceeded to the deserted hamlet.

By the bright and cheerful light of day, I entered the hut in which the body lay, with an unconcern that contrasted curiously with my terrors of the previous day. As may be imagined, I had little sentimental feeling with regard to Rodman, and would much sooner have had his company dead than alive; so that it was with an indifference, of which I felt almost ashamed, that I proceeded to examine the grisly remains in the light of my newly-conceived hopes.

The hat, which I picked up and scrutinised closely, had certainly not been in sea-water, and the shoes were still, in places, shiny with grease; thus contrasting strongly with my own, which were nearly white, and sparkled with salt. The clothing, too, was quite free from the white stains that salt-water produces, and this, with the absence of any signs of rust upon the knife, led me, inevitably, to the conclusion that Rodman had not been in the water at all and consequently could not have swum ashore.

But, if he had not swum ashore, he must have found a more practicable landing-place than the bay which Wilkin had chosen, and, as I reached this conclusion, possibilities of hope began to rise before me, to which I hardly dared to give definite shape.

It was one thing, however, to know that a landing-place existed, and quite another to ascertain its whereabouts. The whole island seemed but a chaos of peaks and precipices, inaccessible to any creature but a bird or a mountain goat, and endless time might be consumed and innumerable dangers faced before a fraction of its coast could be explored.

Nevertheless from this landing-place, wherever it might be, Rodman had contrived to reach the hamlet, and where he had been able to make his way it should be possible for me to retrace his steps, if only I could find out by what route he had come.

I walked out on to the terrace and looked around. Behind the houses the land rose steeply to a second smaller terrace, beyond which the rocks seemed to soar up in a jumble of precipices and crags on which there was hardly foothold for a chamois. But it occurred to me that, since the little river came down from the mountains at the back of the hamlet, it must, unless it fell in a sheer cascade, have excavated for itself some kind of valley; so in the direction of the river I bent my steps, and had not walked above a hundred yards when, as I passed by a mass of the debris thrown down by a recent landslip, I distinguished, very plainly, footprints pointing towards the hamlet. That they were those of Rodman I felt no doubt, for they had been made by a single pair of feet, and I knew that our men – even if they had penetrated so far, which was not likely – had gone away from the boat in parties of three, and would certainly not have separated.

Pursuing the track left by Rodman's feet, I presently came to the mouth of a gorge, in the bottom of which the little river came brawling down from the mountains in a succession of rapids and small cascades. This gorge was much more precipitous than either of those that I had previously traversed, which was to be expected, since it ascended towards the loftiest part of the island.

So rugged and difficult did the ascent appear, that I felt very doubtful of the possibility of climbing it, and I was scrambling up in a very half-hearted and tentative fashion when I came upon a small level space in which the stream had widened out into a shallow pool. And here, in the sodden earth at the margin, among luxuriant masses of the pink-flowered bean-plant were, not only footprints, but, in one place, the impressions of a pair of knees, as of someone who had stooped to drink; and beside them a distinct circle in the muddy earth – evidently the mark made by the anker where it had been set down on its end.

I now had no doubt that I was on the right track, and, greatly encouraged, I started with renewed energy to climb up the narrow gully, regardless of the frowning precipices that overhung my course, or the dangerous, unstable character of the rock, which crumbled beneath my feet, and often broke away in large masses that bounded away into the depths beneath. But it was arduous and very exhausting work, for the rocks, roasting in the burning rays of the sun, were unpleasantly hot to the touch, and the quivering air that rose from them was like the breath of an oven.

In a few minutes I was bathed in perspiration, and as I struggled on, hauling myself up from crag to crag, the sunlight beat down upon me and seemed to dry up my very blood. Time after time did I pause to drink from the stream and splash the cool water over my head and breast, and hardly had I resumed my labour before the dripping sweat had drained me dry, and I was again parched with thirst.

At last I came to the head of the stream, where its waters gushed from the rock, and here I called a halt and not only drank my fill, but let the refreshing liquid trickle over my body until all my clothes were saturated. Then, with deep regret, I bade farewell to the stream, and resumed my progress up the narrow gorge, now arid and bare and hot almost beyond endurance.

I had been climbing upward for about two hours, and had drained the last drop of water from the bottle, when I found the way barred by a sheer cliff which extended right across the ravine, and, in fact, seemed to close it completely. Its height, indeed, was not great, being perhaps less than forty feet; but forty feet of sheer cliff may present as complete a barrier as a precipice a thousand feet high.

But I had not come so far to be turned back by an obstacle that was not absolutely unsurmountable; and when, on the soft earth at the foot of the cliff, I perceived the prints of Rodman's shoes, I decided that, since there had been a way down, there must be a way up. And such a way I presently discovered; for, following without difficulty the line of footprints, I came to a place where the cliff met the side of the gorge at an acute angle; and here it was possible, by taking advantage of the irregularities on both surfaces, to creep up, inch by inch, in the angle. But the ascent was not achieved without much difficulty and danger, and when, at last, I dragged myself over the edge of the cliff, I was utterly exhausted by the long-sustained exertion.

But the struggle was not without its reward. As I rose and looked about me, the change in the aspect of Nature was so great that I could scarce believe my eyes. For here the rugged steepness of the mountain-side gave place to the soft and easy undulation of a tableland, and the arid nakedness of the rocks was changed, as if by magic, into a luxuriance of vegetation at which I stood amazed. At a single step I seemed to have soared from an inferno of hideous desolation into a paradise of beauty. The soft, red earth was clothed with tall grass, amidst which arose multitudes of herbs and bushes, all spangled with flowers, while, here and there, beautiful groups of palm-like fern-trees spread abroad their lacy leaves, each tree crowned with its circlet of spirally-coiled buds like so many green crosiers.

Strangely enough, amidst all this teeming life, the dead trees were clustered as thickly as in the desolate valleys below; but even they were more beautiful and pleasant in their death and decay, for here the leafless branches were clothed in moss of a soft, silvery grey, which draped becomingly the naked limbs with pendant masses that stirred to and fro in the breeze.

Through this strange, remote garden I walked with infinite wonder and delight, now pausing to gather some gay flower and stick it in my belt, and now looking up curiously at the little orange markings on the backs of the fern leaves; and all the while scarce able to believe that this Eden could be part of the desolate, forbidding land over which I had wandered so disconsolately the night before.

Presently I perceived, at the bottom of a dell, a small pool, fed by a running brook, and I hastened towards it that I might slake my thirst and replenish my store of water. Seating myself at the margin of the pool, in the shade of a clump of fern-trees, I dipped up a pannikin full of water and was about to drink, when a large hog appeared suddenly on the opposite side, evidently on the same errand as myself. He did not see me at first, his attention being occupied in finding a comfortable place to drink from, but when a movement of mine attracted his notice, he stared at me with as much astonishment as the countenance of a hog is capable of expressing; his little eyes widened to their utmost limit and his mane bristled up so that I felt quite relieved to think that the pool was between us.

After having gazed at me for a full minute, he appeared to dismiss me from his thoughts, and when he had drunk heartily and with much inelegant snuffling, he sauntered away and I saw him no more. But his appearance put me in mind to examine the muddy ground at the brink of the pool – for though I had no weapons serviceable for hunting, yet it was well to know what supplies the island was capable of yielding – and when I did so, I found it covered with countless prints of feet, not only of pigs but also of goats – some of them, to judge by the size of the spoor, as large as calves – and in one place I saw the impressions of what I took to be some kind of cat.

But it would not be wise to loiter in this garden of Nature, pleasant as it was, for the day was passing apace and the object of my quest was still before me. When, therefore, I had eaten some biscuit and filled my bottle, I set forth across the verdant plateau towards the south side of the island, noting, as I went, that, as a set-off to the rich verdure and the pleasant shade of the fern-trees, the place had been invaded by thousands of the uncouth and foul-smelling gannets, while the burrows by which the ground was honeycombed, told of a teeming population of land-crabs; indeed I saw one of these brutes in a shady place, standing at the mouth of his tunnel and looking like some hideous gnome who had come up from his subterranean dwelling to take a breath of fresh air and a peep at the sunshine.

On the south side the tableland ended abruptly in a series of cliffs and precipices excepting at one place, where a steep ravine with very rugged sides and floor descended like a giant staircase; and down this I took my way, with infinite regret at leaving the shade and beauty of the garden-like plateau, to expose my body once more to the rays of the pitiless sun. Steep as the gorge was, I let myself down without much difficulty from one rock projection to another until, in about half an hour, I came to the head of a good-sized stream, the waters of which I could see for a long way below me, rushing noisily over the rocks and throwing up, here and there, little plumes of spray. As my bottle was by this time empty – for the heated air from the rocks produced an intolerable thirst – I stopped to drink and refill it, and to consider also whether it was advisable to proceed further, seeing that it was well past noon, and that I had no idea what manner of place was below me.

This was a very difficult matter to settle, for if I could not reach the south shore and return to the wreck in one day – and it was by now quite evident that I could not – I should be no better off on the morrow than I was now, and should have had this toilsome journey for nothing. On the other hand, if I went on, I must make up my mind to spend the night without any shelter, for, at the best, I could barely regain the plateau before it was dark; and, pleasant as that place was in the heat of the day, it would be an eerie spot at night, with the quadrupeds roaming about in the gloom and the land-crabs swarming among the grass and bushes. However, I reflected that I might pass the night in one of the dead trees, if I could find one unoccupied by the fierce seabirds, and there I should at least be secure from the crabs; so

I decided to continue my climb down to the shore, and, having taken another drink of water, I resumed my journey.

Before I had travelled another quarter of a mile, I found good reason to rejoice at my decision; for, as I passed over a long slope of powdery debris, I perceived in the soft soil, a line of footprints pointing upward. They had been made by one man and I could feel no doubt that they were Rodman's tracks.

This gave me fresh encouragement and I proceeded in a very hopeful frame of mind, sometimes wading through the torrent and at others making a detour when an easier way presented itself. After half an hour's further climbing I reached a point where the ravine widened out somewhat and made a turn so that the shore below came into view.

And as my eyes fell on the scene thus suddenly unfolded, I halted with an exclamation of joy. The great ocean surges were rolling in, rank behind rank, on to the iron-bound coast, and bursting in thunder at the foot of the cliffs, while sheets of spray flew upward, shrouding the rocks in white mist. But at one spot their furious course was checked by a most singular and artificial-looking structure – apparently a reef or rock, long and narrow in shape, which ran out in a curved line like a small pier, enclosing a space of water in which the great waves died away in harmless ripples.

This remarkable natural haven was, no doubt, dry at low water, but now the tide was nearly full and the waves were breaking heavily against the pier; but, though the spray flew over in clouds, the little haven was quite secure from the surf, and in its most sheltered corner, drawn up high on the beach, lay the dinghy.

After gazing at her for a few moments in half-incredulous delight, I recommenced my climb, my heart bounding with thankfulness and hope and yet harbouring a fear lest the boat should, after all, be damaged and unfit for sea. So eager was I to reach the shore that I had nearly slipped, in my haste, down a low cliff, and I had to restrain my impatience lest I should find myself at the bottom with a broken limb.

At last, leaving the water-course on my left, I ran down the end of the gully and my feet crunched among the stones of the beach.

The first anxious glance showed me that the boat had not suffered any serious injury, and, by the way in which she was secured, it was evident that Rodman had intended to return to her, for a length of rope had been bent on to her painter, and an anchor on the end of this had been carried up the beach and stuck firmly into a cleft in the rocks.

However, to make sure that all was right, I unhooked the anchor, and, as the rising tide had now brought the water lapping around her quarters, I managed, by using my utmost strength, to shove her off into the water and jump on board.

She was perfectly tight and sound, so I ran her on to the beach again and hooked the anchor into the rock as I had found it.

On looking into the stern locker, I found that the biscuit-bag had been opened but very little of the biscuit eaten, and that the water-breaker was still three-parts full; the oars, mast and sail were all in place, and, in fact, the boat was ready for sea at that moment if I had chosen to put out, as I felt half tempted to do. However, the sun was by now not very far above the western horizon, so I decided to spend the night in the boat and consider my future movements at leisure.

The rest of the daylight I occupied in rigging up an awning by means of the sail and mast, in case the night should be wet, and then, having made a few other arrangements for my comfort, I amused myself by walking along the pier. The tide had by this time begun to run out, and I was able to walk to the end of this singular reef, which I now found, to my surprise, to be composed, not of the black rock of which the shore was formed, but of a mass of white coral.

Presently the sun dipped below the horizon and the darkness came on with the suddenness that so surprises the newcomer to the tropics; and no sooner was the daylight gone than the land-crabs began to creep down the slopes of the rocks and crawl about the beach in search of offal dropped by the birds. Hereupon I retired to the boat, where I was secure from their intrusion – for I knew they would not be able to climb up its smooth sides – and, having made a supper of biscuit and water, I lay down to think over my plans before going to sleep.

First I debated the question as to whether I should put off to sea on the morrow as soon as the tide was full – which, by the way, would not be until about four in the afternoon; then I considered what course I should steer on leaving the island – whether I should make for the open sea in the hopes of being picked up by some passing ship or endeavour to reach the coast of South America.

The latter plan I rejected for several reasons. In the first place I had no idea how far away the mainland was, nor what was the character of the coast or the inhabitants (if there were any); nor did I know if there were any ports within a practicable distance to which I might make my way by coasting. In short I should be sailing quite in the dark, and stood to be wrecked on a desert coast or starved in my efforts to reach it.

On the other hand I had seen three vessels in two days, and all, apparently, homeward-bound. Of course I could not expect them to appear regularly with this frequency, but still it looked as if this part of the ocean was a recognised route for shipping, and there seemed a reasonable prospect of my being picked up.

But if I put to sea with the intention of cruising about until some vessel hove in sight, it was most important that I should start with as ample a supply of food and water as might be, for it was impossible to foresee how long I might be drifting about before I was rescued; and as I reflected that the bag that I had left on the wreck contained enough biscuit to last me, at a pinch, for a week, I decided to journey across the island on the morrow and bring it over to the boat.

With this resolution, I turned over and settled myself to sleep, and did not wake until the eastern sky was rosy with the coming dawn.

Having taken down the awning and made everything trim and tidy in the boat, I stuffed my pockets with biscuit, slung on the water-bottle and pannikin and was about to start on my journey when I bethought me that a length of rope might be of service in hoisting the biscuit-bag up the cliff at the north side of the plateau. Accordingly I unrove the halyard from the mast-sheave and unbent it from the traveller, and, coiling it round my shoulders, set off up the gully.

Now that I knew the way, the distance seemed shorter and the ascent easier, and I soon reached the water-course, where I rested for a while and breakfasted. Resuming the climb I presently came out on to the plateau, across which I walked briskly, not loitering as on the day before, to admire its verdure and beauty, but merely stopping at the pool to drink and fill my bottle. Arriving at the cliff, however, I reconnoitred before descending, but finding no better way down than that by which I had climbed up, I made fast the rope to a dead tree which stood within a few feet of the edge, and let myself down easily enough, leaving the rope hanging in readiness for my return.

The rest of the descent was a much less arduous affair than the climb up on the previous day (which was natural enough, seeing that gravity was now all in my favour), and it wanted yet some time to noon when I reached the terrace and ran down to the stream to quench my thirst.

When I came out on the shore the first object that my eyes lighted upon was a large turtle, high and dry on the beach. He saw me at the same moment and immediately began to shuffle off towards the sea; but I pursued and caught him up before he reached the water, and, with a hoist on one side, laid him on his back, where he lay helplessly flapping his flippers until I drew my knife and hacked his head off; indeed he did not stop, even then, but continued to move his limbs slowly to and fro while I stood by with the severed head in my hand, staring at him in no little astonishment, and feeling very like a murderer.

However, here was abundance of meat if I could only manage to cook it, and the next thing was to make a fire. My stock of tinder had been nearly exhausted on the previous night, so, before I could commence, I had to prepare a substitute by fraying out some of the inner bark of one of the dead trees, and, when this was done, it took me near upon half an hour to get a few handfuls of twigs alight; but with the fire once started, my difficulties were at an end, for I had but to build a pile of driftwood and leave it to burn up while I prepared the turtle for cooking. As to the proper manner of doing this, I was, of course, quite ignorant, and so must needs take what seemed the readiest way; which was to cut through the skin at the sides of the breastplate all round, excepting a few inches on one side, and then turn back the breastplate like the lid of a box. Having done this, I cleared out all the entrails, and then, clapping the lid to, set the great shell on the fire; but, since a great deal of heat would be necessary to cook so large a mass, I gathered a further quantity of driftwood and built a large heap over the turtle. In a short time the fresh fuel was in a blaze and a mighty hissing and spluttering came from within, accompanied by an odour so savoury that my mouth watered whenever the breeze bore it in my direction.

The tantalising interval of waiting I employed in making a fresh supply of tinder from a piece of decaying rope that I found on the beach, a portion of which I also unlaid into its separate strands, that I might have the means of carrying away some of the surplus meat – for whatever was left would assuredly be devoured by the crabs. In this way I passed the time until I judge that the turtle would be sufficiently cooked to be eatable, when I kicked away the fire, and, prising up the charred shell with my knife, exposed the interior to view. It was not, perhaps, such a specimen of cookery as might have commended itself to my Lord Mayor or his Aldermen at one of their banquets, but to a famished, castaway mariner, the smoking flesh, swimming in melted fat, seemed fit to furnish a feast for the gods; and though in some parts nearly raw, and in others burnt to a cinder, it was certainly the choicest food that I had had before me since I had left Gravesend.

When I had cut out and laid on the upturned breast-plate, those portions which were most completely cooked, I separated the large masses of underdone flesh from the bones, and, having wrapt them in leaves from the bean plants, buried them in the red embers that they might grill and dry. Then I set the great platter, with its pile of roasted meat, on the ground, and, squatting beside it, fell to with voracious joy.

It was the most delicious food that I have ever tasted; and never, in all my life, have I eaten so much. By the time that colossal meal was brought to a finish by the clearing of the last morsels from the platter, I felt much more inclined for repose and meditation than for the laborious tramp to the wreck. However, as I was still less disposed to enact, for the benefit of the crabs, the part that the turtle had played for mine, I rose and proceeded to remove from the embers the lumps of meat that I had set to grill. They were now black on the outside and covered with ashes, but, regardless of their uninviting appearance, I bored a hole through each with a pointed stick, and, stringing them on the rope-yarn, slung the bundle, of several pounds in weight, over my shoulder and trudged off sluggishly towards the bay.

When I came out opposite the wreck it was near to sunset and the tide was still high, although it was on the ebb; so, as I had walked off my torpor so far as to be able to sit down without falling asleep, I rested for a while beside the water-breaker and refreshed myself with a hearty drink.

At length the sun sank below the sea-line and I judged that the water was now shallow enough to enable me to wade out to the wreck; so, slipping off my clothes, I made them up into a bundle and with them and the bunch of provisions I walked out to my residence.

I had intended to devote this evening to a thorough examination of the contents of the berth with a view to selecting any article that might be useful on my voyage. But when the candle was alight, I found myself more disposed for placid reflection than for active exertion; and after all, I had done a good day's work and was entitled to my reward; so, having cut up some tobacco, I filled my pipe, poured a tot of rum into the pannikin, and, seating myself comfortably in the bunk, smoked with infinite contentment while I reflected upon the uselessness of wealth and the vanity of human ambition.

My ideas on this and cognate subjects grew more and more hazy until the pipe, slipping from my fingers, fell with a loud rattle on to the deck; on which I started up, drained the pannikin, blew out the candle, and wished myself a very good night.

CHAPTER SIXTEEN

In which I play the Eavesdropper

On the following morning I was up betimes, and, to make up for my idleness on the previous night, I set to work at once to search the little cabin thoroughly. The drawers of the chart-table were gone through carefully, the raffle on the deck turned over in detail, and even the few garments hanging on the pegs were taken down and their pockets explored. But, to my disappointment, I found nothing that would be of any material service to me; there were no stores of provisions, no compass of any kind, and the charts, which I examined with eager attention, were all concerned either with the Mediterrean, the North Atlantic or the Indian Ocean. Evidently the ship's people had, as I proposed to do, set out on a boat voyage and had taken with them everything that might be useful in those circumstances. The result was that, when my search was finished, I found myself enriched only to the extent of a few fish-hooks, a dozen empty bottles, a coil of cod-line, and a few articles of clothing, including a tarpaulin coat.

And now, as I made a substantial breakfast of turtle steak, I considered how I should set about preparing the boat for her adventurous voyage.

The most important item was, undoubtedly, water, for though a man might manage to keep body and soul together on the slenderest allowance of food, in these latitudes, under the burning tropic sun, a deficiency of water meant inevitable death, and that of the most terrible kind. There was one breaker already in the boat, but I would not risk putting to sea with that only. Arduous as the task might be, the breaker that was now on the beach must be carried across the island and stowed in the boat also. Yet, as I should have to return to the wreck for the anker, the biscuit-bag and my other things that I intended to take, it would not do to leave my quarters unprovided with water. And here I perceived the value of the despised bottles, which would hold a supply for several days. Taking them up one by one and driving the corks in firmly, I carried them out on to the stern-gallery. Then, when I had stowed in my pockets some pieces of turtle-flesh, I fetched out the coil of cod-line, and, as the tide was still high, though ebbing, took off my clothes, made them into a bundle and attached them to the rope as I had done previously. Passing the coil of line over my head, I flung the bottles into the water and descended quickly by the cable to collect them and carry them ashore before they were borne away by the current, and having deposited them on the beach I went back for my clothes.

The breaker, of course, had to be emptied in order that I should be able to carry it, and, having first filled and corked all the bottles and set them in a row ready for my return, I capsized the barrel and let the water run out. When it was empty, I replaced the bung and made a set of slings with the cod-line, for use on the steep ascent where I should require both hands for climbing, and then, hoisting the breaker on to my shoulder, I set off along the ravine.

On the way I broke off a straight branch from one of the dead trees, by using which as a staff I was able to steady myself on the rough and crumbling surface; and with this aid I reached the north shore with very little fatigue.

After a short rest by the stream, I fixed the breaker by means of its slings on to my shoulders, and addressed myself to the long climb up the northern heights, and in this I found my staff of so much assistance that I marvelled that I had not thought of so simple an expedient before. The way being now familiar seemed much shorter, and I reached the head of the stream in a less-exhausted condition than on the last occasion, in spite of the added weight and encumbrance of the breaker.

The worst part of the climb was between this point and the foot of the cliff, and the heat and exertion were much aggravated by the thin band of cod-line, which cut into my breast like rods of steel. But at length this stage of my pilgrimage was accomplished and I saw before me the face of the cliff with the rope hanging down in the angle.

Here I rested for a few minutes after making fast the rope to the slings of the breaker, and then, having tested the rope by throwing my whole weight on it, I climbed up easily with its aid and drew up the breaker after me.

The remainder of the journey was comparatively easy, though I had to be careful during the descent lest the weight on my shoulders should upset my balance; and I reached the shore considerably earlier than I had on the occasion of my first visit.

As I sat in the boat taking my evening meal of roast turtle, I considered how I should fill the breaker. The water-course fell into the sea in a cascade at a little distance to the eastward – as I could see from the end of the pier – but, as far as I could judge, the place where it poured down on to the beach was not accessible at any state of the tide, so that I should have either to bring the water down a bottleful at a time – which would be an interminable task – or take the breaker up to the nearest part of the stream and bring it down full. Difficult as the latter alternative appeared, I decided to adopt it, for, in the event of its proving impracticable, I could still have recourse to the easier but more tedious method.

As soon as I was sufficiently rested I set to work to carry out my plan while the daylight lasted. The sheet of the sail was of strong, though thin, rope, and about fifteen feet long, and this, I thought, would be of great use in letting the breaker down the steeper places; so I unhitched it from the clew of the sail and coiled it round my neck, and, having once more fixed the breaker on my shoulders, I started up the gully.

I found it possible to reach the water-course at a point somewhat lower down than I had left, it, and, as the water here fell over a ledge of rock, I had no difficulty in filling the breaker; but, when it was full and I attempted to lift it, I was appalled by its weight. Manifestly it was impossible to carry it even the shortest distance, so I made the rope, that I had brought from the boat, fast to the slings, when I was able, either by rolling it, turning it end over end, or hauling it along by the rope, to get it out of the bed of the torrent and along the side of the slope to the gully. From this point there was no difficulty in moving it forward, but a good deal in restraining it from bounding away down the steep declivity and dragging me after it, and I was devoutly thankful when at last it slid down on to the beach. By an almost superhuman effort I hoisted it into the boat where, for the present, I stowed it in the stern sheets, and, as it was now getting dark, I set up the awning and made my arrangements for the night.

As soon as it was light on the following morning, I started on my return journey, in some concern at the appearance of the weather. Ever since my arrival on the island it had been uniformly sunny and indeed sultry, although there had been occasional slight showers of rain in the evenings.

But now the sky was sullen and leaden, and a strong wind was blowing from the south, bringing up a sea that thundered on the shore and sent the spray flying across the haven.

When I reached the plateau, ragged masses of cloud were whirling and eddying around the swaying fern trees and often blotting them out in wreaths of fog.

The north side of the island was, for once, sheltered from the wind, though, now and again, a gust came pouring, down a ravine and moaning among the boughs of the skeleton trees; but when I reached the bay I was met by a gale against which I could scarcely force my way, while the howling of the wind and the roar of the surf combined in a din that was almost deafening. Far out from the shore the sea was white as milk, and even the shallows between the wreck and the beach were covered with small breakers.

I looked at my residence with some misgiving, for it was not yet high water, and if the storm should bring up enough sea to beat away the outer sandbank, I might find the wreck breaking up beneath me. However, I considered that, since by her appearance she must have weathered many a storm before, there was no reason to suppose that she would succumb to this one; so, taking off my clothes less willingly that usual, I gathered up four of the bottles and waded out through the broken water. By the time I had carried all the bottles to the wreck and had made another journey for my clothes, my teeth were chattering with the cold and I was glad to huddle among the blankets in the bunk to get warm.

The tide was full a little before sunset, and I was then able to estimate the force of the surf, which evidently beat right over the sandbank, for I could feel the timbers of the old ship tremble as the breakers struck the wreckage at her bows. But it was clear that the force of the waves was broken, to some extent, by the sandbank, and that no damage was being done, so I dismissed the matter from my mind and amused myself as best I could by considering my plans for the future, and congratulating myself heartily that I was not at sea in the dinghy.

The whole of the next day the gale continued to blow with unabated fury, and the sea rose to such a height that I became seriously alarmed for the safety of the dinghy, while the shocks of the waves upon the crazy fabric in which I was sheltering were so violent that I did not dare to settle down at night until the tide had gone down somewhat.

It was a dreary business sitting idle in the confined cabin or pacing the sloping stern-gallery, watching the birds battling with the wind or listening to the roar of the surf; and the flavour of roast turtle – upon which I subsisted exclusively, in order to save the biscuit for the voyage – became positively nauseous, and I felt myself longing to have a good honest piece of hard tack between my teeth.

When I awoke on the second morning, although the surf was still pounding heavily against the bows of the wreck, the howling of the wind had ceased, and in the intervals between the booming of the breakers, a continuous murmur was audible, accompanied by the drip of water.

I arose, and, stepping through the quarter-gallery, opened the door and looked out. A heavy rain was falling, through which the island loomed dim and grey, and from every projecting part of the wreck the water was dripping and oozing in comfortless streams and runlets though every cranny in the woodwork.

I gazed out discontentedly at the cheerless scene and then, with a sigh, closed the door and went back to the berth, making up my mind to another weary day of imprisonment in my narrow quarters.

Having breakfasted, with little relish, on a lump of turtle-flesh, I wandered, for a while, up and down the berth, looking for something with which to pass away the time. It was too early to begin smoking, there were no books to read, so I reached down some of the charts and unrolled them on the table; but they were of too little interest to engage my attention in my present restless state and I soon replaced them in the rack, and, turning to the scuttle with a yawn, slid back the grimy glass and looked out to seaward.

My yawn came to an end abruptly, and, in a moment, I was all excitement and agitation; for, out in the offing, at a distance of about four miles from the land, a vessel lay hove to under reduced canvas; and though she loomed but dimly through the mist of rain, I had no difficulty in recognising HM sloop-of-war *Asphodel*.

Percival had come back, then, after all! With what object it was impossible to guess, but whatever he had come for, he was not likely to depart without a diligent search for the lost sheep.

I looked again at the ship. It was evident, from the trim of her sails, that a breeze was blowing off shore, although here, in the lee of the island, I had not been able to perceive it; and though, for the present, the surf was too heavy to admit of landing, an off-shore breeze, combined with rain, would soon bring the sea down sufficiently to enable a boat to pass through the breakers.

Hence it was necessary that I should, without delay, come to a decision as to what course I intended to pursue. The simplest and most obvious plan was to go out on to the beach and meet the landing-party, when I should certainly be arrested as a deserter, though my explanations might afterwards be accepted. But this meant a return to the life on board ship from which I had already regarded myself as emancipated, with the probability – indeed almost the certainty – that Percival would make some fresh attempt on my life.

On the other hand could I escape the search-parties? And if so, in what manner? I felt little inclination to set out in the pouring rain for the more distant part of the island, even had it been advisable; which it was not, since I might easily be seen through a glass by someone on the ship, and the direction of my flight ascertained.

Then it was quite possible that the wreck might not be examined, for, looked a from the beach, it did not seem a likely place for a man to take refuge in, when he might, if he pleased, be comfortably housed ashore. But in any case it would be well to explore the wreck further and see what means of concealment she would afford at a pinch.

In the sleeping berth there was a second door which I had not yet opened, as I had assumed that it gave access to the unsavoury main cabin. Such now proved to be the case; but when I mustered courage to face the disgusting stench of the apartment, I found that several other berths opened into it. One of these, which seemed to have been used as a steward's pantry, had a trap in the deck, which I raised, and discovered a ladder leading, apparently, to the hold.

Throwing back the trap I descended, and found myself on the lower deck in the upper division of the hold, beside a yawning hatchway that led to the lower hold. Both cavities were quite light owing to the ruinous state of the forward part of the ship, and I saw at a glance, that if the wreck was searched by a shore party, my only chance of escaping them lay in creeping out forward and hiding among the half-submerged timbers.

Returning up the ladder and replacing the trap, I glanced through the berths on this side of the ship without finding anything of interest, and then went back to my own little cabin, shutting the door after me and opening that of the quarter-gallery, to allow the stench to clear off.

Looking out, once more, through the scuttle, I perceived that the sea was going down fast and that the surf was, even now, not more violent that usual. The rain continued to pour down in torrents, so that, at times, the ship was almost hidden from my view; but, as I was watching her, I suddenly observed that a boat had already put off and was nearly half-way to the shore.

I followed her eagerly with my eyes as she drew nearer and nearer until she reached the edge of the breakers, when the men rested on their oars for some time, and I guessed that a consultation was being held as to the advisability of venturing in. At length the men began to ply their oars again and the boat's head was turned towards the beach, while a figure which I thought I could recognise as Wilkin's, stood up at the steer oar.

Very anxiously did I follow the fortunes of the boat as she plunged boldly into the snowy surf, sometimes vanishing into the trough and at others flinging bow or stern high into the air.

Every moment I expected to see her swamped; but still, as the surges rolled past her, the rhythmical sweep of the oars showed that she still held her own; but, of a sudden, when she was within fifty yards of the shore, a great roller swept up astern of her and burst in a cloud of spray right over her, and when it had passed, I saw the boat, full of water, with the men clinging to her gunwales or supporting themselves by floating oars or spars.

It now seemed to me that the boat was doomed, for if she struck the beach with that weight of water in her, she must inevitably break up instantly; but as she drifted slowly shoreward, I saw a man climb into her and fling the anchor overboard; and, in spite of the seas that broke over him, he retained his position, veering out the line gradually until the boat took the ground.

As the sea swept back in the undertow, the boat heeled over and a great part of the water poured out, and, with her buoyancy partly recovered, she was allowed to drift up on to the beach, when the next wave came in.

The men who had held on to the gunwales now walked up on to the beach, and, with the aid of a rope, dragged ashore those who were clinging to the oars and spars, and who could not gain a footing on the beach without assistance by reason of the undertow. At length everyone seemed to have reached dry land – if it could be so described, with the deluge of rain descending on it – for the party mustered on the beach and I judged from their manner that no one was missing.

Almost immediately the expedition broke up into groups; two men remained by the boat, which they fell to baling out, and the remainder dispersed in parties of three, disappearing up the ravines northward, excepting two officers, who stood near the boat.

Presently the latter began to pace up and down the beach, looking very forlorn and wretched as the rain poured down upon their streaming tarpaulins, and it was evident that they were holding little communication, for they walked some paces apart, each apparently absorbed in his own misery. After about a quarter of an hour of this, pursuing their monotonous walk to and fro with the regularity of a pendulum, one of them halted, and, addressing his companion, pointed to the wreck. They appeared to debate for a while on some matter, and I wondered if they were discussing the probability of my being concealed in the old vessel; then, calling out to the men by the boat and again pointing to the wreck, they started off at a brisk pace in my direction.

So it seemed I was to have visitors after all, and it behoved me to prepare my mansion for their reception.

First, I examined the quarter-gallery minutely, in case I should have left any traces of my occupation; but the marks made by my wet feet on the previous day had now dried and were not to be detected, and of other traces there were none.

I next bestowed my attention upon the sleeping berth, picking up any crumbs of biscuit that I could find, and dusting the table so that no recent marks on it should be visible. Then I removed all my goods, including the biscuit-bag and the anker, to the berth which had the trap in the deck, congratulating myself on having resisted the temptation to smoke on this particular morning – for the odour of tobacco would have betrayed me in a moment – and looked round the little berth in case I should have overlooked anything that might give a hint of my presence. I could find nothing, and yet it seemed that if I could discourage my visitors from entering the berth, it would be well; for their eyes might perceive something that mine had passed over, and, besides, the evidently habitable condition of the berth might offer a suggestion that would lead to further search.

The doors both opened inwards into the berth, and were provided with the usual cabin-hooks to fasten them ajar as well as a bolt apiece. But to bolt the door would be to arouse suspicion and so defeat my object. Glancing around, my eye lighted on a bundle of boarding-pikes that was lashed to a pair of cleats on the partition near the ceiling. Here was the very thing for my purpose. Casting it off from the cleats, I suspended the bundle of pikes by means of the lashings, in a horizontal position with the butts against the end of the bunk, and the points about two inches from the door close to the handle.

I was now quite secure, for the door could be opened no more than a couple of inches, and this would give a view of only a small corner of the berth. To open the door completely it would be necessary to batter it off its hinges.

I had hardly completed these arrangements, when a loud creaking from the stern-gallery announced that my visitors were climbing up the ropes. Putting my head out into the great cabin, I could see their shapes dimly through the encrusted stern-windows, as they pulled themselves over the rail, and the next moment the voice of my cousin Percival came distinctly through the shattered pane:

"This is some kind of shelter, at least, Wigmore, but we may as well try the quarter-gallery; the upper one will be the drier."

They passed along to the entrance to the quarter-gallery, and, as I stood by the door of the berth, ready to retreat, if necessary, I heard them enter and shut themselves in.

"By the Lord," exclaimed Percival, stamping his feet upon the deck, "but 'holy water in a dry house is better than this rain-water out-of-doors.'"

"'Tis not much odds after the sousing we had in that accursed surf," growled Wigmore.

"Is it not then?" rejoined Percival. "I tell you, my friend, enough is as good as a feast. Pah! I am wet to the bone."

"Well," remarked the lieutenant, "we've had a plunge-bath and a shower-bath, and now we are like to have a vapour-bath. I am steaming inside my tarpaulins like a net of fresh-boiled potatoes."

"I wonder how long those rascals will be before they give the view-halloo," said Percival. "They won't loiter in this rain."

"No," replied Wigmore, "but they've got the whole island before them, and our worthy friend will, most likely, have seen the ship and run for his burrow. It may take them all the day and a day or two more to boot."

"That sounds comforting," grunted Percival. "But here are two doors which we may as well look into, for there isn't room in this hole to swing a cat."

I heard them open the door that led into the great cabin and hastily slam it to again.

"My God!" exclaimed Wigmore, hawking and spitting as though he were like to choke, "what an infernal stink! 'Tis like an otter's den or a Yarmouth midden."

The door of the berth was next tried and as it opened back against the boarding-pikes, Wigmore called out in a gasping voice:

"Shut it, shut it, for God's sake, Hawke; we shall be choked," and the door immediately closed.

I now felt moderately secure; so, as I was, myself, nauseated by the effluvia from the great cabin, I shut the inner door softly and opened the scuttle to let out the smell and let in the fresh air. Then I seated myself on the bunk that I might listen at my ease to the conversation of the two officers, which was very clearly audible through the thin bulkhead, as they spoke in their strong and penetrating sea-voices.

"'Tis damned unfortunate," said Percival, "that this rain should have come on to spoil the fun of our jaunt ashore. We might have hunted up some of those pigs and goats and got some fresh meat."

"Yes," replied Wigmore, "'tis a pity, as you say; but this soaking may cool our friend's ardour and induce him to return to the ship – that is if he is still on the island."

"Why, where else should he be?" demanded Percival, sharply.

"He might have been taken off by some passing ship," suggested the lieutenant.

"Fiddlededee!" exclaimed Percival, and I guessed he was thinking of the pit; "no vessels ever put in here."

"A good many ships pass in sight though," rejoined Wigmore; "in fact most of the homeward-bound vessels make the island to get a departure, and he might have made a signal-fire and got taken off. By Jupiter! Hawke," continued the lieutenant, "'twould be deuced awkward for you if he had been picked up by a homeward-bound ship. You would grin on the wrong side of your face if you came home and found our friend sitting on the nest."

"Don't be such a damned croaker. Wigmore," said Percival. "I tell you we shall run him to earth before we have done."

"What do you intend to do if he is brought in?" asked Wigmore. "If I were in your place, I'd run him up to the yard-arm. That would settle matters for good and all."

"It would, with a vengeance," replied Percival, "and I'd do it if I dared. But there will be a good many awkward questions to answer as it is, and this might be one too many. I don't want to build a honeycomb for someone else to suck. No, I'll clap him in irons and put him aboard the Admiral's ship at Jamaica for a court martial, and then if old Jervis doesn't hang him or flog him to death, according to his humane custom, we must hope for the good offices of our old friend Yellow Jack."

"I suppose you are right," said Wigmore, "but 'tis a pity he can't be finished off out of hand. By the way, have you any idea what the Admiral means to do with us?"

"No more than you have," answered Percival. "His letter merely says, 'Proceed to Port Royal without delay.' I expect he is, himself, waiting for further instructions. We may remain on the West India station or we may be sent home. It depends, no doubt, on what the French are up to."

The conversation now drifted into other channels, and, as the subjects were of no interest either to me or to the reader, I need not record them. The time dragged on and the rain continued to fall without intermission, filling the air with its monotonous murmur and the melancholy drip of water.

I speculated uncomfortably on the probable proceedings of the search-parties when they returned from their fruitless errand. It seemed now almost certain that they would explore the wreck before giving up the search, and I was just about to make preparations for a retreat into the submerged portion when my attention was arrested by an exclamation from the lieutenant, who had just opened the door leading out on to the stern-gallery.

"Here come two of the parties, Hawke, and there is Wilkin hailing us."

I looked out of the scuttle and saw a group of six men approaching along the shore. The leader I recognised as the boatswain, who, as the lieutenant had said, was hailing the wreck.

"Any news, Mr Wilkin?" Percival roared from the stern-gallery.

"Are, aye, sir!" shouted Wilkin, "We've found him, sir."

"Found him!" bawled Percival. "Where is he, then?"

"He's dead, sir," was the answer; "we came on his body in an 'ouse."

"Come up here, Mr Wilkin, and let us hear the particulars," and Percival returned with his colleague into the quarter-gallery.

"This is a stroke of fortune for you, Hawke," exclaimed Wigmore. "Everything will be plain sailing now, and I need not say, my dear fellow, that you may depend on me to keep quiet about certain little details."

"I know that" answered Percival gruffly. "You are not more anxious to make a trip to Tyburn than I am."

"You need not speak in that way," rejoined Wigmore. "I meant that you have kept my little affair close and that I shall do the same by yours – from gratitude, Hawke, not from fear of your peaching on me."

"Very well, very well," said Percival. "Let it be as you will; but here they come."

The loud creaking of the stern-gallery was followed by the sound of footsteps, and then I heard the voice of the boatswain:

"Come aboard, sir."

"I am sorry to hear your report, Mr Wilkin," said Percival. "Where did you find the body?"

"We found the skiliton in a sort of ruined 'ouse, sir," replied Wilkin.

"The skeleton!" exclaimed Percival in a startled voice; "you don't mean an actual bare skeleton, surely!"

"I do, sir, indeed. As bare and as clean as the skiliton in a puppet show."

"But my good fellow," expostulated Percival, in a tone of deep disappointment, "the man had only been on the island a week. He couldn't have rotted to a skeleton in that time."

"No, sir," answered Wilkin, "he couldn't; but this here body hadn't rotted; the bones had been picked clean. While we was a-lookin' at the body, we sees something move and out pops a great land-crab as big as your head – the damndest, ugliest-lookin' varmint (beggin' your pardon, sir) as ever you clapped eyes on, and shoots down a hole like one of these here Jack-in-the-boxes. When we comes to look round the place, the ground was like a rabbit-warren – all full of holes. There ain't no doubt, sir, as them crabs had eat him up; but whether dead or alive we couldn't tell."

"But look ye, Mr Wilkin," objected Percival, "if the body was eaten to a skeleton, how could you make out that it was that of Roberts?

"Why, sir, as things happened, that was all plain sailing. First, there was the clothes he was a-wearin', which sartainly came out of our slop-room. Then, on the way, we had looked into the pit where we left Roberts digging, and there we found the rope which he had cast adrift and thrown down to the bottom, and half of a broken knife-blade – here it is, sir. Now we finds, by the side of the body, a broken knife – which is this here – and you see, sir, as the half what we found in the pit, fits it perfectly."

"Yes, that seems pretty conclusive," remarked Percival.

"But that aren't all, sir," continued the boastswain.

"Muffin, what was with us when we came on the body, rekernised the knife – says he gave it to the diseased himself."

"Indeed!" exclaimed Percival, with what seemed to be the liveliest satisfaction; "send him in and let us hear what he has to say."

"Come in, Muffin," the boatswain sang out; and then I heard the sound of shuffling feet and a loud sniff.

"Now, then," exclaimed Wigmore, impatiently, "Speak up to the Captain, man, and don't stand there snivelling and blubbering like a great schoolboy."

"I asks your pardon, sir, but he was my friend, he was," quavered poor Bill in a ridiculous, squeaky voice – at which, for all its absurdity, I felt a big lump rise in my throat – "and how am I a-goin' for to tell his friends? The poor young lady – "

"There that'll do, that'll do," interrupted Percival, who evidently did not like the turn that Bill's lamentations were taking, "we shall all hop off our perches one day or else get knocked off. Tell me how you know this knife."

"Why, d'ye see, sir, I give it to him myself when he was a-sailin,' down the Thames, and I cut his name on the handle – here it is, sir, J – I – M, Jim – not as how his name really were Jim, 'cause that there were only a purser's name; but he told me I was to call him Jim and so I did call him Jim, and I cut Jim on the handle of his knife."

"I see," said Percival. "A very lucid explanation. So he told you you were to call him Jim Roberts?"

"Yes, sir. He didn't seem to want the ship's people to know what his real name was, 'cause, d'ye see, sir, he was a gentleman born."

"Ha! a gentleman, was he? And do you know what was his real name?"

"Why, sir, 'twas the same as your own – Robert Hawke."

"Robert Hawke, hey?" exclaimed Percival, in a tone of surprise. "Do you happen to know where he came from?"

"He lived at Shorne, near Gravesend, sir," answered Bill, "'cause I remembers as he were mixed up in some trouble about a murder there; but he never done it, sir."

"Ah, now I understand," said Percival. "He was suspected of this murder and ran away to sea to be out of the way."

"No, sir, 'twasn't like that," exclaimed Bill. "He was took by the press, along of me, at Gravesend."

"That is so, sir," interposed Wilkin. "We took him and Muffin at the 'Mermaid' in Gravesend. Mr Wigmore will remember as he was in command of the press-gang."

"Oh, he was the man from the 'Mermaid,' was he?" said Wigmore. "Yes, I recollect. We sailed the same night."

'Now tell me, Muffin," said Percival, "have you any proof that this man's name was Robert Hawke?"

"Why, sir," replied Bill, "I see a letter what was wrote to him in that name, and I've seed his watch – 'cause we shared a chest between us. 'Tis a fine gold watch with the picture of a hawk on the back, with his wings spread out like the sign of the Spread Eagle tavern."

"Is that watch on board now?" demanded Percival.

"Yes, sir, I see it this morning when I went to the chest."

"I must see that watch," said Percival, "but I fear that Muffin's story is only too true. How strange are the ways of providence, Wigmore! That unfortunate man, it would seem, was none other than my cousin, Robert. I trust it may turn out otherwise, but I fear there is little doubt; for now that the matter has been mentioned, I seem to recall something familiar in his face, though I had not seen him since he was a child. Well, God's Will be done! Make the signal for the ship to fire a gun, Mr Wigmore."

"There is no need, sir," said Wilkin. "The rest of the men have just now returned to the boat. I expect they weren't able to get far up the mountains."

"Then," said Percival, "let us get off at once. The surf seems quieter now and there is nothing to stay for."

I heard them troop out on the stern walk; the gallery creaked with their weight on the rope; and presently they came into view from the scuttle, tramping along the beach.

I saw the boat launched; watched its perilous passage through the breakers; and as soon as it was safely outside the broken water and the sail was hoisted, I went to the steward's pantry to collect my goods.

When I returned to the berth, the boat was nearly alongside the ship and hands were already aloft loosing the sails.

It was now well past noon and still raining, but the grey pall of the sky was breaking and patches of blue began to appear. With this promise of fair weather before me, I determined to make my way to the haven before dark, if possible, that I might be ready to put to sea at daybreak.

My preparations were soon made. The anker and the remains of the turtle were stowed in the biscuit-bag, a blanket from the bunk rolled up and secured to my shoulders with the lashings from the boarding-pikes, and the pipe, tobacco, and tinder-box secured in my pockets; and it remained only to see the ship clear of the island.

The boat swept alongside and disappeared in the lee of the ship; and a minute later the yards swung round, the main top-sail filled, and the sloop stood away to the westward.

I ran down into the starboard quarter-gallery, the windows of which were broken in places, and watched the beautiful craft as she glided out into the offing, until she vanished behind a jutting headland. Then I fetched my pack, slid down the cable into the shallow pool that the receding tide had left, and waded ashore.

As I ascended the beach, I paused to, look for the last time at the old ship that had given me so kindly a refuge in the hour of my distress. She looked, now, lonely and forlorn in the drizzling rain; and the seabirds, wheeling around her with plaintive cries, seemed to call to me to come back; and it was not without an odd feeling of regret that I at length shouldered my bag and turned my face towards the ravine.

The rain slackened by degrees, and what there was rather refreshed me by keeping me cool and free from the burning thirst that I had found so distressing in my previous journeys. Thus I was able to proceed more briskly than usual, and had reached the top of the cliff before the sun broke through the banks of cloud in the west.

Looking out to sea I could now perceive the *Asphodel* far away towards north-western horizon, stretching away gallantly towards her distant goal. As I stood watching her from my lofty station, I wished that poor, simple, faithful-hearted Bill could have seen me waving him a farewell greeting, so that he could have gone on his way joyful instead of sorrowing. But I comforted myself with the thought that we should meet again in happier circumstances; and with that I hauled up the rope, which I had found still hanging down as I had left it, cast it off from the tree, and, coiling it around my neck, strode off across the plateau.

It was dark before I reached the store, or rather I should say the night had fallen, for the sky was now clear and the stars shining brightly. The boat lay high and dry, broadside on to the beach, at which I was rather alarmed until I had examined her and satisfied myself that she was uninjured. By the starlight I rove the halyard and bent it to the traveller, refastened the sheet to the clew of the sail, and ran up the latter as an awning. Then I supped off turtle and biscuit, drank a tot of rum, smoked a pipe, and, as the tide made and the water came lapping around the bilges of the dinghy, I rolled myself in the blanket and turned in for the night.

CHAPTER SEVENTEEN

In which I encounter a most Genteel Rascal

The first glimmer of dawn brought me out of my blanket, all agog to start on my new adventure. Not that there was any occasion for haste, since the tide was yet a long way out and a wide stretch of shingle intervened between the boat and the margin of the incoming water; but my impatience would not permit me to rest, and before the sun was fairly up, I had fetched in the anchor and stowed it in the bows, coiled down the painter, unshipped the rudder and made all clear for pushing off.

There was a long and irritating interval, during which the tide crept in, inch by inch, and I paced the beach, munching the last of the turtle, the flavour of which suggested that I had finished it none too soon. At length the strip of uncovered shingle had narrowed to less than a dozen yards, and I now addressed myself to the task of turning the boat round stern on to the sea (for, as I have said, the storm had driven her up, broadside on).

By using one of the oars as a lever, I had little trouble in slewing her round, and, by the same means, I continued to shove her down several feet until she was well below high-water mark. Then I stepped on board and waited, watching, with great attention, the behaviour of the sea by the end of the pier.

As the tide rose, the line of surf naturally came nearer the land. At half-tide the seas broke just in a line with the end of the reef, and, in fact, against it, so that it would have been impossible to get the boat out of the little harbour. But, as high water approached, the line of breakers drew in farther and farther and by the time the water began to lap around the boat's stern, there was a space of several yards between the outer edge of the breakers and the end of the pier. Here the waves – dangerously high and steep – swept past the pier-head and spread out fanwise into the harbour, ultimately reaching the shore in oblique lines of small and harmless breakers.

Hence the passage out, although practicable, was by no means without danger, for any failure to manage the boat, after leaving the shelter of the pier, must result in its being drawn into the surf and swamped instantly.

As soon as the stern of the dinghy began to lift to the ripples, I rose and shoved off; and, having turned the boat round, seated myself on the middle thwart and began to pull cautiously along the side of the pier. As I approached the mouth of the harbour, this became far from a comfortable berth, for the middle part of the reef was partly submerged and here the water came over in green masses that fell into the boat in such volumes as threatened to fill her; and I had to pull with all my strength to avoid being swamped before I came to the principal danger.

Suddenly I shot past the pier-head and in an instant was caught by a huge, steep-sided roller, which tossed me into the air with a velocity that took away my breath. For one awful moment I seemed to hang over the raging surf; then I dived as swiftly into the trough and the great wave swept away from me and burst with a roar at barely twenty yards distance.

Instinctively I threw my weight upon the landward oar so as to cant the boat's head somewhat off the shore and thus took the next wave on my bow; but the rollers were so high and steep and moved so swiftly, that I began to fear that I should be carried into the surf by the send of the sea in spite of my efforts. However, once clear of the reef, I put the boat's head straight out to sea, and, after pulling like a galley-slave for about ten minutes, had the satisfaction of finding myself at a safe distance from the breakers.

Even then I did not relax my efforts, but turning westward, pulled obliquely off the shore, so that, presently, I began to open the western side of the island. This brought me somewhat out of the lee of the land – for the wind was, today, blowing from the north – and as soon as I felt the draught of air coming round the headland, I shipped the rudder, stepped the mast, and ran up the sail.

There was a good sailing breeze when I was clear of the west end of the island, and the boat slipped along at a very respectable pace, notwithstanding her rather tubby build; but I was not a little concerned to find that, owing to her light draught, she made a great deal of leeway. Indeed it soon became evident that she would not go to windward at all, for, after a quarter of an hour's sailing on a westerly course, she had fallen away considerably to leeward of the island.

This would not do at all. The principal track of the shipping lay to the northward of the island, and here was I blowing away to the south. At this rate I should be as dependent upon the oars as if I had no sail at all, and, with my small stock of provisions and water, continuous and fatiguing exertion was of all things the most to be avoided.

It was most unfortunate that my small experience of boat-sailing had prevented me from foreseeing this difficulty, since, with the abundant driftwood on the shore, I might easily have made a pair of lee-boards such as the Thames barge-men fit to their shallow craft with such excellent effect. But regrets were useless now, and some remedy had to be devised.

Having lowered the sail, I pulled up one of the bottom boards, a stout piece of oak about five feet long and a foot wide. This would answer as a lee-board, though a rather clumsy one, if I could sling it in position, so I set to work to bore a hole through one end by means of my knife, and a very awkward task I found it. When, after infinite labour, I had made a hole half an inch wide, I detached the cod-line lashings from the breaker and rove them thrice through the hole; then, twisting the three strands of line together, I secured them to the lower end of the mast and dropped the board over the side.

When I now hoisted the sail and brought the boat by the wind, the success of this makeshift contrivance was complete, for, after sailing for half an hour about west-north-west, I not only regained the distance I had lost, but found myself creeping steadily to windward.

I sailed on this course for about three hours, when I dipped the sail and went about, passing the lee-board over to the opposite side; for, on reflection, I had decided to keep in the neighbourhood of the island so that, in the event of bad weather or of my stock of water and provisions running out, I could put in for shelter or to obtain fresh supplies; while by cruising up and down to the northward of the island, I should have as good a chance of being picked up as if I put out into mid-ocean.

Holding on to my new course, east-north-east, I had by noon brought the island directly under my lee at a distance of three or four miles; and, as I cruised along, parallel to the north shore, I amused myself by identifying the terraces and the various spots that I had visited in my wanderings. Possibly from the green patch, which I recognised as the plateau, some vessel was even now visible, though unseen by me down on the sea level.

Slowly the island drifted past and gave place to the blank sea-horizon. It was intensely hot, and, as I lolled in the stern-sheets, listlessly grasping the tiller with one hand and the sheet with the other, the burning sunshine poured down upon me until I was sick with the heat and consumed with thirst. About two o'clock I went about again with the object of getting the shadow of the sail to fall on the spot where I was seated; and this made things so much more endurable that I passed the remainder of the heat of the day in comparative comfort.

As evening approached I began to consider how I should dispose of the boat during the time that I was asleep. It would not do to leave her blowing about at random, for I might find myself driven ashore by the morning, or the sea might rise and swamp her, or a change of wind carry her out of sight of the island. So I decided to rig a floating anchor which would keep her head to the sea and reduce the effect of the wind.

To this end I lowered the sail, and, having unhooked it from the traveller, unstepped the mast. Next, I secured the ends of the halyard below the cleat near the foot of the mast and so made a bridle. On the bight of this I made a clove-hitch through which I passed the end of the painter and knotted it securely; then I flung the mast overboard, and, though the breeze was now but light, the painter soon ran out its full length and brought the boat very comfortably head to sea.

My first night on board was not as comfortable as I could have wished, for, after the restful bunk in the cabin on the wreck, I found the quick, uneasy movement of the boat not a little disturbing. However, I fell asleep after a time, and woke next morning to find the sun already above the horizon and the island about a dozen miles distant and still somewhat to leeward.

In the course of the morning, the wind veered round to the north-west, which enabled me to steer a course a little east-of-north. After some hours of this, the island began to sink astern and a group of rocky islets, which I had seen from the plateau, rose broad on my larboard bow. Considering that I had now travelled far enough away from my base, I lowered the sail and rigged it up as an awning, under which I reclined during the hottest part of the day, keeping a look-out for any vessel that might heave into sight.

After a time, the sultry air, the glare of the sun, the incessant movement of the boat and the monotonous noise of the water washing against her sides, lulled me into a dreamy, half-conscious state in which, I fear, my look-out was forgotten, while my thoughts strayed away from the desolate island and the still more desolate ocean to to sweet Kentish countryside that I was, perhaps, never more to see.

It was now near the end of September; the summer was over, the harvest long since gathered, and pensive autumn, russet-robed and veiled in mist, had stolen into the land to breathe her benediction on the waning year.

Now the sturdy oaks in the lanes would be showing patches of sere and yellow amidst the livelier summer green, and early acorns patter down by the roadside, to be garnered by thrifty squirrels, or lie hidden beneath the leaves until the spring song of the birds called them to put forth their tiny shoots. In my mind's eye, I could see the jovial ploughman turning over the stubble upon the hillside, and hear the crack of his whip and the creak of rusty harness. I could see the charcoal burner by the denuded hop-garden, the oasts peeping above the trees, with wreaths of smoke curling from their cowls, and the mill, perched high upon the common above the village, busy with the fruits of the harvest and creaking merrily in the wind.

And, I saw, too, Mr Leigh, walking his rounds upon the farm with his gun upon his shoulder, and sweet Prudence tending her garden or helping her mother in the stillroom, or perhaps directing the maids in the kitchen and bidding them have an eye to the old black clock on which the little smith with untiring arm beat out the irrevocable seconds.

Then my thoughts wandered away from the present, with its miseries and perils, its yearnings and its hopes, into the dim and shadowy past, until it was dim and shadowy no longer, but fresh with the vividness of reality. As I reviewed the quietly-passing years, so full of tranquil happiness though so empty of events, so different from the stormy times that were to follow, men and things and places started forth unbidden from the recesses of memory, sharp and clear as though no waters of oblivion had ever rolled over them.

Thus vividly did I recall the daily pilgrimage, when, with half a score of the village lads, I would set off with my bulging satchel of books and provisions, down the winding ridgeway and across the fields to the school at Gravesend, with little Prudence trotting by my side, to be duly deposited with the dame who taught her to spell and cipher. And how, as we passed the old church in Milton, we would stop and argue over the new sundial on the porch, that our schoolmaster had made, until we were late for school, and good Mr Giles would threaten us with the rod; and how we would then, with childish cunning, ask him some question about the dial, and chuckle inwardly to see his wrath melt into gracious approval.

And so my musings rambled on through the sweet summer days when I would rove in the woods with little Cousin Prue; and the winter days, when the fields were white and we made slides on the pond by the Dover road; and the Sunday mornings when I would sit in the high-backed pew and forget the droning of the sermon as I gazed, with never-ending fascination, at the stone effigy – stiff and stark – of the mail-clad knight, stretched on his stony couch.

But in all these wandering recollections of the past, as in the pictures of the far-away present, there stood out in high relief a single figure, around which all else seemed but as a background.

That figure was my Cousin Prudence – sweet Prue – who had loved me so truly and whom I was, perhaps, never to see again. And as the thought of her came to me again and again with fresh insistence, there was revealed to me a thing which, in my boyish dullness, I had hardly suspected.

From my very childhood I had dimly realised that Prudence was not to me as other maids. That her unvarying sweetness of temper, her sympathy and self-forgetfulness, her quiet dignity – though she was always merry and bright – and her delicacy of thoughts and speech, made her somehow different from the others. But this I had taken for granted, for was she not my Cousin Prudence – almost my sister?

And I had recognised in my bearing towards her something different, too; a respect and reserve that set her apart. With other girls I had often enough flirted and frolicked as young men do; but never with Prudence. Other girls I had made love to, half-jestingly, and kissed them when no one was about, and thought no harm; but I should never have dreamed of treating Prudence so.

And yet I knew that, in my regard, I would have set her against them all without a thought; for, in my quiet life, she was like a violet in a garden, blooming almost unseen and unheeded, and yet filling it all with sweetness. But this, if I had noticed it, I had put down to our relation as brother and sister. I had assumed that my carefully chosen speech and well-considered conduct in her presence, were but the natural results of brotherly solicitude, and had never guessed their real significance.

But now I knew. Now it was made clear to me that, of all the women in the world, there was but one who could be any concern of mine; that she, who had been weighed in the balance of lifelong intimacy and never once found wanting, was the true complement of my being, disjoined from which I must go through life unmatched and incomplete.

It was, perhaps, a somewhat belated discovery, and the occasion none too opportune; still I was but young and my life lay all before me, if I could only escape from the entanglements that fate seemed to have drawn around me.

And with this thought, I fell to castle-building and planning what I should do when I came home to Shorne, when all my difficulties were surmounted and my perils at an end; and so the long day passed until the afternoon sun came prying under the awning to rouse me from my dreams.

I lowered the awning and stood up, stretching myself. Far away to the north a speck of rosy yellow announced a passing ship, which, had I kept a better look-out, I might have seen in time. But she was now to windward and leaving me too rapidly for any pursuit to be thought of; so, having read myself a severe lecture, I hoisted the sail and set a course towards the island (the peaks of which just rose above the horizon) in order that I might not drift out of sight of it during the night.

Soon after sunset I put out my floating anchor, and, having taken my frugal supper of biscuit and water and smoked a pipe of tobacco, rolled myself in my blanket and lay down to rest; but it was long before I fell asleep, for the confinement of the boat made me restless, and my limbs twitched and started for lack of exercise.

Nevertheless I was tired and worn with the burning heat of the day and the incessant movement of the boat, and when, at last, restlessness was overcome by fatigue, I slept heavily, so that, when I opened my eyes, it was broad day. I raised my head above the gunwale and gazed abroad with a drowsy yawn. The air was breathless and still, and a thick mist, warmed by the rosy light of the morning, brooded over the sea, and shut out alike the sky and the horizon.

The calm water, smooth as oil, heaved softly like the breast of a sleeping child, and lapped, with gentle gurglings under the boat's quarters; while down below the glassy surface, a group of fishes glided stealthily to and fro as though fearful of disturbing the silence of the ocean.

Suddenly my ear caught a sound that seemed to issue out of the fog; a soft, rhythmical creak, like the chafing of a parrel on its mast.

I glanced around, seeking to penetrate the woolly mist, but seeing nothing, until I turned my eyes astern; and then I started up with an exclamation of surprise, for, barely fifty yards distant lay a vessel, becalmed with all sail set and swaying softly to the heave of the sea. Near as she was, the mist had softened her outlines till she seemed airy and unsubstantial as the shadow on a cloud, and with her magnitude exaggerated from the same cause, she looked up against the warm light like a gigantic phantom.

No sooner had my eyes lighted on her than my mind misgave me. She was schooner rigged, and, for all the dimness of the misty light, there was in her aspect a something trim and jaunty which, together with her long spars and spreading pinions, no seaman's eye could mistake. If she was not our nimble friend the pirate, then was I greatly deceived.

I began to consider seriously whether I should not steal away into the fog; but it appeared that I was already observed, for as I went forward to draw in the painter, I caught the sound as of two men talking. Immediately afterwards a hoarse voice hailed me:

"Boat ahoy! There! who are you?"

"I am a castaway seaman," I answered.

"Pull alongside, here, and let us have a look at you."

The tone was disagreeably peremptory but there was nothing for it but to obey; so, having hauled the mast on board, I threw out a pair of oars and paddled up to the schooner's gangway.

As I drew alongside and looked up at the vessel, my misgivings received abundant confirmation. The bulwark rail was lined by above a score of heads and a dozen or so of the crew had climbed into the rigging to get a better view of me.

Never in my life have I looked upon so sinister a group; as I ran my eye along the line of faces, all leering down at me with mocking grins full of malice and ferocity, it seemed to me as if the very cream of rascality must have been skimmed from all the jails of Europe to furnish out the crew for this one vessel. They appeared to be of all nationalities – English, French, Spanish, and even negroes – but, diverse in all else, they had in common an expression of ferocious wickedness that filled me with horror and disgust as I looked at them.

"Waterman ahoy!" sang out one as I came alongside. "What's your fare to Execution Dock?"

A roar of hoarse laughter greeted this specimen of Wapping wit, and a great, red-faced ruffian with a mat of hair streaming over his shoulders, leaped on to the rail and held aloft an eighteen-pound shot.

"Here's a passenger for you, mate," he roared, and was on the point of dashing the shot down on to me, when he was pulled back on the deck by one of the comrades.

"Avast there, you fool," exclaimed the latter; "didn't ye hear that the cap'n wants to see this here cove?"

"Cap'n be damned!" replied the first man. "There's too much cap'n aboard this here blessed hooker. Ain't we all equal, mate, hey?"

"In course we are," rejoined the other, "but that ain't no reason for a-crossin' of the skipper. You come along up, young man," he added, beckoning to me; and I, glad enough to be out of the boat with the chance of having a shot dropped through the bottom, hitched the painter to a chain-plate and skipped up on deck.

The crew crowded round me clamorously, and I had a momentary vision of a rabble of wild dishevelled ruffians, strangely garbed and fierce of aspect; but my conductor grasped me by the arm and drew me quickly through a little door under the break of the poop, down half a dozen stairs, and, throwing open another door ushered me into the great cabin.

As I stood, hat in hand, within the threshold, I stared around me in the utmost astonishment, so different was the scene from what I had anticipated. For the appearance of the crew had prepared me for a display of gaudy squalor, a disorderly mingling of dirt and riches, with suggestions of coarse and drunken debauchery.

How different was the reality! The spacious cabin might have been the abode of some savant or man of letters, rather than a sea-captain

234

– and a robber at that – so prim and correct was the air that pervaded it, so neat and well ordered, so suggestive of cultivated taste. The walls were mostly lined with shelves of books; the forward bulkhead was adorned by a splendid portrait in a gilt frame; the open stern-windows revealed pots of flowers – each furnished with a little tarpaulin cape to protect the soil from the spray – ranged on small balconies; and everything was scrupulously clean and dainty.

But the occupant of this singular abode was even more surprising. Seated in an elbow-chair, with a book on his knee and several others open on the table, as if for reference, was a grave-looking, middle-aged man, primly dressed in a suit of black and wearing a neat, grey wig. His neck-cloth and ruffled shirt were white as snow, his hands daintily clean and well-kept, and his appearance generally marked by the precise care of externals that one might look for in a fashionable attorney or physician.

As I entered with my conductor, he raised a thoughtful, benevolent face and glanced at me inquiringly.

"This is the young man from the boat, captain," observed my companion.

Ha!" said the captain, "so you have been tossing about the sea in an open boat, hey, my man?"

"Yes, sir," I answered.

"The sport of the wind and the wave, hey?" continued the captain, with a quizzical smile. "Like Æneas of old,

" *'multum ille et terris jactatus et alto'*

"H'm!"

"Truly you are right, sir," I answered, adding, rather inconsequently, by way of capping his quotation:

" *'Vi superum, saevae memorem Junonis ob iram';"*

"Ha!" exclaimed the captain, in a tone of pleased surprise, "a scholar, hey? Allow me, sir, to have the honour of shaking you by the hand."

He rose, and, offering his hand with a bow, saluted me ceremoniously.

"But how comes it," said he, "that a man of your parts comes to occupy so lowly a station – for I take it, by your garb, that you serve His Majesty, King George – God bless him! – before the mast? Surely the quarter-deck should be your fitting place."

"My fitting place, sir," I replied, "should be ashore in my own home; but the press willed otherwise."

"The press!" he exclaimed. "Ah, now I understand. Be seated, I pray you, and let me offer the hospitality of my poor abode to a fellow-sufferer from that infamous institution."

"The company wants to know what you're a-going to do with this here young cove," said the man who had brought me down.

"Inquisitive dogs, Starbuck," commented the captain; "always prying, always prying."

"They wants him chucked overboard," continued Starbuck.

"Do they indeed?" said the captain in an indulgent tone. "Playful rogues! They love their simple jests. Tell them, Starbuck, that I shall show myself on the poop after breakfast and my guest will take the air in my company."

"You'd better mind your eye, captain, if you do," said Starbuck. "They means to send this here cove for a swim and they wouldn't make no bones about rushin' the poop."

"And is that so?" said the captain, in mild surprise. "Well, it is my usual custom to mind my eye, as you phrase it; but speak to them, my dear Starbuck; entreat them not to agitate me. I shall be encumbered with pistols, you know, and an agitated man with pistols is a most unsafe neighbour. Why, do you know, sir," he added, turning to me, "I have known a pistol, in such circumstances, to explode without warning, to the surprise, and I may add, to the discomfort, of such persons as chanced to be in a right line with the axis of the barrel."

Here I caught the eye of Starbuck, winking violently, as that worthy turned to take his departure, his face suffused with a grin of delighted admiration; and as the door closed behind him, the captain's countenance relaxed into a dry smile.

"A rebellious family, this of mine, sir," said he. "Truculent rogues, sir, and mostly fools to boot; but shall we to breakfast? 'Tis past nine of the clock." Here he drew from his fob a magnificent gold watch and gazed pensively at its jewelled dial; then, observing my admiration, he held it out to me with the pride of a connoisseur.

"A fine timepiece, sir," he remarked; "quite a work of high art; utility and beauty combined. I had it of a Spanish nobleman, a great and worthy man, sir, now, no doubt, in Abraham's bosom, where timepieces are superfluous – nay, where they would be impertinent, as presuming to divide, with their puny mechanism, the immeasurable expanse of eternity."

"Your friend bequeathed it to you as a souvenir?" I suggested.

"Why not exactly, not exactly," he replied; "though indeed he passed away from among us shortly after the toy came into my possession. In fact, he had the misfortune to slip overboard – a most melancholy affair – but such, my dear sir, is man – a mere transitory shadow, the blossom of a day. 'For the wind' – or in this case, the water – 'passeth over him and he is gone; and the place thereof shall know him no more!' "

He slipped the watch back into his fob with a sigh, and jerked the bell-rope, whereupon a young negro thrust his head in at the door.

"Breakfast, Quassie," said the captain, "breakfast one time. Fine breakfast, plenty chop, you sabby?"

"Me sabby, sah," replied Quassie, withdrawing his head; and immediately there issued from the adjacent pantry the pleasant clink of china.

"Circumstances," observed my host, as the negro deftly set out the table furniture, "circumstances would seem to render unnecessary a formal introduction, but nevertheless I shall venture to present myself by name to my honoured guest. Ishmael Parradine, sir, your most obedient servant, and commander of the free-trader *Autolycus*."

He bowed ceremoniously with his hand spread out on his shirt ruffle and I hastened to introduce myself:

"I am called James Roberts," said I, "ordinary seaman of His Majesty's sloop-of-war *Asphodel*."

"The handsome ship, I take it," said Captain Parradine, "that did me the honour of accompanying me some distance, a week or two since."

I replied that his conjecture was correct.

"Ha!" said he, "a very fine craft, sir, and a charming picture she made, as she came round the north point of the island. I trust your worthy captain suffered no inconvenience from the little mishap that my awkwardness occasioned."

"Why," I replied, laughing, "I am afraid it upset a little plan of his, somewhat."

"I feared it, I feared it," sighed the captain. "But breakfast waits. Pray be seated and let me serve you with such poor fare as my table affords."

I took the chair which he indicated and glanced round the table, astonished alike at the luxury and profusion of the "poor fare," and the richness of the appointments. Ham, chicken, fresh eggs, and numberless preserved dainties stimulated the appetite, while the eye was regaled by the spectacle of the magnificent plate and costly china set out upon a damask cloth of snowy whiteness.

"And now, my dear Æneas," said the captain, as he filled a dainty porcelain cup from a silver coffee-pot, "tell me of your wanderings on the wide ocean, of your solitary communings with mermaids and tritons, with bluff old Neptune and the 'cerulean Proteus'

> " 'Magnum qui piscibus aequor
> Et juncto bipedum curru metitur equorum.' "

I smiled, as elegantly as is possible to a man whose mouth is filled with boiled chicken and soft biscuit, and replied that I had not encountered any of the worthies to whom he referred, and that, as to mermaids, my acquaintance was limited to a tavern of that name.

"Ha! The 'Mermaid'!" he exclaimed. "Sacred and immortal sigh! How it carried one's thoughts back to 'rare Ben Jonson' and his jovial crew – Beaumont and Massinger and even the undying Will.

> "What things have we seen
> Done at the Mermaid!"

"You are right there, sir, indeed," said I with a grim laugh; and I then told him the story of my impressment at Gravesend, to which he listened with deep attention, informing me, when I had finished, that he, also, had been pressed into the King's service.

He next questioned me about the manner of my leaving the ship, whereupon I gave him an account of my life on the island and subsequent escape from it. As I proceeded with my recital, his interest became so great that he pushed aside his plate that he might give me his undivided attention, and presently he rose from the table and fetched from an inlaid cabinet a small sheet of paper, which, when he laid it before me, I had no difficulty in recognising as a chart of the island.

"Now show me, Mr Roberts," said he, "the exact position of this haven that you discovered."

"'Tis here," said I, pointing to the place, "a couple of hundred yards west of the cascade."

"And would it be safe, think you, for a large boat – say a ship's launch?"

"Undoubtedly," I answered, "with a full tide and sufficient hands to work her."

"That is well to know," said he, with evident satisfaction; then laying a piece of blank paper on the table and handing me a pen, he begged me to draw him a rough sketch of the pier and entrance.

This I did, and after he had asked me a few more questions, he pinned my sketch to the chart and returned the latter to the cabinet.

"To turn to another subject," said he, reseating himself, "can you tell me if your people found any – ha – property on the island?"

"There was nothing in the pit," I replied; "that I can vouch for."

"And so can I," he rejoined with a smile. "But did they search nowhere else?"

"I feel convinced they did not," I answered. "There was not enough time before they left, and, moreover, I found no traces of any excavation when I was on the island."

He fetched out the chart once more and laid it before me.

"Show me," he said, "what places you visited."

I traced on the chart the routes of my various journeys, describing the features of the places, while he peered over my shoulder with eager attention.

"And you saw no signs of the ground having been disturbed in any of these places?" said he, as I finished.

"None whatever."

"Excellent!" he exclaimed. "My crew will be infinitely obliged to you, for you will have saved them a disagreeable landing through the surf. We were bound for the island when we had the good fortune to encounter you, intending to see for ourselves whether our little savings had been tampered with. But this mission is now unnecessary, as I will presently announce to the company. However, the calm still continues," he added, looking out of the stern-windows, "so we may finish our breakfast first."

When the meal was over – such a meal as I had not taken since I left my home at Shorne – the captain rang the bell, and, taking from the cabinet four silver-mounted pistols, laid them on the cushioned window-seat and regarded them pensively.

"What a contrary world it is, Mr Roberts," said he. "We lament the brief span afforded to us in our earthly pilgrimage and then we employ our ephemeral existence in making and using instruments to abbreviate further the lives of our fellows. Strange inconsistency!"

He reached down from a shelf a powder-flask and a leathern bag of balls, with which he proceeded to load the pistols in a very methodical and scientific fashion, clearing the vents with a large pin and finally filling the pans with fine mealed power. Then he wound around his middle a red silk sash, through which he passed the pistols, and once more looked out through the window.

"The mist rises, Mr Roberts," said he, "and the breeze is not far off. Let us go up and take the air."

He led me out of the door and up a pair of stairs on to the poop, from whence we were able to look down upon the whole of the main deck.

Here was a scene of disorder which appeared very strange to me after the discipline to which I had been accustomed. The unwashed deck, marked with many a dark and sinister stain, was filled with a rabble of unkempt ruffians, tricked out in all kinds of gaudy finery, but dirty and slovenly to the last degree, with their ragged hair streaming loose upon their shoulders and their beards long and matted, or plaited into tails, or curled into preposterous ringlets. Most of them wore large earrings, and many had great brooches and jewelled pins stuck into their frowsy shirts, while chains, and necklaces bearing pendants and even crucifixes, adorned necks that would have better fitted a hempen collar. Taken as a whole, they were the most repulsive villains that it has ever been my lot to see collected together.

As soon as we appeared, the whole mob surged aft talking loudly in half a dozen different languages, and making as if they would rush up the poop-ladder.

Observing this the captain advanced to the rail at the break, and, taking off his hat, raised his hand to command silence.

"My respected comrades," said he, as soon as he could make himself heard, "I have very gratifying news to impart, which I have but just learned from this gentleman, who does us the honour of accepting our hospitality. You will be pleased to hear that our little store is untouched. This gentleman was dispatched by the commander of His Majesty's ship to examine the pit, and he was, by some mischance, left behind when the vessel sailed. He assures me that no other excavation was made, and that he has seen no signs of the ground being disturbed, although I have satisfied myself that he has passed the locality of our store more than once. Hence there is, now, no need for us to revisit the spot, and we may proceed on our voyage without delay."

"What's a-going to be done with this here stranger?" demanded one of the crew as the captain finished his discourse and resumed his hat.

"Ah!" shouted another, "is he a-going to join the company or a-going overboard?"

"These are matters," answered the captain, "that shall be duly considered and settled to the satisfaction of all." He raised his hat once more and bowed to the company, and observing the last speaker to shake his fist at the poop, he smiled benevolently and kissed his hand.

"Let us walk," he said, drawing out one of his pistols to polish it with his handkerchief; "'twill presently be too hot, so we must take our exercise while we may."

We continued to pace the poop for half an hour, keeping on the same side of the long brass traverse gun that occupied the centre, and, during this time, my host conversed with easy fluency on a variety of topics; but I noticed that he never for a moment let his attention stray from the head of the poop ladder, and that one or other of the pistols required polishing as long as we remained on deck.

Chapter Eighteen

In which the Schooner is brought to her Berth

The remainder of this, my first day on board the pirate, I spent in the cabin, for the captain, having made his little demonstration of authority, did not appear to think it desirable to obtrude me further upon the notice of the crew.

Shortly after we came below, the fog having lifted completely and a light breeze having sprung up, Starbuck entered the cabin to report.

"The fog's cleared up, captain," said he, "and a nice little breeze a-tricklin' out of the nor'-west."

"Anything in sight?" inquired Parradine.

"Nary a rag nor a stick," answered Starbuck.

"Then, my dear Starbuck," said the captain, "we will shape a course north-east and set everything that will draw. A good look-out should be kept, Starbuck. Perhaps one of the gentleman-adventurers might wish to ascend 'the high and giddy mast'; the prospect from the topgallant yard, for instance, would be found most extensive and delightful."

"Right you are, captain," answered Starbuck, cocking his eye at me with a broad grin. "The crew," he continued, "is in a rare takin' about this here young fellow. They says as he has got to join or swim."

"Join or swim, eh?" repeated the Captain. "Merry knaves, merry knaves. Well, we will consider, Starbuck; I will put the case to our guest."

"Do you think," I asked, when Starbuck had retired, "that your crew would prefer that I should go adrift in my boat again?"

"I think not," was the reply; "nor should I desire to see such an expedient adopted. To their swinish intellects the alternatives, 'join or swim,' seem the only ones possible. They are but poor ignorant louts, Mr Roberts, whom we should pity even if we despise;

"'For knowledge to their eyes her ample page
Rich with the spoils of time did ne'er unroll.'

They must be led by the hand, sir (though 'tis a dirty hand); must be governed by the more potent and cultivated mind. What would your wishes be?"

"I should prefer to be put aboard some homeward-bound vessel," I answered, "or else set ashore at some frequented port."

"As to the former," said Parradine, "I fear that the peculiarities of our trade might render it difficult of accomplishment. As to the latter it may be done if we temporise with these ruffians until we make our port. In any case you must not join – nor swim," he added with a benevolent smile.

"May I ask whither you are bound?" I inquired.

"Our destination is a salubrious spot which I am acquainted with in the Sierra Leone River, where we propose to heave down and effect a few repairs. I had thought of Madagascar, but 'tis too far afield, and is, moreover, the common rendezvous of a parcel of rascally picaroons; so I preferred Sierra Leone. The schooner is not foul, as you may judge by her sailing, but there is some oozing below the waterline, and we think it well to adopt the new and excellent plan of sheathing her with copper."

"But surely," said I, "there is no copper sheathing to be had at Sierra Leone."

"You are perfectly correct, sir," replied the captain: "but the fact is we have recently had the good fortune to acquire, on most advantageous terms, a quantity of copper plates, with which we propose to sheath the vessel ourselves."

"And how long do you think it will take you to reach Sierra Leone?" I asked.

"In these latitudes," he answered, "the winds are fickle, especially under the line, but ours is a nimble craft, and if we are fortunate we may enter the river within a fortnight."

This was better than I had expected, though my position, meanwhile, was by no means all that I could have desired. I could not see how the demands of the crew were to be set aside, although it was manifest that Captain Parradine, in spite of his suave and oily manner, was a man of immovable resolution and unbounded courage, coolness, and resource.

Nor did I find it easy to explain his attitude towards me. A mere chance stranger, an ocean waif, I could be of no concern to him; and yet, unless he was deceiving me, he was prepared to oppose the wishes of the entire crew of ruthless scoundrels to whom he was a servant rather than a commander, for what? Simply to preserve me from the stigma of piracy. The thing was incomprehensible, and I could not banish from my mind a suspicion that under the cloak of pretended friendship, he concealed some treacherous design.

Towards evening Starbuck paid us another visit.

"Crump has the first watch," said he. "Shall I send him down or will you give me the orders for the night?"

"Tell him, with my compliments, Starbuck, to keep a bright look-out and heave the log now and again, and keep the reckoning carefully if he has to alter the course."

"Right, captain," said Starbuck; them after a pause, "What about this young man? The company says they wants to know without any more backin' and fillin'."

"I will confer with them in the morning," said Parradine calmly.

"They ain't in a pleasant frame of mind, captain," said Starbuck. "I wouldn't be surprised if some bedevilment was afoot."

"Ha!" exclaimed the captain, looking up quickly from the chart over which he was poring, "think ye so, my dear Starbuck. Well, we must be prepared; we must set the alarum. Tell Crump that we are setting the alarum in case he should wish to speak to me in his watch. And you let the fact leak out, 'twould be no harm. An accident would be such an unspeakably shocking thing."

"I'll tell Crump, and let someone overhear me," replied Starbuck with a chuckle. "They won't want no badger-drorin', I'll answer for it," and he departed, gurgling with inward mirth.

Shortly afterwards the captain proceeded to set the alarum, and a very curious process it was. Taking from a drawer in the cabinet a very large and powerful blunderbuss, he cleaned out its vent with great care, oiled the lock and examined the flint. Then he poured into it an enormous charge of powder, and, having secured this with several wads, filled up the barrel with about three-quarters of a pound of buckshot, mixed with slugs and pistol balls, and crammed another wad on top of all; and when he had primed it liberally with fine, mealed powder, he lashed this formidable engine of destruction to a large cleat − apparently fixed for the purpose − on the side of the cabin about two feet from the deck, in such a position that its muzzle pointed at the opening of the door.

"You will observe, sir," he remarked, setting the door ajar and peering out through the opening, "that the position is a very commanding one."

It certainly was. The door was in an angle, and as it opened one looked straight down the passage, or alleyway, leading from the main deck, the whole length of which would be raked by the fire of the blunderbuss. There was not a particle of shelter, even if an attacking party used a long spar to push open the door, and the position was, as the captain had said, strategically perfect.

The blunderbuss, then, being placed in position, Captain Parradine proceeded to attach to the trigger a thin line which was rove through two small pulley-blocks, one behind the gun and one fixed to a hook on the ceiling. To the end of the line was attached a seven-pound hand-lead which the captain propped up near the top of the door.

The alarum was now set and promised to be highly effective. As it stood, the door could be opened without difficulty for about six inches, but if that amount were exceeded, down would topple the lead, the blunderbuss would explode, and the entire length of the passage would be swept by a hail of missiles.

"Do you often set your alarum?" I inquired, as my host stepped back and viewed his invention with a satisfied smile.

"Not often," he replied. "On occasions when little misunderstandings arise, such as the present, I am led to take this precaution; but they are rare. On one of these occasions, not long since, a most regrettable accident occurred; for the silly fellows, in their high-spirited, frolicsome way, must needs burst into the cabin at midnight. A dreadful explosion followed, and it pains me to recall that many suffered injury – some, indeed, were cut off from among us – at which I was the more afflicted from being, as one might say, the innocent cause of the mishap."

Nothing happened that night, however, the former "mishap" having, no doubt, produced a certain moral effect, and I rose in the morning to find the schooner bowling along merrily to the song of the south-east trade wind.

After breakfast the captain went on deck to discuss my affairs with the company. He did not inform me what had passed, merely remarking that "he had settled that little affair for the present"; but I was relieved to find, when I ascended to the poop, that the crew made no further demonstrations of hostility, but, on the contrary, seemed disposed to treat me with a kind of ferocious amiability.

So, by degrees, I settled down into my place as a recognised supernumerary, with no definite duties, in great bodily comfort, and with nothing to disturb my peace of mind, excepting the fear that we might fall in with some defenceless merchantman or encounter one of His Majesty's cruisers; in which latter case I had little hope of escaping the doom that would overtake the rest of the crew.

We were singularly fortunate in the weather, for the trade wind followed us to within a few degrees of the line; and even then we were never quite becalmed, but, by carefully husbanding every cat's paw that stirred the tropic sea, we crawled foot by foot across the sweltering Doldrums until we were abreast of Cape Palmas.

This was on the thirteenth day out from the island, and the same afternoon we felt the first faint breath of the north-east trade wind, blowing cool and fresh off the mainland of Africa.

That evening, as the captain and I sat at the table with a bottle of burgundy before us, conversing on various topics relating to literature and the fine arts, my host having filled my glass and his own, leaned across the table and addressed me in low tone and with a decision and directness in strong contrast to his usual sententious affectation.

"Mr Roberts," said he, "I have a certain matter to put before you which is of vital moment to us both, and for this reason, and also that I conceive you to be a man worthy of trust, I shall speak without reserve, relying on your discretion and secrecy.

"I have learned today from Starbuck – who, though he is the company's quarter-master, is yet entirely faithful to me – that the crew have decided to depose me – fools that they are.

"Their intention is to allow me to direct the refitting of the schooner and bring her out to sea, and, as soon as we are clear of the land, take the first opportunity of putting a bullet through me. Now I have managed to quell temporary and partial revolts, time and again; but this is an organised plot. They are tired of me and want a commander of their own kind, which means that it is time for me to go.

> " 'Lusisti satis, edisti satis, atque bibisti;
> Tempus est tibi abire.' "

(He could not resist the temptation to quote, even in this council of war).

"Now, as to yourself. You may fitly say to me, in the words of the faithful Ruth, 'whither thou goest, I go' – and that will be overboard unless we have a care. If you would see your home again, you must cast in your lot with mine for the present, and, when I give the word, we must act together."

"Have you settled on any definite course of action?" I asked.

"No," he answered, "I shall wait an opportunity; and when the proper moment arrives, I shall go forth, even like unto the patriarch Lot – and convey a few trifles with me."

"Can you explain," I inquired, "why your crew have taken this sudden resolution against you?"

"It is not sudden," he replied. "I have been looking for an explosion for months past. You must perceive that there could be no sympathy between me and the rabble of illiterate ruffians that form the company; and the incongruity between our natures and habits has ever been a source of mutual distrust. And there is one little matter in particular that has aggravated their suspicions of me – and not without reason. You must know that it has been our custom, from time to time, to deposit the proceeds of our cruises in certain hiding-places on shore! Now the men in general have been content to conceal the whole of the goods, bringing to sea with them nothing but a few gold pieces for play, and such jewellery as they chose to wear on their persons. I, on the other hand, have been accustomed to bring to sea and keep in my cabin all the gold and jewels that fell to my share, having them packed in small and portable cases. This proceeding of mine they have viewed with deep distrust, and, despite the most plausible explanations, have persisted in regarding it as proof of an intention on my part to decamp – in which surmise they have been entirely correct; for it has always, since I entered the trade, been my fixed purpose to retire, in due course, with a modest competency, and spend the remainder of my life in the society of persons of cultivation, amidst the delights of gentle and rural surroundings. My worthy company propose to acquire, by summary measures, the reversion of my small property; but, with your esteemed support, I have little doubt of disappointing them. By the way, are you disposed to join me in a small adventure?"

"Of what kind?" I asked.

"Why, I have mentioned that a substantial deposit of valuable property is lying unclaimed on a certain island. Now this landing-place of yours would make it moderately easy for two resolute men to remove the whole to a place of safety. I have considered a plan and should have great pleasure in submitting it for your approval. What say you? 'Tis a great property – indeed I may say 'twould be a fortune for each of us."

"I am not ambitious to be rich, Captain Parradine," said I, "and I should be loath to meddle with goods to which I have no claim. In any projects for your escape from this vessel you may look to me for loyal and hearty support, but as to this adventure, I must confess that it is not to my liking."

"As you will, my friend," rejoined Parradine, a little coolly, and I assumed that he was annoyed at my implied condemnation of his mode of life, for he sipped his wine with a thoughtful and abstracted air, and did not speak again for some time.

"Is not Sierra Leone a place somewhat frequented by shipping?" I asked presently.

"A goodly number of vessels put in there to wood and water," he replied, "especially slavers from Senegal and Gambia or from Cape Mount and the Windward Coast. 'Twas formerly a great rendezvous for pirates, for the anchorage is excellent and one can land in a ship's boat; but 'tis now principally resorted to by slavers and other Guineamen."

"Do you know many of the slavers?" I inquired.

"I have made the acquaintance of quite a number of them," he answered, with a dry smile.

"Then," said I, "you may, perchance, have met one, Enoch Murking, who trades upon this coast."

"Murking!" mused Parradine, tapping his forehead with his forefinger.

"The master of a ship called the *Charity*," I added.

"Oh! The *Charity*!" exclaimed my host. "Yes, yes. Enoch Murking, ha! ha! Yes, I remember him; a godly soul and well nourished, if I mistake not,

" 'Justice in fair, round belly with good capon lines.'

I remember him, indeed, and I make no doubt he remembers me."

He chuckled at the recollection (the nature of which I had little difficulty in guessing at) and was so much amused that his good humour was completely restored; and he sat for a long time before we turned in, regaling me with stories of the Guinea trade, by some of which I was much more entertained than edified.

The following morning as we sat at breakfast the captain addressed to me a few more words of warning and instruction.

"We are now, Mr Roberts," said he, "close upon our destination, and I must exhort you to consider our position most earnestly. We must show no inkling of suspicion, no hint of distrust; we must go about our business of refitting with every sign of eager interest in the schooner's welfare. We must be assiduous ourselves and must insist on the utmost assiduity in others. You understand me?"

I assured him that I fully grasped the situation and would follow his instructions to the letter.

Shortly afterwards we ascended to the deck and the spectacle that there unfolded itself to my vision filled me with admiration and delight. We were close in to the land, having just rounded the wooden promontory of Cape Sierra Leone. On our right hand lay the high ground of the Cape, clothed in the richest verdure down to the very water's edge, where lofty strangely-shaped trees and clumps of graceful palms gave to the landscape an aspect at once unfamiliar and gorgeous with tropic luxuriance. Behind the Cape the land rose until the low peaks of the Sierra closed in the view, and over all extended the rich mantle of green tinged with blue.

On the left hand a low-lying shore jutted out and receded, and straight ahead lay the wide expanse of land-locked water, its calm surface supporting a fleet of anchored vessels.

The tide was running in as we entered, and the schooner glided swiftly along the shore, now opening some little hamlet and now losing it again behind a grove of trees, and soon we began to draw near the anchorage. I saw the captain scrutinising the vessels with unconcealed anxiety, and it was with profound relief that I presently heard him report that there were no vessels of war among them.

As we held on our way without shortening sail, it was not long before we found ourselves among the shipping; and it was not difficult to see that our appearance excited considerable interest; for, whenever we passed near to a vessel, the entire crew could be seen watching us, the officers mounted on the poop with spy-glasses and the men on the forecastle or in the lower rigging.

"What can be the meaning of that noise?" I asked as we passed a large snow, from which proceeded a most dismal clanking, mingled with groans and shouts.

"They are exercising the slaves," answered Parradine. "The poor devils are made to jump in their chains, to keep them in condition; and, in case they should fail to dance and sing with due cheerfulness, a seaman stands by, ready to encourage them with a few strokes of the cat."

"'Tis a most abominable traffic," I exclaimed, "and a disgrace to our country, which boasts of the freedom of its people."

"You are right, Mr Roberts," he agreed, "though the boast is but an empty one, as you and I can testify. But 'tis a scurvy trade, as you say, this slaving, though mighty profitable, let me tell you. Here is another of them if I mistake not."

He indicated a small ship that we were approaching, and, as I turned to look at her, I started.

"Why," I exclaimed, "'tis the *Charity* – Mr Murking's ship."

"I believe you are correct, sir," said Parradine. "I seem to distinguish the touching allegorical group under her bowsprit. Yes, yes, ha! ha!" he continued as we swept past the lumpish, ill-favoured craft, "and do I not perceive, upon the poop, the attenuated form of our graceful and godly friend?"

It was Murking beyond all doubt, his unwieldy figure appearing even more enormous in a white linen coat. He stared at us as we passed, and suddenly diving below, reappeared with a telescope, which he levelled at our poop and through which he was still examining us when he grew small in the distance.

"Some chord of memory has been touched, I surmise," remarked Parradine, with a smile, as he looked back at the diminishing white figure. "The good ship *Autolycus* is not unknown to fame."

"Let us hope," I said, "that no cruiser will come into the river while Murking is about."

"Ah! That I grant you, would be highly unpleasant," answered the captain, "though, thanks to the press, the traders give His Majesty's ships nearly as wide a berth as I should. But methinks I perceive another acquaintance of mine – yes, and the recognition is mutual."

He pointed, as he spoke, to smart-looking polacre brig, from which a boat was putting out into the fairway, and, as the schooner and the boat approached, a man was seen standing in the stern-sheets of the latter, waving a handkerchief.

"Luff up and back the topsail, Starbuck," shouted Parradine; "here is someone who wishes to speak to us."

The topsail was set aback immediately, and, as the schooner's way deadened, the boat shot alongside and the man who had made the signal scrambled into the main chains and ran up on to the poop.

"Fortune is kind indeed, my dear Cotter," exclaimed Parradine, shaking the stranger's hand cordially, "to send my old comrade to welcome me on my arrival."

"Aye, captain," replied Cotter, "she's always kind to you. But you've only just caught me."

"Why, when do you sail?" asked the captain anxiously.

"I shall drop down on the ebb," answered Cotter. "There's a lading of black ivory waiting for me now at Cape Mount."

Parradine took the stranger apart, out of my hearing, and the two men conversed earnestly and hurriedly for a few minutes. Then our visitor, with an anxious glance over the taffrail at the receding anchorage, disengaged himself.

"I must be off, captain," said he, "or we shall never get back against this tide. You may depend on me, so far," he added in a lower tone, but, remember, I can't stay after I have shipped the goods. Black ivory is a perishable cargo."

With this he dropped down into the boat, and, as he pushed off, the topsail-yards were swung and the schooner gathered way again.

"An old quarter-master of mine," remarked the captain, "and now master of that extremely elegant brig. A simple, honest soul, to whom I trust I may have the honour of presenting you shortly. We now approach our destination, and I would again impress on you the necessity of preserving an appearance of cheerful alacrity. The mangrove already begins to close in on us, and in half an hour I hope we shall be in our berth."

The scene was changing rapidly as we advanced. The broad, lake-like estuary was narrowing into the proportions of a not very wide river, and on either hand the banks were hidden by what looked like a tall hedge of a sad, colourless green. The trees which formed this hedge seemed to grow out of the water and to be destitute of trunks, and, as the river narrowed, I perceived that they stood upon a strange tangle of submerged roots.

Nearer and nearer the melancholy walls of sage-coloured foliage approached, hemming us in by degrees, until a turn of the river carried us out of sight of the estuary and nothing was to be seen but an unbroken expanse of leaves and branches.

The wall of vegetation that shut out the view also intercepted the breeze, and the schooner now drifted helplessly though swiftly, on the tide, with her sails hanging motionless from the spars.

"Bend a tripping-line on to the bower-anchor, Starbuck," said the captain, "and let go enough cable to drag lightly."

The order was quickly carried out. The anchor splashed into the water, and the vessel soon came round head to the tide stream and so continued to drift up, stern foremost, with just enough drag of the anchor to render her obedient to the helm.

In this manner we proceeded for about half an hour with gradually diminishing speed – for it was near upon high water and the tide was beginning to slacken – when, just after we had rounded a rather abrupt bend in the river, there appeared on the larboard side a narrow opening in the mangrove – apparently the mouth of a creek.

"Give her another dozen fathoms of cable," sang out the captain; and, as the rope ran out through the hawse-hole, the anchor took hold of the ground, and the schooner brought up just above the opening.

"Now, gentlemen, if you please," said the captain, bending urbanely over the poop-rail to address the crew, " '*Ars longa, vita brevis,*' and also 'Time and tide wait for no man.' We must get our warps out and take her in to her berth on the top of the tide. I would suggest that if the pinnace were lowered into her native element the warps might be carried into the creek with conveniency and dispatch."

The grinning seamen, with many a wink and nudge at their commander's fine phrases, hoisted out the pinnace and brought her to the gangway. Two or three coils of rope were flung into her, when the captain, motioning me to follow him, descended the poop-ladder and stepped down into the boat.

The opening in the mangrove extended as a straight, narrow passage for about a hundred yards; then it made a sharp turn and widened out considerably until it ended at a hard, or beach, at the foot of a slopping bank, on which a number of tall timber trees grew. From one side of the beach a spit of land ran out for some twenty yards, and I judged – correctly as it presently turned out – that the captain intended to run the schooner alongside of this. We pulled up the passage as far as the bend, and, when the captain had examined the beach from this position, one of the warps was made fast to the roots of the mangrove and we pulled back to the schooner, paying out the rope as we went.

By this time the tide was slack; so, having carried the end of the warp on board, we manned the capstan and hoisted up the anchor; then all hands tailed on to the warp, to the pull of which the schooner was soon creeping up the passage, with her yard-arms stirring the foliage on either side.

As we approached the bend in the creek, the pinnace was sent out ahead with two more warps, one of which was secured to a tree above the beach; and by hauling on these handsomely, the schooner was presently brought alongside the spit, where she took the ground, with her jibboom overhanging the margin of the beach.

In this berth we were completely enclosed by the mangrove and invisible from the river, and I could not but admire the judgment with which the locality had been selected; for, if any other vessel had chanced to ascend the river, it was in the highest degree improbable that our existence would have been discovered.

The captain was not slow to put into practice those principles which he had so strongly inculcated; for, pausing in his labours only to snatch a hasty meal, he urged forward the work with the greatest eagerness and enthusiasm. No sooner had the vessel taken the ground than all the spars were swung out to starboard to cant her over towards the spit; and the instant that the men had finished their dinner he was out on the deck spurring them on to renewed exertions. A long spar was rigged as a derrick, with which to hoist out the contents of the hold; the hatches were removed; a gang of men sent below; another stationed on deck to heave at the hoisting tackle, and a third party sent ashore on to the spit.

Then commenced the work of hoisting out the ballast. This was in the form of lead pigs – a costly material (but what matters the cost of a thing that is never paid for?) though highly efficient for the purpose – and a quantity of copper plates, which were to be used for the sheathing, had been used in a similar fashion. These were now hooked on to the tackle by the gang of men below, hoisted up by those on deck, and, having been swung out-board, were received by the men on shore and neatly built up into a stack on the end of the spit.

Bearing in mind the captain's advice I threw myself into the work with a degree of energy that won the warmest approval of the pirate crew, heaving at the fall of the tackle as though my life depended on the speed with which the task was accomplished.

To do the rascals justice they were by no means backward at the labour, arduous as it was in the steamy, oppressive air of the mangrove swamp, but worked with a will that surprised me, calling for no rest and but little refreshment until the evening mists began to steal along the dull surface of the water. By that time all the copper plates were ashore and the stack of lead pigs had grown to a size that was quite impressive, when the weight of the material was considered.

When the day's work was finished, the captain showed a prudent indulgence by bringing up from the lazarette a small cask of Madeira which he presented to the crew with his compliments, that they might spend a pleasant evening; which they apparently did, for the creek resounded with their songs, shouts and laughter until the mosquitoes came out in swarms and drove them down into the 'tween-decks.

That night, as we sat perspiring in the cabin over a bottle of Canary, the captain was unusually silent and thoughtful. Considering that he was probably maturing his scheme for our escape, I did not disturb him with any attempts at conversation, but occupied myself with my own thoughts.

"This has been a pleasant and peaceful halting-place in life's pilgrimage," said Parradine at length, sipping his wine and gazing round the trim, well-furnished apartment. "Many a quiet hour has slipped away while I have sat in this cabin, like a hermit in his cell, holding sweet converse with the master minds of a dead-and-gone age; hours that have glided past as softly as the shadow that creeps over the face of a sundial upon a summer's day. Well, well! Those hours are gone, Mr Roberts, and cannot be recalled except by memory; out of the void they came, bringing their joys and their sorrows (fleeting and ephemeral as themselves) to be gathered in with the great harvest of Time.

" 'Tempora labuntur, quae nobis pereunt et imputantur.'

But they were pleasant times, believe me, sir, full of serene content and lofty meditation, when I have sat here with the flowers peeping in at the window, and old Ocean murmuring his soft refrain without. Here has the pastoral song of sweet-tongued Virgil come to me from the shade of the spreading beech-tree, telling me of rustling leaves and lowing herds and all things rustic and peaceful.

" 'Haec super arvorum cultu pecorumque canebam
    Et super arboribus';

Yes, sir; not to Tityrus alone were those melodious numbers sung, but also to Ishmael Parradine, swaying in his sea-parlour, twenty centuries distant."

Being somewhat overpowered by this outburst on my host's part I made no reply, but merely pushed the bottle towards him, when he refilled his glass and mine and presently resumed:

"Those quiet hours of study and reflection will be to me among the most delightful of recollections, and so 'tis wise and good to dwell upon them; for should we not rise superior to fickle fortune if, like the sundial of which I spoke, we let the storm-cloud pass unnoted and mark the sunshine only. So would I do, and, in memory at least, let the dark days fade forthwith into oblivion and leave me no remembrances save those of summer pleasure.

" *'Horas non numero nisi serenas.'*

'Tis a wise man's resolution and shall be mine.

"But why do I speak in this strain? you are doubtless asking yourself. I will answer you. It is because already I read the 'Finis' at the end of one volume of my life, and, as yet, I cannot see the title-page of the next. I am like one turning out of a comfortable inn to wend his way upon an unknown road; and you may believe me, Mr Roberts, that when a man has reached my years, he does not set out upon such a journey without many a wistful look behind. I am looking my last upon the little home that has sheltered me for so long; for this, Mr Roberts, is, I trust, our last night on board. Where we shall be tomorrow night, God alone can tell."

"Then you intend that we shall escape tomorrow," I asked eagerly.

"That is my purpose, if a fitting opportunity should occur, as I have little doubt it will."

"And have you any plans for our disposal after leaving the schooner?"

"I have many," he replied somewhat curtly, "but 'twere idle to discuss them, since our actions must be, after all, determined by chance circumstances."

Seeing that he evidently did not wish to take me into his confidence, I turned the conversation into other channels; and after we had sat talking for another half-hour, we turned in to rest, so that we might be ready to resume the unloading at daybreak.

CHAPTER NINETEEN

In which Captain Parradine calls Checkmate

When I came out on to the poop soon after daybreak, the schooner was enveloped in a dense white mist, very chilly and damp, by which even the mangrove was completely hidden; but as the sun rose the mist gradually melted away, and, one after another, the different objects emerged, thin and shadowy at first, but growing more distinct by degrees, until the whole of the creek was visible. And a very singular appearance it presented, though, indeed, I had little leisure to observe it; for, no sooner had we swallowed a hasty breakfast than the work of swaying out the ballast commenced again; but in the brief pauses in our labour I took the opportunity to gaze about me, and never, I thought, had I looked upon a stranger spectacle.

The tide was now low, and, where the yellow water had been, was an expanse of slimy grey mud, out of which arose, on either side the forest of mangrove, the whole dense mass of trees raised high above the surface on tall stilted roots. The appearance – indeed the reality – was that of a vast plantation raised on piles, or as if a multitude of pollard trees had been stood on their heads and made to support a forest of erect saplings.

The roots themselves were coated with grey mud and encrusted with thick-shelled, misshapen oysters; and small, purple-bodied crabs crawled over them and roamed up the branches far overhead, perching among the leaves in the most incongruous manner, and endeavouring, unsuccessfully, to pry into the bird's nests, which hung, like small globular baskets, from the festoons of creepers that trailed from bough to bough.

The surface of the mud was tenanted by a multitude of creatures which, at first, I took to be frogs, as they hopped or walked somewhat after the same fashion as those reptiles; but, when I examined them through a glass, I was astonished to find that they were fish – somewhat like a gurnet in shape, but furnished with two legs like the hind-legs of a toad, with which they were able to take short hops or walk quite briskly. They moved for the most part in regular processions, each party composed, apparently, of an entire family, for at the head marched a large fish – probably the patriarch or grandfather – followed by his relations in a diminishing scale until the rear was brought up by a rabble of tiny fishlings no larger than minnows, waddling along at the top of their speed to keep up with their elders.

By the time we had been at work three hours, everything of weight had been hove out of the hold and landed; not only the ballast, but also a great store of round shot, and bags of grape and langridge. All that now remained was the powder in the magazine and the provisions in the lazarette, and these it had been decided not to put ashore.

The tide had now begun to run up the creek, and as the water rose around the schooner she floated like a bladder; so that I was surprised that the weight of her guns and top-hamper did not capsize her; from which accident, I suppose, she was saved by her great beam and the flatness of her floor. As she rose the slack of the warp was taken in from time to time, and at high water two large ropes were passed out through the hawse-holes and carried ashore. Then the whole ship's company landed with powerful tackles, and, when these had been clapped on to the ropes, they all tailed on to the falls and hauled together; by which the schooner was dragged forward until her forefoot was on the beach.

"Now, gentlemen," said the captain, "we will get the boats ashore out of the way, and then we can take a little midday siesta before commencing the unromantic pastime of scraping."

There were five boats in all, four of them being large and heavy, as required for boarding purposes, while the fifth was the jolly-boat – a small, light craft, sharper and swifter than such boats usually are.

The pinnace was already in the water, and, with our large crew, it was not long before the rest were afloat. Just as the little fleet was moving off shorewards, the captain called out, as if by an afterthought:

"We will keep the jolly-boat under the stern, if you please. I shall want to examine the schooner's sides before the tide runs out."

The jolly-boat was accordingly made fast to the taffrail, while the others were conveyed ashore, with the tools required for the afternoon's work; and presently they were all drawn up, high and dry, on the beach.

"Now I think we may take a short spell of repose, gentlemen," the captain sang out, "and refresh ourselves for our afternoon's labours."

The men trooped up the beach and sat or lay down in groups in the shade of the trees, leaving the schooner untenanted save for the captain, myself, and the black servant, Quassie.

"I think our opportunity has come, Mr Roberts," said Parradine, as he watched the men settling down to rest under the trees, "but we must be prompt, for the tide is ebbing fast and the creek will soon be dry. Come below and I will show you what is to be done."

We descended to the cabin, where I perceived four small, iron-bound cases ranged along the stern. Each was furnished with strong beckets, or rope handles, and, though none of them was more than eighteen inches long, when I lifted them, at the captain's desire, I was astonished at their weight.

"These contain my little fortune," said Parradine, "for my books I must leave with these unlettered ruffians. They are to be lowered into the jolly-boat with this watch-tackle, the sheaves of which I have oiled well that they may run silently. Hook the tackle on to the dead-light staple above the window and lower the cases one by one when I give the word, and be careful to make no noise. Now I am going to examine the schooner's sides, that Quassie and I may get into the boat without arousing suspicion. Do you have everything in readiness so that no time be lost."

With this he departed and I heard him walk along the poop, overhead, to the taffrail, where he evidently cast off the boat's painter, for the next moment she was drawn away from under the stern.

As soon as he was gone, I set about my task, being as anxious as he not to lose this chance of escaping. Opening one of the windows, I took the flower-pots from their place on the little balcony and set them on the floor. Then I hooked the double block of the tackle on to the staple above the window and the single, or lower block on to the becket of one of the cases. I had hardly completed these preparations when the boat appeared round the schooner's quarter, rowed by Quassie, while the captain stood up in the stern-sheets holding in his hand a scraper with which he had apparently been testing the vessel's sides.

As the boat backed in under the counter, he grasped a rudder-chain and looked up.

"Now Mr Roberts," sad he softly, "lower away as quietly as you can."

I hauled on the fall of the tackle, and, as the case ascended through the window, I eased it over the balcony, and then lowered. The well-greased sheaves of the tackle ran almost without noise, and when I felt the rope slacken, I looked out and saw the captain disengage the hook from the case, which lay snugly in the bottom of the boat.

Hauling up the tackle I hooked on the second case, and soon had the satisfaction of seeing it safely deposited beside the first; and so with the third, which I was just in the act of lowering, when I heard a hoarse shout from the shore:

"Hullo, there! What's a-doin'? I say, mates, they're a-lettin something down into the jolly-boat."

"Never mind the other case," shouted the captain; "come down yourself."

But he had already unhooked the tackle from the one I had just lowered, and, as I was loath that he should be the loser by his solicitude for me, I hauled it up quickly, regardless now of the noise, hooked on the last case, and let it run down.

"Quick, for your life!" he shouted, looking up anxiously as he disengaged the hook once more; "they are coming down the beach," and, as an uproar of angry voices caught my ear, I climbed out through the window, and, grasping the four ropes of the tackle, slid down into the boat.

"Pull away!" exclaimed the captain, giving the boat a vigorous shove off, and seating himself in the stern. "The sooner we are out of pistol shot the better."

Neither the negro nor I required any urging to exert our utmost strength at the oars, for the pirates were swarming up the shore-ropes, and already several had gained the deck and were running aft. As they reached the poop I saw them, to my unspeakable horror, slew round the long gun and train it on the boat. That gun, as I knew, was kept loaded, and as I watched the bloodthirsty villain of a gunner squinting along the barrel at us, I gave myself up for lost; for with his reputed skill as a marksman he could hardly miss us at so short a range.

I saw the tompion whipped out of the muzzle, and the apron removed; and then the gunner, having taken a final aim, held a pistol to the touch-hole of the gun.

I waited, with my heart in my mouth, for the explosion that was to blow us out of the water, while Quassie shrieked aloud. There was a flash from the pistol, a report, and a small wreath of smoke, but the great gun had not spoken, and as the smoke cleared away I saw the gunner frantically digging into the vent-hole, while several men rushed down the poop-ladder.

A few moments later they reappeared carrying muskets and priming them as they ran, while one man emptied a powder-flask on the vent of the gun; but just as the muskets were being levelled at us, the boat swept round the bend of the creek and entered the passage into the river. The loud report of a volley of muskets reached our ears, and the bullets hummed so close around us that several leaves came fluttering down into the boat; but none struck us, and after this demonstration we heard no more from our invisible enemies.

"'Tis mighty fortunate," said I, "that the gun missed fire."

"The gun?" said Parradine; "did they endeavour to fire the gun at us?"

"That they did," I answered; "but Providence favoured us, for by some chance the charge failed to ignite, and the gun missed fire."

"Ha!" said the captain thoughtfully; "missed fire, hey? A trifling dampness of the powder, no doubt, would account for the mishap. Perchance a cup of water that I carelessly spilled down the vent last night may have occasioned it. But 'twas as well, for while our friends were amusing themselves with the gun, their minds were diverted from the more dangerous subject of muskets and pistols."

"I suppose we shall have the rascals on our heels very shortly," said I, pulling at my oar with the energy of desperation.

"I think not," replied the captain. "The tide was ebbing fast when the boats were drawn up on the beach; by now there is a dozen yards of dry mud between them and the creek, and even if it were possible to carry the heavy boats over the mud, there is not now enough water in the creek to float them. In this light boat we were only just in time. Look at the blade of your own oar, for instance."

I lifted the oar, and then perceived that the blade was covered with black mud, into which I had been driving it at each stroke without observing the fact in my excitement.

We now emerged into the main river, and were immediately caught up by the swift tide stream and whirled along past the walls of mangrove at a speed that promised to give us a good start, even if we were pursued. But no signs of our enemies were to be heard and, at the captain's suggestion, Quassie and I moderated our exertions.

"Do you think," I asked presently, "that the men will refloat the schooner and sail out in search of us?"

"'Twould not be possible at present," replied the captain. "Yesterday was the top of the spring tide, and for the next six days every tide will be lower than the last. Now, seeing that we hove her fairly high and dry, she will not float again until the next spring tide, nearly a fortnight hence, by which time, I trust, we shall be far to seek."

"You have shown your customary foresight, I observe," said I, laughing, "and doubtless the remainder of the programme is arranged with like completeness. May I ask whither we are now bound?"

"Why, there it is, sir," he answered. "The chance meeting with my old friend Cotter made me hope to have all things settled to a nicety; but, as you heard him say, he was off to Cape Mount, and must have sailed out on the ebb yesterday. At Cape Mount he will remain a day or two, but he is no laggard, as I know well, and his brig is as nimble as her master. We may catch him before he sails, but 'tis more likely that we find him gone."

"How far is it to Cape Mount?" I asked.

"A matter of three hundred and fifty miles," he answered, "and an easy journey at that, for the north-east trade is a fair wind all the way, and it seldom fails one entirely north of Cape Palmas."

"Could we not make the passage in the boat?" I inquired.

"We could," answered the captain, "but 'twould take us between three and four days at the best, sailing night and day; indeed we should probably take longer, for though the weather is fair enough at this time of year, the sea is very large outside, and a boat's sail is becalmed half of the time by the high billows. Even a slow ship, having her sails constantly filled, would cover the distance much more quickly."

"What do you propose to do, then?" said I.

"I shall speak to some of the slavers in the anchorage," he replied, "and offer a round sum for a passage to Cape Mount. The passage-money will go into the captain's pocket, so there will probably be little difficulty."

"Perhaps Mr Murking would take pity on us," I suggested, with a laugh.

"Ah, good, pious soul!" said the captain, highly amused, as he always was at the mention of Murking's name. "'Twould be a work of charity indeed, and, as the holy á Kempis truly observes, 'He alone is truly great who is great in Charity.' But if 'charity covereth a multitude of sins' – as I doubt not she does at this moment – she is a dull sailer, and I would fain be carried to my destination by some less full-bosomed craft."

At this moment we rounded the last bend of the river, and the broad, land-locked water lay before us. Simultaneously we felt the cool breeze, and, by the captain's direction, Quassie and I unshipped our oars and hoisted the sail, when the light boat, impelled by wind and tide, sped over the calm water in gallant style.

As we weathered the island that lies near the middle of the great harbour, we came in sight of the anchorage, and Parradine peered eagerly under the foot of the sail.

"There is a ship that seems to be getting ready to weigh," said he, "and if I mistake not the cut of the rags that she is hanging out from her spars she is that very *Charity* of which we were speaking."

I looked under the sail at the distant vessel, and a single glance convinced me that the captain was right in his surmise.

"And why not the *Charity*, if she is going our way?" I asked. "Will she not do as well as another?"

The captain pondered a while.

"Why, the fact is," said he at length, "that Mr Murking and I have met before, and that in circumstances less profitable to him than to me. But on those occasions I have been accustomed to take some trifling precautions against recognition, and as I judge by our friend's obliquity of expression that his eyesight is none of the best, 'tis just possible that he may fail to recognise an old acquaintance; in which case I should refrain from jogging his memory. Yes, if he sails our way I will take the risk; that is if you are willing, for he will hardly have forgotten you."

"Oh, as to me!" I answered cheerfully, "he will welcome me with open arms. He still thinks me a fugitive from justice, worth two hundred pounds, and will regard me as the very apple of his eye."

The captain laughed with great enjoyment.

"Here is a truly humorous situation," chuckled he; "and now I would not change the *Charity* for the swiftest craft in the harbour."

While we had been talking the *Charity* had set her sails and was apparently ready to weigh, and I feared we should miss her, after all, when I noticed a shore boat pulling towards her, in the stern of which was a bulky white figure. We watched the boat run alongside the ship, we saw the white-clad figure ascend to the deck, and then, as the boat pushed off, the clink of the capstan-pawl was borne to our ears, announcing that the anchor was being hove in. Before it had broken out, however, we were within hailing distance, and, lowering the sail and mast, ran the jolly-boat alongside at the gangway.

Murking, who was on the quarter-deck, came and looked down at us with sour curiosity.

"Well," said he, "what do you want?"

"Good day to you, sir," said Parradine suavely, as he climbed the side, followed closely by me; "Captain Murking, if I am not misinformed."

"You are not misinformed, sir," replied Murking, apparently comprehending Parradine and me simultaneously with his respective eyes. Suddenly the effective eye travelled my way, whereupon Murking stared at me in the greatest astonishment.

"Gracious Heaven!" he exclaimed, "do my eyes deceive me, or is it really Mr Roberts?"

"'Tis the same, sir," I answered, "miraculously preserved to throw himself once more upon your" – I was about to say charity, but corrected the phrase to "hospitality."

"And in what manner can I be of service to you and your friend?" inquired Murking, thawing with suspicious suddenness.

"We would venture to inquire whither you are bound?" interrupted Parradine.

"I am bound for Annambo, on the Gold Coast," replied Murking.

"Then in that case," said Parradine, "we would crave a passage as far as Cape Mount, if you would do us so great a favour, and I shall have great pleasure in being answerable for any charges that you may make in respect of our accommodation."

"Be pleased, sir, to consider my ship and myself entirely at your service," said Murking, with a bow; "and now, as the anchor is aweigh, 'twould be well if the boatman should hand up your baggage and push off."

"The negro, sir, is my servant," said Parradine, "and the boat is mine, since I must needs buy her to obtain the use of her, and the cases are too heavy to hand up the side."

"I understand, sir," said Murking – with more truth, I suspect, than he intended to convey – "the cases shall be carefully hoisted on board, and we shall find room for the boat too."

A couple of sailors were told off to hoist up the cases with a stout rope, and then, as the davits at the stern were unoccupied, the jolly-boat was hauled up under the taffrail.

"You would wish to stow the cases in the great cabin, no doubt," said Murking.

"I should certainly prefer it, if I might be so indulged," answered Parradine.

"Then, sir," rejoined Murking, "let us convey them thither."

With this he caught up one of the cases by its becket and staggered off to a door under the break of the poop. I took another and followed, and Parradine, rather to my surprise – for he was a slight-looking man, though squarely built – picked up the remaining two and marched after us without any particular show of exertion.

The great cabin of the *Charity*, which was half a dozen steps below the level of the main deck, furnished great contrast to that of the pirate schooner. Clean and neat it certainly was, for a shipmaster needs be orderly in his habits if he would make existence tolerable in the confined space of a single apartment, but yet there was in its aspect something coarse and sordid. The table was bare, the chairs no better than those of a village alehouse; the bookshelf contained a few shabby volumes – navigation tables, sailing directions, a Bible, and one or two account books – the chart-table displayed a quadrant case and a chronometer, and the walls were garnished with bunches of handcuffs, shackles, and iron collars, so that the place looked like a turnkey's office. The dreadful suggestiveness of these latter objects was emphasised by piles of iron chain coiled down in the corners, and especially by a row of half a dozen instruments suspended from pegs on the forward bulkhead, in which I recognised my old acquaintance, the thumb-screws.

But it was not the eye alone that was the channel of disagreeable impressions in this retreat; the air itself was pervaded by a subtle effluvium – which I had already noticed on deck – of a most penetrating and repulsive character, at which I had observed Captain Parradine to make a wry face as he entered.

As soon as we had deposited the cases on the deck by the bulkhead, Murking excused himself, with a hint that he would prefer us to remain in the cabin.

"Pray, gentlemen," said he, "be seated, and consider this humble abode as your own; and you will pardon me if I leave you for a while to attend to the affairs of the ship."

"Bah!" exclaimed Parradine, as Murking left the cabin, "what a foul, stinking traffic is this! Thank God the breeze is on the quarter. Come to the window, Mr Roberts, and let us breathe the pure air. When I look at that greasy, hypocritical villain I feel a new-born kindness to my deserted flock on the schooner. Beasts of prey they are indeed, and savage enough at that; but this fellow is a mere mawworm, a bot, a devourer of living flesh."

He spat out of the window and flung himself into a chair with an expression of infinite disgust, and so remained for a while staring out at the verdant slope of the land and the dwindling anchorage.

"Our friend," said Parradine presently, "has quicker wits than I had bargained for. He knew me at the first glance."

"I had that impression myself," said I.

"Yes," pursued the captain, "he knew us and judged we might be made to yield a profit. Did you note his sudden suavity? Did you observe how courteously he refrained from inconvenient questions? Why, he has not even inquired my name unless he has by this put the question to Quassie, and learned that his guest is Mr James Dawson."

Here he smiled genially, for by this name we had agreed that he was to be called, and the black had received most emphatic instructions to that effect.

"He is a deep villain, is this pious host of ours," continued Parradine, "and purposes, no doubt, to play us some scurvy trick. Aye, I warrant his fat brain is busy with our affairs at this very moment!

Well, well. We are not babes in the wood, neither, and perchance we may clap a deuce on his knave, after all. But we must watch him like a cat at a mouse-hole."

"He will have to make his plans quickly," said I, "seeing that you purpose to leave him so soon."

"*I* purpose?" said the captain inquiringly. "Do you not purpose also to ship with my friend Cotter?"

"Whither is he bound?" I asked.

"To the Havana," answered Parradine; "but I shall probably leave him at Barbadoes."

"For my part," said I, "seeing that the *Asphodel* is cruising in those waters, and will probably stop every slaver for the purpose of impressing part of the crew, I shall give the West Indies a wide berth."

"Think again, my friend," said Parradine. "At one of the islands I could buy a small fishing craft which you and I and Quassie could work without assistance, with which we could proceed to our island, berth in your haven, and fill up at our leisure with enough valuable property to enable us to live in luxury for the rest of our days. 'Tis a great opportunity, Mr Roberts."

"It is, I grant you," I replied, "and most handsome of you to offer to share so valuable a booty with a penniless waif such as I am. But my whole desire is to return to my home, and that I shall best accomplish by staying here, if Mr Murking will have me, until I may escape on to some homeward-bound vessel."

The captain seemed greatly concerned at my resolution, and urged me repeatedly to abandon it in favour of his scheme; and I found it the more difficult to resist his solicitations inasmuch as he discovered a very evident and sincere regard for me. But I remained firm, choosing to encounter any danger rather than that of again falling into the hands of my cousin Percival.

After a time, during which the slaves had been exercised and fed, as we judged by the clank of chains and the scufflings and shouts from the deck, Mr Murking returned and invited us to take the air on the poop; whither we repaired gladly enough, thankful to exchange the musty foulness of the cabin for the fresh breeze.

Here Captain Parradine entered freely into conversation with our host, explaining to him the nature of his arrangements with Cotter; in which Murking promised to assist him to the best of his ability.

"And you, Mr Roberts, do you also leave us at Cape Mount?"

"That, sir, rests with you," I replied. "If you could make use of me I should like to remain with you until I could exchange into a homeward-bound ship."

"You are welcome to stay as long as you please," said Murking. "But why exchange? Why not make the round voyage and return with me?"

"'Tis generous of you to make so liberal an offer, Captain Murking," said I, "but I have had my fill of wandering, and long to look once more on my native land."

"Indeed!" said Murking, in manifest surprise. "Then it shall be as you wish, and if you desire to earn your commons whilst you are with me, I shall have no difficulty in finding you occupation."

I thanked him for his complaisance, and my position on board being now settled, the subject dropped, and the conversation turned into other channels.

The *Charity* was, as has been said, but a dull sailer, being both clumsy in her hull and under-sparred; but, with the breeze over the quarter, and her studding-sails set, she squelched along over the big, quiet billows at a quite respectable pace, and I hoped that we should be in good time to catch the polacre. Nevertheless Captain Parradine seemed far from satisfied, for, as the mountains of Sierra Leone gave place to a low-lying shore, and as this shore receded and presently vanished below the horizon to the east, he began to fidget around the binnacle and stare at the compass-dial with evident uneasiness. About noon on the second day he climbed to the fore-topgallant cross-trees with a spy-glass, ostensibly for the purpose of seeing if any sail was in sight, and when he came down I saw that he was highly dissatisfied.

"This fellow wishes me to miss my passage," said he. "We are right out of sight of land."

Shortly afterwards Murking came out on to the quarter-deck, and Parradine at once accosted him.

"You are a careful navigator, Captain Murking," he remarked; "you are giving the land a mighty wide berth."

"Too wide, think you?" asked Murking suavely. "Well, perhaps you are right, though I like to keep a good offing on this coast. However, we will steer in a couple of points, for we must not cause you to miss your assignation through excessive caution."

The course was accordingly altered, so that the ship followed the south-easterly trend of the coast, and gradually approached the land, which, towards evening on the third day, was visible from the tops.

"We should make Cape Mount at dawn," said Parradine, who had been examining the coast from the mizzen-top, "and we might have been there this morning if a reasonable course had been steered. We must be up betimes, Mr Roberts, for Murking intends to do us a mischief of some kind, though I fancy he has not yet made a definite plan. Why not change your mind, my dear friend, and come with me?" he continued earnestly. "You will find no British-bound ships on this coast, for all the slavers make for the West Indies, and surely 'twould be better to risk meeting the frigate than to remain shipmates with Judas Iscariot."

My mind, however, was firmly made up, and I told him so; on which he shrugged his shoulders, and we retired for the night.

It was still dark when the watchful Parradine came to my bunk and shook me by the shoulder.

"Come, rouse out, Mr Roberts," said he; "'tis past five of the clock, and time we were on deck."

I turned out, and, slipping into my clothes, followed him on to the quarter-deck; but, early as we were, Murking had been beforehand with us, for we found him already busy with the leadsman in the mizzen channel.

"You are early afoot, sir," he remarked dryly, not greatly pleased at his guest's alertness.

"Yes," answered Parradine; "I am anxious to know my fate."

He had not long to wait, for the dawn was already appearing in the east, and in a few minutes it was broad day, as is the way in the tropics. As the light waxed, we all looked eagerly to the eastward, and soon we could make out, over the larboard bow, the rounded outline of a hill crowning an inconspicuous promontory.

"Cape Mount!" exclaimed Parradine, pointing to the hill, "and there is Cotter, too, so we shall be in time, after all."

We were none too soon, however, for, as we approached the roadstead, the brig was seen to be casting loose her sails. A little more delay on Murking's part, and we had missed her.

"What is it that interests our worthy host so greatly?" said Parradine, for Murking had mounted the poop and was examining some object with close attention through a glass; "a sail, hey?" he added, peering over the bulwark.

I followed the direction in which he pointed, and perceived that a vessel was coming up close-hauled from the south.

"No spy-glass is needed to make out what she is," he continued, gazing at the approaching ship with great disfavour; "a corvette, beyond all doubt."

"Well, she will not pass anywhere near us," said I, "unless she alters her course."

"We shall see," answered Parradine, keeping his eye covertly on Murking; and even as he spoke the latter descended from the poop and walked forward, where he remained for some time in earnest conference with the mate – a small, harmless, rather foolish man named Batten.

The corvette was distant some five or six miles, and heading to pass a mile or two outside of us, while the brig lay in shore, and was now within a couple of miles, so that it was time to alter our course if we were to close with her.

"Would it not be well to steer in shore now, sir?" asked Parradine, as Murking came aft, "otherwise we shall fall dead to leeward of the brig."

"In one moment, sir, I will attend to you," replied Murking, and with this he bustled away towards the cabin.

"Hum!" said Parradine, frowning; "methinks I smell a rat. We are now nearly abreast of the brig, and in a few minutes we shall have her in the wind's eye. More-over I think I see Mr Batten casting loose one of the forward guns. Look ye, Mr Roberts," he added, taking from his pocket a couple of little flags, rolled up ready for hoisting, "if you would serve me, run these two pendants up to the mizzen-royal-masthead if I do not return in five minutes with Mr Murking. Will you do this for me?"

"Certainly I will," I replied, taking the flags and pocketing them.

"I thank you, sir," said he, "and for the last time, will you not change your mind and come with me? No? You will not? Then adieu and God bless you!"

He walked away with a calm and deliberate step towards the cabin, and, even as he disappeared, Mr Batten came aft and ascended to the poop, where I saw him bend the ensign on to the signal halyards at the peak. As he hauled on the line and the flag blew out, I observed that he bent it on with the union downwards, and, supposing him to have made a mistake, I ran up on the poop.

"Why, Mr Batten," said I, "you have hoisted the ensign upside down."

He regarded me with an expression half sulky and half shamefaced.

"I've got my orders, I have," says he.

"What! to make a signal of distress?"

"Aye," he answered, "I've got my orders," and with that he slunk down the poop-ladder and retired forward.

It being now perfectly evident that some mischief was afoot, I thought it best to make my signal without further delay; so I drew from my pocket the two little flags – which I now saw were of bright yellow China silk, very delicate and thin – bent them on to the signal halyards of the mizzen-mast and ran them up. As the two little balls reached the truck, I jerked the line and they blew out in the form of streamers of a very unexpected length and size; and almost at the same moment the report of a gun sang out from the *Charity's* deck.

The effect of these proceedings immediately became apparent. The brig, which we had passed at a distance of about a mile and a half, had already mast-headed her sails and had been heaving up her anchor in a leisurely fashion, as I could tell by the slow clink of the capstan-pawls; but no sooner had our gun been fired than this sound changed into a continuous rattle, showing that the hands were running the capstan round at the top of its speed. Simultaneously a boat was lowered from the quarter, and was veered away to the scope of a long towline.

In a couple of minutes the brig had her anchor out of the ground, and, canting her head off shore, began to run down towards the *Charity*, towing the boat astern. She was evidently an exceedingly fast vessel, and, with the light breeze that was then blowing, she overhauled us as though we had been at anchor. Down she came, almost dead before the wind, growing larger every moment, until she passed across our wake within a cable's length; and, at this moment, the boat's crew let go the towline and, putting out four oars, began to pull swiftly after us.

The report of the gun rang out again, which caused me to look round at our own deck, and there I saw that a very curious reception was being prepared for the approaching boat; for at each gangway there was assembled a party of seamen armed with cutlasses and handspikes while Mr Batten stood amidships giving directions.

"What is this, Mr Batten?" I asked, running down on to the quarter-deck, "you know Mr Cotter's vessel, don't you?"

"I've got my orders, I have," said Batten, sulkily. "No one ain't to be allowed to board this here ship."

I glanced round until my eye lighted on an iron belaying pin, of which I made a mental note with a view to possible contingencies; but I made no reply, and we all waited in an uneasy silence for the boat to come alongside.

"We're a-givin' em a long pull," one of the men remarked presently. "I didn't know as the old *Charity* were such a flyer."

His comrades laughed gruffly at the notion of the *Charity*'s nimbleness, and there was another pause, during which the brig glided past, shortening sail as she drew ahead, with her people crowded along the rail staring at us.

"Them pore fellers must be gettin' tired," said the sailor who had spoken before; "they can't ketch us up. Whereabouts are they?"

He thrust his head over the rail and stared down the ship's side.

I can't see 'em nowheres," said he.

There was another long pause, during which the men amused themselves by pretended attacks on one another with their cutlasses, and Batten stood with his back towards me, whistling.

Suddenly one of the sailors burst into a shout of laughter and pointed with his cutlass; his comrades ran to the side and looked over and shouted with laughter too. Mr Batten stood on tiptoe to peer over the bulwark and his face extended into a broad grin, and I, looking over the shoulders of the sailors, broke into a joyous laugh.

For there was the brig's boat, pulling away from our quarter as fast as four good ash staves could drive her. And there was Captain Parradine, standing up in the stern sheets, hat in hand, bowing like a dancing master. I jumped up into the main rigging and waved my hat to him, whereupon he lifted up the cases, one after the other, to show me that all was well. Then he kissed his hand thrice and sat down and I seemed to hear him murmur "Nunc dimittis."

"He's cut off the old fox's brush this time," observed one of the sailors, with unconcealed satisfaction. "I wonder if he give him a trouncing."

"Lord!" exclaimed another. "To think of trouncin' the old man! I'd like to a' seen him a-doin' it. 'T would be like a-thumpin' a bag of dog's-body."

"He must have got out of the stern window, Mr Roberts," said Batten, all his sulkiness gone now, and his countenance beaming with unholy joy; "'tis an odd thing this. I had best go and ask the captain what is to be done next."

He slouched off towards the cabin while I followed, with somewhat wistful eyes, the receding boat. Soon she drew alongside the brig; the crew climbed up the side, the cases were hauled on board, and the boat rose to the davits.

Then the sails of the brig were sheeted home and she lay on her course to the west; and as, by degrees, the space widened between us, my eye followed, with an emotion that surprised me, a diminutive figure at her taffrail. Smaller and smaller it grew as the brig drew out to sea until at last it vanished in the distance; and so passed out of my ken one of the politest and most lovable knaves that ever emptied a purse.

CHAPTER TWENTY

In which I show much Valour and little Discretion

I was still standing at the foot of the poop-stairs with my elbow on the rail, watching the dwindling brig, when Mr Batten came behind me and touched me on the shoulder.

"Here is a strange thing, Mr Roberts," said he. "I had to burst open the cabin door before I could get in and I can't find the captain nowheres. He ain't in the cabin and he ain't in his sleeping berth."

"Nonsense, Mr Batten," said I, smiling, "you must have overlooked him."

"That, sir," said Batten earnestly, "would be impossible. Consider his size, sir. 'Tis my opinion," he continued, "that Mr Dawson has thrown him into the sea."

Now this was precisely my own opinion, and I must confess that I was not deeply afflicted at the thought; but considering it best to make sure of the matter, I proposed that we should search the after-quarters together.

We accordingly repaired to the cabin, the appearance of which certainly suggested that it had been the scene of stirring events, for both the chairs were overturned and a number of articles were strewn about the floor, among them being a large pistol, which I observed was not one of Parradine's and from which I noticed the ramrod was missing.

Undoubtedly Murking was not in the cabin, nor was he in his sleeping berth, which had apparently not been entered, since nothing was disturbed. We examined two other berths that communicated with the great cabin, but in neither of them was there any trace of the missing ship-master.

"There can be no doubt, Mr Roberts," said Batten, when we returned to the cabin and stood gazing out of the open window, "that Mr Murking has gone overboard, though how Mr Dawson got him through that window is more than I can understand."

"Listen," said I. "What is that noise?" for a muffled groan caught my ear, apparently proceeding from somewhere below the floor of the cabin.

"'Tis someone in that lazarette!" exclaimed Batten. "It cannot be – " here he thrust his finger through a ring in the floor and lifted up the flap of the hatchway. We both peered down into the dark cavity, from which arose the noisome stench of the bilge – a slaver's bilge – and at the foot of the ladder we dimly descried a shape which instinct told us was that of the lost sheep.

Batten instantly scrambled down the ladder while I lay on the deck and reached down to help; and so, between us, we presently hauled and hoisted the unfortunate Murking up through the hatchway and deposited him on the cabin floor. He was in a pitiable state, his face swollen and purple and streaming with sweat, while his eyes seemed to be starting from their sockets. The ramrod of a pistol was lashed in his mouth as a gag, his hands were secured behind his back with a pair of his own handcuffs, and his feet were confined by a pair of shackles.

While Batten was unfastening the lashing that secured the gag, I unlocked the manacles with a key that I picked up from the floor, whereupon Murking, having recovered the use of his hands and mouth, rose to his feet.

"Where is he?" he panted hoarsely, as a stream of bloody foam trickled down his chin. "Where is that murderous villain?" and without waiting for an answer, he waddled away, as fast as the leg-shackles would permit, towards the deck, followed by Batten and me.

Now, at the moment when we emerged together on to the quarter-deck, there arose above the rail at the gangway, a large face, very red and wrathful, surmounted by an old white beaver hat. The face appertained to an officer of His Majesty's navy, as appeared when its owner stepped down on to the deck, and a very irritable gentleman he seemed to be, for he scowled at us and the crew as though moved by an urgent desire to order us six dozen apiece out of hand.

"Well," he snorted, glaring at Murking, "where is the master of this old stink box?"

"I am the master of this vessel, sir," said Murking stiffly.

"You!" shouted the lieutenant, glaring more fiercely than before, "Why, what do you do here? You're more fit for the Greenland trade – fill your own oil tubs – no need for sticking whales – look like a whale yourself – doesn't he, Simmons?" (This was addressed to a midshipman who had followed him on to the deck.)

"Sir," said Murking, "I made a signal – "

"I know you did," interrupted the lieutenant, "like your damned impudence – don't stand there squinting at me! and what do you mean by dancing about in leg-shackles before a king's officer – like some confounded mountebank?"

"Sir," said Murking, "I made a signal – "

"You said that before," interrupted the officer.

"And I say it again!" roared Murking, purple with fury.

"Very well, I'm not deaf," shouted the lieutenant, who did not appear to be dumb either.

"I made a signal," continued Murking, "to let you know that I had a most notorious pirate on board."

"All right," said the officer, "bring him out."

"He's gone, sir," said Murking.

"Gone!" shrieked the lieutenant, "you said you had him on board. How can he be on board if he's gone? You've brought me on a fool's errand, you infernal old blubber-bag."

"I wished to explain, sir – " said Murking.

"Then explain and be hanged to you. Well?"

"– That he made his escape on that brig in the offing – " continued Murking.

"What?" exclaimed that lieutenant. "Do you say that vessel is a pirate?"

"No, sir, I do not," replied Murking.

"Then what the devil do you mean?" demanded the officer, fairly skipping on the deck with irritation.

"I mean that the pirate took a passage on board my ship," said Murking, "and that – "

"You harboured a pirate, did you?" interrupted the officer.

"No, I did not harbour him, sir," exclaimed Murking.

"Yes, you did," said the lieutenant.

"I say I did not, sir," roared Murking.

"Why did you connive at his escape," demanded the other.

"Connive!" screamed Murking, "I connive at his escape? Look at me, sir."

"I am looking at you," said the officer, "and mighty little I like your looks. Why did you let that pirate go?"

"I did not let him go, sir," replied Murking. "He bound and gagged me, sir, and escaped from my cabin window; and he took with him a bag containing three hundred guineas, sir, My own property."

"'Tis his own property now," remarked the lieutenant, grinning.

"I demand justice, sir," exclaimed Murking huskily. "The man is on board that brig and she is not yet gone too far to be overtaken."

"Why, confound you," spluttered the lieutenant, "do you take me for a Bow Street runner? Are the king's ships to go scouring the sea after every dirty thief that makes off with a handful of guineas? Muster your hands, sir."

"I trust you are not proposing to impress any of my crew," exclaimed Murking in great trepidation; "we are short-handed already."

"So are we," said the lieutenant.

"And the men are inclined to be sickly, too," added Murking.

"'Tis no wonder," answered the officer, "with the stink that is coming up that grating; 'twould make a polecat heave. Turn up the hands smartly, sir."

The hands were, in fact, all on deck, and Murking sulkily ordered them to toe a line.

"Did you ever see such a pack of Wapping rats, Simmons?" exclaimed the lieutenant running his eye disdainfully down the line; "who is that great hulking fellow, sir?" he added, pointing to me.

"He is my clerk, sir," answered Murking, "and is not a seafaring man."

"We could soon make a seaman of him," remarked the lieutenant, to my great uneasiness.

"His services are indispensable to me in my trade," said Murking earnestly, "and he is landsman, as I have said."

The officer looked at me suspiciously, but as I had exchanged my ragged seaman's clothing for a suit that Parradine had given me, there was nothing in my appearance to throw discredit on Murking's statement. He therefore passed me over, with a growl of discontent, and, picking out a dozen of the most capable-looking men, ordered them to fetch up their chests and get into the boat.

"I protest, sir," exclaimed Murking in great distress, "you are not leaving us sufficient hands to work the ship. In this trade, 'tis highly dangerous to have so small a crew."

"No doubt," was the answer; "you should have shipped more hands. Now you rascals, down with ye into the boat or I'll send up a boatswain's mate to help you with his starter."

At this threat the pressed men scrambled over the rail in uncommon haste; and, when he had seen them safely stowed in the boat, the officer bestowed a parting scowl on Murking and followed.

"This is infamous," exclaimed Murking – in which I heartily agreed with him; "we have not enough men left to manage the slaves who are on board, and there are a hundred and fifty more blacks now waiting for shipment at Winnebah."

"Perhaps," I suggested, "if you sent a boat to the corvette, her commander might give you some redress."

"More likely he would impress the boat's crew," growled Murking. He flung away in passion, and when he had removed the inconvenient shackles, fell to abusing the seamen, cursing them for a parcel of idle dogs in language which accorded ill with his professions of piety. He was evidently much put out – which was not to be wondered at – and being naturally of a savage and malignant temper, did not fail to visit his anger on all who were subject to him, no matter how free from offence their conduct might be.

Presently, as he was cruising about the deck, seeking excuses for fault-finding, he spied my signal pendants, which had been left flying from the masthead.

"What rags are those fluttering aloft, Mr Batten?" he asked, squinting up at the streamers.

"I don't know, sir," replied Batten, staring aloft in great surprise – for I had managed to run up the signal unobserved by him – I didn't hoist them."

"You didn't hoist them, you idiot!" exclaimed Murkings, fetching him a thump that sent him staggering backwards, "are you not the mate of this ship?"

"Yes, I am," answered Batten, rubbing his head, "and I wish I wasn't."

"I hoisted those pendants, sir," said I.

"With what object?" demanded Murking.

"I did so at Mr Dawson's request. They were, I suppose, a private signal to Captain Cotter."

"So you aided your rascally confederate to escape, did you?" exclaimed Murking furiously. "You were in the plot too – as I suspected."

He advanced to me with his fist raised as though he would deal with me as he had with Mr Batten.

"You had better not, Mr Murking," said I. "I am not your mate, remember."

On this he thought better of his intention, and instead of striking, fell to reviling me.

"'Twas an ill day for me," said he, "when I admitted such a pair of cut-throats on my ship. But I might have known what to expect from such villains."

"For what has happened, Mr Murking," I said "you have only yourself to thank. You sought to betray, for your own gain, a man who had trusted himself in your hands, and to whom you had passed your promise, and you fell into your own snare. You have no sympathy from me, though Mr Dawson be all that you say."

"What?" bawled Murking, "do you flout me to my face, you worthless runagate? You who – " here he checked himself suddenly and I guessed that he had been on the point of disclosing his intentions towards me.

"But why do I waste words on you?" he continued, "when the day's work is yet to do and you are lounging about with idle hands? Get to your duties, sir, and bear a hand at lifting the gratings. 'Tis time the blacks were fed, Mr Batten."

Batten hurried away, glad enough to escape, and I joined a group of seamen who were about to lift the gratings that covered the hatchways. A more unsavoury task I was never set to, for the hot reek that arose from the hold was foul beyond the stench of the filthiest and most neglected pig-sty.

When the gratings were off, the male slaves were assisted up the ladders, and as they crawled on to the deck, I was moved with pity at their miserable condition. They were shackled together in pairs, the right leg of one bound to the left leg of another, and the whole gang was confined by a long chain attached to the iron collars that all of them wore.

As soon as they were on deck, the women and children were let out of the after hold, and, being unshackled, made their way on deck without assistance and seated themselves at a little distance from the men.

As I was helping the poor wretches out of the hatch-ways, I noticed Quassie, Captain Parradine's servant, standing hard by, watching his unfortunate countrymen with an expression of placid curiosity.

"Why, Quassie," said I, "has your master left you behind after all?"

"No, sah," replied Quassie, "he no leave me. I stay. I Cape Coast man. Dis ship he go for Cape Coast, den I go for my country."

At this moment the cook and his mates appeared, carrying great tubs filled with a mess of shelled beans and rice and buckets of soup.

These delicacies, being shovelled into wooden bowls, were set before the slaves, and the latter were commanded to eat.

Poor wretches! They had little pleasure in their food, being fresh from the noisome hold, and, moreover, but lately torn away from their homes and families. Yet they mostly took their food diligently, bitter experience having taught them that the slave-master will brook no voluntary starvation by which the quality of his cattle may be injured. While the meal was in progress Murking walked the deck in sullen silence, swinging in his hand a whip of twisted bull-hide; and if any slave showed a failing appetite, the brutal villain would fetch him such a cut across his naked shoulders as would set him a-gobbling for his life, while tears of agony and despair streamed down his face into the bowl.

I looked on at this scene with a growing desire to thrust my thumbs into Mr Murking's neck-cloth and strangle him out of hand; and I was not the less disgusted to observe that Quassie, who was an interested spectator of the banquet, greeted each cut of the whip with loud chuckles of amusement.

His amusement, however, was short-lived, for his laughter attracted the notice of Captain Murking — who had apparently not observed him before.

"Who is this fellow?" inquired Murking, glaring at the negro.

"I Captain Parradine — I mean Mr Dawson — servant," explained Quassie with a bland grin.

"Ah," said Murking, "that is who you are, eh? Mr Batten, you know what to do."

"Yes, sir," replied Batten, beckoning to a group of sailors; and even while the negro was gaping around in stupid surprise, he was seized from behind, his smart clothes stripped off and a collar and shackles clapped on. The whole thing was done with such speed and dexterity that the unfortunate black found himself stark naked and shackled to a fellow-captive before he had realised what was happening.

Then, indeed, his lamentations were terrible to witness; he screamed, blubbered, and wrenched at his shackles with passionate fury, until a few cuts from Mr Murking's whip convinced him of the necessity of submission; when he subsided into muffled whimperings that were even more moving than his former extravagance of grief.

During the whole time that these scenes were enacting, I had been furtively observing the conduct of one of the slaves who had, apparently, escaped Murking's notice, being somewhat concealed by the mainmast. He was a man of great·stature and very fierce and resolute of aspect – as, indeed, were many of our men-slaves; for they were mostly of the nation called Coromantees, who are accounted the boldest of all the negroes and very dangerous to handle. This man, then, I had been watching, but so as not to direct attention to him, and had observed that his food remained untested, which made me fear that he would presently fall under the lash of Mr Murking's whip. Batten also had observed him but for the same reason, perhaps, had forborne to speak, though, when Murking's attention was occupied elsewhere, he made impatient gestures to the man to eat his food. At length, however, the captain, in crossing the deck, came opposite the defaulter, and, as his glance fell on the bowl of untouched food, he halted and glared at the slave with unspeakable malignancy.

"Why, how is this, Mr Batten," he exclaimed furiously. "This beast has not taken a mouthful of his ration."

"No, sah," exclaimed the slave passionately, "I no chop him. I no be bush man, same like de oder slave; I scholar man; I speak white man talk. I come dis ship wid my wife for buy goods. Den you catch me, you panyar me; you tink you sell me for slave. But you no fit sell me. I no take chop, den I die. You no sell me."

Here, then, was another example of Murking's treachery. This poor devil – apparently a respectable native trader – had been lured on board for the ostensible purpose of bartering his produce for European articles of trade. Then he had been kidnapped and thrust down into the hold to be spirited away to the slave marts of the West Indies.

Verily, Parradine was right; a pirate, who was ready to give and take hard knocks, was quite a respectable character compared with a sneaking man-stealer like the pious captain of the *Charity*.

As the man finished speaking, Murking's face took an expression truly diabolical.

"You will die, will you, my friend?" said he. "That is as may be, but, let me tell you it shall not be of starvation. There is your food, you black beast! Eat it this instant or, by the living God, I'll strip every rag of flesh from your bones."

He waited for a few seconds, and then, as the man made no sign of obeying, he brought down the heavy, hide whip with all his strength upon the naked back of his victim.

A broad, bleeding weal marked the place where the blow had fallen, and the man, with a slight shudder, set his teeth and grunted.

Again and again the terrible whip descended, and, at each stroke, Murking seemed to grow more furious, while a dark stream of blood trickled down the man's back, and the startled slaves on either side looked on askance, with terrified glances, as they crammed the food into their mouths and bolted it in entire handfuls.

"Stop! Mr Murking," I exclaimed. "Hold your hand, for God's sake. This is no work for a Christian man."

"Stand away," he roared hoarsely, and flourished the whip as though he would strike at me; which, if he had done, I had stove in his skull then and there.

"'Tis no use to kill the man, sir," said Batten. "Why not try the *speculum oris*?"

Murking paused, breathing hard, and wiping the sweat from his face.

"Very well," said he, "fetch me one – and bring a screw also."

Batten hurried off to the cabin and returned shortly carrying a thumb-screw and an instrument somewhat like a massive pair of compasses, the legs of which could be forced apart by turning the winged head of a screw. The latter instrument Murking seized and endeavoured to thrust its pointed end between the jaws of his wretched victim; but, though he used such violence that the man's mouth was all bruised and bloody, the poor wretch held his teeth resolutely clenched so that it was impossible to insert the end of the wedge.

At this moment one of the women who had been looking on at this dreadful scene with passionate gestures of grief and horror, rushed forward and flung herself at Murking's feet, clasping his ankles with her hands, while the tears streamed down her face.

"Master! I beg you!" she exclaimed piteously, "no kill him! He be my husband; s' pose I beg him, he take his chop. No kill him, master!"

Murking cast a baleful glance at the poor creature and kicked her savagely away from him. Then, snatching up the whip, he slashed her heavily across the breast.

This outrage had the effect of rousing the slave, who had borne his own sufferings in grim silence, and he sat up glaring ferociously at his tormentor.

"You white pig!" he shouted. "You flog my wife! S' pose I catch you for my country I cut you up small-small, I make patakoo chop you."

"Hum," said Murking with a mirthless smile, like that of Satan himself, "bring me that woman, you lazy rogues, and hold her down in front of this son of Belial."

The sailors thus addressed came forward with manifest unwillingness, dragging the frightened woman, whom they laid down on the deck in the place that the captain indicated.

"Now hold her tightly," said Murking. "Grasp her knees and elbows securely. So."

He caught up the thumb-screw, and, slipping the woman's thumbs dexterously into the holes, began to turn the screw slowly, leering into the husband's face with a horrible, devilish smile.

For a moment the woman stared at Murking with an expression of terrified bewilderment; then her eyes seemed to start from their sockets and a scream of mortal agony burst from her lips.

This was beyond endurance. While the previous horrors had been enacting, my anger had mounted by degrees until I could scarce control myself; yet I had forborne to interfere, having no authority on board. But this thing was not to be borne. Regardless of the consequences, I pushed the men aside, and, gathering all my strength for the blow, fetched Mr Murking such a buffet as sent him rolling over and over across the deck. Then I relaxed the screw, and, plucking the instrument from the woman's hands, tossed this devil's plaything into the sea.

Murking lay still for a few moments, half stunned by the blow, and the seaman looked from him to me as if doubtful what to do. Presently, however, the captain sat up still dazed, and, slowly rising to his feet, looked round as one in a dream. But a few seconds seemed to restore him, and then he strode towards me – though he did not come within arm's length.

"You mutinous villain!" he exclaimed, huskily, "you cut-throat gallows-bird! You shall pay for this. Aye! You shall dance on the air at Tyburn yet, my fine friend. Seize me this fellow!" he shouted, turning suddenly on the bewildered sailors: "do you hear me? Seize him and make him secure like the other cattle."

"Sorry for do it, mate," said a burly seaman, stepping up to me, "but orders is orders and you'd best take it quiet."

He grasped my arm firmly, but without roughness, while a dozen more sailors gathered round; and, as I realised the uselessness of resisting, and perceived, moreover, that the men were but doing their duty, I remained passive in their hands while they fitted me with a pair of handcuffs and secured my ankles with shackles.

"Now," said Murking, "fix him on a collar, make him fast to the chain and down with him into the hold."

"You don't mean into the slave-room, sir," expostulated Batten.

"Yes, I do," shouted Murking, "let him lie with his friends in the men's room."

"Remember, sir, that he is an Englishman," said Batten.

"An Englishman!" bawled Murking. "He is an escaped murderer, delivered into my hands to be given up to justice; that is what he is. I know him of old. And he is a confederate of that pirate scoundrel, as you know, yourself. Down with him into the hold, I say, and if you thwart me, Mr Batten, by God, you shall go down with him."

"Look ye, Cap'n Murking," said the sailor who had pinioned me, stepping between me and the captain, "there ain't no white man a-going into the slave-room on this here ship, is there, mates?"

A chorus of approving growls showed that the men were of one opinion on this subject.

"Don't argue with me, you mutinous hogs," exclaimed Murking furiously, "or I'll clap you all in irons. Fix on the collar and I'll pitch him down myself."

"As to a-puttin' us in irons," said the sailor, calmly, "that is all damned nonsense, d'ye see; you can't work the ship without a crew. And if there's any more jaw we casts this young fellow loose and lets him fend for hisself; so now you've got your bearings and you can set your course."

"Do you refuse to do your duty, Mr Batten," demanded Murking.

"I shall obey all your lawful commands, sir," answered Batten; "but you know what would happen if we were boarded by a king's officer and a white man found in our slave-room."

Murking reflected for a few moments. It was evident that the men would not permit him to carry out his infernal plan, and perhaps, as his anger cooled somewhat, he perceived that such a course of action bid fair, not only to deprive him of his reward for delivering me up, but also to expose him to serious danger in the probable event of my death.

However this may have been, he made a show of yielding to the wishes of the crew.

"You are mighty tender," he growled, "about this worthless ruffian. But you shall be humoured, though you deserve it as little as he does. Stow him in the spare berth, Mr Batten, and make him secure – but I will come with you and see to that myself."

I was led into the cabin, where Murking unlocked one of the two berths that were kept vacant for possible passengers – the other had been occupied by Parradine and me – and, throwing it open, thrust me in. It was quite bare of furniture, the standing bed being unprovided even with a mattress, and there was no seat but the floor.

"Here," said Murking, "this murderous scoundrel will be berthed like a gentleman, and you can go away with your dirty consciences at rest."

Batten and the sailors who had escorted me aft, accepting this as a dismissal, retired, and Murking stood in the doorway regarding me with complacent malice.

"You thought," he observed presently, "when you fled from my house, that you had escaped, and that your crimes would go unpunished. But Providence has ordered things otherwise in its infinite wisdom. By what means I know not (though it seems to me almost a miracle) the Lord has delivered you into my hand, and I shall hold you fast, I warrant you, until the time comes for you to pay the penalty of your sins."

He raised his eyes to Heaven – or, more strictly speaking, to the opposite corners of the ceiling – and then, lowering them, bestowed on me a glance of triumphant malevolence.

I was greatly tempted to tell him the real state of the case, but, reflecting that Mr Colville's two hundred guineas' reward was now the chief security for my being kept alive, I resolved to keep my own counsel on the matter, and made him no reply; and so he went away, locking the door and removing the key.

I was now left to my own reflections, which were certainly none of the most agreeable. The berth was small, dark and insufferably hot, and, as I walked up and down the narrow space of deck with short steps and a hideous clanking of my shackles, I found the confinement irksome to the last degree, and looked forward with dismay to the months that must elapse before the *Charity* would crawl up to her berth off Rotherhithe. The prospect of being cooped up all that dreary time in this stuffy, evil-smelling den, was truly appalling, and again and again I found myself lamenting, with unavailing regrets, that I had not thrown in my lot with the pirate captain, from whom I might easily have separated at the first West Indian port at which the polacre touched. Presently, becoming weary of the little steps that I must needs take by reason of my shackles, I sat down on the floor and fell into a brown study.

It seemed as though there was to be no end to my misfortunes; no sooner was I clear of one peril than I fell instantly into another. On that fateful day when poor Will Colville met his death, my good fortune seemed to have left me suddenly and for good, and ever since I had been as one haunted by an evil spirit, or under a curse.

What was to be the end of it all? Clearly, if Murking carried out his threat and held me in durance, fettered and manacled, in this sweltering dungeon, while the *Charity* crawled half-way round the world and back again, there could be but one end of it; sooner or later I should be dropped over the side, to lay my bones on the bed of the Atlantic.

I had remained thus solitary and wrapped in gloomy reflections for near upon five glasses – as I could tell by hearing them struck upon the ship's bell – when I heard footsteps approaching and the key was inserted into the lock.

As the door opened, I perceived that my visitors were two of the sailors, and that they were bringing me some food, of which I was sorely in need, having taken nothing since the preceding evening.

"Sorry to bring you such scurvy rations, mate," said one of them, with rough sympathy, "but the old fox stood by whiles it were served out, so we hadn't no chice."

He set down a bowl and a pannikin of water, and I then perceived that the former contained an ordinary slave's ration.

"'Tain't so bad as what it might be," said the seaman, pointing to the bowl; 'tis shrimp soup today, with rice and beans, and that's better than what they serves out to the hands aboard a king's ship, I can tell you."

I was fully aware of this, and without more ado, fell to upon the rough victuals with an appetite unimpaired by my misadventures.

"Couldn't I have the handcuffs off to take my food?" I asked.

"Old man says not," answered the seaman. "We asked him, but he wouldn't agree to it nohow. That was a rare thump as you give him. My eye! but it did my heart good to see it."

"It didn't do his heart good, though," chuckled the other sailor, "nor his head neither."

"No," agreed the first speaker, "and it won't do you no good, young man. 'Tis mighty unsafe for to thrash a shipmaster on his own deck."

To these observations I made no reply, being fully occupied in disposing of the victuals, which, despite the inconvenience of the handcuffs, I managed pretty expeditiously.

When I had finished, the sailors took the empty bowl and pannikin and went away, and I was once more left to myself. But the meal, coarse as it was, had refreshed me, and I was now in a far less dismal frame of mind. The resiliency of youth asserted itself, and already I began to form projects for escaping from my captivity; and though, as may be supposed, they were not of a very practicable nature, yet they served to while away the time, and, moreover, caused me to consider every contingency that might arise, with so much completeness, that I should be the better prepared for action if any chance of escape presented itself.

My visitors came to me again twice during this day, and I certainly had nothing to complain of in respect of food, for my diet was the same as that of the slaves; and though these unfortunate captives were subjected to numberless cruelties and hardships, there were few slave-masters who were so blind to their own interests as to stint their rations. Indeed the danger, in my case, was of the opposite kind, for I bid fair, if my appetite continued as hearty as it was at present, to wax overfed and gross for lack of exercise.

My last meal was taken by the light of a lanthorn, and I spun it out as long as I could for the pleasure of having something to look at. When it was finished, and I was once more left in darkness, the time dragged on more wearily than ever; and though I endeavoured to amuse myself by following in imagination the doings of the crew on deck, noting the passage of the ship's day as the bell was struck at each turning of the glass, the ennui became at last intolerable; and, as eight bells announced the setting of the first watch, I flung myself down upon the hard plank bed and sought to forget my weariness in sleep.

But in this I was for a long time unsuccessful. The berth was stifling hot and the effluvia from the hold filtered in through every cranny in the deck and bulkheads. Moreover, the handcuffs prevented me from settling into a comfortable posture, and at each restless movement the leg-irons clanked with a horrid noise and clattered on the plank bed.

But everything has an end, and so it was with this weary and distressful night. By degrees my thoughts began to ramble into more pleasant scenes; the hard bed grew less uneasy, the shackles less obtrusive; the hot, foul air and the lurching of the ship faded from consciousness, and at last, to me, as to my fellow-captives in the hold, sleep came with its brief reprieve, casting open the dungeon door that was to close again with the coming of the day.

CHAPTER TWENTY-ONE

In which Mr Murking pilots the Charity to her last Berth

The days of my captivity dragged on with a dreary sameness and a monotony of discomfort that furnished little matter to record. Each sultry day was succeeded by a sweltering night, through which I shifted and turned uneasily on my hard bed, sometimes sleeping, sometimes wakeful, and often dreaming strange, disturbed dreams. The only pleasant time in the whole round day was that between midnight and dawn, when the air had cooled down and I enjoyed the unwonted luxury of huddling in a corner of the bunk and shivering with the cold.

My food was brought to me regularly, and, though my appetite soon fell off, I looked forward eagerly to each meal; for the few minutes' chat with the sailors made a very agreeable break in the long day. Sometimes Mr Batten came with them, and, in his simple way, would try to hearten me up that I might not give way to despair.

Not that I was at all disposed to abandon hope. On the contrary, as I grew somewhat accustomed to my captivity, and even, in a way, reconciled to it, I encouraged myself constantly by contriving plans for my escape; of which the most promising one involved a certain degree of violence towards my host. It was Mr Murking's custom to look in on me once or twice in every day to satisfy himself, no doubt, as to my condition; and it occurred to me that, if I could contrive to unfasten my handcuffs – and on examining the fastenings carefully, this did not seem impossible – I might lie in wait for him, and, using the manacles as a weapon, batter in his skull with them, after which I thought it likely that the sailors would permit me to go off in Captain Parradine's boat. I have sometimes regretted that I did not carry out this plan, but, doubtless, it was better that things should have happened as they did.

On the evening of the sixth day of my imprisonment I was waiting for the arrival of my last meal, with the anxiety of a caged animal which knows that its feeding time is approaching. The food was due at three bells in the second dog-watch and two bells had been struck some time before.

As last the chimes sounded from the deck, and, immediately after, I heard steps approaching. The key turned in the lock, the door was flung open, and the sailors entered, followed by Mr Batten.

"Here's your supper, Mr Roberts," said the latter, cheerily. "'Tis a sort of lobscouse made of shrimp soup and biscuit – not bad fare, let me tell you, for I've supped off it myself. You must try to stow away a bigger lading than you did this morning, or Mr Murking will be complaining."

"Let me have a run on deck and a breath of fresh air, Mr Batten," said I, "and I'll soon empty the bowl."

"Ah," replied Batten, "we must talk about that when we get to sea. Things will be better then, Mr Roberts, depend on it. The captain will let you out when we are clear of the coast, I make no doubt."

"When do you suppose we shall leave the coast?" I asked.

"Why," answered Batten, "we passed Cape Three Points at six bells this afternoon. In the morning we shall be off Cape Coast or Annamabo, and by this time tomorrow we'll have our hook down in the Winnebah roads. 'Twill take us two days to ship the slaves, and then 'tis off we go for Barbadoes with a hold full of roaring Coromantee boys – and I hope to God they'll keep the peace; for three hundred Coromantees are no joke with a small crew like ours."

"Are these Coromantees very turbulent folk, then?" I asked.

"Aye, sir," answered one of the sailors, "that they be. Mighty different is these here Gold Coast blacks from the Brass River or

Bonny people. Lor' bless you, they'll cut your throat or pitch you overboard without so much as 'by your leave.' "

"Yes," said Batten, "they are fine people and fetch a good price, for they are strong and hardy, but very fierce and courageous, and as cunning as a pack of monkeys."

By this time I had finished my meal, so Batten took the bowl from me, and, having once more exhorted me to keep a brave heart, ushered the sailors out and locked the door.

It was long before I fell asleep that night, for Batten's encouraging words had given me new hope, and I lay revolving new schemes for escape until near upon midnight. Then I began to doze, and presently sank into a troubled sleep filled with all manner of strange dreams; in some of which I was back in my home, in others wandering about the island or aboard the pirate schooner, and at last I found myself carrying out my plan of attacking Mr Murking.

I had aimed a blow at his head with the swinging handcuffs, and missed him. Then we had grappled and I was whirling him around, dashing him against the sides of the berth and clanking my shackles in the most horrid manner, while the sailors who had come to his assistance thundered at the door and bulkhead with a deafening noise.

Suddenly a loud report rang out, and I awoke with a start, to realise in an instant of amazement that the noises of my dreams were no mere figment of the brain, but real sounds that had worked themselves into the imaginary scenes.

The whole ship was shaken by a mighty uproar. Stampings and tramplings on the deck, shouts and screams, the rattle of chains and the din of fire-arms, mingled in the most infernal hubbub. Footsteps ran to and fro over my head on the poop; the crash of bursting woodwork and shattering glass and china resounded from the cabin; the bulkheads shook and trembled and naked fists beat from time to time on my door.

Of a sudden a strange calm fell upon the vessel. The footsteps ceased, the shouts died away, the chains were silent, and a most singular hush succeeded to the deafening uproar.

I sat up in my bunk and listened, not without a certain vague uneasiness.

For fully a couple of minutes the silence continued; then it was broken by a terrible yell as of someone in mortal agony, followed by a peal of wild laughter.

Again there was an interval of silence, during which I sat listening, breathless and trembling, and again that awful scream pealed forth, until, as I seemed to recognise the voice, my hair stirred and a chilly sweat broke out upon my forehead.

A dozen times, or more, the horrible cry was repeated, and each time a thunderous shout of laughter followed. Then the shriek grew more continuous, now drowned by the ringing laughter and now rising with piercing acuteness above all other sounds.

Presently it subsided into a strange muffled wail that grew weaker and fainter by degrees until it ceased altogether, and there was another interval of silence.

Then there came to my ears a most unearthly sound as of a multitude of voices chanting a psalm; and yet it was not quite like a psalm, neither – indeed 'twas not like any melody that I had ever heard, for it rambled from one note to another in the strangest and most unexpected fashion; and, though the rhythm was quick, yet the air was full of wild and melancholy cadences. But the melody was repeated again and again as in the psalms that are sung in our churches, and at the end of each figure, there was a sound as if a great number of persons had clapped their hands together.

Even as I was listening, like one in a dream, to the rising and falling of this weird music, soft footsteps approached my door and the key was turned in the lock. I leaped from the bed, ready to defend myself, when the door opened and I beheld, with no little astonishment, the slave on whose behalf I had quarrelled with Murking. He stood on the threshold, a tall, dignified figure, though naked, dirty and haggard, and I saw that his wife waited outside, glancing nervously towards the quarter-deck. The man saluted me gravely and entered, followed by the woman, who, as she crossed the threshold, made a low curtsy, and, placing her hands together, murmured some words that sounded like "yah woora."

"We come, sah," said the man, "for set you free. We set ourself free, den we tink about you. We say 'Mastah he get soft heart, he sorry for black man, he try for help him; so black man he sorry for mastah, he try for help him!' Dis key he fit for unlock de handcuff; A'b'nábah" – this was addressed to his wife – "you unlock dem leg-iron."

He inserted the key into the handcuffs while his wife knelt to unlock the shackles; in a few moments the fetters fell apart, and I was free.

The negro looked out of the door towards the entrance to the cabin and listened.

"Now we go," said he, drawing the key from the outside of the door and inserting it on the inside; "dis place good for you. You stay and lock de door. Plenty of my country people live for deck. Dis day dey smell blood; s'pose dey see you, p'raps dey kill you. You wait here. Soon we take boat, we go 'shore. Cape Coast quite near, Annamabo quite near; all we Cape Coast and Annamabo people. When we go, all quiet; den you go on deck. Plenty ship at Cape Coast. Dey look you; dey send boat for fetch you. Now we go. God bress you, sah!"

He went out, and his wife, having made another low curtsy, followed; when I proceeded to act on his advice, and, shutting the door, turned the key.

For some considerable time I waited, listening to the various sounds from the quarter-deck and the poop overhead, and speculating on what had occurred. On the whole I was not a little elated at regaining my liberty, and, though I was somewhat disturbed by the thought of what had probably happened to the crew, the little that I had seen of the ways of a slaver had prepared me to regard without deep concern any mishaps that might occur in the conduct of the trade. Men who elect to make a living by consigning hundreds of their fellow-creatures to death or lifelong captivity, have little to complain of if they meet occasionally with hard knocks and rough handling.

Presently I was able to distinguish, above the general uproar, the creak of heavy tackles, and I judged that the boats were being lowered.

The *Charity* was provided with three boats of her own, of which one, the long boat, was of large size, as is usual in slavers, and there was the schooner's jolly-boat in addition; but with all these, it seemed to me impossible that the entire party of slaves could be conveyed ashore in a single journey, and I began to fear that the landing of the escaped slaves might prove a protracted business.

By degrees the noise from the deck grew less, and a confused murmur of voices seemed to come from outside the ship, accompanied by sundry thumpings on the vessel's side.

Then these sounds became more faint and presently died away altogether, and nothing was to be heard but the ordinary creaking of bulkheads and timbers as the ship rolled softly on the swell. After listening for a time, with the growing conviction that the slaves were really gone, I unlocked the door and peered out cautiously into the cabin.

The place was completely wrecked; the furniture smashed, the windows shattered, and the floor strewn with a litter of broken china mingled with the contents of chests and lockers.

Still no sound was to be heard; and, gathering courage from the stillness that reigned over all, I passed through the cabin and stepped out on to the quarter-deck.

The slaves had gone and the ship appeared to be deserted.

But, though no living being moved upon the silent deck, the space enclosed by the high bulwarks was not untenanted; for here and there, sprawling limply upon the blood-stained planks, were the corpses of those who had fallen in the fray. In all there were twelve – seven being members of the crew, and five negroes – and from the way in which they were huddled together between the fore and main-masts it appeared that the slaughter had taken place in the first, rush, when the slaves broke out of the hold.

I glanced quickly at the prostrate forms, as they lay in all sorts of strange and contorted postures, gathered together in grisly companionship; but my attention was speedily diverted from them to a figure that reposed stiffly on the main grating.

It was Mr Murking; and, as I looked on his hideous corpse, I realised, with a shudder, the significance of those horrible cries that I had heard.

He was stretched at full length upon the grating, to which he was secured by lashings. His wrists were confined by a pair of handcuffs and his thumbs were clamped tightly in a thumb-screw, from the joints of which there oozed, even yet, a thin trickle of blood.

His face – bloated, dusky, and set in a wild stare of agony and terror – was frightful to look upon; the mouth was wide open, the jaws forced apart in a dreadful gape by a screw-gag. As to the manner of his death, it was obvious enough; an iron collar had been fixed around his fat neck, and, being many sizes too small, had embedded itself in the flesh and strangled him – as was evident from the protruding tongue, the swollen, blackened face, and the eyes starting out from their sockets.

I stood by the grating looking down with a dreadful fascination upon the hideous face, which, with it squinting stare and bulging eyes, irresistibly recalled the aspect of the great land-crab that had so terrified me on the island; and, though my flesh seemed to creep as I looked, I could not muster one jot of pity or compunction. As he had sown, so had he reaped; nor was the harvest one whit beyond his deserts. Not indeed, by mere death, nor even by the agony that had preceded it, could the price of his evil deeds be paid; for in his very ruin, the consequences of his avarice and wickedness had fallen upon many who never stood to share in his gains. Not alone from many hundreds of despairing toilers in far-away plantations, or from scores of the forgotten dead, whose bones lay in the ooze of the ocean's floor, but even from this very deck the cry for justice arose from the victims of his greed.

At this point in my reflections I aroused suddenly from my contemplation of the dead shipmaster, as the question flashed into my mind, "What of the others? Is there anyone living on the ship beside myself?"

There were six dead seamen on the deck besides Murking. What had become of the rest of the crew?

I ran to the side and looked over, thinking they might have escaped in a boat. The ship was about five miles distant from a green and pleasant coast with grassy uplands rolling away inland, and two considerable towns on the shore. One of these, which lay a few miles to the westward, I judged, from what the slave had said, to be Cape Coast, for I could see a large building like a castle, close to the sea, and in the roadstead a number of vessels lay at anchor. The other town, which was a little distance to the east, was smaller, and had a low, whitewashed fort on the shore; and I now perceived that the slaves were making towards it, from which I concluded that this was Annamabo.

A glance at the retreating slaves showed that they were in possession of all the four boats, and also made clear the means by which they had managed to escape in a single party. The boats were loaded as deeply as was safe, with the women and children, and with a number of men sufficient to work the oars; the remainder swam alongside or supported themselves by ropes.

This arrangement naturally hindered them from rapid movement, and they were proceeding shoreward at a very deliberate pace, being even now hardly a mile away from the ship.

The remainder of the crew, then, had not escaped in a boat; whence it followed that they had either been flung overboard or driven below.

I ran forward to the forecastle hatch, which was closed and fastened by a peg thrust through the staple. Drawing out the peg, I slid back the hatch, when there immediately poured up in my face a dense cloud of smoke. I drew back with a start, and fell to coughing and choking, but, recovering myself in an instant, I shut my mouth and peered down the hatchway; when I perceived dimly through the smoke and darkness a number of motionless forms huddled together at the foot of the ladder.

For one moment I hesitated, as volumes of fat black smoke poured out through the narrow opening and set me once more coughing and gasping; then, having taken a deep breath and shut my mouth tight, I dropped down the ladder, caught up the first man that I could lay hold of, hoisted him on to my shoulders and climbed up again.

Having deposited the man on the deck, where he lay without movement or sign of life, I descended once more and brought up another inanimate body, and so on until six limp, motionless bodies were laid out abaft the hatchway; and all the time, the black smoke continued to roll up in ever-increasing volumes. I was about to descend for the seventh time, although I was, by now, faint, giddy and half-stupefied by the suffocating fumes, when a portion of the bulkhead fell in with a shower of sparks, and a sheet of flame shot through into the forecastle and rose through the hatchway. There was nothing for it but to slide the hatch to and trust that the men who were still below were already dead; and, when I had done, this, I turned my attention to those whom I had rescued.

The six men, one of whom I now perceived to be the mate, lay quite still where I had set them down, and I began to fear that they were all dead and that I had my pains for nothing. However, I ran to the scuttle-butt and fetched a dipper full of water, with which I sprinkled the face of each in turn; and presently I had the satisfaction of seeing Batten and another man make a slight movement of the chest. Thereupon I dashed some more water in their faces, which had the effect of making them catch at their breath with a kind of sigh; and then, when they had breathed a few times, each, in turn, opened his eyes. I now redoubled my efforts to restore the other four, but in spite of all that I could do, none of them showed any sign of reviving, and I was forced, with much reluctance, to conclude that they were dead.

An ominous crackling from beneath the hatch warned me to remove the two living men from so dangerous a neighbourhood; so I dragged them aft to the quarter-deck, and when I had again soused them plentifully with water, they were so far revived as to be able to sit up against the bulwark, although they were still quite dazed and stupid.

Our position was now a most alarming one. The fire, which had evidently broken out in the store-room forward, had fairly taken hold of the ship, for, even as I was dragging the seaman on to the quarter-deck, the fore-scuttle had fallen in and a huge column of smoke, reddened with flame, shot aloft, while thin wisps of vapour began to rise through the gratings of the forehold.

I mounted the poop and looked towards the anchorage at Cape Coast to see if our condition had been observed by any of the anchored vessels. One of them, which appeared to me to be the corvette which had boarded us, had already cast loose her sails, and, by the speed with which they were being mast-headed, I judged that our danger had been seen and understood. Indeed it could hardly have been otherwise if any watch were kept, for the *Charity*, left to herself without guidance from the helm and with her braces hanging slack, had brought to, and was slowly drifting to leeward with most of her canvas aback and her yards swinging to and fro at each heave of the swell. The appearance of the ship, together with the shoreward procession of boats – apart from the smoke that rose from the fore-deck – could scarcely fail to make clear to any nautical observer, what had happened.

The morning was very calm and the surface of the sea of a glassy smoothness, beneath which the swell from the ocean rolled in long regular billows.

There was so little breeze that the columns of smoke from the forecastle rose nearly straight into the air; but what little there was appeared to come from the west, so that the corvette lay almost dead to windward. Nevertheless the man-of-war was between three and four miles distant, and though, as I watched her, studding-sails were set on both sides alow and aloft, until she seemed a veritable cloud of canvas, yet I feared that in this light air she could hardly reach us before the *Charity* would be ablaze from stem to stern.

The two men whom I had rescued had by now revived sufficiently to be able to take in the position of affairs to some extent. Batten staggered to his feet and stared dreamily at the column of smoke.

"The ship's on fire, Mr Roberts," said he looking up at me.

"Yes," I answered, "and here comes the corvette to take us off. But I fear she will hardly be in time. What do you think we had best do?"

"We had better lower a boat," said he.

"The boats are all gone, Mr Batten," said I. "The slaves have put off in them," and I pointed to the procession that was now approaching the shore.

"Oh, aye," said Batten, slowly recovering his not very brilliant wits and gazing first at the slaves and then at the corvette, "well then we must stay where we are."

"Where is the powder stowed?" I asked.

"In the after-hold," he replied. "The magazine is just abaft the trade-room."

This was so far satisfactory, as the fire was at present confined to the fore part of the ship. Yet some measures for our safety would have to be taken, and that pretty soon, for the large empty spaces of the slave-rooms would allow the flames to find their way aft much more quickly than would have been the case if the hold had been filled with cargo.

"I think we had better get the gratings overboard," said I. "Then if the fire spreads aft before the corvette comes up, we can get on them and shove off. They will keep us afloat until we are picked up."

"You are quite right, Mr Roberts," said Batten; "the gratings will keep us afloat. But are we three all that's left?" he added gazing about the deck with a bewildered air.

"There are our shipmates, Mr Batten" said I, pointing to the corpses that lay about the deck, "excepting a few who are in the forecastle."

"God! What a slaughter!" exclaimed Batten, in an awe-stricken voice. "I feared something would happen with all those Coromantee devils on board. And there is Mr Murking too – he's quiet enough now; but, good Lord! how he did holler! I could hear him down in the forepeak just as if he'd been close alongside."

At this moment a great tongue of flame leapt up through the forecastle hatch and speedily caught the foot of the foresail, and in less than a minute the whole of the canvas on the foremast was in a blaze.

"Off with the fore-gratings!" I exclaimed. "There's no time to lose; we shall have the mast tumbling about our ears in another minute or two."

We ran to the fore-hatch, through which the smoke was now raising in a dense cloud, and, lifting the gratings, carried them to the gangway, when, having secured each with a good length of rope, we hoisted them over and dropped them into the water.

One of the main gratings was occupied, as I have said, with Murking's corpse, and with this none of us was disposed to meddle; but we secured the other one and dropped it overboard; and, having now three gratings towing alongside, we were at liberty to leave the ship as soon as it became unsafe to stay longer.

On looking again at the corvette, which had crept up towards us at surprising speed, considering the lightness of the breeze, I perceived that her boats were being lowered, and that one of them – apparently a fast cutter – was already pulling in our direction.

It appeared that the corvette's people had seen us cast the gratings overboard and had thus realised that there were still some persons left on the burning ship.

We all ascended to the poop, and, taking up the most conspicuous positions, waved our hands and neckerchiefs to the approaching boat; a useless proceeding indeed since the speed with which the oars rose and fell showed us that the crew, stirred by the seaman's natural sympathy with sufferers from the greatest of marine disasters, were putting forth their utmost strength in the effort to reach us.

"Smoke's a-comin' out of the main hatch, sir," said the seaman, speaking for the first time since I had hoisted him out of the forecastle.

"Aye, you're right, Watkins," said Batten;" 'Tis time for us to go, Mr Roberts, if we don't want to be blown out."

At this moment the foremast, no longer supported by the burning rigging, fell with a terrific crash, bringing down with it the maintopmast, the spars and sails of which, clattering down with a noise like the discharge of a broadside, buried the forepart of the deck in their ruin and almost immediately burst into a blaze.

'Twas indeed time for us to go, and we lost mighty little in taking our departure.

Slipping down the ropes by which the gratings were secured alongside, we took our respective places, lying down upon the frail rafts that our weight should not cause them to capsize, and, casting loose the ropes, pushed off.

The gratings bore our weight well enough in that quiet sea, and we had been safe enough but for one thing, which was, that in our hurry to escape we had neglected to provide ourselves with any means of propelling the gratings. This oversight now threatened to be our undoing, for, owing to the lightness of the breeze, the *Charity* made so little drift to leeward that we remained nearly stationary with respect to her and within a couple of dozen yards of her side. We did indeed make slight shift to paddle with our hands – though not without some risk of upsetting the gratings – but with all our efforts the distance between us and the burning ship seemed to increase but by inches.

"The mainmast is afire," remarked Watkins cheerfully, after we had been paddling for some minutes like a party of paralytic turtles; "we'll get it presently."

We were, in fact, "getting it" to some extent already, for the burning sails and spars sent up showers of sparks and shreds of blazing canvas, which began to descend on us in most unwelcome profusion; and as the sails on the mizzen-mast had now caught, we fell to speculating, with no little anxiety, as to which side it was likely to take in its fall.

Suddenly there reached my ears the quick rumble of oars, and, as my grating was lifted on the swell, I caught a momentary glimpse, before I sank again into the glassy valley, of the corvette's boat, rushing towards us in a cloud of spray.

A few moments later she swept alongside of us and a rasping voice, which I had heard before, sang out impatiently:

"Come along, man, come along; don't lie sprawling there like a sick frog on a cabbage leaf."

The exhortation was addressed to Batten, who, fearful of capsizing his grating, clung to it in desperation and stared helplessly at the boat, until one of the sailors reached out a boat-hook and dragged him off into the water, when he was promptly seized and hoisted on board. The boat-hook was next extended to Watkins, and, while he was being assisted, rather unceremoniously, to embark, I slipped off my grating and swam to the boat, into which I was immediately hauled by a couple of seamen.

"Any more people on board?" inquired the lieutenant, giving Batten a shake to quicken his wits.

"None but dead men, sir," answered Batten; "we are all that's left of the ship's company."

"Give way, then," shouted the officer; and the sailors, who evidently liked the looks of the *Charity* as little as did their commander, bent to their oars and pulled the boat away even faster than she had come.

Our rescuers had arrived none too soon. Before we were a couple of hundred yards distant from the burning ship, sheets of flame arose from the main deck, and showers of flaming fragments of wood and canvas flew aloft and descended into the sea around, while the mizzen-mast wrapped in a shroud of fire, swayed for a few moments and then came down with a mighty crash immediately over the place where our gratings were afloat.

"Did you carry any stern chasers?" asked the officer.

"No, sir," answered Batten.

"Then we'll keep in a line with the stern for the present," observed the lieutenant; and he accordingly steered the boat past the *Charity*'s quarter until we could see the smoke pouring out of the stern windows.

In this position, and at a safe distance, the men were ordered to lie on their oars, and all hands fell to watching in solemn silence the progress of the conflagration. The ship was now a mere hulk; but, though all her top hamper was gone, the huge column of smoke, lighted at its base with flame, that rose from her decks and spread aloft like a gigantic tree, made her loom up colossal and majestic.

Suddenly there was a loud report, followed quickly by another. The forecastle guns had exploded, and we could see the shot hopping away across the sea, throwing little white plumes of spray where they had touched the water. The lieutenant's precaution had not been unnecessary.

We were sitting gazing with fascinated eyes at the burning ship, and waiting for the explosion of the broadside guns, when, in an instant, the entire vessel burst into a sheet of flame and appeared to rise bodily, and then dissolve into a countless multitude of flying fragments. A dull roar came across the sea and struck us a palpable blow. Great masses of timber and metal soared high into the air, where they remained poised for an instant, apparently motionless.

Then they descended in an avalanche into the sea around and disappeared; and the *Charity* was gone as though she had never been. Where she had floated but a few moments before was the empty sea; and above it an enormous ball of smoke, which moved majestically to leeward, spreading out slowly until it hung, like a great black pall, over the scene of the tragedy.

With one accord, as it seemed, the occupants of the boat drew a deep breath.

"There's a fine funeral for Enoch Murking," remarked Batten.

"Enoch!" exclaimed the officer, "Was that his name? The fat man? Why his godfathers and godmothers must have had the gift of prophecy."

"Aye, sir," said Watkins, "he's gone aloft, sure enough, but I doubt if he ain't mistook his destination. I reckon his charter-party's made out for a different port."

"Silence, you rascal!" exclaimed the lieutenant, "How dare you trifle with sacred things in this ribald fashion. Give way, there," and he sat up stiffly as the men once more bent to their oars.

The corvette, as soon as she had lowered her boats, had hove to, and now lay about a mile to windward of the other two boats, the crews of which, having seen us picked up by the cutter, had remained resting on their oars, looking on at the burning of the *Charity*; we overtook them as we returned, and the three boats pulled back to the ship in company.

"How many have you got, Lamb?" asked the officer who commanded the launch, bringing his boat alongside the cutter.

"Only three," answered the lieutenant; "two seamen and the clerk."

"Oh, you've got the clerk, have you?" said the other, grinning. "He'll be quite useful aboard, won't he? Be able to keep the washing books and write the men's letters for 'em."

The two officers laughed and Mr Lamb regarded me with an expression that occasioned me some uneasiness. Clearly I had been spoken about on board the corvette, though in what connection it was impossible to guess; and no further light was thrown upon the matter by the officers, for the launch sheered off and allowed the cutter to pass her.

As we approached the man-of-war, I looked at her with a sailor's interest and curiosity. She was considerably smaller than the *Asphodel* and of a sharper build with finer lines, especially forward; her shape suggested a very smart and speedy craft, as did also her long spars, and my first survey of her gave me a very favourable impression.

"Well, Mr Clerk," said the lieutenant, who had been watching me as I examined the little warship, "what think you of the corvette?"

"A pretty ship, sir, and looks like a smart sailer," I answered.

"Quite right," he answered, "so as you like her looks jump aboard."

We swept alongside the gangway as he spoke, and he skipped up the side, hardly touching the man-ropes, and signed for me to follow.

CHAPTER TWENTY-TWO

In which I return to an Old Haunt

As soon as I reached the deck Mr Lamb turned on me sharply, looking mighty fierce.

"We've no use for quill-drivers aboard ship, you know," said he, "and you've got to earn your passage. What can you do? You don't look like a landsman."

"I can do the duty of an ordinary seaman, sir," I answered.

"Ah, I thought so," said he. "Here, Simmons; just have this young gentleman's name entered in the ship's books as an ordinary seaman, and remember, my friend, that this is a king's ship, not a stinking slave-wagon, and behave accordingly."

I promised to bear the circumstance in mind, and, having saluted the lieutenant, followed the midshipman to the purser's quarters, where I was duly enrolled as a member of the crew of His Majesty's sloop-of-war *Naiad*.

The corvette, as soon as she had hoisted in her boats, commenced to beat up for her anchorage, a process that, as the breeze continued light, consumed the best part of the morning. When the anchor had been let go opposite the castle, and the sails stowed, the hands were piped to dinner, greatly to my satisfaction, for I had tasted no food since the preceding evening; and I now had an opportunity of making the acquaintance of my messmates. Some of them, indeed, I had seen already, for they were part of the consignment that Mr Lamb had brought from the *Charity*; and the rest were rough, good-natured, simple fellows of the same type as the occupants of the 'tween-decks of the *Asphodel* or any other king's ship.

"This here is a bit of a change for you, Mr Roberts," observed one of the *Charity's* men, as we gathered round the little mess-table.

"And a mighty pleasant change, too, let me tell you," I answered; and then as the man looked surprised, I gave an account of the events that had occurred on the slaver since they had left, to which the men around the table listened open-mouthed.

"Darn me!" exclaimed a hairy sea-monster, who sat opposite to me, fetching the little table a thump that set the platters dancing, "Darn me if I wouldn't a-given the rascal a drubbing myself! You did quite right, my lad, and acted like a freeborn Briton. But, look ye," he added, suddenly changing his tone, "don't ye be a-fallin' across the hawse of any of the officers aboard *this* ship. 'Twould be no matter of a-clappin' ye in the bilboes, here; 'twould mean runnin' ye up to the yard-arm; so just mind your eye, mate."

I thanked my friend for his advice and promised to refrain from battering my superior officers, and the talk then turned upon the domestic affairs of the ship and the prospects of the voyage.

The *Naiad*, I gathered, was an eminently comfortable ship, for my messmates spoke well, not only of the vessel herself and her officers, but even of the provisions, which were certainly unusually good for a ship of war, as I had already discovered. This was all very pleasant hearing, especially when one considered what an inferno a king's ship can be under brutal officers and with uneatable provisions; but the item of news that rejoiced me most was that the ship was at present taking in fresh meat, vegetables and water preparatory to sailing for England.

After dinner all hands were mustered to help in unloading the canoes that came off from the shore loaded with limes, bananas, soursops and other fruit of the country, as well as beef and goat's flesh; and a very cherry party we made, for everyone was in high glee at the prospect of bidding farewell to this torrid and sickly coast. By sunset we had got all the fresh stores on board excepting a part of the water, the shipping of which was expected to take some time, as the casks had to be brought out singly in canoes; and though these little craft – each of which was fashioned very neatly out of a single log of wood – were exceedingly staunch and buoyant, yet the surf that broke on the beach, under the castle wall, rendered it unsafe for them to put off with a heavy lading.

That night I enjoyed the unwonted luxury of a sound, unbroken sleep, and never before had I fully appreciated the comfort of a hammock. The 'tween-decks were remarkably airy – much more so than those of the *Asphodel*, though the latter contrasted favourably enough in this respect with a ship of the line —, and as a small anchor-watch only was set, I had the full night in. Consequently I turned out in the morning mightily refreshed, and fell to cheerfully upon the holystone, driving it up and down the sanded deck with such goodwill as drew a smile of approbation from the lieutenant of the watch.

At daybreak the canoes began to arrive alongside with the water-casks, and the work of hoisting in the latter commenced, and proceeded without intermission until nearly ten o'clock, when the welcome news was circulated that the last cask was on board. All hands were now on the very tiptoe of expectation, and when Mr Lamb appeared on the quarter-deck with his speaking-trumpet tucked under his arm, every man was at his station ready to leap into the rigging at the word.

"Cast loose the sails," said the lieutenant; and as the entire crew made a simultaneous rush for the shrouds, and flew aloft in a body, like a troop of monkeys, his red, wrathful face broke into a grim smile.

"Lazy, overfed rascals," he growled; "they can be smart enough when they've got the Tavern under their lee."

Smart enough indeed they were. The gaskets were off in a twinkling, and the creamy-white canvas fell in great dropping masses, almost simultaneously from every yard on the ship.

"Heave short!" said Mr Lamb, as the hands came tumbling down the ratlines or sliding down the back stays.

The capstan bars were shipped, the messenger was passed, the "jollies" took their places, and the fifers inflated their chests. Then from the latter burst forth the cheerful strains of "Drops of Brandy" – not without a certain prophetic significance – and the marines began to stamp round the capstan, while the top-men looked on with grins of happiness.

As the cable came in, the hands tailed on to the halyards, and the ship opened out her white petals like a flower bursting into bloom. The anchor broke out of the ground, the "jollies" broke into a trot, and the fifers grew purple in the face in their frantic struggle to keep pace with them.

At last all the preparations were completed; the well-scrubbed anchor was laid to rest upon the bill-board, the shank-painters were secured as though they were never again to be cast off, the yards were trimmed, ropes flemished down, and His Majesty's sloop-of-war *Naiad* stood out to sea with her flying jibboom pointing west-south-west.

That afternoon, as I was engaged with a party of men, tautening up the lanyards of the lee rigging, a corporal of marines came forward, looking about as if in search of someone.

"Is there any man here of the name of Roberts?" he asked.

I informed him that that was my name, for by my old title I had been entered in the ship's books.

"Then you've got to come along o' me to the captain's cabin," said he.

"What's in the wing?" I asked, as I followed him aft.

"Can't say as I rightly knows," he answered, adding encouragingly, "but you'll soon find out, I reckon."

I descended to the cabin – for the *Naiad* was a flush-decked ship – in the wake of my conductor, and found three officers seated at the table with writing materials set before them. One of these was Mr Lamb; another I recognised as the lieutenant who had charge of the morning watch, and the third – who sat at the head of the table – I judged to be the commander; or, to give him his courtesy title, the captain.

I had not seen him before, and my first impression was highly favourable. He was an elderly man, with snow-white hair, which he wore, rather needlessly, powdered. His face was round and ruddy, and of a most gentle, benevolent cast; indeed, he looked more like a country clergyman than a naval officer, and contrasted oddly with his irascible first lieutenant.

"James Roberts," said the latter, casting upon me a most ferocious glare, "Captain Maitland has sent for you to ask you a few questions. Do you ever tell the truth, sir?"

"'Tis my ordinary custom, sir," I answered, preserving my gravity with some difficulty.

"Then you may follow your usual practice on this occasion," said Mr Lamb.

"Certainly, by all means," said the captain.

"Be good enough," continued Mr Lamb, "to inform the captain how long you had been on board the slaver when I boarded her."

"Three days, sir," I replied.

"And you were the master's clerk?"

"I had been appointed clerk the previous evening."

"And you were a landsman?" demanded the lieutenant, glancing at the captain.

"That was not my statement, sir," I objected.

"Aha, a sea-lawyer, methinks!" said Mr Lamb. "You heard the master tell me a lie, and you did not contradict him."

"'Twas not for me, sir, to contradict the master of the ship," I answered, "and, moreover, when he had seen me last I was a landsman."

"There is a good deal in what he says," observed the captain mildly.

"Plausible, sir, plausible," answered Mr Lamb.

"Now," he continued, fiercely, "tell us who the man was who came on board the slaver with you."

This was an awkward question, and I paused before replying.

"That's right!" exclaimed Mr Lamb; "think before you speak. Don't tell the wrong lie."

"He was a man, sir," said I, "to whom I was under great obligations."

"Shared up liberally, did he? H'm! Was that man a pirate, sir, or was he not?"

"My impression, sir, is that he was a pirate," I answered.

"Your impression!" exclaimed Mr Lamb, with a scornful laugh; "come, sir, tell us how you came to be in this man's company."

I reflected for a moment, and decided that the wisest plan was to tell the whole truth, sparing my friends as much as possible. I accordingly gave the officers an account of all that had happened to me since I was taken by the press-gang at Gravesend, reserving nothing but my relationship to Percival, and my presence on the occasion of his second visit to the island.

The three men listened with close attention as I related my adventures, and when I had concluded the captain bestowed on me an approving smile.

"A very clear and connected story," he observed.

"Yes, sir," said Mr Lamb; "one tale is good till another is heard."

"Yes, that is true, too," agreed the captain.

"This fellow," continued Mr Lamb, "is, by his own admission, a runaway seaman from one of His Majesty's ships. He has also been for some three weeks an associate of pirates – one may even say a member of the crew of a pirate ship."

"There is a good deal of truth in what you say, Mr Lamb," said the captain.

"That being the case," pursued the lieutenant, "I submit, sir, that he is liable to arrest as a pirate and a deserter from His Majesty's navy."

"Undoubted, undoubtedly," assented the captain.

"I beg to point out, sir," said I, "that I did not leave my ship, but that the ship left me."

"That, of course, makes a great differences Mr Lamb," said the captain.

"A mere excuse, sir," snorted Lamb, "and, moreover, who would believe the word of a deserter. The rascals are always ready enough with an explanation."

"Quite so, quite so!" said the captain; "I entirely agree with you."

"Then, as to the pirate, you stayed on board of your own free will, did you not?" demanded the lieutenant.

"No, sir," I answered; "I asked to be allowed to go away in the boat, and was refused."

"Yes, you see, Mr Lamb," said the captain, "he asked to be allowed to go and was refused. He could do no more, could he?"

"Asked!" exclaimed Lamb. "He should have gone without asking."

"Of course he should," agreed the captain. "You should have gone; why didn't you go?"

"I was not permitted, sir," I replied.

"Well, if he was not permitted to go," said the captain, "why he had to stay, you know, Mr Lamb."

"The fact remains, sir," said Lamb, doggedly, "that he was at large on board a pirate for near upon three weeks. 'Tis a felony, at least."

"I fear it is," said the captain.

"And he should, by rights, be confined in irons and delivered up to justice," said Lamb.

"No doubt," agreed the captain; "that would be the proper course."

I interposed at this point to express the hope that I should not be confined in fetters, pointing out that the precaution was unnecessary, as it was impossible for me to escape, and I was willing to do my duty. I remarked, further, that I had only been released from confinement on the morning when the *Charity* was lost.

"What!" exclaimed Mr Lamb, "were you in irons on board the slaver?"

"I was, sir," I answered, and proceeded to give an account of my assault on Murking, and the consequences which followed it, to which Mr Lamb listened attentively, with a warlike gleam in his fierce blue eye.

"Why, now," says he, "here is a pretty mutinous, fire-eating rascal that we have taken on board. We shall be getting our heads broken next. Not but what that slaving villain deserved all he got; I'll say that."

"Undoubtedly, Mr Lamb," said the captain, "he richly deserved it, though it was certainly highly insubordinate conduct on the part of this young man. But what do you suggest that we should do? Do you think the prisoner should be confined in irons? It seems a needlessly severe measure."

"We should lose a seaman by putting him in irons," said the second lieutenant, "and he is a smart fellow, and willing, too."

"Well," Mr Lamb conceded, "perhaps he might be allowed his liberty as long as he behaves well. He can't run away while we are at sea, and he could be secured when we come into port. After all, 'tis our business to hand him over to justice, not to punish him, especially as he has not been tried."

"Very well, then," said the captain; "let that be our decision. The man is to be at large until we enter our port."

On this I was dismissed, and returned to the deck greatly relieved, though the prospect of being haled before a justice on a charge of piracy was not altogether to my taste, nor was that of being claimed as a deserter from the King's navy. But these matters lay in the future, and so I put them out of my mind and went about my duties.

The *Naiad* having obtained an offing of about twenty miles, sailed parallel to the coast until she was clear of Cape Palmas, when she bade farewell to the land, and stood out into the Atlantic on a north-westerly course, passing outside the Cape Verde islands, which we sighted on the ninth day after leaving Cape Coast. This was the last we saw of Africa or its islands, for we passed some distance to the westward of the Canaries, giving the land a wide berth, and carrying a good sailing breeze with us all the way. About the latitude of Cape Finisterre we were overtaken by a moderate gale from the south-west, before which we scudded under reefed topsails for a couple of days, and this brought us fairly into the chops of the Channel.

It was somewhere to the north of Brest, I think, that we struck soundings, and never shall I forget the thrill with which I watched the men haul up the deep-sea lead and examine the shells and sea-rubbish that stuck to the arming. It was evening, and though the gale had nearly blown itself out, there was still a good deal of wind and a very heavy sea rolling up from the ocean; but when we had seen those homely fragments upon the lead, and knew that the "Channel of old England" lay ahead, we shook out the reefs joyously and snapped our fingers at the blustering weather.

Next morning, about ten o'clock, we sighted Start Point, and, taking a fresh departure, bore up west-north-west and joined the stream of homeward-bound shipping that was moving up Channel. Late in the evening we saw Portland Bill over the bow, and when the sun rose on the following morning, its light fell upon the high chalk cliffs of Beachy Head.

The wind had by now veered round to the north-west, and we found it mighty cold after the sultry air of the Tropics; but we cared nothing for that, for the winter sun shone brightly, and our native land lay close aboard; and we hailed with delight every order that sent us aloft, whence we could look out across the busy Channel and gladden our eyes with the sight of the white cliffs and homely green fields of Old England.

It was late in the evening when we rounded the South Foreland and saw the crowded Downs ahead of us, and the daylight had gone – greatly to my regret – before we let go our anchor. But, late as it was, the cable had hardly run out before a galley-punt, with a crew of hardy Deal boatmen, came groping alongside to give us the news and see if anyone was wishing to go ashore.

The news seemed somewhat to disappoint the people of the *Naiad*, who had been under the impression that war had already been declared. It now appeared that England was still at peace with the French, though the relations had become such that ships of war were being recalled in large numbers from the more distant foreign stations – a fact which, when I heard of it, caused me to speculate concerning the whereabouts of the *Asphodel*.

The Deal boat was ordered to remain alongside to convey the captain ashore, and presently our commander appeared, swathed in a heavy boat-cloak, and descended into her, when she pushed off into the darkness. He did not return to the ship until daybreak on the following morning, when we had just finished holystoning the deck and were blowing upon our fingers to warm them; but within a couple of minutes of his coming on board, the order was passed to heave up the anchor.

The north-west wind had now given place to a biting north-easter which struck us as uncommonly keen when we lay out on the yards to cast loose the sails, and we looked down with some envy at the marines, tramping round the capstan to the music of the fife. The ebb-tide having just commenced to run out through the Downs, we had to pass round the South Sand Head to get an offing, and then for an hour or two we sailed on a northerly course with the Goodwins, white and threatening under our lee.

When once we were clear of the North Foreland, however, we had a fair wind, and, presently, a fair tide also; and with our studding-sails set, we slipped along at so good a pace that when we anchored for the night, we were some miles to the westward of the Nore.

I now began to speculate, with considerable interest, on the course that the commander intended to pursue in regard to me. Since the consultation in the cabin, nothing had passed. I was nominally under arrest, but had gone about my duties and enjoyed the same privileges as the other men. The *Naiad* had proved an eminently comfortable ship; punishments were rare on board and many little concessions were made to the men, by which life was rendered more pleasant. Even Mr Lamb, for all his rasping voice and blustering manner, was really a kind and considerate officer, and not a little liked by the crew; while the petty officers, taking their tone from their superiors, refrained from bullying and worrying the men, and kept their colts in their pockets.

At daybreak next morning we got under way, and, the north-easter still continuing, all sail was crowded on, and we crept up slowly over the ebb-tide. The low shores of Canvey Island and the flat marshlands of Essex and Kent slipped past, until the ship rounded Hope Point, and began to work her way against the swiftly-running tide up the Lower Hope.

Presently we passed the mouth of Cliffe Creek, and I looked from the beacon across to the little village of East Tilbury, on the opposite side of the river, and thought of that evening – years ago it seemed, as I recalled it – when I had sneaked away on board the *Tally Ho*, a despairing fugitive, with the hounds of justice baying after me from the shore.

A few minutes more and we turned into Gravesend Reach, and there, rising above the flats that bordered the river, was Shorne itself, with the old mill upon the hill-top full in sight, and its sails turning merrily in the breeze. I hardly dared trust myself to look lest my emotions should burst all bounds and shame me before my shipmates; and yet I could not but steal a glance now and then as I thought that Prudence was there, and, perchance, even now looking at our ship through her old spy-glass.

The anchorage was very full, several king's ships being moored among the merchantmen and coasters, and as we crawled up the fairway, each of these was eagerly examined by our men.

"There's the old *Tartar*," said one. "My brother Bill's aboard of her. I thought she were in the West Indies, but I reckon she has been recalled, same as what we have."

"That's about it, mate," said another. "There's the *Centaur*; we saw her at Ascension; but who's that there donkey-frigate just ahead?"

The men scrutinised the vessel we were approaching, and as we opened her broadside, one of them exclaimed:

"I knows her; she's the *Asphodel*" – he pronounced the word "ass-fodle," assuming, it would appear, a connection between the ship's name and her build – "my cousin Tom was aboard of her before he shipped on the *Ajax*."

A single glance at the vessel showed me that the fellow was right. It was the *Asphodel*, sure enough, and a very handsome ship she looked, with her sails neatly furled, her yards squared to a nicety, and a row of snowy hammocks along her rail. We passed her slowly, though the tide was beginning to run slack, and so close that I was able to recognise many of the men who stared at us over the hammock-nettings.

As I was surveying her, I suddenly became aware that Mr Lamb was standing within a few feet of me on the other side of the invisible line that terminates the quarter-deck on a corvette, and was watching me with a grim smile.

"I see you are having a look at your old ship, Roberts," said he, as I caught his eye. "Would you like to be put aboard of her?"

"No thank you, sir," I answered; "she was a comfortable ship, but I like the *Naiad* better."

"Ha! you won't like her so well presently," said he. "The captain says you must be put in irons as soon as the anchor goes down."

"I am sorry for that, sir," said I.

"I dare say you are," he answered, "but it has to be. You were entered in the ship's log as a pirate, and you'll have to be given up to justice; and you'll need to be put in irons because 'twould be so mighty easy to make off here in the river. You could just skip overboard and strike out for the shore, and you'd be off before we could get a boat lowered."

"I don't think, sir, that there is any evidence on which to convict me," I said.

"Possibly not," he replied, "but I judge your actions by what I should do in your place, and I warrant you I would give the gaols a wide berth if it were only a matter of swimming a hundred yards or so."

With this he turned on his heel and walked away aft, leaving me to act upon what I could only regard as a pretty broad hint. There was undoubtedly a great deal of truth in what he had said. Gaols were places to be avoided at all risks, and here, in Gravesend Reach, I had only to drop overboard to run a very fair chance of getting away into the town before any pursuit could be started. Yet I hesitated to make the attempt, not so much on account of the risk, as that, being at large, I was in a measure on parole; and so I let the opportunity slip, and we passed on to Northfleet Hope, with its level stretches of marshland where pursuit would be easy.

Before we reached Greenhithe the flood-tide overtook us, and we slipped up Long Reach at a great pace, threading our way among a crowd of colliers, hoys, and merchant vessels that had hove up their anchors when the tide turned. One after another the familiar landmarks on the river-bank glided past – Purfleet, Erith, Woolwich –

until as we turned south from Bugsby's Hole the forest of masts that marked the Pool of London rose across the marshes.

We were approaching the head of Blackwall Reach when Mr Lamb once more accosted me.

"There's a sight that should make you thoughtful, Roberts," said he.

He nodded as a he spoke towards the low shore of the Isle of Dogs, where I could see a row of gibbets, now half-submerged by the rising tide, each bearing a corpse that hung in chains, with its feet but a few inches above the surface of the water.

"That's how pirates are dealt with," said Mr Lamb. "'Tis a short shrift and speedy promotion that waits for the bold sea rover when he falls into the hands of justice."

With this pleasant reminder he stumped away aft, and presently began to roar out orders for shortening sail. I ran aloft for the last time, and as I stood in the foot-ropes rolling up the fore-topgalllant sail, I looked down upon the stately façade of Greenwich Hospital, and saw the tower of Limehouse Church looming up over the land.

A little to the north of Deptford Creek the helm was put over, and the topsail-yards trimmed, and as the ship swung round head to stream the anchor fell with a heavy splash into the yellow water.

While the hands were still aloft furling the topsails, the master-at-arms approached me, accompanied by the armourer, bearing a pair of leg-irons.

"We've got to clap these here irons on to your legs, Jim Roberts," said the former, with an apologetic grimace at the shackles. "Seems a scurvy way for to finish up a cruise, but you knows more about it than what we do."

He conducted me below into the 'tween-decks, where the irons were secured on to my ankles, and I was left, seated on a chest, to meditate on my condition, while the crew were set to smartening up the ship and putting her into harbour trim.

My confinement was of a singularly informal character, for when supper-time came I took my meal in the mess-berth in the usual way, receiving the ordinary rations and the customary allowance of rum, and my messmates chatted with me as though nothing had occurred out of the common. But when the hammocks were piped down I received another visit from the master-at-arms, who was accompanied this time by a ship's corporal bearing a battle lanthorn.

"You've got come on deck, Mr Lamb says," he observed; "you ain't safe down here; you might be a-slippin' out through the hawse-holes."

This was a most extraordinary proceeding, for, since the ship was in port, only an anchor watch would be set and it was pretty certain that the men composing it would seek out sheltered spots and go to sleep until they were relieved.

"Come, now, move yourself," said the master-at-arms; "and look ye, my lad, you walk up that ladder carefully, or you'll have them irons a-droppin' off."

I glanced back, and by the light of the lanthorn I could see that the faces of both men beamed with the broadest of grins; indeed, I had already been struck by the surprising roominess of the leg-irons, the bands of which seemed to have been originally made to fit the ankles of some contumacious elephant.

"Here you are, young man," said the master-at-arms, indicating a little shelter that had been rigged up against the after side of the galley; "you jest stow yourself in there and keep quiet, d'ye see, or you'll be wakin' up the watch."

The corporal threw the light of the lanthorn into the shelter, and, as I seated myself, the two men retired chuckling audibly.

I now proceeded to examine my shackles more closely, and found that they were, in fact, only kept on by my shoes, for, when I removed the latter, the hoops slipped quite easily over my heels. I replaced them for the present, in case any rounds of inspection should be made, and settled myself in my shelter to wait until the ship was quiet and all hands had turned in. The men who formed the first watch were evidently excited by their return home, for they stood around a gun and yarned and argued with the greatest animation, though in suppressed voices, until I could have gone out and knocked their heads together.

The officer of the watch, too, seemed restless and I could hear him, and sometimes see him, stumping up and down the quarter-deck, whistling softly or stopping to look over the side at the lights of the town of Greenwich.

So the time passed. Every quarter of an hour the chime of a church clock – that of the parish church of Greenwich, I suppose – was borne upon the breeze, telling me that the precious minutes were slipping away. Nine o'clock, half-past nine, ten o'clock struck, and still the mumbling conversation went on, and still the officer continued to pace the deck.

A quarter-past ten! More then half of the first watch was gone, and I began to grow seriously uneasy. What if the men of the middle watch should prove wakeful too?

As I was thus reflecting, the officer yawned loudly, and paused in his walk, and, on peering out, I saw him seat himself behind one of the quarter-deck guns.

His yawn seemed to remind the sailors that they were wasting precious time, for I heard one of them remark:

"Well, brothers, I reckon we've about had our fill of jawing. Here's for a nap."

The proposed change of entertainment appeared to commend itself to the rest, for very shortly, the talking ceased, and when I looked out, first on one side and then on the other, I could see nothing but a foot here and there projecting beyond the carriage of a gun.

The moon was shining, though not very brightly, and I determined to wait until a mass of cloud – which was approaching it – had obscured its light, for at present everything about the deck was quite plainly visible. Meanwhile I proceeded with my preparations.

Slipping off my shoes I drew the irons over my feet and laid them down very quietly on the deck. Next, as I reflected that I should want my shoes as soon as I was ashore, I searched my pockets for a piece of spunyarn – an article that a sailor is seldom unprovided with – and having found a little hank of about two fathoms, I secured the shoes to my back by passing the spunyarn round my waist.

These arrangements concluded, I looked out once more. The cloud had crept over the moon, and the deck was shrouded in darkness. Not a soul was to be seen, and occasional snore proceeded from the neighbourhood of one of the forecastle guns.

I stepped out of my shelter, and having looked quickly up and down the deck, crept into the deeper gloom under the bulwark and stole aft, stooping to pass under the muzzles of the guns.

When I reached the main rigging, I stood up, and, climbing noiselessly over the hammock-nettings, let myself down into the channel, and dropping over the edge, slid down one of the preventer-platers. Here for a moment I hung by one arm; then I let go and dropped, striking the ship's side and rebounding into the water.

The first plunge into the icy river completely took away my breath, and I sank two or three fathoms before I recovered myself sufficiently to strike out. When I came to the surface and shook the water out of my eyes and ears, I was just passing the ship's quarter, and I could hear the officer, calling loudly to the watch.

"Come, rouse up there!" he shouted. "What was that splash? Somebody's gone overboard."

The tide carried me swiftly away from the vessel, and I heard no more, though I saw a lanthorn lowered over the stern a minute or so later; but I was in no condition to take notice of any possible pursuit, for the water was so intensely cold that already I began to feel my limbs stiffening and my hands and feet benumbed, and I knew that my only chance was to make direct for the shore. Accordingly I struck out with all my strength, guiding myself by observing the direction in which I was carried past the anchored vessels.

But short as was the distance that I had to cover, I began to fear that it was beyond my strength. The exhausting effect of the cold was a thing I had not allowed for, and I found my strokes growing slower and slower, and my breathing more laboured, until I felt as though I must let the tide carry me whithersoever it would.

Of a sudden, just as I was on the point of giving up, my foot struck the submerged wooden steps of a causeway; I grasped them with the tenacity of a drowning man, drew myself up, and stood upon the slimy platform, shivering and wretched, but safe.

My first act was to untie the spunyarn and slip on my shoes; then I walked up the causeway, passed through a kind of archway or tunnel, and down a flight of stone stairs into a narrow street that ran parallel to the river.

It was now that the idea of pursuit first occurred to me, and I perceived the necessity of putting as great a distance as possible between me and the ship. I looked up and down the deserted street, and, making my decision in an instant, turned to the right and set off at a run.

The street along which I ran was at first much like that of a waterside village, with houses here and there, and large spaces of fields and gardens between; but soon the houses became closer together, and the aspect of the place more townlike, and after I had been running for about a quarter of an hour I came out into a wider space, in the middle of which was a church. As I slackened my pace and looked up at the steeple, I recognised it in an instant. It was the church of St Mary, Rotherhithe. Oddly enough, it had fallen out that in my flight from the corvette I had returned along the very street which I had traversed with poor Bill Muffin on the morning when I had fled from Mr Murking's house. The house now lay within a few minutes' walk of where I stood, and it seemed as if Fate were guiding me towards it.

And why not? Murking was there no longer, and as to Rebecca she would certainly not betray me, and would most likely give me shelter for the moment.

Reflecting thus, and considering the fact that I had no other friend or refuge within reach, I made the resolution to seek out Rebecca and throw myself upon her compassion.

No sooner had I reached this decision than I began to step out briskly in the direction of the house; but as I walked on, I suddenly bethought me that, at this late hour, Rebecca would most likely have gone to bed, and that the noise I should have to make to arouse her would be a source of great danger if I were pursued, since, the whole neighbourhood would become aware of my arrival. Hence I decided to approach the house from the rear, whence I had left it, and, if nobody was stirring, to keep quiet until the morning.

I now began to look very closely at the houses on my left hand, anxious lest I should miss the narrow alley through which I had formerly fled; and this I very nearly did, after all, so inconspicuous was it in the shadow of the houses.

But when I had made sure of it, I passed under the archway and up the little lane until I came to the wall at the end of Mr Murking's garden, which I identified without difficulty by the single buttress that ran up the middle of it. I stood and looked up at the high wall, and wished for the friendly ladder which had helped me over on the last occasion; however, I was now a sailor, and if there was no ladder there was at least the buttress, which was rather narrow and projecting, and so afforded a fairly good hold.

Having listened for a moment to make sure that no one was approaching, I raised my hands as high as I could reach, and, grasping the angles of the buttress, drew myself up a little. Then I caught the buttress between my knees, and shifted my hands up a few inches, and so by degrees I crept up until I was atop of the wall.

Here I sat and surveyed the house, making a little noise with my heels to ascertain if any watch-dog was kept. There was no light in any of the windows, nor any sign of life either in house or garden, so I dropped down and walked softly up the path.

Now that I had ceased running my wet clothes made me dreadfully chilly, and I looked forward with some dismay to spending the long winter's night without shelter; indeed my teeth began to chatter so horribly that I was almost resolved to rouse up Rebecca at all costs, when my eye fell upon a small outhouse built against the wall near the well, and I thought it wise to explore it and see if it would shelter me sufficiently to prevent me from catching my death of cold.

On looking in, I perceived that the little house contained a quantity of rubbish and disused household furniture and utensils, while at one end were a number of empty sacks and a heap of straw. This, I thought, would answer my requirements well enough for the present, so I entered and shut the door, finding sufficient light from the moonbeams that slanted in through crevices in the woodwork to enable me to make my arrangements for the night.

These were of the simplest character. Having spread some of the sacks upon a portion of the straw by way of a bed, I got into one of the other sacks and pulled the rest of the straw in a heap on top of me. Over this I laid the remainder of the sacks as a coverlet, and then crept to the very bottom of the one that I was in – as a caddis worm retires into his tube. In a very few minutes I was as hot as I cared to be, and steaming like a new-boiled patato, and in yet a few minutes more I was sound asleep.

CHAPTER TWENTY-THREE

In which I come to an Anchor at the Bell Inn

I slept on very comfortably in my warm nest for about four hours, when, as is usually the way with seamen newly come ashore, I awoke, expecting to be roused out to take my watch. As I stirred, the straw above me rustled, and I then recollected where I was, upon which I turned over in great enjoyment of the warmth and composed myself for sleep again. The force of habit, however, was so strong that I did not fall into a sound slumber, but dozed and dreamed and woke up at intervals until I heard a church clock strike six, and a few minutes afterwards the sound of bolts being drawn back and the creak of opening shutters.

I crept out from my bed, and, pushing the door of the outhouse a few inches open, peeped forth. It was still quite dark, but a light flitted about inside the window that faced the garden, and presently the door opened, and I perceived my old friend Rebecca approaching down the flagged path with a lighted candle in one hand and a bucket in the other. She set the candle down in a sheltered corner by the well, and, having hooked the bucket on to the rope, flung back the flap and gave the handle a turn. Her back was towards me, and, as she let go the handle and the bucket descended, I took advantage of the noise made by the revolving axle to squeeze out of the doorway and slip past her; and, while she was peering down into the well, I ran up the path, holding my shoes in my hand, and entered the door, which she had left ajar.

I stepped into the house on tiptoe, and proceeded stealthily, thinking there might be someone about besides Rebecca, but when I made my way to the kitchen I found it empty, and a new-lit fire crackling in the grate. Having slipped my feet into my shoes, I drew a stool to the fire, and, reaching down a great pair of bellows from the wall, fell to coaxing the fire to burn more brightly, for the morning was mighty raw, and the kitchen as cold as a vault; and I was thus engaged when I saw the light approaching outside the window and heard Rebecca push open the back door.

As she entered the kitchen and perceived me, she stopped dead, and uttered a cry of amazement; and so remained for some moments standing staring at me as if petrified, while I went on blowing the fire and watched her out of the corner of my eye.

Presently she set down the bucket, very deliberately, and reaching a large broom out of a corner, advanced slowly towards me with the weapon poised, looking uncommonly formidable.

"Why, Mistress Rebecca!" said I, laughing heartily at her warlike attitude, "here is a pretty welcome to offer to an old friend! Do you not remember James Roberts?"

"Roberts!" exclaimed Rebecca, still keeping the broom pointed at me, "I thought it had been some blackamoor! Aye, now I see 'tis that same good-for-nothing; and what do you do here, sir, and how came you into my kitchen?"

"Come, come, Mistress Rebecca," said I, "give me some better greeting than that. Are we not old acquaintances and good friends too?"

I laid down the bellows, and stepping across to her, regardless of the threatening broom, kissed her affectionately, and got a hearty cuff of the head for my pains.

"If you do that again I'll scratch your face," said she. I did it again, on which she struck out viciously with the broom, though I suffered no great bodily injury from her assault.

"How did you get into my kitchen?" she demanded, when I had retired out of range of her weapon to renew the parley from a safe distance.

"I will tell you that presently," said I, "and a great deal more. Many strange things have happened since I left this house, Rebecca; things that you will be very surprised to hear. Let us get the breakfast ready, and then I will tell you all my adventures."

"Who cares for your adventures?" snorted Rebecca. "'Tis no concern of mine where you have been gadding about, or what mischief you have been after."

"My adventures concern you more than you think," said I.

"Indeed!" said she, her curiosity getting the better of her fierceness for a moment. "Well, don't stand there babbling like a fool; fill the kettle."

A truce having been thus tacitly arrived at, I proceeded to fill the kettle from the bucket, spilling a good deal of water on the floor in the process, and receiving the gratifying information that I was a clumsy booby. Meanwhile Rebecca placed a large frying-pan on the fire, and slapped into it two enormous gammon rashers, which soon began to hiss and splutter and emit a most delicious fragrance.

"You've been in the water again," said Rebecca suddenly, with a disdainful glance at my clothes and shoes.

I admitted the accusation.

"Never saw such a man," she muttered; "'tis a regular water spaniel. You've been foreign, too, haven't you?" she added, with a searching look at my brown face.

"Yes," I answered, "I have been to Africa."

"Africa, eh?" said she. "Well, don't sniff at the bacon like that. Are those the manners you learn in foreign parts?"

I excused myself, remarking that bacon was a novelty to me, and Rebecca continued to bustle about, dividing her attention between the table, the frying-pan, and the kettle, which was singing on the trivet. At last everything was ready, the cloth laid, the china set out, the little silver teapot warmed, dried, and aired, and the inlaid caddy brought forth from the cupboard. Then the tea was made and the bacon dished up, and we sat down to breakfast, Rebecca reserving for herself a shred about two inches square cut from one of the rashers, and putting the remainder on my plate, regardless of my protests and entreaties for a fairer division.

Gourmets who seek their chief pleasures at the table, commonly take an entirely wrong method of achieving their aim, multiplying dishes and striving to tickle their jaded plates with rich and rare delicacies and curious wines; whereas, if they would really know what sensations food is capable of yielding, they should spend a month or two in the 'tween decks of a king's ship, dieting upon beef that has grown old in the cask, and musty biscuit full of the worm. Then when they had grown to eat such fare with appetite, they should sit down before a smoking gammon rasher, with new-baked bread and fragrant tea, and I warrant them to snap their fingers at all the kick-shaws and dainties that load the table of the epicure.

Rebecca sat pecking at her food and gloating over my voraciousness with true womanly satisfaction, though I could see that she was on tenter-hooks to hear my story; so that when I had finished the bacon, and eaten little more than half of a quartern loaf, I declared myself fully satisfied, though, to speak the truth, I could have finished the bread to the last crust.

"Very well," said Rebecca, pouring herself out a fresh cup of tea, "if you can eat no more let us hear these wonderful adventures of yours."

Hereupon I plunged into my story without further preamble, starting from the time when I had fled from the house after receiving her warning, and going through my impressment, my life on the island, my sojourn on the pirate schooner, and the events that befell on board the *Charity*, and bringing my narrative up to the very moment when she had found me in the kitchen.

To all of this she listened with profound attention, and many a little exclamation of surprise, and when I came to speak of Murking's terrible death, I could see that she was deeply shocked, for she wiped her eyes with her apron, though in a surreptitious manner, as if half ashamed; and when I had finished my story she would have me tell her over again how the slaves broke out and wreaked their vengeance upon her employer.

"Well, well," she said, wiping her eyes again as I concluded, "God rest his soul – if he had one, which I sometimes doubted. 'Tis worse than thumb-screws by this time, I fear, and hotter than Guinea, too. He was a bad man, Mr Roberts; a very bad man, and yet he had his virtues; no one could have enjoyed a fried black-pudding more than he did, and he was the best judge of tripe that I ever knew."

She was silent for a time, and sat looking thoughtfully at the fire, evidently following out some train of reflection. The nature of her meditations appeared presently, as she concluded aloud:

"Yes, yes, 'tis all for the best, no doubt. I never could have thought of Mr Murking as a cherubim; his figure would have been quite unsuitable."

It was certainly difficult to imagine the late shipmaster in the character referred to, and I agreed with Rebecca in her conclusion; on which she aroused from her reverie and asked me somewhat pointedly what I meant to do.

"Why, I mean to get me home this very day," I answered. "After all these months, I am pining for a sight of my Cousin Prudence."

"You keep a fair appetite, notwithstanding," said Rebecca, with a grim smile, "and I notice 'tis your cousin you are so mighty anxious to see, and not the kind uncle and aunt who have brought you up and cared for you."

On which I felt my face flush hot, and no doubt looked very foolish; but I answered stoutly that Prudence was more to me than all the word beside, and that, please God, so it should always be, though I lived to be as old as Methusalem.

Rebecca smiled on me indulgently and with a certain sad wistfulness, as I thought.

"So we talk and so we think, when the heart is young," said she; "and perchance 'tis the best wisdom after all; for if we can go on thinking so, then the heart shall keep young and laugh at the white hairs and the crow's feet. Well, lad, you shall see your cousin and I'll wish you God speed, for, if all you have told me be true, she is worthy of the love of an honest man; and that," concluded Rebecca, with an abrupt return to her usual manner, "is more than can be said for most of them."

"I suppose," said I, presently, "that I had better catch the tilt-boat down to Gravesend."

"I suppose you'll do nothing of the kind," answered Rebecca, tartly, "and don't interrupt me with your chatter. I'm thinking."

I hoped that she would conduct her thinking with reasonable expedition, for I was in a fever to be off.

"Now," said she, after in interval, in which I had fidgeted about the kitchen in a state of almost unbearable impatience, "listen to me and don't keep shuffling round the room like a dancing bear learning its steps. I am not going to let you leave this house. Several ships are fitting out in Deptford Dockyard, and several more, that have left the yard, are waiting in the river to make up their crews, and as you saw yourself there are more ships down at Gravesend – your own among them. Every waterside street is patrolled by the press-gangs, and no seafaring man dares show his nose out of doors. If you stir out of this house, with your brown face and your sailor's clothes, you will be snapped up before you have gone a quarter of a mile – overgrown baby that you are. I tell you, this country is as bad as that Guinea Coast that you come from, except that there they press women and children as well as men. Besides, you are to remember that you are not only a seaman, but a deserter and a pirate to boot. Now attend to me. You shall give me a note to your cousin or your uncle and I will go down to Shorne. When they know your whereabouts and condition, your friends can bring you proper clothes and make the necessary arrangements for getting you home in safety."

As she finished speaking, I stepped round the table and kissed her, on which she smacked my face – but not very hard.

"Rebecca," said I, "you are an angel. All that you say is perfectly true and I had thought of it – "

"Then why did you talk of going by the tilt-boat?" she interrupted.

"What else was there for me to do?" I demanded.

"Bah!" said Rebecca. "Rubbish! How am I to get to Shorne?"

"You could catch the tilt-boat as it comes down from the Pool, and take the Rochester coach from Gravesend."

"'Twould be quicker," said Rebecca, "to walk across to the Dover road and catch the Rochester coach. There would be time. Where should they set me down?"

"At the crossroads by Pipes Place," I answered, "a mile this side of Gad's Hill," and I directed her how to find the village.

"That will do," said she, "and mind, you are not to stir out of the house – not even into the garden – and 'twould be best not to answer the door if anyone knocks. I am used to leave the house empty when I have to go abroad."

With this she retired upstairs, and returned in an astonishingly short space of time, clad in a warm cloak and hood and ready for the journey.

I handed her a little note that I had written whilst she was preparing to start, which she placed in an under pocket for security.

"Clear the table and wash up the crockery as soon as I am gone," said she, "and don't leave the cover off the bread-pan."

I promised to carry out all her instructions to the letter; but she cut me short in the middle of my speech, and before I had time to wish her adieu, the street door slammed and I was alone in the house.

Straightway I cleared away the remains of our breakfast as I had been commanded and made everything snug and tidy, and then began to browse about in search of something to help me to pass the time until Rebecca should return. First I visited the sitting-room in which I had enjoyed the society of Mr Murking, and there took down from the shelf and examined one by one, the pious books which had apparently formed his ordinary reading; but, though I trust I am as good a Christian a becomes my station, and heartily reverence the holy gentlemen who write these works, yet I have never discovered much pleasure in the reading of sermons or commentaries. Accordingly, I replaced the books on their shelves and continued my tour of inspection.

As my eye fell on the cupboard door, it occurred to me that I should like to see if Mr Colville's proclamation was still there, and then I bethought me of the blue jar in which the key used to be kept, and I ran down to the kitchen to look for it. The jar was still in the same place, and when I put my hand into it, there was the key, as of old, which I took and carried upstairs. I had now no scruple about opening the cupboard, seeing that its owner was no more and that I had a specific end in view; so I unlocked it without hesitation, and, when the door opened the first thing that met my eye was the proclamation itself.

I read the document through with a smile, now that its terrors were extinct, and, thinking that I would beg it of Rebecca anon, put it back, and was about to close the door, when I noticed a row of volumes at the back of the cupboard. I reached one out and found it to be a book of plays, whereupon I drew out the others, which were of a similar character, and took them down to look over by the kitchen fire. They turned out to be the plays of Ford and Wycherly, and were certainly most admirably suited to furnish an antidote to the sermons; for the jests in them were as coarse as those that I had been accustomed to hear in the 'tween-decks, and not half so witty for the most part. But one very curious fact I noted in these books, which was this, viz., that whereas the sermons had been so delicately handled that they were as fresh and clean as when they were new, these plays were soiled on nearly every page with greasy thumb-marks, which I seemed, somehow, to associate with fried black-pudding.

With these books I contrived to pass the time very tolerably, sitting by the fire in company with a large black cat, who had appeared mysteriously from some unknown hiding-place, and who, though somewhat stiff in manner at first, had come to view me with amiable toleration, after I had provided him with a light luncheon. Nor was I without other comforts, for my ditty-bag, which I was wearing when I was arrested, contained, among other sailor's treasures, the pipe that I had found on the wreck, and a goodly lump of tobacco; so that I was able to smoke, and did so, notwithstanding the manifest disapproval of the cat.

In these occupations, and the preparation of a midday meal, the washing of the crockery and the replenishment of the coal-box the hours slipped past until the short winter's day came to an end and I had to continue my reading by the firelight. The solemn-faced clock in the corner showed that it was half-past four and I began to look for Rebecca's return, though she might easily be an hour or two longer if she met with any delays on the road. I made up the fire, filled the kettle, and laid the table for a meal, and then, finding that I cared no more for the plays, took the volumes upstairs and replaced them in the cupboard.

Five o'clock passed – half-past five – six o'clock; and now I began to grow so impatient that I could no longer sit by the fire, but must needs wander about the house like some unquiet spirit.

About half-past six, as I was returning to the kitchen to make up the fire and see that the kettle was boiling, I heard the sound of wheels approaching up the street, and thought that Rebecca was returning in state. But the vehicle stopped before it reached our house, and in my disappointment I seized the poker and made so violent an attack upon the fire that the cat retreated under the table in alarm. While I was thus occupied, I heard the street door slam, and leaped to my feet. The poker fell from my hand with a crash; the cat shot under the pot board as though fired from a carronade; the kitchen door burst open, and the firelight fell upon my Cousin Prudence.

In an instant her arms were around my neck and her cheek pressed to mine, and she was sobbing and laughing in the same breath, in the strange fashion that women have when overwrought.

As to me, I was so taken aback with the suddenness of it all that I had not a word to say, and could do naught but fall to kissing her; which, indeed, answered the purpose better than speech, and was so agreeable withal, that there is no saying how long I should have continued, had she not stopped me and hauled off out of range in some confusion – though she still held my hands and smiled in my face with infinite affection.

"This is a joyful day for us all, Robert," said she. "'Tis as though you had come back to us from the grave."

"So it seems to me," I answered. "There has been many a time when I have doubted if I should ever look upon this dear face again."

"And how rejoiced father and mother will be," said Prudence. "Your little note, which I left for them, will turn their mourning into thanksgiving and joy."

"Were they from home, then, when Rebecca arrived?" I asked.

"Yes, they were gone to Mr Crowhurst's, the lawyer's," answered Prudence; "but I forgot," she added, "that you know nothing of what has been happening. We are staying in town, at the 'Bell,' in Holborn, near by Furnival's Inn. 'Twas there Rebecca found me – and that reminds me that we must not let her stay upstairs in the cold."

"No, indeed," said I, "after her long journey, too, and all taken for us."

I lighted the candle and gave it to her with a parting kiss as she ran off, and then set to work to warm the teapot, though I did not dare to make the tea. I had just finished this task when the two women came down, and very pretty it was to see Prudence enter the kitchen with her arm around her stolid companion, and Rebecca striving hard to look fierce, and failing miserably.

"I suppose," said the latter, "you are used to drink rum or brandy at this hour; but there is none here, so you will have to make shift with a dish of tea."

She examined the pot critically, feeling it all over with her hand, and then proceeded to make the tea with the air of a high-priest performing some sacrificial rite, and, having brought forth two large wax candles and set them alight on the table, bade us draw up our chairs.

"No doubt," said she, "your father and mother, Miss, will be highly rejoiced to see this scapegrace – though 'tis more than he deserves."

"Truly they will," replied Prudence; "they were inconsolable when the tidings of his death were brought to us. Indeed," she added, with a fond glance at me, "he was the apple of our eye."

"H'm," grunted Rebecca, with a sniff. "Whose eye?"

"I mean," said Prudence –

"I know what you mean," said Rebecca, smiling grimly. "Don't tell me."

At which Prudence blushed somewhat, though she cast a roguish look at me, and evidently cared not a straw for Rebecca's sarcasms.

At this point I became aware that Prudence was clad in mourning garments, and asked, rather foolishly, if there had been a death in the family.

"Why 'tis for you, you gaby," she answered, between laughing and crying, adding, "but there shall soon be a change, I promise you."

"Aye," agreed Rebecca, "I warrant me there will. 'Tis the white satin and the wreath she is thinking of now."

"Rebecca," exclaimed Prudence sternly, as her cheeks flushed scarlet, "if I hear any more of your impudence, I will fetch you a sound rap on the head with you own teapot. And you, sir," she added, turning upon me suddenly, "need not sit there grinning and encouraging her. This is not the 'tween-decks you will please remember."

"Who was it that brought you the report of my death?" I asked.

"Who!" she exclaimed, reddening now with anger at the recollection, "who would it be but that lying villain, Percival? He told us that you had shipped in a false name, had deserted on an island, and that when they sent a search-party for you, your body was found. It seemed as if there could be no doubt as to the facts."

"I see," said I. "And then my identity was discovered by certain articles found in my chest. Was it not so?"

"'Twas exactly what he said," I said. Meanwhile, what else have you to tell me?"

"I have something to tell you," she answered, "that will surprise you greatly – unless you have already guessed the truth. Do you remember how, in the letter I sent you at the 'Mermaid,' I said that I had some wonderful news to impart? Well, 'twas this: that your cousins Wilfrid and Hubert, while returning from Italy, had been caught in a terrible storm and drowned at sea, and that poor Sir Thomas was so broken with his loss, that he took to his bed and died within the month."

I gave a low whistle through my teeth.

"This is news with a vengeance, Prue," said I, "and makes clear to me many things that I had not understood. But poor Percival! He has counted his chickens so carefully. And now, to find that the eggs are addled after all! 'Twill be a bitter blow."

"Yes, the black-hearted villain!" exclaimed Prudence. "He thinks he is standing in your shoes already."

At this moment the noise of wheels was audible in the street, and immediately there came a knock at the door.

"That will be the coach," said Prudence. "I bade the man return for us in half an hour. You have no baggage, I suppose," she added with a smile.

"But I have," I answered, "and a mighty saucy one too," on which Prudence pinched me and we made our way to the front door, where we found Rebecca peering up and down the street in search of press-gangs.

"All seems to be clear," she said, "and I have told the coachman to drive straight away from the waterside. In with you before you are caught again."

Prudence and I embraced her tenderly and entered the coach, and, as I glanced out through the window, I saw her standing at the threshold, wiping her eyes with her apron.

"'Tis a lonely life for the poor soul," said Prudence, who had also seen her, "and she so full of love and goodness. She must not be left there, Robin, dear."

"That she shall not, Prue," I answered, warmly; "you may trust me for that."

The coach moved slowly through the dark and narrow streets of Rotherhithe, jolting most uncomfortably over the uneven roads and squeezing against posts, palings and even the houses themselves.

For some time Prudence and I sat side by side in the darkness without speaking, each wrapped in meditation on the strange and startling events of the last few hours.

Presently, as the coach struggled out into the wider streets to the south, I slipped my arm around my companion, and, drawing her closer to me, began to speak of that which was of far more moment to me than the prospect of wealth and greatness that had so suddenly opened.

"Prudence," said I, "you have told me some wonderful news tonight, which I have liked well enough to hear; but there is something else that I would know from your lips – something that I have thought about often in the troubled days that are past. I would ask you, little cousin, how is it with you and me after this long separation?"

"What mean you, Robin?" she asked faintly.

"I mean this, dear Prue," I answered; "when I went away, we were but boy and girl, though as fond as any two cousins could be. But I have come back a man with the full knowledge of what you have been, and are, to me; with the knowledge that under my boyish fondness lay hidden a man's passion, which is hidden no longer, but made manifest by suffering and separation.

"In my wanderings and misfortunes I have heartened myself with the thought that when I came home you would marry me, and so recompense me for all the ills I had put up with, though, indeed, I am not good enough for you, unless my love be held a sufficient merit. What say you dearest?"

"I say," answered Prudence, "that there must be no more of this. As we are, so must we continue. You must not speak to me of marriage."

"Good God, Prue!" I gasped, trembling with a new and horrible fear, "am I too late, then? Is your promise or your heart given already?"

"No! No!" she exclaimed hastily, indeed not. Oh! Robin, how could you think it? But you forget that you are now a great gentleman and I but a simple country maid – a farmer's daughter – and am no match for you."

I drew a deep breath of relief.

"Is that all?" said I. "Sure, Prue dearest, you are making much ado about nothing. Why the parson will mend that for us out of hand; for you have but to marry me and you are forthwith a great lady, and not a pin to choose between us in point of station."

Prudence laughed a nervous, shaky little laugh.

"Sea air and the sprightly society of the 'tween-decks would seem to have sharpened your wits, Robert; but truly, dear cousin, you must put this matter out of your thoughts. You will want no homespun bride in your mansion. Be patient and you shall marry some fine lady of your own rank who shall be a fitting mate for you."

"That I will be hanged if I do," I exclaimed. "What! Because I am like to become a fine gentleman, which I never asked or wished to be, am I to be denied that which I wish for more than all the world beside. Think you I am going to sell my birthright — the right to choose my own mate — for a scurvy sackful of guineas and a few yards of land? Not I, I promise you. No, sweetheart, let us have done with these cross-purposes. I love you as truly as ever woman could wish to be loved, and you love me too — you shall not deny it. Fortune holds out to us this great gift which she offers to so few. Let us take it and be thankful."

She crept a little closer to me but spoke not a word.

"Prue," said I, as a hollow rumble under the coach told me that we were crossing the river, "we are on the bridge and shall soon be at the inn. Say it, dear heart, say it in my ear — 'tis but one little word, yet it shall hold us faithful and true till death do us part."

She hesitated for an instant more, then drew my head down and laid her cheek against mine.

"I have said 'no' twice," she murmured softly, "and nearly broke my heart in the saying it. Now must I yield since I cannot endure again to put away my heart's desire. Robin, I am yours, body and soul; and that I have been, if you had but known it, for many a year past."

How shall I tell of the tide of happiness that swept through me, and sent my heart carolling aloft like a lark in the spring sunshine? 'Tis beyond speech — even as it was then; and naught could I do but gather my new-won treasure in my arms and hold my peace, lest I should weep from sheer excess of joy. So we sat, hand in hand, without speaking, hidden from one another by the darkness of the coach, yet linked in infinite sympathy and mutual bliss, and both of us mightily astonished to find the 'Bell' in Holborn so short a distance from London Bridge.

"Do not tell them tonight, Robin," said Prudence, as the coach turned into the inn-yard; "I would give my mother the news when we are alone."

I kissed her once more and gave her my promise to respect her wishes, and having opened the door and leaped out, turned to assist her to alight; and as I did so, I perceived Mr Leigh descending the stairs from the gallery, three at a time, in a series of highly undignified bounds and hops.

In a moment he had me in his arms and had bestowed a dozen hearty kisses on my cheek, while the tears ran down his rosy face.

"And is it thou, indeed, my dearest boy?" he exclaimed in a shaky voice, half-way between a sob and a chuckle, "come back to us, when we were wearing the willow, to be the light and life of our home, as of old? My faith!" he added, holding me at arm's length to get the better view of me, "but you are none the worse for your wanderings; 'tis a fine man you are growing, Robin, lad, and fit to be a lord. Hath Prue told you of your fortune? But of course she hath. And here is your aunt – 'tis he, Martha, right enough; 'tis our own Robin come back!"

My aunt was descending the stairs slowly and wiping her eyes as she came. I ran up to her and caught her in my arms, when she wept quietly on my shoulder as I led her back to the gallery. I was profoundly affected by the deep affection displayed by these, my dear kinsfolk, and not a little ashamed in my heart to have given so little thought to them. But 'tis the way of youth – and perhaps 'tis the right way. The song of the young bird is for his mate, not for the parents who have nurtured him as he cowered, unfledged and helpless in the nest.

In the gallery we found an elderly gentleman of most magnificent aspect, who, at once, reminded me of the turkey-cock that was used to lord it over the farmyard at Shorne; principally, I think, because of his florid complexion and the purple bloom upon his nose and a something warlike and commanding in his carriage. He wore a large wig, well powdered, and his dress, though quiet in tone, was that of a man of fashion, while his ruffled shirt was of the finest and as white as snow.

"Come, come, good people," said he, tapping the lid of a gold snuff-box and helping himself to a pinch with extreme daintiness, "these sacred emotions are not to be exhibited to the gaping crowd in an inn-yard. Let us within where we can welcome our honoured guest as befits his station. Your servant, Sir Robert; permit me to present myself to you. Augustus Crowhurst, sir, at your service – and I may add, *in* your service – for I am the attorney to the estate, and the executor of the will of the late Sir Thomas, your lamented uncle."

I bowed to the lawyer and we all proceeded to the room that Mr Leigh had engaged, where my aunt at once pressed me to partake of food; and when I had declined, much to the relief of Mr Crowhurst (who had already supped), the lawyer rang for the landlord, with whom he remained for some time in earnest consultation by the door. The result of their debate presently appeared when the landlord re-entered, walking delicately on tiptoe, bearing in a cradle an ancient and crusted bottle, at which he gazed fearfully, as though he expected it to explode.

"You have come, sir," said Mr Crowhurst, when he had critically examined the cork, which the landlord offered for his inspection, "most opportunely; for your cousin, Captain Hawke, is but lately returned from the West Indies, but has already entered his claim to the estate. He has offered to furnish evidence of your decease and has, in fact, appointed to visit me at my chambers tomorrow and bring with him the necessary witnesses. Therefore, sir, since your story must needs be a long one, and it is desirable that we be in possession of all the facts, in view of tomorrow's interview, I venture to propose that you give us an account of your adventures."

"Aye," agreed my uncle, "You must have had some queer experiences and seen some strange sights, Robin, since you were spirited away from us, and we are all agog to hear you tell of them. Let us draw up to the fire – 'tis chilly sitting by the table – and we will clink a glass and you shall tell us your story. Bring the bottle, Martha, while I carry the chairs."

"Nay, for God's sake, have a care – permit me, Madam," exclaimed Mr Crowhurst, taking possession of the bottle and carrying it, as a priest might bear some holy relic in a religious procession; "kindly place the small table by the fire, Sir Robert – not too close – so – that will do very well."

We seated ourselves around the blazing sea-coal fire, Mr Crowhurst filled our glasses, my uncle called for a clean pipe and some tobacco, and I plunged into my narrative, with my aunt on one side, holding my hand, and my sweet Prudence on the other with her arm drawn through mine.

There is no need for me to repeat the exclamations of astonishment, pity, or anger with which the various episodes of my story were greeted; how Prudence wept when I told of the way in which Rebecca had befriended me; how Mr Crowhurst laughed at my account of Percival's visit to the wreck, until we had to loosen his neck-cloth; or how he pronounced Captain Parradine "a prime fellow and a credit to his rascally profession." Let it suffice to say that they all listened as though spellbound, and only interrupted me to clamour for more details; so that, by the time I had finished, it was past eleven o'clock by Mr Crowhurst's splendid gold repeater, and Mr Crowhurst himself was in that condition that he could not decide whether he should call for a fourth bottle or send for a chair.

Mr Leigh decided for him, and when it was announced that the chair was waiting in the yard, the lawyer rose and bade us a very ceremonious adieu.

"I shall bid my tailor wait upon you in the morning, Sir Robert," said he, "for we cannot have you seen abroad in your present garb – not but what it becomes you admirably," he added, with a bow that caused him to sit down on the edge of the table. "But 'tis not seemly and 'tis not safe."

Mr Leigh and I saw him to his chair, and he departed wreathed in smiles and kissing his hand to a post-boy whom he apparently mistook for my uncle. We then returned to the fire and sat a little longer talking over my adventures until I began to yawn, despite the presence of my sweetheart; whereupon Mr Leigh would have me bid the ladies "good night," and carried me to the room where I was to sleep. And here he left me with his blessing, bidding me sleep well that I might have my wits about me on the morrow.

CHAPTER TWENTY-FOUR

In which my Cousin Percival makes a Discovery

A soft, persuasive tapping at my chamber door aroused me early on the following morning, and I went to the window and looked out. An elegantly dressed gentleman was standing in the galley refreshing himself with a modest pinch of snuff from a tortoise-shell box, and taking the opportunity to adjust his wig with the aid of a small mirror in the lid. As he seemed to be about to repeat his summons, I opened the door and asked what was his pleasure.

He made a low bow when he saw me, and removed his hat with a flourish.

"I received, sir," said he, "a message from Mr Crowhurst this morning, bidding me to wait upon your worship, to advise your worship in the matter of raiment. Mr Crowhurst is pleased to acquaint me that your worship is lately returned from a voyage, and is in need of habiliments suitable to your honourable and exalted station."

"Mr Crowhurst spoke, last evening, of sending his tailor to me," said I, rather embarrassed by the magnificence of my visitor. "May I venture to inquire if – " I paused in some confusion, doubtful if this courtly gentleman were not some friend of Mr Crowhurst's; but he came to my relief with the answer "Your worship's surmise is entirely correct. It is my happiness to enjoy the privilege of draping the figure of my learned and distinguished patron, and I hope to have the felicity of placing my humble services at your worship's disposal in a like manner and with equally, or even more, fortunate results."

"In that case," I said, "I will ask you to please to walk in; for, doubtless you will wish to take some measurements."

"It will certainly," said he, entering with a bow and a flourish, "be desirable that I ascertain the dimensions of your worship's noble and distinguished person, if your worship will forgive me for putting you to that trouble."

"'Tis no trouble at all, sir," said I, shutting the door and shooting the bolt.

My noble and distinguished person was, at the moment, disguised in a ragged shirt and a pair of duck trousers, both well stained by the slime and ooze of the river, and I suggested that he might desire me to divest myself of them.

"God forbid, sir!" he exclaimed, raising his hands in horror, "God forbid that I should so intrude upon your worship's modesty – to say naught of the inclemency of the weather. Though, mark you, sir, I am not denying that your worship would doubtless appear to greater advantage in that, the garb of our earliest forefathers, than clothed in the choicest productions of sartorial art. But 'tis an artificial age, sir. May I trouble your worship to open the mouth, fill the lungs, and pronounce the syllables 'ha-hum' slowly. 'Twill assist me in determining the circumference of your worshipful bosom."

I followed his instructions; that is to say, I opened my mouth and filled my lungs, and was about to pronounce the mystic syllables, when I was suddenly overcome by the absurdity of the situation and burst into a shout of laughter; whereat my visitor was deeply scandalised and I was fain to apologise, remarking that I was last fitted out by the sail-maker, whose methods were more summary.

The tailor was evidently disconcerted by the levity with which I had viewed his proceedings, for he set about his business in silence, handling his tape with uncommon skill and entering the measurements in a small pocket-book. When he had finished, he complimented me warmly upon my proportions, and informed me that he had a suit by him that would fit me well enough, until there should be time to have one made to my exact measure.

"'Tis a poor thing for one of your worship's quality," said he, "though 'twas made for a young nobleman. But he had the misfortune to fall in a duel before it could be sent home, and so it was left on my hands. I will send it to your worship presently, together with all necessary appointments, so that your worship may be able to go abroad and take the air. And if I may not seem to presume too much, I would observe that your worship's hands are somewhat stained, apparently with tar, which detracts from their natural grace and symmetry, as well as being a thought unusual in gentleman of quality. If I might presume to advise, I would suggest that a mixture of clarified butter and silver sand applied vigorously, would probably restore to the integument its pristine purity of colour."

With this well-meant and really useful piece of advice, my gentleman took his leave, and I fell to scrubbing myself, that my person, at least, might be clean if my clothing was soiled. When I had made myself as presentable as circumstances permitted, I betook me to our sitting-room, where I found all the family assembled and the breakfast ready.

As I entered, my aunt ran to me and flung her arms around my neck.

"Prudence hath told me all, Robin," said she, kissing me on the cheek, "and the news hath given me more joy than I can tell – not for the sake of the great alliance, though I am far from insensible of the condescension, but because my mother's eye hath seen for years, and especially since your late troubles, that she loved you; and since I knew my dear maid to have a heart too steadfast to change, I feared, when we heard of your great fortune, that she had lost you; and I looked to see her, like many another poor loving soul, wend on her earthly pilgrimage a lonely spinster, widowed though unwed, with only the empty husk to feed her love withal. And now, dearest boy, 'tis all changed. In the fulfilment of her love, my life is fulfilled; and, when my time comes, I can go to my rest, saying, 'Lord, now lettest Thou Thy servant depart in peace'; for I know thee, too, Robin, and that she shall find thee a true man, and shall no more need the care of a father or a mother."

I kissed my aunt and stroked her hair, in which a few silvery threads nestled amongst the chestnut, like the first russet among the green leaves when the autumn is approaching.

"Mother, dear," said I – "for so I must call you now, and so you have been to me, and shall be – you need have never a moment's doubt that I shall duly prize and cherish the treasure that you are giving to me. Indeed, though I should give myself up to be her slave, and think of naught but her service, I could never repay her for the mere pleasure of looking upon her sweet face. And let us have no more talk of condescension; for I know well enough that I am but a poor country lout, and not half good enough for so lovely a maid, and one so good and so clever too."

During this conversation Mr Leigh took numerous and extravagant pinches of snuff, a luxury to which he was but little accustomed, and, as a result, burst into a violent fit of sneezing; after which he wiped his eyes with a great red handkerchief and grasped me by the hand.

"Rob, my lad," said he, heartily, "thou hast acted the part of a man, as I knew thou wouldst. And let me tell thee, boy, thou hast chosen the better part, and shalt have thy reward. I will say no more."

"You need say no more, uncle," said I, "having spoken but the truth, except that had I acted otherwise I should have shown myself a brainless fribble. As to this greatness as my aunt calls it – being but so much pelf and an empty name – before I would have let it turn me one hair's breadth from my happiness, I would have flung the whole trumpery to Percival and gone back to whistle at the plough's tail. And now, if Prue has a kiss for her man to cheer him upon a winter's morning, we will fall to upon the victuals, for I perceive that I have something of my sea appetite still."

We accordingly drew up to the table, and I made such an attack upon the food as filled my aunt with admiration, though I had had a pretty good twist in the old days.

"My faith, Robin," said Mr Leigh, laughing at my voracity, "'tis well thou hast come into a fortune. Thou wouldst have eaten us out of house and home."

While we were yet at breakfast a messenger arrived with a note from Mr Crowhurst, bidding us come to his chambers in Lincoln's Inn at two of the clock; "and I would pray you to be punctual," said he, "for I would not have you meet my other visitors until the appointed time. There will be great doings here, and I can promise you some sport with Cousin Percival."

"I trust he will let poor Percival down as lightly as may be," said I, "for I cannot but feel sorry for him, rascal as he is. He cares for the estate so much more than I do, and has made so sure of it; and besides," I added, with a glance at Prudence, "I stand to gain so much more than he ever did."

"'Twill be a bitter pill, certainly," said Mr Leigh; "but he must bolt it down and make the best of it."

As soon as breakfast was finished I called for butter and silver sand, and retired to my chamber to scour the tar-stains from my hands; and with this task I was still engaged when the tailor made his appearance, followed by a porter carrying a large bundle.

He seemed mightily flattered to perceive that I had acted so readily upon his advice, and was pleased to compliment me upon the appearance of my hands, when I had dried them; for his recipe had, indeed, answered to perfection, and they were now quite clean though brown from the sun and hard from handling ropes.

The porter carried in the bundle and opened it, when my friend proceeded to take out the various articles that it contained and lay them on the bed for my inspection. They were all very fine, and yet I was pleased to see that they were not too fine; for I had feared that my good friend had meant to send me abroad tricked out as I had seen some of the exquisites from the inn window. There was a fine cambric shirt, a plum-coloured suit with gilt buttons, a handsome laced waistcoat, silk stockings and several pairs of shoes for me to try on. There were also two or three hats and a clouded cane with a gold top, as well as a few minor necessaries, including a snuff-box, which I rejected at once, despite the tailor's protests.

"There, sir," said the latter, wagging his head from side to side as he surveyed the articles displayed on the bed. "I trust your worship may contrive to make a respectable appearance, with the aid of these poor trifles, until a suitable outfit can be prepared. Perhaps I may even experience the happiness of receiving your worship's commands this very morning."

He retired to wait in the gallery and I made haste to array myself, finding the suit to fit me passably, though a trifle strait in places, and the rest of the garments all that could be desired. When I was dressed and had fitted on a pair of shoes and a hat to my liking, I called him in, when he entered and walked round me with knitted brows, like a sculptor surveying a newly-finished statue.

"'Twill pass," was his decision, after he had made the circuit half a dozen times, "though it does but indifferent justice to your worship's figure, and I would pray your worship not to mention my name in connection with it. If your worship will authorise me to prepare a suitable outfit for a gentleman of quality, I shall have great pleasure in submitting specimens and putting the work in hand forthwith. Or, if your worship would do me the honour to visit me at my humble abode at Great Queen Street near by Drury Lane, that would be even better."

I accepted the latter proposal, and having made a note of the address, wished the tailor "good morning" and left him to gather up the rejected articles while I betook myself to the sitting-room.

"My faith!" exclaimed Mr Leigh, as I entered, "here is a fine gentleman indeed! This is more like our own Robin, hey, Prue?"

"Truly, father," replied Prudence, with a mischievous smile, " 'fine feathers make fine birds.' And since we make so brave an appearance and have no more occasion to fear the press, shall we not go forth and look at the town? You see, Robin, I have doffed my mourning and put on my finery to match yours."

"Aye," chuckled Mr Leigh," "you are as gay as a pair of tom-tits on a May morning – and a very apt comparison too," he added, with the sudden conviction that he had said a clever thing without intending it.

Accordingly we all sallied forth to stroll about the town and look at the sights; down Holborn Hill and on to Newgate, where we stood and watched the workmen taking down the gallows, and Mr Leigh had a silk handkerchief and an empty purse taken from his pocket; down the old Bailey to Ludgate Hill and into St Paul's – which Prudence had never seen before – and along Cheapside, where we gaped at the shops and the people, until it was time to return; when we walked back to the "Bell," by way of the Fleet Market.

After dinner we betook ourselves, in no little excitement, to Mr Crowhurst's chambers, which were in Old Square, Lincoln's Inn; and we had had so much care not to be late, that the clock had but just struck the half-hour when we passed through the archway from Chancery Lane. However, the lawyer seemed in no way discomposed by our premature arrival, for when we were ushered into his room, we found him seated at a table, surrounded by documents, in an atmosphere charged with the mingled aroma of snuff and sherry.

"You are punctual with a vengeance," he remarked, as he rose to welcome us, "but 'tis better so. The matter must be disposed of today, so we had best make suitable preparation. Your story, Sir Robert, was so full of interest – so romantic, in fact – and the circumstances in which it was told, so agreeable, that I find I have not so clear a notion of the sequence of events as I should wish; I will therefore trouble you to refresh my memory and allow me to take a few notes."

He spread out a sheet of paper and proceeded to make a digest of my statement, filling in the dates and localities with careful precision. This consumed a good deal of time, and we had but just finished when the manservant entered to announce that Captain Hawke and Mr Wigmore had arrived with several seamen.

Mr Crowhurst rose and drew back a curtain that concealed a small doorway behind his table, within which a chair had been placed.

"Do me the favour, Sir Robert," said he, "to take a seat in this chair, and do not leave it or make any sound until I ring my hand-bell. Then I will ask you to step out and show yourself."

I did not much admire this arrangement, by which it seemed that I was to play the eavesdropper, and said so, with some warmth.

"Your must be guided by me, my dear sir," replied Mr Crowhurst a little stiffly. "I am conducting this business, in your interest and that of the estate, and must choose my own methods – for which, you will please remember, you are in no way responsible."

I felt that I could make no further objection, so, with a somewhat ill grace, I stepped into the doorway and seated myself; when the lawyer shut me in with the curtain.

In a few minutes I heard the door open and the sound of footsteps, as of several persons entering the room, and then the strong sea voice of my cousin Percival addressing the lawyer.

"I wish you good afternoon, sir. You have given me an unexpected pleasure in providing so much company. I had supposed I was come on my own business."

"So far, sir, you were right; but Mr Leigh considers that the question is one in which his ward, Robert Hawke, is somewhat interested, and I agree with him."

"H'm," said Percival. "I fear his ward's interest in this, and all other earthly matters, lapsed some time ago."

"So I understood from your letter," replied Mr Crowhurst; "and, as I informed you in my reply, if you can bring forward convincing proof of Sir Robert's decease, I shall advise Mr Leigh, and other persons interested, not to oppose your claim."

"You are very good, sir," said Percival, dryly, "to offer to present me with that which is already my own. But I will proceed to business, merely remarking that I consider the presence here, of these persons, an unwarrantable impertinence."

"As you will, sir," replied the lawyer; "and now, as you say, to business. I have here your letter containing, as I take it, the substance of your statement, which sets forth that Sir Robert Hawke shipped as a seaman on board the sloop-of-war *Asphodel* on the 25th of July in this present year seventeen hundred and ninety-one, in the name of James Roberts. What evidence have you to offer as to that statement?"

"Here is Mr Wigmore, my first lieutenant, and Mr Wilkin, my boatswain, who were with the press-gang that took him."

"Ha!" said Mr Crowhurst. "He was pressed, was he? You did not mention that."

"I confined my statement to that of material facts," answered Percival; "and it is my intention to do so on this occasion likewise."

"And a very proper course," said Mr Crowhurst. "Your name, sir, is − ?"

"Edward Wigmore," replied that gentleman.

"Edward Wigmore," repeated the lawyer, who was apparently committing the statement to writing, "a lieutenant of His Majesty's navy, does hereby declare and affirm in manner following, that is to say − "

"That I commanded a press-gang on the day mentioned by Captain Hawke and that I took a man who gave the name of James Roberts, outside the Mermaid Inn at Gravesend."

There was a pause during which the lawyer's pen squeaked over the paper.

"Had you instructions to take any particular person?" asked Mr Crowhurst.

"That question is not relevant to the inquiry," interrupted Percival. "We are dealing with the matter of identity."

"You are quite correct, sir," admitted the lawyer. "Now as to this man, Mr Wigmore, was he a seaman?"

"He was stated to be, by a man who was taken with him, and who is present, but it turned out, I think, that he was not."

"I see," said the lawyer. "Now we will hear Mr Wilkin if you please."

Wilkin accordingly made his statement, which agreed with that of the lieutenant, and, being asked if he had any special instructions, was about to reply, when Percival interposed.

"That question is not material to the inquiry," said he, "and you are not to answer, Mr Wilkin."

"We now come to the landing on a certain island, Mr Wigmore," pursued the lawyer blandly, "which took place, I observe, on the twentieth of October. You accompanied Captain Hawke on that occasion, I believe?"

"I did, sir,"

"Is it usual for the captain and the first lieutenant to be absent from the ship together?"

"That question is impertinent and irrelevant," exclaimed Percival.

"Is it so?" said Mr Crowhurst, mildly; "then we will leave it. Was the man called James Roberts with you on that occasion?"

"He was."

"Did he return to the ship with you?"

"He did not."

"Where was he when you last saw him?"

"He was digging in a pit in which it was supposed the pirates had deposited their booty."

"Had he the means of getting out of that pit?"

"Certainly he had. The rope by which he let himself down was left for him to haul himself up again."

"How long did you wait after making the recall signal?"

"We waited a quarter of an hour after everyone else had come down to the boat, firing muskets every few minutes."

"You sent no one to search for him?"

"No. The ship was making urgent signals of a suspicious sail in sight. We had no time to waste on searching for runaway seamen."

"Quite so, quite so," said Mr Crowhurst. "You have heard Mr Wigmore's statement, Mr Wilkin. Do you corroborate it?"

"I do, sir," answered the boatswain. "'Tis true, every word."

"Very well," said Mr Crowhurst; "then we come to the finding of the body, which, I think, occurred on the twenty-seventh of October. Was it not so, Mr Wilkin?"

"Quite right, sir!" answered Wilkin, "and it happened this here way. I goes ashore along of the captain and Mr Wigmore, and a damned wet morning it were — a-rainin' cats and dogs. When we lands, the boat's crew is broke up into search-parties, and I goes off with one of 'em and takes along with me this man William Muffin, what was pressed aboard at Gravesend with James Roberts. I makes my way to the pit, because that was where I see the missing man last, and, seeing half a knife-blade a-laying in the mud at the bottom, I goes down to fetch it and have a look round."

"I see," said Mr Crowhurst; "you let yourself down by the rope?"

"Why no, I didn't," said Wilkin, "'cause the rope were lying in a heap at the bottom; but I lets myself down by means of some foot-holes as the diseased seemed to have cut in the side – and broke off his knife a-doin' of it."

"What a very remarkable thing!" exclaimed the lawyer. "Can you account for his having cut those foot-holes?"

"The hitch that made the rope fast to the tree above, must have slipped and let the line down atop of him."

"But isn't that very singular, for the hitch to have slipped?" demanded Mr Crowhurst.

"Why 'tis a darned rum go, and that's the fact," answered Wilkin, "seeing as how it were all fast when he went down."

"Amazing!" said Mr Crowhurst, "however, we will not delay you. Pray proceed."

"Well," continued Wilkin, "we goes on to the north shore and walks along in the rain without seeing anything, until we comes to the ashes of a fire, with the bones and shell of a turtle close by. Then we walks on further and comes to the ruins of some small houses, and we starts to overhaul 'em one by one. At last, in one house, we finds a body – or rather a skiliton, for the flesh had all been eat off the bones by land-crabs; we see one of the crabs run down a hole close by the body."

"But how could you identify a skeleton?" asked Mr Crowhurst, "for I understand that you determined this body to be that of James Roberts."

"Why d'ye see, sir, there was the clothes – all torn to rags they was, but we rekernised 'em as the ship's slops. And then we found a knife by the body. It were broken in half and the half blade what we saw in the pit fitted it igzactly – 'cause I sent Muffin down for it on the way back and we tried the two pieces. Then Bill Muffin rekernised the knife, being as how he bought it out of the purser's stores and give it to the diseased and carved the diseased's name on the handle, and there it were. And the sheath what was on the belt what the skiliton was wearing, hadn't got no knife in it. So we knowed that the skiliton were that of James Roberts."

"Very well reasoned, Mr Wilkin, and very clearly told," said Mr Crowhurst. "May I have the knife and the other articles, Captain Hawke? Thank you. Now Mr Muffin, you are quite certain this is the knife you gave your shipmate, Roberts?"

"There can't be no doubt, sir," answered Bill, in a melancholy voice; "I wish there could, but d'ye see, I cut his name on the haft – J – I – M, Jim, and there it is if you look, sir, J – I – M, Jim."

"Yes, you are quite right; the name is there as you say. And now I will ask you something else; I gather, from the captain's letter that you were acquainted with this James Roberts before you were pressed, and knew his real name."

"Yes, sir. His name was properly Robert Hawke, as I knew from Toby Rooke, and also from seeing the name on a bill offering a reward for a-giving of him up on a charge of murder – but that was all my eye, d'ye see, 'cause he never done it at all – and giving a description of a gold watch which I have seen in his possession – which is that same watch as you now have in your hand, which was took by me out of his sea-chest after his death, in the presence of the captain and Mr Wigmore."

"That watch belonged to the late Robert Hawke, I believe, Mr Leigh," said Percival. "Would you kindly examine it and satisfy yourself?"

"'Tis his watch, sir," replied my uncle, curtly.

"Is there any more evidence to be offered, Captain Hawke?" asked the lawyer.

"What more would you have, sir?" demanded Percival. "The testimony that has been given is enough for any court of law, I should think."

"Then in that case," said Mr Crowhurst, 'I will ask the witnesses to append their signatures to their respective depositions and the business will be concluded."

I heard the squeak of the quill as the witnesses, one after the other, signed the documents, and then the jingle of keys and the opening and closing of a heavy lid or door; by which I inferred that the papers had been forthwith consigned to a strong box.

"May I ask if you are satisfied of the death of my late cousin, Robert Hawke?" Percival asked after a short pause.

"I am not," answered Mr Crowhurst. "It is my opinion that he is yet alive."

"Yet alive!" exclaimed Percival, incredulously. "Why, sir, you must be mad. What reason can you have for so preposterous an opinion in the face of all this evidence to the contrary?"

"I will show you," answered the lawyer.

The hand-bell tinkled softly, whereupon I rose from my chair, feeling uncommonly foolish and awkward, and, drawing back the curtain, stepped into the room.

My entrance was greeted by a deathly silence, and for an appreciable interval no one moved or even seemed to breathe. The four strangers remained fixed in the postures of amazement into which they had fallen, and my cousin became, in a moment, so aged and haggard in aspect that I was moved by pity for him.

"And what, sir," said he, at length, in a strange, husky voice, "may be the meaning of this masquerade? Who is this person?"

"This, sir," replied Mr Crowhurst, "is Sir Robert Hawke – lately, as I understand, known as James Roberts."

"Indeed!" exclaimed Percival, starting from his chair with a furious scowl on his pale face, "then there is no time to be lost. Do you hear, Mr Wilkin? This is the deserter, Roberts. Fetch in the other men from the lobby and arrest him at once."

Mr Crowhurst reached out his hand and seized a small cord that hung beside the bell-rope.

"Stop!" said he, as the boatswain rose, with mighty little alacrity, from his chair. "Let me advise you to commit no such folly here."

"Who asks for your advice, sir," thundered Percival. "Do your duty, Mr Wilkin."

"Captain Hawke," said the lawyer quietly, drawing the cord tight as he spoke, "if any violence is attempted, I promise you that you and Mr Wigmore shall be lodged in Newgate within an hour."

"What do you mean by that, sir," demanded Percival, while I noticed that Mr Wigmore's face lengthened perceptibly.

"I mean this," replied Mr Crowhurst, in the same quiet and even tone; "that your present intentions have been foreseen and provided for. My chief clerk is, at this moment, waiting out in the square, in readiness for a signal, which will be made the instant I pull this cord. He has in his pocket a sworn information charging you and Mr Wigmore with conspiracy, and making mention of another little matter which the lieutenant will understand" (here Mr Wigmore's face assumed a pale olive green tint). "On my making the signal, the gates of the inn will be shut and the watch posted, and my clerk will lay the information before a justice who is waiting to receive it. I assure you, sir, that nothing has been neglected."

Percival was visibly taken aback and sat down again with his hands thrust into his breeches pockets, whilst he glowered at the lawyer.

"You talk very glibly of conspiracy, my friend," said he, "but 'tis mere brag. What have you against me?"

"Sir," answered the lawyer, blandly, "I had a complete case, with abundant evidence, before you came here; and now, there are your boatswain's depositions, made before witnesses, and containing matter which, alone, is sufficient to send you to the gallows or the pillory, or on a trip overseas in a new capacity according to the discretion of the learned judge."

Percival shifted uneasily in his chair.

"This is all talk," said he; "you know you can do nothing."

"Why what folly is this," exclaimed the lawyer, impatiently. "You have behaved like a scoundrel and now you are acting like a fool. You have gambled for the title and you have lost. Here is Sir Robert, in full possession, and you are out of it. He may prosecute you or he may not; but if you continue thus you will force his hand. And, mark you, the prosecution rests not with him alone. This crime is now known to several persons, and you are at the mercy of any one of them, so beware! If any mischance, whatsoever, befall Sir Robert, in that moment the law will be put into motion. And now, sir, I will wish you a very good day."

Percival rose abruptly, without a word or a look at us, and stalked out of the room, followed closely by the crestfallen lieutenant.

As soon as they were gone, I exchanged greetings with my late shipmates, embracing Bill affectionately – to his utter confusion – and shaking the honest boatswain warmly by the hand.

"This here's a rum start and no mistake, Jim – S' Robert I means," said Bill, beaming with happiness, and blushing to find himself in such great company. "I reckon we made a false departure with that there skiliton, Mr Wilkin."

"'Twas very fortunate for me that you did," I replied, "as you will agree when I spin you my yarn. But tell me, Bill, are you satisfied to remain on a king's ship or would you like to leave the Service?"

Bill scratched his head with an embarrassed air.

"Why d'ye see, Jim – S'Robert I means – 'twouldn' do for me to be a-talkin' afore the bo'sn about slippin' my tow rope."

"Sartinly not," agreed Wilkin, stolidly.

"But," continued Bill, "There's Biddy what you see at the 'Mermaid.' Now I would like to marry Biddy, that I would."

"Of course he would," interposed Prudence, shaking his hand warmly, "and he shall. She is a sweet girl, Robin – but you know that – and she is as fond of him as – I am sure he deserves."

"Is she though, miss," exclaimed Bill, grinning shyly and blushing to the colour of a beetroot, "I didn't know that" – which was a wicked falsehood on Bill's part.

"What say you, Mr Crowhurst?" I asked; "Bill's impressment was quite irregular as he was the mate of a ship at the time."

"Why in that case," replied the lawyer, "we might obtain his discharge – by the use of a little influence. A good deal can be done at the Admiralty, by influence," he added with a dry smile.

Bill bowed his acknowledgements, and, when I had shaken his hand once more, he was led away by the boatswain, still bowing and on the broad grin.

"Already, you see," said Mr Crowhurst, with a smile, "you begin to find the advantages of your position. You can now render your humble friend this great service and make him a free man once more."

"Yes, Robin dear," said Prudence eagerly, "and you can do something more. You can give these two good honest souls a wedding gift – a trim little vessel of their own, and then Bill will be the master of his ship and safe from the dreadful press-gang."

"There is an idea for you," said Mr Crowhurst, laughing genially at my sweetheart's enthusiasm. "Mistress Prudence will help you to get rid of your fortune, never fear."

"I shall thank her to do so if she can think of so pleasant a way of accomplishing the object," said I, for the notion of setting up poor Bill as a shipmaster and owner pleased me uncommonly.

"Well, well," commented the lawyer, "a gentleman of fortune might spend his wealth to less advantage than in making simple, honest folk happy. But, speaking of your fortune, there are one or two matters on which I would confer with you in private, and, as I was proposing to accompany you to your town house in Bloomsbury Square, I would suggest that Mr and Mrs Leigh and Miss Prudence precede us thither. We will follow you very shortly, dear people – indeed we shall be there nearly as soon as yourselves."

On this hint my uncle and aunt and Prudence left us to make their way to Bloomsbury, and as soon as we were alone, the attorney opened his business without preamble.

"I understand," said he, "that you propose to marry Miss Leigh."

"That is so," I answered.

"'Tis what the worldly-wise would call a poor match," said Mr Crowhurst; "but the worldly-wise do so often overreach themselves in their wisdom, that one is glad to see a man act squarely on his own convictions and instincts. I approve your choice entirely and believe you will never, for an instant, repent it; but I must ask you what is to be done about the settlement."

"I should wish you to act as though Miss Leigh were a lady of fortune," I answered, "and you may confer with my uncle on the subject. But 'tis of little moment, so that my wife receive suitable provision, for we are, as it were, one family with one common interest."

"That is all I wished to know," said Mr Crowhurst; "so now, if you please, we will follow our friends."

We sallied forth together, turning out into Lincoln's Inn Fields, and making for the archway under the house of the Sardinian Ambassador. We had gone but a little way, however, when we perceived a considerable crowd of people approaching, and Mr Crowhurst stopped to ask a man, who was running on ahead, what was the cause of the gathering.

"'Tis a gentleman has shot himself," was the answer, "and they are carrying away the body."

"Hey!" exclaimed the lawyer, "shot himself, you say? Let us see the corpse."

We pushed, together, through the crowd until we came to a party of men carrying a shutter, on which lay a motionless form covered with a sheet of sacking.

"Let us see the face, my friends," said Mr Crowhurst in an authoritative tone, and taking a quick side-glance at me.

One of the bearers drew back the cloth and uncovered the face. 'Twas that of my cousin Percival.

CHAPTER TWENTY-FOUR

In which the Bells are rung in Shorne Steeple

There is, as I took occasion to remark at the beginning of this narrative, a certain misfortune that besets a writer like myself, which is this: that he is, by the nature of things, forced to restrict his recital to those circumstances that give him the least pleasure to look back upon.

For, whereas he may ask the reader to accompany him in all his perils and hardships; to follow him whilst he is buffeted by adverse winds and tossed about upon a sea of uncertainties and disappointments; he cannot invite him to share the sweet repose and tranquil happiness that comes to him, at length, as the reward of his travail. It is the character of peril and adversity to be accompanied by tumultuous action, which stirs the passions of the listener to their recital; while happiness and prosperity are apt to have their being amidst circumstances so quiet and placid as to leave naught to tell.

To such a period my story is now approaching; and, as I see the end of my task draw near, I am like a mariner, casting his eye towards the watch-glass to note the dwindling sand that heralds his release from duty. My glass, too, is running out. The sand trickles through apace; the little cone above grows smaller and more hollow, and soon the bulb will stand empty. Twice a dozen times has that glass been turned, and now 'tis set for the last watch; and so I will crave the reader's pardon for this digression and get back to my narrative.

'Twas New Year's Day in the year seventeen hundred and ninety-two; a calm, sunny day with a promise of spring that awakened the birds in the bare trees to a hopeful chirruping, and brought out the crows to rummage among the furrows in the ploughed fields. The river, down in the valley below the rising ground of Shorne, repeated the soft winter blue of the sky, and distant sails glowed a rosy yellow through the haze.

Already the smith had shut up his forge, and set out with his journeyman and apprentices to tend the bell-ropes up at the church; for the smith was an expert bell-ringer and meant, on this, my wedding-day, to ring out a triple bob major – or as near to that achievement as the furnishing of the belfry would allow. Already the post-chaise that was to bear me away with my bride, was lurking behind a rick in the farm-yard, while the horses gorged joyously in the stable. Already Bill Muffin, with well greased pig-tail and covered with blushes, was seated in the kitchen with the self-possessed Biddy, smiling benignantly at the little smith upon the clock, or joking with Toby Rooke (who had come up from the creek, as he grimly expressed it "to see his mate turned off").

For Bill was to be married today, too, having caught eagerly at my suggestion to that effect, remarking, with great wisdom, that "seein' as how the ways was greased, he might as well be launched at the same time; though 't was for all the world like a-sendin' a billy-boy slidin' down astern of a seventy-four."

I strolled away alone to wait at the church, leaving the house in a pleasant ferment, with Mr Leigh wandering from room to room, and Prudence, flushed and happy, flitting to and fro, pursued relentlessly by Rebecca (now transplanted from Rotherhithe and flourishing amazingly in her new surroundings).

Along the ridgeway, exchanging cheerful greetings with the villagers at their doorways, across the little common on the hill-top, where the old mill stood idle and becalmed, and so down the steep pathway to the church.

All the world seemed gay this morning as if in sympathy with my own happiness. The aged yew in the churchyard wore a holiday dress all spangled with red-gold berries, which the birds picked off and devoured with chirps of enjoyment; and even the Good Samaritan upon the tombstone near the porch, seemed to burst forth into extra lavishness in the matter of oil and wine, fairly turning his flask bottom upwards over the sufferer's elbow in the exuberance of his generosity.

The church – which I now revisited for the first time since my return – was empty (for the bell-ringers were yet girding up their loins at the 'Crown' hard by), and as I looked upon the well-remembered scene, I seemed to breathe an atmosphere of ancient peace, of calm untroubled by the turmoil of the world without. There lay the knight in his battered armour, as of old, slumbering through the centuries upon his stony couch; still, with pathetic pride reminding the stranger that he was Li: Eine: Seigneur: De: Roundale:, and still making his pathetic appeal, Dieu: De: Sa: Alme: Eit: Merchy. And there was the great pendulum, drooping far below the belfry ceiling, swaying slowly with measured beat, as it grudgingly told out the seconds "that perish for us and are reckoned," and making me think of Captain Parradine and his wise advice to "count not the hours unless they be sunny."

All was unchanged from my childhood and would be still unchanged when my name was but a memory and my life as a tale that is told. While I was a wanderer upon the broad ocean, a castaway upon the island, a prisoner on the slave-ship, the knight had slumbered on, and the clock had told, with monotonous voice, of the passage of the fleeting hours.

My meditations were interrupted at this point by the arrival of Bill Muffin accompanied by Toby, of whom the former remarked that the coach was at the house and that he "cleared out when he heard the order passed to the coachman to heave short." He likewise informed me in a hoarse whisper that the parson was in the vestry "a-getting ready for to knock away the dog-shores and launch us down the ways."

Even as he was speaking, the sound of wheels was heard, which put him in such a flutter that he fell to whistling "Nancy Dawson" until he was brought up short by Toby. The people filed into the church and took their places; the bell-ringers followed, wiping their mouths, and as I stepped through the porch, the wedding party entered the churchyard, led by my sturdy uncle, beaming and joyous and mighty proud, as he well might be, of the beautiful maid by his side.

As to my sweet Prudence, how shall I speak of her? How convey her dainty loveliness, her modest dignity, as she came up the path upon her father's arm; serious of mien, though her eyes were shining with the happiness that she strove not to conceal.

And now the words are spoken – the solemn, beautiful words, that so many utter with deep emotion and think so little upon in the years that follow. The covenant is made of a love that shall endure even unto death, of a faithfulness that shall be unbroken through good report and evil report; the dream of my troubled manhood has become a reality and the utmost desire of my heart is fulfilled.

Here, at the summit of my happiness, while the bells in the ancient steeple send forth their cheery clamour, calling upon the rustic in the fields and the woodman in the copse to pause in their labours and rejoice with me, let me bid farewell to the patient reader who has journeyed with me so far afield. In the days of my bitter adversity we met, and since then have sailed together through many a stormy passage. Peril, suffering and hope deferred have endured through many a weary month, and now we part, having witnessed the fulfilment of that prophecy uttered by Prudence on the Chadwell marshes, when the clouds of misfortune were darkest, that "He that goeth forth and weepeth shall doubtless come again with rejoicing."

R Austin Freeman

The D'Arblay Mystery

When a man is found floating beneath the skin of a green-skimmed pond one morning, Dr Thorndyke becomes embroiled in an astonishing case. This wickedly entertaining detective fiction reveals that the victim was murdered through a lethal injection and someone out there is trying a cover-up.

Dr Thorndyke Intervenes

What would you do if you opened a package to find a man's head? What would you do if the headless corpse had been swapped for a case of bullion? What would you do if you knew a brutal murderer was out there, somewhere, and waiting for you? Some people would run. Dr Thorndyke intervenes.

R Austin Freeman

Felo De Se

John Gillam was a gambler. John Gillam faced financial ruin and was the victim of a sinister blackmail attempt. John Gillam is now dead. In this exceptional mystery, Dr Thorndyke is brought in to untangle the secrecy surrounding the death of John Gillam, a man not known for insanity and thoughts of suicide.

Flighty Phyllis

Chronicling the adventures and misadventures of Phyllis Dudley, Richard Austin Freeman brings to life a charming character always getting into scrapes. From impersonating a man to discovering mysterious trap doors, *Flighty Phyllis* is an entertaining glimpse at the times and trials of a wayward woman.

R Austin Freeman

Helen Vardon's Confession

Through the open door of a library, Helen Vardon hears an argument that changes her life forever. Helen's father and a man called Otway argue over missing funds in a trust one night. Otway proposes a marriage between him and Helen in exchange for his co-operation and silence. What transpires is a captivating tale of blackmail, fraud and death. Dr Thorndyke is left to piece together the clues in this enticing mystery.

Mr Pottermack's Oversight

Mr Pottermack is a law-abiding, settled homebody who has nothing to hide until the appearance of the shadowy Lewison, a gambler and blackmailer with an incredible story. It appears that Pottermack is in fact a runaway prisoner, convicted of fraud, and Lewison is about to spill the beans unless he receives a large bribe in return for his silence. But Pottermack protests his innocence, and resolves to shut Lewison up once and for all. Will he do it? And if he does, will he get away with it?

OTHER TITLES BY R AUSTIN FREEMAN AVAILABLE DIRECT
FROM HOUSE OF STRATUS

Quantity		£	$(US)	$(CAN)	€
☐	A CERTAIN DR THORNDYKE	6.99	11.50	16.95	11.50
☐	THE D'ARBLAY MYSTERY	6.99	11.50	16.95	11.50
☐	DR THORNDYKE INTERVENES	6.99	11.50	16.95	11.50
☐	DR THORNDYKE'S CASEBOOK	6.99	11.50	16.95	11.50
☐	THE EYE OF OSIRIS	6.99	11.50	16.95	11.50
☐	FELO DE SE	6.99	11.50	16.95	11.50
☐	FLIGHTY PHYLLIS	6.99	11.50	16.95	11.50
☐	THE GOLDEN POOL: THE STORY OF A FORGOTTEN MINE	6.99	11.50	16.95	11.50
☐	THE GREAT PORTRAIT MYSTERY	6.99	11.50	16.95	11.50
☐	HELEN VARDON'S CONFESSION	6.99	11.50	16.95	11.50

ALL HOUSE OF STRATUS BOOKS ARE AVAILABLE FROM GOOD BOOKSHOPS
OR DIRECT FROM THE PUBLISHER:

Internet: **www.houseofstratus.com** including author interviews, reviews, features.

Email: **sales@houseofstratus.com** please quote author, title and credit card details.

OTHER TITLES BY R AUSTIN FREEMAN AVAILABLE DIRECT
FROM HOUSE OF STRATUS

Quantity	£	$(US)	$(CAN)	€
Mr Polton Explains	6.99	11.50	16.95	11.50
Mr Pottermack's Oversight	6.99	11.50	16.95	11.50
The Mystery of 31 New Inn	6.99	11.50	16.95	11.50
The Mystery of Angelina Frood	6.99	11.50	16.95	11.50
The Penrose Mystery	6.99	11.50	16.95	11.50
The Puzzle Lock	6.99	11.50	16.95	11.50
The Red Thumb Mark	6.99	11.50	16.95	11.50
The Shadow of the Wolf	6.99	11.50	16.95	11.50
A Silent Witness	6.99	11.50	16.95	11.50
The Singing Bone	6.99	11.50	16.95	11.50

ALL HOUSE OF STRATUS BOOKS ARE AVAILABLE FROM GOOD BOOKSHOPS
OR DIRECT FROM THE PUBLISHER:

Hotline: UK ONLY: **0800 169 1780**, please quote author, title and credit card details.
INTERNATIONAL: **+44 (0) 20 7494 6400**, please quote author, title, and credit card details.

Send to: **House of Stratus Sales Department**
24c Old Burlington Street
London
W1X 1RL
UK

Please allow for postage costs charged per order plus an amount per book as set out in the tables below:

	£(Sterling)	$(US)	$(CAN)	€(Euros)
Cost per order				
UK	2.00	3.00	4.50	3.30
Europe	3.00	4.50	6.75	5.00
North America	3.00	4.50	6.75	5.00
Rest of World	3.00	4.50	6.75	5.00
Additional cost per book				
UK	0.50	0.75	1.15	0.85
Europe	1.00	1.50	2.30	1.70
North America	2.00	3.00	4.60	3.40
Rest of World	2.50	3.75	5.75	4.25

PLEASE SEND CHEQUE, POSTAL ORDER (STERLING ONLY), EUROCHEQUE, OR INTERNATIONAL MONEY ORDER (PLEASE CIRCLE METHOD OF PAYMENT YOU WISH TO USE)
MAKE PAYABLE TO: STRATUS HOLDINGS plc

Cost of book(s): —————————— Example: 3 x books at £6.99 each: £20.97

Cost of order: —————————— Example: £2.00 (Delivery to UK address)

Additional cost per book: ————— Example: 3 x £0.50: £1.50

Order total including postage: ——— Example: £24.47

Please tick currency you wish to use and add total amount of order:

☐ £ (Sterling)   ☐ $ (US)   ☐ $ (CAN)   ☐ € (EUROS)

VISA, MASTERCARD, SWITCH, AMEX, SOLO, JCB:

☐ ☐ ☐ ☐ ☐ ☐ ☐ ☐ ☐ ☐ ☐ ☐ ☐ ☐ ☐ ☐ ☐ ☐ ☐ ☐

Issue number (Switch only):

☐ ☐ ☐

Start Date: **Expiry Date:**

☐☐ / ☐☐   ☐☐ / ☐☐

Signature: ————————————

NAME: ————————————————————

ADDRESS: ——————————————————

——————————————————

POSTCODE: ——————

Please allow 28 days for delivery.

Prices subject to change without notice.
Please tick box if you do not wish to receive any additional information. ☐

House of Stratus publishes many other titles in this genre; please check our website (**www.houseofstratus.com**) for more details.